# Twisted Wrister

*Book 7 in The Playmakers Series®*

BY G.K. BRADY

Copyright © 2021 by G.K. Brady.

All rights reserved

This book is a work of fiction. Names, characters, places, and incidents are the product of the author's imagination or are used fictitiously. Any resemblance to actual events, locales, or persons, living or dead, is coincidental.

No part of this book may be reproduced, or stored in a retrieval system, or transmitted in any form or by any means, electronic, mechanical, photocopying, recording, or otherwise, without express written permission of the publisher.

Without in any way limiting the author's and publisher's exclusive rights under copyright, any use of this publication to "train" generative artificial intelligence (AI) technologies to generate text is expressly prohibited. The author reserves all rights to license uses of this work for generative AI training and development of machine learning language models.

978-1-7363606-6-8

Cover design by Getcovers
Cover model Colton R. by Wander Aguiar Photography, LLC
Edited by Jenny Quinlan, Historical Editorial
Proofread by Word Servings
Trefoil Publishing

# Contents

# *Dedication*

*For Aunt Kay and Uncle Mac, whose commitment and affection for one another gave me hope and showed me what a truly loving relationship looks like. You were the best role models ever, and I miss you every single day.*

# Chapter 1
# Been There, Dumped That

Blake Barrett resisted the urge to give the redhead chewing on his bottom lip a little backward nudge into the hallway so he could close his door. Unlike hockey, where his skill set was innate, his social fumbling at times like these was downright squirm-worthy. Manners he had—his mother had made sure of that—but helping a woman with her coat was a far cry from trying to maneuver her out the door after he'd just had sex with her. "Hey, thanks for letting me bang you. Would you please leave now so I can catch a few hours of sleep before practice?"

Awkward as fuck.

Usually, he was the one leaving. No, *usually* he wasn't sleeping with a stranger. Yeah, that.

"Sherry, I need my lip back if I'm going to get any sleep," he teased, second-guessing his approach. Too light? Too harsh? Should he act like the gentleman ingrained in him, or should he be a dick? Did politeness even count in this situation? A year after earning a permanent job in the big league, this whole puck-bunny phenomenon still mystified him. He wasn't particularly outgoing or funny, and while he wasn't ugly, he was no better looking than the next guy. Was it *him* or his job that drew them in? His buddies all told him not to worry about it, to go with it and enjoy, but he wasn't sure he'd ever get there.

Sherry raked pointy nails through her long mane and pouted at him. "Is that all you have to say after what happened?"

His mind flashed to the horror of accidentally pulling out Sherry's extensions when he'd been in the throes ... talk about killing the moment. But honestly, how could he have known her hair was fake?

"Uh, I'm sorry about the hair," he repeated for the hundredth time since the mortifying incident.

"You're forgiven, lover, but that's not what I was talking about." Sherry hooked a long leg over his hip and grabbed his ass. "I'm talking about what happened between us."

*Shit. Did something more than sex and Olympic hair-pulling happen between us?*

She spared him blurting out a painful "Thanks for a great time tonight" when she said, "You've got all the right moves, handsome, but we need to work on that kiss of yours. One more nibble. Let Sherry show you how to kiss the *right* way."

*Wait. What?*

Her tongue thrust into his mouth, and he nearly choked. It was a big tongue and an active one, performing a thorough tonsil-swabbing. Was that the *right* way?

A very loud throat clear made both their heads turn. A woman stood about ten feet away, and her eyes swept them from head to toe. He suddenly realized he only wore boxers—he hadn't expected to see anyone else out here at 3:00 a.m., especially not with only four units per floor—and her assessing glare made him more self-conscious than he already was. Maybe because he was half-naked, sucking face with a woman he barely knew, who had just dropped the bomb on him that he couldn't kiss.

The woman in the hallway had a short froth of brown curls, with a stature and demeanor to match.

"Excuuuse me," she said in a frosty tone, "but maybe you should move your wrestling match inside?"

Sherry pulled away and covered her mouth and the giggle escaping it. "I have to go anyway." She spun toward the elevator, blowing him a kiss over her shoulder. “Bye, Blakey. Call me. We’ll pick back up with your lessons.”

He frowned after her, his eyes straying toward her exaggeratedly swinging ass before shooting back to the Curly One tapping her foot.

“Done ogling? Can I get to my apartment?” Curly huffed.

He straightened, pretending he wasn’t clad in only his underwear. Time to fight attitude with attitude. “Who’s stopping you?” Then he gave her his best middle-of-the-night smile, hoping he didn’t resemble a nutso slasher.

She made a rigid lifting motion with her hand. “You’re kinda blocking the way.”

He glanced around. Apparently, he’d stepped into the hallway without realizing it. At six-two and two hundred pounds, he was big—his teammates had dubbed him “Bear”—but not so big she couldn’t get around him. She was just trying to be a pain. No, she *was* being a pain. The girl looked to be wound so tight she might pop a few springs, and it showed in the twist of her mouth and the narrowed eyes behind her black-rimmed glasses. Dressed in a starchy blue-and-white-striped button-down shirt, navy slacks, and black flats, she probably moved like her stiff clothes. Where the hell was she coming from so late anyway? Not clubbing—not dressed like *that*. Maybe she’d had a fight with the boyfriend, which would explain her snippiness. She’d moved in only weeks ago, and until now he’d never met her—never even *seen* her—and he knew nothing about her, other than his roommate had a huge hard-on for her. Exactly why, he had no idea.

Taking a step backward into his doorway, he swept his hand grandly. “Please.” If his mother could see him, she’d be proud. Well, except for the half-naked part … and the part that preceded it. He could practically hear her slurring in his head, “Always use your best manners, Blake. Make your mama proud.” Making her proud was hit-or-miss depending on whether she noticed, which in turn depended on her level of inebriation.

With a roll of her eyes, Curly strode past him with a scowl that made her look as though she’d sucked down an entire box of Sour

Patch Kids. For reasons beyond his comprehension, he surrendered to a rare impulse and decided to needle her.

"Did you have fun tonight?" he called after her, a smirk tugging the corners of his mouth.

Slowly, she turned on her heel. "What?"

Crossing his arms, he tucked his hands in his armpits. "Obviously, you're getting back from a night out. Did you have fun?" He enunciated the last words slowly. Mom would *not* be proud; he was in dick mode, which was unusual for him.

Curly jutted out a hip and perched her fist on it. Daggers shot from her eyes. "Not that it's any of your concern, but my 'night out' was actually the conclusion of a long day at work."

Surprise had him rocking on the balls of his feet. Okay, so he'd made a few wrong assumptions. In his defense, she looked more like a business professional, not a bartender or a waitress or a swing-shift kind of worker—the kind of jobs that clocked out in the wee hours. Maybe she was a nurse, but then she'd be wearing scrubs, right? Curiosity got the best of him. "What do you do?"

"I do plenty. What I *don't* do is talk to strange, half-dressed men in hallways in the middle of the night."

"So what kind of men *do* you talk to in hallways in the middle of the night?"

He hadn't noticed before, but the hand not fused to her hip dangled at her side. She brought that arm up and flourished some kind of compact canister she pointed at his face, her index finger poised to depress the top.

Internal systems all came online at once, and he threw up his hands and backed away. "Whoa, whoa, whoa! Take it easy, for Christ's sake! No threat here, so put away the mace."

She lowered her arm, and he blew out a relieved breath, though his heart was pounding against his rib cage like it wanted to escape. He let out a mirthless laugh. "Damn, didn't mean to get off on the wrong foot. We're neighbors. We should be planning movie night or the next barbecue." He went for a look of contrition.

Whether or not it had an effect on her would remain a mystery because she wheeled, presenting him her back.

"Uh, good night?" he ventured.

As she inserted her key in her lock, she cut him a glare. "Good night ... *Blakey*." The slam of her door cut off the possibility of any more conversation.

"That woman could stand a lecture from Mom," he muttered as he softly closed his own door behind him. A few more cleansing breaths, and his heart rate finally slowed. He ambled to the loft's floor-to-ceiling windows and took in the glittering carpet of lights stretched out in front of him. He nearly pinched himself. Again. Blake Barrett couldn't believe his luck. Correction: his life. Because it wasn't luck that had put him smack in the middle of a luxury apartment with panoramic views of the Rocky Mountains, nor had it gotten him a fat bank account or accolades for his recent play. He'd earned every single thing he had with pools of his sweat and blood.

"Goddamn, what the hell are you doing, Barrett?" The rasp of his roommate and best friend, Owen Ferguson, nearly shot Blake out of his shorts. "First you keep me up by pounding some skank, and now you're trolling the fucking hallway? Never mind what a stupid idea it is to bring a hookup home, or that the walls are *not* soundproof. Do you have any idea what time it is? Some of us need our shut-eye before practice, dude."

"Sorry about the noise, man," Blake grumbled.

Ferguson let out a condescending laugh. "Yeah, well, at least you closed the deal this time. Or maybe she did the closing for you. Whatever, it's not like you get lucky all that much, so good for you for a change."

Blake bristled. Fergs was a few months older, which placed him at Blake's ripe age of twenty-four, but damned if he didn't take every opportunity to act like he was light years ahead of Blake in pretty much every facet of life—even in hockey, and *especially* with women. Ever since Blake had beat Fergs in face-offs percentage, his childhood buddy had been sour grapes. They hadn't had a good old-fashioned knock-down drag-out in years, but the temptation to bust Ferguson's chops had been gathering a head of steam lately. But not tonight; Blake was too exhausted for combat, physical or otherwise.

With an inner headshake, he directed his focus elsewhere. "The noise in the hallway was all the new neighbor. She fucking pulled a can of mace on me!"

"Why?"

"Damned if I know. All I did was ask if she'd had a nice night. You'd think I'd made a threatening move."

A hint of a grin tugged Ferguson's mouth. "Obviously, she doesn't know you, or she'd know you don't *have* a move, threatening or otherwise."

Blake ignored the jab.

A few beats later, Fergs threw him off when he said, "So what was she wearing tonight?"

"Who?" Fergs had been with him when Sherry had first approached. Had he already forgotten the hot pink number cut down to there and the tiny skirt that had been so tight it had been nearly impossible to peel off? Truth be told, Blake had had little idea which one of them she was interested in until Fergs left to use the john and she'd pushed herself up against Blake and started running her long nails all over him. Her blatant signals had been unmistakable—even for him.

Ferguson let out an exasperated breath, bringing him back to the condo's living room. "The hot-as-fuck little brunette who pulled the mace on you. Jesus, picturing her going all cavewoman makes her even hotter, her hair all wild and shit. What was she wearing?"

"How would I know? Chick was grumpy as hell." *Was* Curly hot? Blake's hotness-alert system had been turned to its lowest setting, and even if it had been cranked up to a higher level, the mace pointed at his face would have knocked out the power to his meter.

Ferguson's eyebrows bounced. "She's not grumpy around me. No sir, she's all smiles. Real pretty ones too. Must be the power of the Fergs. And never mind about what she was wearing. I'll let my imagination fill in the blanks. By the way, your sister called tonight."

Blake's stomach acid began a familiar slow churn. He tended to get frosty when it came to his little sister. Amanda showed way too much interest in Ferguson, and Blake suspected that interest was returned—she was a living, breathing female after all, and Fergs didn't require much beyond that—though if Fergs *was* interested, he was subtle about it. Thank God Amanda was back in school in Hawaii and not in the guest bedroom, where she'd been for a few weeks this past summer.

"What's she calling *you* for? And what time did she call?" His voice came out in a warning growl.

Amanda hadn't called *him*. Or had she? Come to think of it, he hadn't checked his phone since getting distracted by Sherry. But no one messed with Amanda, *especially* not one of his womanizing teammates.

"Said she couldn't reach you," this particular womanizing teammate said. "Sounded to me like you were blowing your wad right about then, so being the good friend I am, I left you alone. You're welcome." He paused to yawn. "She said it wasn't urgent, but she wants you to call her in the morning."

"So *not* right now?"

"No, she said it can wait." Ferguson let out a low chuckle. "You know how she always forgets the time difference, bro. It was nine or ten o'clock where she is, so it was still early."

Why did hearing Ferguson relay this information stick in Blake's craw? Because *he* should have been the one taking Amanda's call—that's what good brothers did—instead of getting the old teakettle to whistle, no matter how much he'd needed to let off steam.

Ferguson stifled another yawn. "I'm out. We riding to the rink together?"

"Yeah," Blake replied absently.

"Okay. See you in a few."

As Blake trundled off to his room on one side of the sprawling condo, questions spun in his head. Amanda never called just to call. She always had a purpose, and that purpose usually centered around their mom. Maybe she wanted to give him good news this time: she'd visited Mom in rehab, and she was doing really well and was so grateful Blake had almost bodily hauled her there himself. *Yeah, right.* More likely, Amanda was calling to let him know Mom had ditched—again.

He muttered a curse. As his thoughts swung in that direction, growing louder, they jolted him to full wakefulness. Any lingering effects from the post-sex fog had long since evaporated, and now a cold, steely spike of dread wedged itself inside his chest.

# Chapter 2

# Mace in the Hole

Michaela Wagner shut the door behind her and sagged against it. As her heart slammed against her rib cage, she wondered what the hell had come over her. She'd never pulled pepper spray on anyone in her life—had never needed to, thank God. And she hadn't needed to this time either. At least, she hadn't felt threatened, just annoyed beyond reason. As for acting tough, she didn't even know if the damn thing still functioned. Her doting father had given it to her years ago when she'd gone off to college—to protect her from the "hooligans" on campus, and later, in law school. And to this day he fretted, which was annoyingly sweet. He simply could not wrap his head around the fact that she didn't hang out in jails all day. Moreover, while her job might one day bring her into contact with criminals of the white-collar variety, it was doubtful she'd ever rub shoulders with the sort of "unsavory folk" her dad envisioned. She was a real estate lawyer working on ho-hum contracts with everyday clients. Yes, she loved real estate law—it's why she'd specialized in it—but the kind she worked on was ... dull. And never-ending.

Except for one client, Michaela hadn't acquired any of her business herself. She'd merely inherited the higher-ups' dregs.

Hours from now, she'd hit the reset button and down a few gallons of coffee before plugging back in at work, ready to deliver another sixteen-plus hours. And while she could barely keep from drowning under the weight of the work, the partners collected the praise and the paychecks. But that was fine, she reminded herself. She was in the dues-paying cycle of her career.

Still, being the most junior of all the junior attorneys was killing her social life, and she wanted some balance, damn it! Did her fun side live and breathe under the mountain of to-wits and therefores? She'd mothballed vibrant, fun Michaela so long ago she wasn't sure that part of her still existed. She missed that girl.

That very thinking was what had led her to tonight's fiasco, which had in turn led her into that awful pepper spray-threatening mood. She cringed with embarrassment. Never mind that she'd semi-fibbed to the guy about being at work. Well, she *had* come from the office, even if she hadn't spent the entire time clocking work hours. Excuses aside, how was she ever going to apologize to the big guy for her bad behavior?

With a tired sigh, she pushed away from the door, kicking off her shoes and dropping her purse as she wandered deeper into the empty space she hadn't yet grown accustomed to. It wasn't so much empty as it was minimalist sterile, all white and gray high-end furnishings that looked wholly uninviting and uncomfortable. They weren't bad once you perched on them, but she simply didn't *want* to. Saturday would change that, though, when she moved in the red leather couch and sank her bones into it.

She advanced cautiously into the darkened apartment. Couldn't find the light switch, couldn't find—*Ow! Mmph! Found the damn chair leg.* With a breathless curse, she plopped into the hard-angled offending chair and massaged her big toe.

Buzzing sounded on the floor behind her, and she got up, keeping her weight off her damaged foot as she inched her way toward the purse she'd dropped.

A text glowed in the dark. *How did it go?*

With an eye-roll, she tapped out, *Why are you asking me at 3 a.m.?*

*Because it's not 3 a.m. here. It's 11 a.m., and inquiring minds need to be fed details.*

Michaela laughed in spite of her throbbing toe and her disheveled ego. Best friends since middle school, Michaela and Fiona had a bond that couldn't be broken. No matter what, her bestie always knew what to say and when to say it, whether it was to pick Michaela up or kick her ass. They were closer than she was to her own sisters—if she had any sisters. Pretend ones that lived in an only child's active imagination didn't count, she was pretty sure.

Michaela: *You're going to be disappointed, GF. No deets to report. The whole thing was a big suckaroo.*

Fiona: *So you didn't find the one?*

Michaela: *Nope. If he's out there, he's not hanging out at speed-dating events. Unlike me, he's way too smart for that idiocy. Come to think of it, I'm pretty sure he's not out there. Period.*

Fiona: *Oh, he's out there. He's just waiting for you to find him.*

Easy for Fiona to say. She'd found "the one"—and a rich one too—the summer before law school when they'd donned backpacks and bummed around Europe. Fiona had literally fallen into his lap on the Eurail in Italy, and now she seemed to be forever exploring lands halfway across the globe with him instead of practicing law beside Michaela. How selfish of her! What had happened to the blood-sister oath they'd taken that night they'd decided to find out what getting drunk was all about? Didn't that promise trump a man, even if he was the perfect one for Fiona? Sheesh.

Michaela: *He's either the proverbial needle in a haystack or his white charger came up lame.*

Fiona: *Nah, he's just getting it shod, lololol.*

Michaela's phone rang, and she picked up, lifted by the sound of her best friend's voice but still feigning annoyance. "I'm trying to sleep, you know."

"I won't keep you long. Just thought it'd be easier if we chatted. Besides, I needed to hear the tone of your voice to know how serious this is."

"Very serious. Speed dating is *not* the answer. In fact, it sucks balls. It's worse than the dating apps, if you can believe that." Phone to her ear, Michaela meandered back to the two-story-high living space and stared out at Denver's sparkling skyline. "I tried my damnedest tonight, Fi. Honest, I did. I got myself psyched up for a big adventure, but it was a complete letdown, and I ended up going back to the office and falling asleep on my desk. The closest I came to anything meaningful was almost licking a guy's head."

"Whoa! *That* sounds like an adventure to me! He must have left quite an impression if you were considering going down on him. In a crowd no less."

Michaela burst out with an errant laugh. "Get your mind out of the gutter! Not *that* head. The head I'm talking about had a bad comb-over. A few of his greasy hairs were waving in the air with static electricity, and I felt sorry for him. Thought I could slap some spit on those puppies and tame them. That way maybe he'd get lucky ... with someone else."

"Ohhhh. Got it. So speed dating isn't like a bag of M&Ms?"

"Huh?"

"A rainbow of yummy choices. You don't know which one to start with. Work with me here!" she said in an exasperated tone.

"Too tired, Fi."

"So all that effort and you left without even getting a name?"

The dark, polished wood floor had an array of light faux fur rugs, and Michaela stepped to one and dug her toes into the softness. "I gave my number to one guy—only because I didn't want to disappoint the hostess—but God, I hope he doesn't call. I'll have to invent an excuse to get out of seeing him, and you *know* how much I hate lying."

"Have I ever told you that while honesty is an honorable trait, it's impractical for an attorney?"

"A million times. Now it's a million and one."

"Well, at least you got out and tried to meet people. I'm proud of you, Micky-Dub. You need to do more of that. Find your fun in the sun, your mojo in ... can't think of a word that rhymes."

"The dojo," Michaela filled in for her. "And no, I'm not signing up for some dojo class so I can wear a white robe and badly fitting capris in order meet men."

"Huh. Good point. How are you liking your new digs?"

Michaela winced once more as she recalled pulling out the pepper spray on her neighbor. "Good, but I might have blown any chance at neighborly relations. I kinda threatened one of the guys next door just now."

"*What?* Like *just* now? Did he try to attack you? Have you called the police?"

"Uh, it wasn't exactly his fault." *Good thing* he *didn't call the police.*

"Uh-oh. I feel a confession coming. What did you do, Mick?"

Michaela explained quickly—not that there was much to tell anyway. "Oh well," she said on a humorless laugh. "Just another guy who thinks I'm out of control."

"Hey, leave Anders molding in the past. It's where he belongs. So this neighbor. Is he cute?"

Michaela puffed her cheeks and blew out a breath. "I don't know, Fi, and honestly it doesn't matter because he's already taken. He was making out with some woman in the hallway. After she left him standing there, he tried to make conversation. Which is weird, don't you think? All I wanted to do was get inside, so I kinda ... went Terminator on him. The only thing I noticed about his face was his panicky expression. I do have a vague impression of a junior version of Chad Michael Murray—complete with the smirk—before I pulled out the spray." *So* not *my type. That sculpted body, though. I'd like it to be my type.* She'd never been with anybody quite that ... chiseled.

"You're cracking, Micky-Dub. You need to get laid!"

"What I need is my best friend home to dole out hugs. How much longer are you and James planning to traipse around Europe?"

"Another month or so. We'll be home in time for Thanksgiving. For what it's worth, you get an *A* for effort, Mick. You were brave to try the speed-dating thing. I never would have gotten up the nerve to do something so ... so daring. Don't forget, the right man is out there. Hell, he might even be next door! Whoops! Or not."

Michaela barked out a laugh. "I miss you, Fifi."

"Miss you too, girlfriend. Now get some sleep, but don't forget what I said. Think opportunity. Think fun! Be bold! Let's find you a man! Love you."

"Love you too, Fi."

Michaela chuckled to herself. *Next door? Yeah, scratch that.* Another wave of guilt had her shaking her head. God, what a way to say hello! She headed for the bedroom, turning over various apologies in her head. What if she baked him some cookies and left them at his door with a note explaining her evil twin had been the pepper spray-wielding maniac?

Oh hell. The guy was merely a neighbor, and only temporarily. She'd be moving out in a few months, and she owed him zip. Considering the redhead rubbing herself all over him like a catnip-crazed feline, he'd probably already forgotten Michaela's mini-meltdown because, hello, he'd had his hands full. Very full.

The image of the couple yanked her firmly back to the hotel ballroom and the myriad desperate people searching for their match, like plugs looking for the right sockets to connect with so that electricity could race through them. Ha! She'd have to write that analogy down in her journal ... if she ever started keeping one.

Maybe if she *had* been bold ... What if she'd dressed provocatively, like the redhead or some of the other women at the event? No, she would have been even *more* uncomfortable, and the choice in men wouldn't have changed.

Her mother's voice floated through her head, telling her if she expected to land a man who wasn't a total loser, she needed to tuck her brain away for a while. "Men are intimidated by women who are smarter and more successful than they are," her mom had warned more than once. Did that mean she should dumb herself down? No. If her smarts were too much to handle, well, that was *his* loss. Michaela had thought herself clever once, doing an end-around and picking someone smarter and more successful than she was, and look what a disaster *that* had turned out to be.

Ah, motherly advice. Because Michaela was an only child, she had grown up routinely bombarded with all kinds of guidance—helpful and not so helpful—from her elderly, well-intentioned parents. But the constant barrage wasn't all bad: it had pushed her out of the nest early and brought her to Colorado from Kansas, where, at barely seventeen, she'd begun her first year of college at CU Boulder, speeding through her undergrad coursework and conquering law school ahead of schedule. And she was proud of that accomplishment, damn it! Besides, Fiona was smarter and she'd landed her Prince Charming, who treated her as though she walked on water.

So why was Michaela different? Was it a lack of choices, like tonight's epic failure? Or was it her? Was she too picky? Too intense? Too unappealing? These questions were not new. She'd been asking them since Anders had shocked everyone by getting married two years ago.

Another thought popped into her head—apparently, she wasn't getting to sleep anytime soon—and dragged her mind back to the couple getting it on next door. What had the woman meant about "lessons"? Salsa? Mixology? Sex? Nah, he didn't look like a guy who needed lessons in sex. Probably could teach them, though. At least *someone* in this building was getting some action, she grumbled to herself.

"And time to put *that* distracting thought away," she said aloud, followed by, "Barbecues and movie night, my hiney. Oh great. And now you're talking to yourself." Fiona was right. She needed to get laid.

As Michaela got ready for bed, she brushed out the goo that held her unruly curls in check so she didn't end up resembling a dandelion. Removing her glasses, she eyed her reflection in the mirror. Fuzzy hair aside, she was attractive, wasn't she? So why didn't she *feel* attractive? *Because it's 3:00 a.m. and you're exhausted!* And why, oh why, couldn't she find someone who appreciated her the way she was? She *thought* she'd found him once, but she'd been wrong ... like so many of her guesses when it came to men.

"Stop beating yourself up," she told her reflection in a Spanish accent. "You don't need no stinking man." With that, she executed a plucky pivot and blew herself a kiss. "He needs *you.*" *Whoever he is.*

# Chapter 3

# A Couch Is a Hard Thing to Move

Days later, Michaela sat in her office, shutting down her computer, when Brad Hewitt stuck his head in.

"Working on Saturday?"

Her knee-jerk reaction was to toss out a dry "obviously," but then she remembered this was Brad, and she softened her tone. "Actually, I was just heading out to meet a client."

"Ah. And here I thought you were getting your ducks in a row for the Fenton account."

Benjamin Fenton, a big-time land developer, had been Steadman's client for nearly two decades. But Steadman, the law firm's patriarch, was looking to cut back his workload, and he was offering to personally mentor one of the junior attorneys—essentially grooming them to take over the account after Steadman retired. A plum opportunity, for sure, that offered lots of billable hours. And while every junior attorney in the firm was vying for the chance, Michaela was in a good position to win it because of her real estate focus. If she could win the Fenton account, she might fast-track to a partnership.

Brad was a junior attorney too, though six months more senior—a fact he never brought up, never rubbed in her face, unlike a few of the other juniors at Steadman, Hart & Fast. Of course, he wasn't the face-rubbing type, nor was he trying to land the Fenton account, which meant he and Michaela weren't competing against one another. He was a reserved guy, bordering on milquetoast, with dark hair and expressive brown eyes that gave him an almost feminine appearance. And they were his best feature. What he lacked in physical appeal he made up for with a quick mind and quiet tenacity. Michaela respected him, liked him, could talk to him endlessly about the nuances of law, but that's as far as it went. For Brad, however, she suspected he nurtured hope for a romance that would never bloom.

Offering her a tentative smile, he paused to clear his throat. "What a coincidence. I'm leaving too. Would you care to have lunch?"

She had sidestepped a number of halting almost-invitations from him, but today she didn't need to search for a genuine excuse. "Can't. I have to pick up my new, er, used couch, and April's meeting me at my place."

Those dark brows of his knotted together. "You guys hang out together? But she's your assistant." A hint of puzzlement creased the corners of his mouth.

Though she knew he didn't mean it the way it sounded—like she shouldn't be hobnobbing with the "help"—she bit back the urge to explain that April had merely offered to do her a favor. "We're running an errand together," she said instead, hoping he interpreted it as a work errand, consequently freeing her from swerving around a fib.

"Oh. Well, perhaps ... that is ... What are you doing for dinner?" he blurted.

Michaela's heart tugged. He'd never been so bold before. "Brad, I'm afraid—"

Beads of sweat dotted his forehead, and he swiped a pale, puffy hand across it. She flinched inside, knowing what the invitation must have cost the socially awkward man, and she raced to fill the silence. "Thank you, but—"

Her phone chimed, and she picked up. *Saved by the bell!* "Hi, Paige. Yes, I'm heading your way right now. See you soon." She ended the call and looked up at Brad with a vague smile. “Can’t keep a client waiting. Gotta go.”

Brad stammered out an unintelligible answer. Michaela shot up from her desk, gathered up her things, and flipped off the light switch, all while dodging Brad—in more ways than one—on her way out the door. Increasing her stride, she called, “Have a good weekend, Brad,” over her shoulder, locking out an image of him gaping after her.

*God, I hope I didn’t hurt his feelings.* Once inside her Toyota Tundra, she glided through traffic as she headed toward the 7th Avenue Historic District in Denver. Fifteen minutes later, she pulled into a private alley and parked in the driveway belonging to a gorgeous stone-and-stucco manor. Before she could hop out, the garage door lifted, revealing a big man, a slighter man, one tiny woman, and a red couch.

“Hi, Paige,” Michaela called to her favorite client, the lone one she had brought to the firm. Petite Paige Miller, Denver real estate mogul and owner of Anderson Homes, smiled her dazzling, dimpled smile and did a Vanna White-like sweep toward the couch. At odds with her diminutive frame was the protruding belly swelling nearly as wide as she was tall. Beside her stood her towering husband, Beckett Miller.

“Hi, Mick,” she greeted. Only special people called Michaela by her nickname; Paige was special. “It’s all yours.” The couch was a leftover from a redecorating project for a wealthy client that Paige’s associate, Mia Morales, had been handling. The client hadn’t wanted the piece in the end, and Paige had called Michaela. Paige had also arranged the house-sitting gig in the gorgeous luxury condo Michaela had just moved into. Yeah, Paige was *very* special.

Michaela leaned in to give her a squeeze, trying to avoid her baby bump but somehow not managing to. “Oh, I’m so sorry!”

Paige waved her off. “It’s okay. I bump into everything, so I’m used to it. I feel like I’m hatching two Butterball turkeys instead of a pair of peanut-sized babies.”

Beckett chuckled. “You’d think she’d tip over, right?” He leaned down and kissed her temple and caressed said turkey-hatching center with a sweet look that about melted Michaela’s knees. “Need a back massage when we’re done here, pixie?” he murmured low, but Michaela’s tuned-in ears caught it.

She could barely contain a swoony sigh. *I want someone who wants to give me massages ... and who looks at* me *like that.* Clearing her throat, she grinned at Beckett, whom she’d met a half-dozen times before and really liked. After he introduced the other guy, one of the college hockey players Beckett coached, Michaela thanked them profusely for being her moving crew—from the garage to the back of her truck.

The young guy asked if she wanted his help when she reached the condo.

“I got this,” Michaela scoffed, ignoring her toe that, after last night’s run-in with the chair, still pulsed like a red beacon on top of an emergency vehicle.

“You sure? This sucker’s heavy.” Beckett arched a skeptical eyebrow above his glasses and flashed her a smile. In that moment, she pictured the reformed ladies’ man barely crooking his pinkie to have women falling all over him in his pre-Paige playboy days; even the glasses had a way of enhancing rather than detracting from the package.

Smooth operators had never been Michaela’s thing, and apparently they hadn’t been Paige’s either, but he’d won her over anyway—probably with those back massages and a plethora of other sweet deeds. Now *those* were Michaela’s thing, but they were as hard to find as a chilled martini at a Mormon church service.

“Thanks, but I have help when I get to the condo.” She’d tested it before and was fairly certain she and April could handle it. *Slide if off the tailgate, scoot it into the lobby, into the elevator, and scoot some more down the hallway into the condo. Piece of pie.* Besides, she didn’t want to put the Millers out more than she had already.

While the men loaded the couch into the Tundra, Paige leaned in and said in a conspiratorial whisper, "Beck has a coaching buddy who recently turned single. Super nice guy. He wants to get back out there, and he likes smart women, so I thought of you. Interested in being set up on a blind date?" Her auburn eyebrows bounced with mischief.

Hmm. Did Beckett's "buddy" have that whole handsome jock thing going too? If so, he might be a garden-variety babe magnet not cut from the let-me-bring-you-breakfast-in-bed bolt because, hello, he was *newly single*.

As if reading her mind, Paige helpfully added, "He's older, so a little more mature. Steady."

Before Michaela had a chance to process further, Paige ran on. "We're having an informal gathering, and Scott will be there. Join us, and you can see for yourself if he's anyone you might be interested in getting to know. Very low-key, no pressure."

"Uh ..."

Paige winked a pale green eye. "I won't tell him. That way you can check him out on your own terms."

Fiona's voice floated through Michaela's head. *"Think opportunity! Think fun!"*

"Sure. Why not?" Michaela finally choked out. "I'd be happy to come."

An hour later, Scott the Single was the last thing on Michaela's mind as she sucked in air, folded over the arm of the sofa she and April had managed to wedge in the doorframe. Her toe was shouting at her about stubborn pride and how she should have taken the college guy up on his offer to help.

As if to reinforce the thought, April climbed over her end and panted, her silky black ponytail sliding over her shoulder. "So you had a big muscly hockey player at your disposal, and you said no?"

"I didn't want to have to drive him back," Michaela mumbled into the couch's cushy seat.

"*I* could have driven him back, Miss Mick. I bet he was really built and really, really cute." April was forever on the lookout for

Prince Charming and, unlike Michaela, seemed to find a possible candidate every weekend. Oh. Because April actually *went* out.

Michaela lifted her head and shook it. “Way too young for you, April.”

April gave her a wolfish grin. “Naw, more like trainable. And a hockey player. Lots of stamina.” She fanned herself with her hand.

“Okay, mind out of the gutter and back on the problem at hand.” Namely, maneuvering the much-heavier-than-she-remembered red beast into her apartment. 3D puzzling, figuring out how to make things fit, had never been her strong suit, but she wasn’t the sort to run from a challenge. Besides, she couldn’t just leave the couch where it was. She dropped her face back into the cushion with a grunt.

“What are you doing, Miss Mick?”

“Strategizing. We need to figure out how we’re going to accomplish this muscular feat with strength neither of us has.” When April didn’t come right back with a snarky remark, Michaela lifted her head ... in time to hear a deep voice reverberate behind her.

“Uh, can I help?”

She bolted upright and turned in time to catch her 3:00 a.m. neighbor eyeing her Lycra-covered rear. Remembering how he’d ogled his date’s butt, she pegged him for an ass man. Then again, she *had* been offering it up, so to speak. His eyes shot up to hers, guilt plastered all over his face, and he gave her a sheepish half-smile. Damn.

# Chapter 4
# HOWDY NEIGHBOR

God, Blake hated to destroy the visual by talking to it, but he couldn't continue gawking at the beautifully rounded butt because it was taunting him and conjuring all kinds of dirty scenarios in his head.

"Hey!" a woman with a long black ponytail piped up from the other side of the red couch. Distracted as he was, he hadn't noticed her, and her sharp greeting made him snap to and consider a salute. Or was that unbridled enthusiasm on her part? Mom's lectures about good manners aside, the woman currently assessing him was one more solid reason he couldn't keep staring at the bite-worthy ass on display in front of him. The woman who belonged to said flawless ass hinged at the waist and swung herself into an upright position. Pivoting crisply, she nearly fell on that perfect butt of hers. Brown fluffy curls framed wide gray eyes peeping through schoolteacher, black-rimmed glasses.

"It's you!" she exclaimed, and not in a good way. She tugged at the hem of her neon body-hugging, long-sleeved running shirt, looking like she wanted to cover up. Instead, she managed to pull it tighter and accentuate other parts of her anatomy that were also perfect. God, he loved spandex or whatever the hell fabric was clinging to her curves. Another tug—of her sleeve this time—and he glimpsed a green vine adorned with delicate red flowers above her wrist right before she covered it.

So Curly was into tattoos? Unexpected. Not that he'd expected anything from her. Nope, not a thing. That would have meant he'd given her a thought after their run-in, which he hadn't. Well, none he'd openly admit to himself.

He dipped his shoulder, letting his gym bag slide off and thud to the floor. "Yep, it's me, and it looks like you're having a logistics issue."

"Yes!" said the Asian-looking woman. "Do you think you could help us get this into her apartment?" Curly opened and closed her mouth a few times, the motion reminiscent of the largemouth bass he used to chase as a kid in Oregon.

Curly's gaze lifted over his shoulder and focused on something—or someone—beyond. A beat later, Blake understood when Ferguson called, "Be happy to, ladies," from behind him.

Soon his roommate was crowding him, zeroing in on Curly. "I'm Owen Ferguson," he announced, as if she'd recognize the name.

Apparently, she didn't. She jabbed her thumb over her shoulder. "That's April Joon, and I'm Michaela Wagner."

Ferguson's slow smile—the one he used liberally on women he viewed as prey—spread over his face as he swept his gaze from Curly's knees to her neck. "Michaela. That's a beautiful name."

Blake held back his gag reflex. Michaela perched her hands on her hips, her expression utterly blank. Was she charmed by that shit? Was the girl charmed by *anything*? Doubtful, just as it was doubtful she had a sense of humor. Not that Blake gave a rat's rear end.

Michaela turned her attention on him, arched an expectant eyebrow, and let out a cute little chuckle. "And you are?"

Huh. If he wasn't mistaken, an unexpected sense of mischief had just made an appearance.

Before he could answer, Ferguson palmed his shoulder with one hand and pointed with the other. "I'm with stupid here." Then he laughed at his own not-funny joke. It died a quick death in his throat when no one else laughed.

"I'm Blake. Barrett. We're your neighbors." Yeah, he was playing right into Ferguson's description of him: stupid.

Michaela broke out a huge smile and extended her hand, which he took without thinking. "Blake Barrett," she chirped, "I'm happy to meet you because, boy oh boy, do I owe you a big fat apology."

Stunned didn't begin to describe his reaction. Utterly disarmed, the first thought to reach his muddled brain was, "Okay. *Now* I get what Fergs likes about this girl because, damn, she has a beautiful smile." He never got to the second thought.

"I'm, um, really sorry about the thing with ... I shouldn't have pointed the pepper spray at you. Totally uncalled for. I've been trying to figure out a way to apologize ever since." She glanced down at her hand—the one he was still shaking. "May I have my hand back now? I need it to move the couch." Her smile turned downright impish.

*Crap!* He dropped her hand as though an electrical shock had just buzzed up his arm. "Sorry! Uh, no apology needed. We'll take care of the couch. Where do you want it?"

Ferguson guffawed in Michaela's general direction. "Yeah, I heard you about maced him the other night. Somebody shoulda done it a long time ago."

*"What?"* April shrieked.

Michaela's shoulders pulled up around her ears, and a look of horror mixed with contrition overcame her features. Though he was sure the little ball-buster could take care of herself, Blake's better-mannered side felt a pull to bail her out.

"Nah, it was just a joke," he tossed out. "Two tired people bumping into each other in a dark hallway at three o'clock in the morning. She had her keys in her hand, and my vision was a little bleary. Eye-to-brain disconnect."

She grimaced and opened her mouth, to say what, he wasn't sure because he cut her off. "Therefore, I owe *you* an apology. Hey, did you know that half your brain is involved with sight? And the human eye stays the same size from the time we're born, but our ears and nose keep growing?" He grinned at her to complete the charade.

Ferguson tapped his arm impatiently. He'd been on the receiving end of Blake's useless bits of trivia for years. "C'mon, meat. Let's do this." He brushed Michaela on his way to the other end of the couch, though there was plenty of room to maneuver around her. She jumped back and eyeballed Blake as if trying to calculate whether he'd pull the same move. *No worries, Curly. I have no intention of getting that close, even if your ass and tits* are *perfect. Not that I noticed. Except I totally did. I'm a guy. It's a reflex, like breathing*.

She mouthed, "Thank you," throwing him off balance again.

He hoisted his end of the couch with an overabundance of force before he realized Ferguson was doing squat on his end. Correction. He was executing some weird slow-mo fingers-in-his-hair move like he was a model posing for a shot. Giving April the flirt face, he paused, grabbed the back of his T-shirt, and tugged it off over his head.

*Oh, for fuck's sake! Like that's not an obvious ploy to show off.*

If April's saucer-sized stare and gaping mouth were any indication, Ferguson's antics were effective. Michaela, on the other hand, narrowed her eyes at Blake and jabbed a thumb toward Fergs. "Does he always do this?" In that instant, she netted a few points on Blake's likability chart.

"Pretty much *all* the time," he grumbled.

"Hey, I just showered, and I don't want to leave any sweat stains on my fresh T-shirt," Ferguson fake-protested.

He and Fergs maneuvered the couch into the apartment, with Ferguson exaggerating every flex and curl of his exposed muscles, meaning Blake did most of the moving. After they got it into place, Ferguson performed a back-of-the-hand swipe over his forehead. "Phew! That was a workout."

"Seriously?" Blake chuffed. Guy hadn't broken a sweat—probably because he hadn't done any work—and he threw Blake a fuck-you look.

Oblivious to their silent signals, Michaela said, “Thank you guys so much. I think the couch would have been stuck there for a week without your help. When I leave in six months, I’ll be sure to hire movers to deal with it.”

“No problem,” Blake muttered as his gaze swept her condo. With only four units per floor, each one offered a corner view, and this one looked out at the northern mountains and a neighboring building. It was sparsely furnished, though the effect seemed intentional, and those furnishings it held looked sleek and really expensive. Cold. It struck him that the buttery red couch was the only item in the place that seemed to suit her, though he knew nothing about her—except she carried mace and wasn’t afraid to use it.

Ferguson’s true objective became unmistakably clear when he flashed her a grin. “How about showing your gratitude with some paybacks?”

Michaela folded her arms across her chest, making no effort to conceal a skeptical smirk. “Like what?”

Fergs made no move to put his shirt back on, but she kept her eyes steady on his, unlike April, who had yet to stop drifting her fangirl gaze all over him. Fergs reached up and smoothed the back of his neck, flexing his bicep in the process. Jesus, where did the dude learn this shit? Blake had never seen him put on the ridiculous bodybuilder porn poses before. He must have been *really* hot for this chick, even if he seemed to be putting on the act for her friend.

“I was thinking,” Fergs drawled. “There’s this great little bar on the corner—”

“The Detour?” Michaela offered.

Ferguson’s smile grew wider. “Yeah. You know it?”

Michaela shook her head, and her dark brown curls bounced around her heart-shaped face. That’s when Blake noticed a dusting of freckles across the bridge of her nose. “Not really. I’ve walked by a few times since moving here, but I’ve never been inside.”

"We need to change that. Right now. Let's get on down there. My treat."

Michaela's eyes slid toward Blake, and her brows pulled together in a question mark. She started to speak, but Fergs cut her off. "Nah, he doesn't drink."

April seemed to emerge from her trance. "I do!"

After an awkward beat, Fergs feigned enthusiasm. "Good! The more, the merrier."

Michaela kept her eyes leveled on Blake. Humor sparkled in their depths. "What about you? You don't ever go to bars? And you don't drink … anything? Not even water?" Then she winced. "I should at least bake you some cookies after … Buying you a drink is the least I can do. Would you join us?" She blinked at him, waiting for an answer.

How could he say no? Besides being rude, he had nothing planned—well, except calling his mom like he'd promised his sister he would after she had begged him during their conversation this morning. But he could easily put off that unpleasantness for a few more hours, even if the obligation was pressing on him like a determined defenseman. One quick drink, he told himself, and he'd head back to the condo and make the call he dreaded.

In his peripheral vision, April directed a puzzled expression at him while Fergs glowered. That glower made up Blake's mind for him. "Did you know that North America's Great Lakes contain twenty percent of all the water found in the world's freshwater lakes? But to answer your questions, I go to bars, and I drink water, among other things. Typically, it's club soda or Coke and lime, though I've been known to throw back a glass of something on special occasions."

"Really?" Ferguson challenged. "Haven't seen an occasion special enough for you to pull that stick out of your ass in a loooong time."

Ferguson was verging on jackassery, triggering a few unpleasant thoughts inside of Blake, so he pretended he hadn't heard him.

Michaela raised a sculpted eyebrow. He didn't know her well enough to answer the question dancing in her eyes, namely why he didn't drink. The question she asked, though, wasn't the one he expected. Another assumption shot down. "Did he rope you into being his roommate to get a built-in designated driver?"

"No," Blake retorted, more for Ferguson's sake than Michaela's. "It's because he couldn't meet girls any other way." *Shit. That wasn't only a lie, but it came off sounding cocky as hell.* Then again, he wasn't trying to impress anyone, so what did it matter how he came off? He executed an inner shrug.

Apparently, it mattered to Ferguson, as the deepening scowl on his face proved. While he scooped up his T-shirt and yanked it on, Michaela slid her mouth to the side, looking thoughtfully at Blake. "Obviously, *you* don't need help meeting girls." She pressed her lips together as if stifling a laugh.

A flush of embarrassment rose up Blake's neck. Was that a compliment? No, she had to be yanking his chain over catching him with Sherry. As his flush practically flamed, he detected a flicker of something undecipherable in her eyes. He wasn't adept at reading women in the first place, and women like her were as mysterious as the reasons why Hollywood kept remaking *Spiderman*. Michaela Wagner was an anomaly in his world, where the women he met were usually in bars and were on a mission to notch a hockey player into their proverbial bedposts.

Rarely, like a few nights ago with Sherry, he found himself in the sack, though most times he avoided encounters altogether because—like a few nights ago with Sherry—an element of clumsiness inevitably arose that left him feeling inept.

The four of them ambled out of the building toward the corner bar, Ferguson crowding Michaela's side while Blake and April brought up the rear. Fergs poured on the charm, flashing Michaela one smile after another while nearly tripping over his feet in his overattentiveness. Michaela returned those smiles with brilliant ones of her own, apparently enjoying Ferguson's interest.

April yanked Blake back to the present when she tapped Michaela's arm. "Hey, you never told me what happened with the speed dating the other night."

Michaela's eyes fired daggers over her shoulder, and her lips formed a tight, menacing line. "Filter?" she growled.

April's nose lifted a few inches. "Of all people, you should know I have no clue what that is."

Five minutes later, they sat at ninety-degree angles from one another at one corner of the bar, Fergs bookending Michaela on one side and Blake making up the second bookend beside April.

Grinning, Fergs leaned in close to Michaela. She didn't move away. "Speed dating? Really? Why?"

She huffed out a breath that lifted the curls from her forehead. "Let's just drop it."

Dropping it was the last thing Ferguson seemed to want to do, so Blake interjected. "Did you know that speed dating was invented by a rabbi in 1999?"

Michaela side-eyed him. "Remind me to invite you the next time I have to play Trivial Pursuit."

When the bartender asked for their drink orders, Michaela pointed at Blake and announced, "I'm buying his." He gave the pretty blond bartender a discreet swiping motion with his hand—his own sign language for "no way"—and she flashed him a grin, mouthing, "Got it."

Their drinks came, and Fergs raised his pint of brew. "Here's to meeting new neighbors."

Michaela clinked his glass with her own pint. "To new neighbors willing to move couches." She sent a nod Blake's way, and he nodded back while he touched glasses with April.

"I guess assistants who give up their Saturdays don't make the grade," April deadpanned before chasing a healthy swallow of her beer.

Michaela patted April's shoulder. "Thank you, Apes. You're the best." Then she stage-whispered, "Even if you do spill my personal secrets."

Ferguson chuckled. “How long have you two known each other?”

April’s dark eyes rose to the ceiling. “Well, let’s see. I was assigned to her back in May, so that would make it”—she dropped her eyes even with Michaela’s—“six months now?”

Blake stirred his drink with the dinky straw. “Assigned?”

“April and I work together,” Michaela offered.

“She’s my boss,” April corrected.

“Where do you guys work?” asked Ferguson.

“A local law firm,” Michaela answered. “Steadman, Hart & Fast.”

“You’re an attorney?” Blake and Ferguson both blurted in unison.

Calculating gray eyes—no, their shimmer made them appear more silver than gray—seemed to appraise them from behind those librarian glasses of hers. “Is that a problem?”

Impressed and utterly intimidated, Blake stammered. “No, uh, of course not. It’s just ... I mean, you seem kinda young to be an attorney.” He hadn’t pegged her for a smart attorney—hadn’t pegged her for *anything*—and his tongue was oddly tied in knots, so he silently sipped his club soda.

“So you chase down ambulances?” Fergs threw out.

Something fiery flashed in Michaela’s silvery eyes.

April smirked. “Hardly. You’re dealing with a real estate lawyer here, not someone who works for ‘The Strong Arm.’ But don’t get into an argument with her.”

Anyone who watched TV or listened to the radio in Denver knew the moniker “The Strong Arm” belonged to a local personal injury lawyer, and Blake nodded his understanding.

“Yeah? That’s cool. What exactly does a real estate lawyer do?” Ferguson was all smooth confidence.

“I work mostly on contracts for the higher-ups and their clients,” Michaela replied. “I have a long way to go to earn my stripes.”

Ferguson’s phone rang, and he excused himself.

His curiosity piqued, Blake asked, “Is that why you were working so late the other night?”

April leaned in conspiratorially. “No, she was speed dating, remember?”

Michaela’s eyes flared once more. Sore subject, apparently. “What do *you* do?” she asked Blake.

How much to tell her? Hell, she was his neighbor, and soon she’d be dating Ferguson, so there was no reason to hold back. It wasn’t as if she’d start salivating all over him as soon as she learned what he did for a living. Still, he glanced over his shoulder and dropped his voice. “Owen and I play hockey.”

“Hockey? Well, that explains the bods.” April batted her boss’s arm, and Blake stifled a smirk. She then turned in her seat and faced him. “What team do you play for?”

Sucking in a breath, he braced himself. “The Colorado Blizzard.”

Michaela’s gaze shot to his. “The Blizzard?” Her eyes widened. “Oh. *Oh!* You’re with the big-boy team. None of this minor-leaguer stuff.”

He nearly let loose a laugh. “Yeah, I guess you could call it that. Do you know hockey?”

She shook her head. “Not a thing. Well, that’s not true. I know there’s an ice rink and sticks and a rubber disk that skaters chase. And lots of blood. Some of the attorneys in my firm are nuts about the sport, and I pick up a little here and there.”

April began looking around as if bored, so he directed his question to Michaela. “If I may be so bold, you may not be picking up the right stuff. There’s not that much blood. Back in the day, guys used to fight a lot more than they do now.”

Michaela propped her elbows on the bar and leaned forward. “Is that where the saying ‘I was at a fight the other night, and a hockey game broke out’ came from?”

“Maybe,” he chuckled. “Haven’t heard that one before. Do you follow any sports?”

“Not really. I don’t have time. Besides, I’d rather play them than watch.”

"Yeah? What do you play?"

"Used to. In high school and college, I shot competitively. Mostly 3-Gun."

Blake's body jerked involuntarily, and he sat back. *Whoa. Knew you were a ball-buster, but a ball-buster with a gun or three? Shit!*

She seemed to read his mind, and she laughed. "Do you know what 3-Gun is?" When he shook his head, she went on. "It's a best-shooter competition involving a rifle, a pistol, and a shotgun."

"You competed with all three?"

"Yep."

"Were you any good?" He winced inside at his own incredulous tone.

"I won a few trophies." There was that impish look again, and it told him there was a lot more behind "a few trophies."

"Huh. I've always wanted to learn."

She pulled her arms off the bar and straightened. "I haven't been to the range in a while, but next time I go, you're welcome to come along. Maybe that'll help make up for the other night."

He nodded dumbly, wondering if letting a small woman teach him how to shoot meant turning in his man card. "Sounds ... interesting."

April blew out a breath. "Okay. I've been patient long enough. What happened with the speed dating?"

Michaela's cheeks flushed a deep pink.

"C'mon, you met twenty-some-odd hot guys. Prince Charming had to be in the mix," April pressed. "Wait. Is *that* why you looked so tired the next morning?"

The fact that Michaela appeared to be squirming in her seat didn't keep Blake from jumping into the fray. He was damn curious himself. "Why do you speed date?"

"I don't *speed date,*" she snapped. "I tried it once. Just once. It's in the past."

"In the past as in two nights ago?"

April whacked his arm. "Yeah. See what I put up with?" The smirk on her face told him she didn't mind putting up with Michaela.

Ferguson's reappearance busted up the fascinating conversation. He withdrew his wallet and fished bills from it. "Hey, uh, that was my mom. My grandma fell, and Mom took her to the emergency room. They're there now, waiting to see a doc."

Michaela's eyes went round. "Is she okay?"

"Mom thinks so, but she banged up her arm pretty good, so I said I'd head on over." He pointed at the bills. "This should cover this round and the next." He looked Michaela dead in the eye. "I really hate to leave. This was fun. I'd like to do it again sometime soon." While the girls thanked him, he motioned Blake to follow him.

Blake tapped the bar. "Be right back. Hold my seat."

"Make sure they get back okay, and make sure no one puts the moves on Michaela, got it?" Ferguson said as they strode through the bar.

Should Blake tell him the little 3-Gun winner didn't need his protection? Nah. "What was up with all that flexing shit you pulled back at her place?"

Ferguson grinned and pointed both index fingers at his stomach. "Hey, I work hard for this body. May as well use it to my advantage whenever I can."

"Yeah, well, you looked like an idiot. And FYI, I don't think she was impressed."

"No thanks to you, dumbass." Then his grin widened. "Isn't she great? An attorney. Who'd have thunk it?" And his grin dropped. "Do you think she's into me?"

Blake shoved his hands into the pockets of his warm-up pants to keep from throwing them in the air. "I have no idea. Ask her."

Ferguson seemed to weigh the idea. "No, too soon. We're still getting to know each other." An earnest look overcame his face. "What if she's the *one*, Bear?"

Blake couldn't believe he was having this conversation, and he wanted out. *The one?* What was this, high school? *Princess*

*Bride?* "Might want to leave this one alone. She's not like the girls you usually go for."

Fergs frowned. "How can you tell? You barely know her."

"And neither do you. For one, she seems—I don't know—wound a little tight."

Ferguson's seriousness fled, and his eyebrows rode up and down his forehead. "And I'm just the guy to loosen her up." He backhanded Blake's chest. "Now get back over there before some douche tries to steal my girl."

# Chapter 5

# MICKY-DUB WANTS TO COME OUT AND PLAY

Michaela tried not to visualize wrapping her hands around April's neck and throttling her after hearing the same question about speed dating for the third time—and coincidentally, just as Blake retook his seat. *Oh goody. He got to hear it too.*

The tightness in her own tone pricked her ears. "Please leave it alone, April. I'm not talking about it here." Nothing like having your humiliations trotted out to total strangers. Maybe she'd let the boss-employee line blur a bit too much. Thank God for both of them the bartender chose that moment to ask if they were ready for another round.

Michaela's dormant wild side, prodded by her irritation with April, perked up. "Yes! And I need something stronger. A Chopin martini with a twist of lemon, please." When was the last time she'd ordered a martini in the middle of the day? Never. Suddenly, she was that cartoon character carrying a devil on one shoulder and an angel on the other. In her case, the devil was Fun Michaela, and the angel was Hardworking Michaela, the woman driven to prove herself the most dedicated worker and therefore worthy of the Fenton account.

The bartender didn't bat an eye at her order. Blake seemed to give her a cool appraisal, and April shot her a curious glance. Still nursing her first beer, April politely declined while Blake looked around uncertainly, as if he wasn't sure whether he should stay or go. In the end, he gave the bartender a nod.

"Does this mean you're actually going to take the rest of Saturday off?" April asked Michaela.

Michaela pondered for a beat, then gave in to the devil whispering in her ear about having fun. "I think I might."

"Whoa! That's the first time I've seen you do that since I started working for you."

"I guess there's a first time for everything." Sheesh! It wasn't as if Michaela was taking the whole weekend off. No, she'd put in double hours tomorrow. Today she'd relax, even if the guilt killed her, damn it!

April tapped her shoulder. "Well, all I can say is it's about time you took a day off." She looped her purse strap over her shoulder. "I've got a hot date tonight, so I'm heading home." A rare look of contrition overtook her features. "Sorry for badgering you about the ... well, never mind."

Michaela blinked at her.

"Need anything before I go?" April continued.

"Nope. I'm good." Michaela's brain registered that April's expression had switched to full-blown apology, and she softened her tone. "Thanks for your help today. I really do appreciate you giving up part of your Saturday."

That seemed to bring sunshine back into April's smile. "It was fun." Giving Blake a breezy good-bye, she sailed out of the bar. The bartender deposited Michaela's martini and slid a fresh club soda in front of Blake. Just the two of them perched on barstools at each corner of the bar now, perpendicular, their knees nearly touching. She raised her frosty glass. "And now you know why I tried speed dating."

A look of confusion came over him, but he raised his glass anyway and took a drink. "I do?"

She tipped the delicate rim to her lips and sipped. *So good.* "Yes, you do. It's because there's no time in my life for meeting people outside of work." She let out a sigh. "I figured I had nothing to lose if I gave it a try. Dating apps are ... a pain. First of all, the personality evaluations take forever to fill out, then you spend *more* time trying to figure out if the ... potential date ... is who and what they say they are. Not until you finally meet them do you discover they're nothing like their profiles. It's enough to drive the hearts and flowers out of a dedicated romantic." The one advantage she didn't share, though, was that the romantic optimist in her could take her time looking at a picture—or five—and pretend the face smiling at her from the screen was "the one" ... from a safe distance. Disappointment never happened until fantasy met reality.

Blake twirled his glass on the bar.

*Gah, he thinks I'm out of my mind. And from what he's seen so far, can't say as I blame him.* She took another drink and licked her lips. God, that tasted good. "I'm guessing you wouldn't know, though, huh? I mean, who needs dating apps when women are falling all over you?"

He shook his head, the cocky SOB. But he surprised her when he said, "It's not really like that, and time is in short supply for me too. Practices, team meetings, games, being on the road, scrambling to take care of real-life details when I'm back in town. I'm not complaining. I love what I do, but it makes it hard to find someone I can relate to, much less keep a relationship going with that someone."

Michaela frowned and took another sip. "So ... no girlfriend? I thought maybe the woman the other night ..." *Whose face you were practically sucking off.* She let the rest of the thought dissolve in the chilled vodka.

One corner of his mouth quirked. "No, no girlfriend."

Michaela nodded. "Ah. Got it."

They sat in comfortable silence for several beats. When Michaela raised her martini glass once more, she realized it was nearly empty. This probably explained what came out of her mouth next. "This is personal, so tell me to shut up if you don't want to answer. I promise I won't be offended."

He lifted expectant eyes to hers. They were light and large, but she couldn't tell the color.

Downing the last drops of her cocktail, she barreled ahead. "I'm curious. It sounded to me as if she—the girl from the other night—might be open for starting something. Obviously, you found her attractive enough to bring home. Do you plan on seeing her again? Or were you looking for strictly a one-night stand, end of story?" She rested her gaze on him, taking in a somewhat boyish face. Boyish, yet his jaw, which was dotted with reddish-blond stubble, was strong and square. Short, messy blond hair stuck out in places, as if he'd just taken a shower and hadn't bothered with it afterward. A handsome guy—almost *too* handsome—and definitely not her type. Not that she really had a *type*; she simply knew he wasn't it. Maybe it was his age, which, judging by that youthful appearance of his, had to be way less than hers. She preferred mature men, men who'd been around the block at least once and had their shit together.

He chuckled mildly. "I feel like I'm being cross-examined. And it *is* none of your business, but what the hell, I'll tell you anyway." He paused on a sigh. "The brutal truth is she's the type of woman I usually meet—it just seems to work that way—and don't get me wrong. I don't have a relationship phobia or anything, and she was nice, fun, but we really didn't have much in common."

"Beyond wanting a physical connection for the night," she finished for him.

A small smile curved a very generous mouth. "Yeah, that. Which I'm guessing makes me a total dick." He gave her a tentative look, like he was waiting for her to pass judgment. But something struck her about what he said and the way he said it, and she backpedaled from her earlier conclusion that he was young. Maybe it was the deep timbre of his voice, or the light lines creasing his forehead and the corners of his eyes that she hadn't noticed before. He threw back half his drink, and her eye was drawn to his neck as the liquid slipped down his throat. He had a powerful neck, beautifully masculine, and it was attached to powerful shoulders. For a deviant moment, she wondered if his muscles were as nice as his show-off roommate's had been. What a turnoff *that* had been! Did guys think that crap worked?

"No, not a dick," she finally said. "It makes you human. We all need that intimate connection from time to time."

Surprise flickered in his wide eyes, though he didn't say anything.

From out of nowhere, the bartender deposited two more drinks in front of them. Now that she'd given herself permission to take the rest of the day off, she was ready to get down! Throwing back another cocktail seemed like the perfect start.

"Do you mind if I ask you another personal question?" she asked Blake after the bartender walked away.

"Go for it," he encouraged.

"In order to ask it, I have to give up some personal information of my own, so bear with me." She grinned at him. "And of course, feel free to stop me at any time." She paused to clear her throat and toggle back into serious mode, sort of a hazy space at the moment. "I lived with someone for five years. His name was Anders—probably still is." A little giggle escaped her, and she got herself back under control. "Anyway, we talked about getting married. It was one of those vague someday things, but I always assumed ... which was probably my first mistake. You know what they say about assuming." He was watching her patiently, a corner of his mouth tipping upward, so she got herself back on track again. "One day he came home and out of the blue said, 'Micky, this isn't working.' Then he launched into this speech about how he wasn't ready to get married, wasn't even sure he was mature enough to be in a committed relationship, and how unfair it was to hold me back, but he still loved me, blah, blah, blah. The way he talked made me think he was suggesting a separation of sorts, and I assumed—there it is again—there was a chance it was temporary and we'd eventually get back together. I was shocked at first, but I told myself he needed to figure things out and that he'd realize he couldn't live without me. Well, imagine my surprise when, five months later, the guy who wasn't sure he could be in a long-term relationship met someone and married her! He knew her a tenth of the time we knew each other before he committed to the most long-term relationship of all."

"Jesus, I'm sorry."

She flapped a hand at him and sipped her martini. "No, don't be, because that's not the point. The point is this, and it's what leads me to my question. I know, finally, right?" She shook her head on a laugh.

The question slipped from her grasp, and she frowned while she rummaged about her martini-logged brain for it. He arched an eyebrow.

"My question. Oh crap. I forgot what it was." Then she giggled again. She *never* giggled.

"Micky?" he asked.

"Yes?"

"No, I mean, is that a nickname?"

"Oh! Yes, it is. Or was. Back in the day when I was more fun. Only a handful of friends call me that nowadays."

"Uh, can I get you something to eat?" Concern was plastered all over his handsome face.

"No, I don't like bar food."

"Well, how about I walk you home and we get you something to eat there?"

"Don't have anything in my fridge."

He signaled the bartender. "That's okay. I do, and it's healthier than bar food."

Before she knew what had hit her, she was outside, squinting against pale October sunshine, putting one foot in front of the other. A warm hand rested on the small of her back from time to time, guiding her, and after what seemed like forever, they'd completed the half-block walk to their building.

"Oh, that's right! You live here too." She was just sober enough to understand she sounded like a twelve-year-old and that inebriated people were never as lucid-sounding or as funny to sober ones as they were to themselves. Except she wasn't drunk, was she?

"Why don't you drink?" she blurted as they stepped onto the elevator. Whoa! Elevators brought on a serious case of the spins, apparently. She staggered after him when the doors opened onto their hallway, focused on staying upright. She hadn't been this dizzy since college.

"It's a long story," he answered as he unlocked his door. He swung it open so she could walk through first. God! On the one hand, she loved men who acted like gentlemen, but on the other hand, she hoped like hell the spins weren't causing her to drunk-stumble because, hello, no way could she hide it when she was in front of him.

He cuffed her upper arm lightly—she *must* have been drunk-stumbling—and steered her toward a huge dark brown couch that looked like it could swallow her whole. *A whale of a couch! And such guy furniture.*

"Have a seat," his deep, disembodied voice said. "I'm going to cook us up something. Anything in particular you like or don't like or can't eat?"

"Nope. I do not discriminate against food." *Or anyone else*, she thought fuzzily.

The couch was big and masculine and soooo cushy. She fell gently to the side, curled up in a ball, and relaxed into the cushions. *So comfy*.

# Chapter 6

# That Loud Knock Is Opportunity

Michaela had no idea how much time had passed when she stirred to the sounds and smells of cooking. A pillow had been tucked under her head, and a blanket covered her body.

*Omigod! How long have I been out?* She sat up, and the spins returned. *Not that long, apparently.* A bottle of water sat on the coffee table in front of her, a droplet carving a path through the condensation clinging to the plastic. She uncapped it and chugged, then cast her glance to the pillow to be sure she hadn't left drool behind. Because really, did she need to add that to her already horrifyingly embarrassing behavior?

"You're awake." Blake's voice startled her, and she whipped her head to see him holding two plates with steam rising off of them. "Fried rice," he announced way too cheerfully. "It's a little healthier than the normal version, but I figured the rice would do you some good." He slid the plate onto the coffee table in front of her, and the aroma wafted up her nose. Her stomach rumbled in appreciation. When was the last time she'd eaten?

He placed his own serving in front of a different couch that sat perpendicular and handed her a fork, a paper napkin, and her glasses.

When she didn't put on the glasses, he gave her a puzzled look. "Don't you need those?"

"What? Oh. No. I can see just fine without them." She picked up her plate, placed it on her lap, and attacked the mound of yellowy-brown rice jumbled with veggies, strips of egg, and ... toasted pine nuts? Weird, but it tasted delicious, and she let out an errant moan.

"I'm sorry. I don't normally do that," she muttered.

"Do what? Moan when you're eating?" She didn't miss the amusement in his eyes. He had very expressive eyes. Green, maybe. Or gray.

"No, not that. What I meant was, I don't normally get drunk in the middle of the day. Not that I get drunk at night either!" She stuffed a forkful of rice in her mouth to keep herself from talking ... or staring at his eyes.

A chuckle escaped him. It was a warm sound that spread up her spine and made her relax all over, made her feel like she could ... just ... breathe. "It's okay," he said. "Sometimes we just need to step outside the box and cut loose."

*Not so sure about that.* She shoveled in another forkful of rice and chewed. "I don't think I thanked you for letting me use your body today."

His eyes flew to hers, and he looked all kinds of confused.

She backpedaled. "Your muscle. For the couch." She quickly added, "You and your roommate."

"You thanked me plenty already." One corner of his mouth lifted. "Does this mean you only wanted me for my body?"

"Um, I guess it does."

He cast his eyes to his plate, but not before she caught a flush of embarrassment on his face. Her stomach twitched. *Time to steer this in a different direction.* "This is really, really good. Did you cook it all by yourself?" She winced at the way the question sounded. For a woman who was supposed to be good with her words, she was seriously lagging.

Her comment elicited another chuckle. "I did cook it all by myself. Even cut up the ingredients. I try to cook as much as possible, but the schedule makes it tough. I like cooking. It's cathartic, helps me relax. The six-foot Wolf range was the main reason I rented this condo." He waved his hand vaguely behind him toward the open gourmet kitchen and yes, a humongous stainless range. "Did you know that wild rice really isn't rice?"

"Um, no, I did not know that."

"So did you ever remember your question?"

Truly puzzled, she rested her fork on her half-empty plate. "What question? If you're talking about the one where I asked if you guys are roommates because you can be his DD, then I think I know my answer. He picked you because you can cook."

His gaze dipped to his food again, and the look she glimpsed was endearingly bashful. "Thanks," he mumbled.

She found herself wanting to put him at ease. "Have you and your roommate known each other long?"

He raised his eyes to hers. "Ferguson? Since we were kids."

*That's right! Ferguson ... the Flexer.* "How's living together when you play on the same team?"

"Usually, it's pretty easy. We share rides, hang out together."

"I hear a 'but' in there."

He stood abruptly, taking his plate with him, and extended his hand. "Seconds?"

"No, thanks. I'll just finish this. Unless you have to-go containers." He seemed to scrutinize her, as if he wasn't sure whether she was serious, and she rushed to say, "The part about the to-go is a joke."

Not even a minute later, he was back, his plate heaped with the rice concoction.

"Sorry," she murmured. "I didn't mean to pry." Man, she was screwing up left and right here! Normally, she could get people to relax around her, but apparently not this guy. Probably because she was coming off like an airhead.

Without looking at her, he shook his head. "No, you didn't. It's just ..." When he raised his eyes to hers again, his face held a pained expression. "He and I are both centers. Do you know what that is?"

She shrugged. "Not really, but I assume you're in the center of something team-related."

He rewarded her with a warm, genuine grin. "That's as good an answer as I've heard. Must be why you get paid the big bucks."

"Ha! If only. So you're centers and ..."

"We each center what's called a line. On the line, there are two wings, one on each side."

"So three altogether."

"Correct. On the back end, there are two defensemen." The quickening cadence of his speech tipped her off that he was in his element now. "In all, five players from each team are on the ice at the same time. Six when you count the goalie, for a total of twelve between the two teams. Unless one team's killing off a penalty, or we're in overtime, and then—"

Her confusion must have shown all over her face because he stopped suddenly, then continued with, "Never mind. Back to the centers. Typically, there are four lines on each team. You have your first line, your second, and so forth. The top two lines get the most ice time, and every guy wants more ice time."

"Therefore a player wants to be on the first or second line?" She told herself to project a "got it" look, but truth be told, a real estate contract made more sense to her. "Do you all get to take turns at it?"

"Yes, every man wants to earn his way to the top line, and no, we don't get to 'take turns.' You have to work your way up, show that you have more skill and grit than the other guy. Or if a top line center gets injured, you might have an opportunity to center that line."

"Okay. So injury equals opportunity. Got it."

He seemed to short-circuit for an instant. "Never looked at it exactly that way before, but yeah, that's about right. You don't want guys to get injured, but that is one way to prove yourself. Anyway, we have a fantastic first-line center, Gage Nelson, and he's not going anywhere. Until lately, Owen was on the second line, and I was third line. But that changed just recently when

Coach switched it up. I'm on the second line now, and Owen dropped to third."

She pointed her fork at him. "Ah. And that's not something you can simply leave behind at the office?"

There was that grin again, though she had no idea what he was grinning at. "Usually, we refer to it as leaving it on the ice, but that's a good analogy."

She nodded, warmed by the grin still aimed at her. "You two are competing for the same job, and I'm guessing things are little strained at home." Her eyes took a turn around the open, two-story space that mirrored her own loft.

His smile slid, and he blew out a breath. "Yeah, you could say that."

"That's gotta be hard. There's a competition at my office right now, and it's pitched every junior attorney against each other. It gets contentious, but none of us has to live together. Plus, you're friends, and I can only imagine how that complicates things."

"It doesn't help. Tell me about the competition at your office. Are you in the running?"

"Yes, I think so." She explained about vying for the big contract. When she finished, he pointed at her glasses where they lay on the coffee table. "So what's up with the glasses? You said you don't need them."

Could she tell him? Sure, she could. He already thought she was nuts anyway. "I don't. I see just fine." She held the glasses out to him. "Here. They're clear. See for yourself."

He put them on and looked around the room. They were too small for his face, and the round frames gave him a bug-eyed look. "Seriously? Then why do you wear them?"

She burst out with a laugh. "I graduated early, and for years people told me I looked like I had just started high school. As an attorney, you need to appear credible. Looking like a kid is a big handicap. I was goofing around and tried on a friend's glasses one day, and she told me they made me look older. So I got a clear pair, and guess what? Instant cred."

"Get out! Really?"

He handed them back to her, and she put them on and pushed them up on the bridge of her nose. "I'm not kidding. Sad, I know, but true. Plus, I get the added bonus that they make me look smart." She held her arms wide. "Right?" She turned her torso this way and that, quickly adding, "If you disagree, please keep it to yourself."

Lacing his hands behind his head, he leaned back and smirked; she tried not to notice how squared-off and well cut he was. "I'd lay odds you'll beat out everyone at your firm and land that contract without breaking a sweat."

*Aw, that's just ... God, that's sweet.* Normally, she'd take a remark like that for what it was: a platitude. But coming from him, it didn't sound like it. Then again, maybe the lingering martini effect was holding sway over logic.

Telling herself it was time to go, she snatched off her glasses and stood with her now empty plate. "Thank you so much for the rice—it was what the doctor ordered—and thank you for ... well, for taking care of me. I hope I wasn't too big a nuisance. Honestly, I usually don't do things like that. Now I have more red ink on my ledger, as Natasha Romanoff would say, and I need to balance it out," she babbled. "I really should go and let you get back to whatever you need to get back to. Can I help you clean up?"

He had risen when she had, and now he took her plate and added it to his own. "No. I got this."

She followed him to a large kitchen island, where he placed the plates in an oversized sink. Considering the delicious meal he'd just whipped up, the kitchen was surprisingly neat—unlike her kitchen whenever she cooked. The guy was a catch ... for someone much younger ... or when he finally became an adult.

The realization led her back to the other night when she'd first laid eyes on him. "So the other night, when, ah, I made the unfortunate decision to threaten you ..."

A laugh rumbled through him. "You didn't exactly threaten me."

They faced each other at one corner of the island, about four feet apart. "Well, maybe you didn't find me threatening, but I was *trying* my damnedest to threaten you. Guess I need to work on my scary face."

"Better work *real* hard, Curly. And grow a few inches while you're at it." He leveled a look at her she couldn't read, but intuition told her there was a lot packed behind it, and he wasn't planning on unpacking anytime soon. Suddenly, he didn't look quite as young as he had mere moments before.

"Well, anyway, the other night your, ah, date said something about lessons, and I was curious—"

He scratched the back of his neck. "You heard that, huh? Ouch. Yeah."

She flipped her glasses on top of her crown. "Why ouch?"

He laced his fingers again, placing them on top of his head, and closed his eyes briefly before opening them back up. *Green. Light green, like my favorite wall color, fern.* "She said I needed kissing lessons."

Michaela spat out a laugh, and those green eyes of his turned icy. "No, no, I'm not laughing at you," she gulped. "It's just ... I find that a little hard to believe, based on what I saw. You looked like you knew what you were doing, and I didn't hear her complain. Just saying."

His hands slid off his head, and his shoulders eased.

She parked her fists on her hips. "Know what I think? I think she wants to see you again, and she planted that little seed of doubt so you'd call her."

"Really?"

"Really."

He let out a mirthless laugh. "Christ, I wish I could figure out how a woman's brain works. It's so damn complicated."

"And I'm trying to figure out the male brain. Maybe we can help each other out." She grinned.

"Help each other out how?" A semblance of a sly smile curved his mouth.

While she'd been thinking they could exchange secrets about the inner workings of each gender's brain, a different idea smacked her. The martinis were definitely in charge, and she decided that, for better or worse, she would let them run wherever they wanted to take her. If nothing else, she had a story to share with Fiona.

Raising her hands, she gave him a come-here motion. "Like this. Show me what you got."

His eyes went wide. "Excuse me?"

"Kiss me," she said. "Let's see if you need lessons or not." What the hell possessed her? *Martinis.* "I want to help you out, and this will erase some of that red ink on my ledger."

He took a tentative step toward her. "Uh ..." The sly smile was still there, though a little less sure.

She rolled her eyes. "Come on. I *know* you're not shy. Not after what I witnessed."

"It's not that, it's just—"

"Look, it's not like we're attracted to each other, so you can relax. This is purely educational. Nonsexual."

He chuckled. "Nonsexual is kissing my mom or my sister. No offense, but you don't remind me of either one."

"No offense taken. In fact, I'd say that's an offhanded compliment. Nothing against the women in your family, of course."

"Of course."

"So. Show me what you got, hockey player." She was enjoying egging him on a little too much. He didn't look like he minded, though.

"All right, Curly, since you insist." He closed the gap and looked down at her, hesitating. "What do I do with my hands?"

"What do you *usually* do with your hands?" Vaguely, she became aware her heart rate had kicked up, and a delightful heat was rolling off of him and wrapping itself around her.

"Uh, not sure I've ever really thought about it."

"Then just put them where they want to go naturally. Shoulders, waist, wherever. Well, stay away from ... you know, the girlie parts."

"Got it. No girlie parts." He looked like he was holding back a snicker—or twelve.

Oh so lightly, she slid her hands up his chest and rested them on his shoulders, chiding herself for enjoying the feel of his hard planes beneath her touch.

He glanced down at one of those hands.

"I've never really thought about it either, but I guess my hands are doing what comes naturally," she said.

They both burst into laughter and pulled apart.

"See? Totally nonsexual," she giggled.

"Yeah, right." He pulled in a breath and placed his hands on her waist. They were big, strong, with a heat imprint she'd feel for days. "Okay. Let's do this."

Rising up on tiptoe, she canted her head. They locked eyes—and burst out in laughter again. Her laugh, unfortunately, escaped in the form of a very unladylike snort.

When she caught her breath, she said, "Maybe we should call it quits. This is obviously not working."

"Chicken," he challenged. "I don't like quitting. Let's give it one more try."

Tacitly, she accepted that challenge; she was no quitter either. They returned to their previous poses, but this time when she pushed up on her toes, he lowered his mouth to hers. It was a quick, chaste kiss. Not enough to gauge his technique, but enough that she felt the promise behind it. He pulled back, and, holding his half-lidded gaze, she lifted her finger to his chin and drew him back down again.

There was nothing chaste or quick about the kiss that followed.

# Chapter 7

# The Art of Parsing

The clattering of Michaela's glasses on the floor had Blake wrenching himself away from the press of her body, and not a moment too soon. Staying in that lip-lock with her a second longer would have surely betrayed the inconvenient manifestation of what the kiss did to him.

*Holy fuck!*

Plus, the annoying little voice that kept telling him he shouldn't be kissing the girl Ferguson wanted had reached a feverishly shrill pitch.

His breathing ragged, chest pounding, he opened his eyes to find her dazed silver ones looking up at him. Though he'd pulled away, he kept his hands on her upper back and in her hair, where they'd landed sometime during a long, wet, consuming fusion of their mouths.

"How did I do?" he rasped.

She blinked as though awakening and put another inch of space between them. Her eyes traveled around the room, reminding him of someone trying to get her bearings. He was right there with her, his mind a drunken, dizzy, spinning top. A scatter of confused emotions skated circles in his head. Lust, guilt, desire, alarm at his lack of control.

"I, uh,"—she paused to clear her throat—"I have good news for you. There's absolutely nothing wrong with your kissing."

He swallowed hard. “Good to know.” Reluctantly, he let his hands slide off her as his senses reeled from the plus-ten stun factor they’d just withstood. He bent to pick up her glasses and handed them to her.

“I stand by my, uh, initial, um, whatever I said about her wanting to see you again.” Her eyes landed squarely on his. “You don’t need lessons. You’re just fine.” She patted his chest. Though it was more of a sisterly gesture, it was far too short. He wanted her hand back, and he found himself craving a touch that was more ... intimate.

Good thing she moved to pick up her stuff—he had no clue what—and headed for the door. All of him wanted her to stay, which was a bad, bad thing. Unsure what to say or what to do, he blurted out, “Did you know that two-thirds of people tilt their head to the right when they kiss?” *Oh Jesus! Way to show her what a total dumbass you are.*

“Interesting,” she mumbled as she scurried to leave. “Well, good-bye. Thanks for ... thanks.” The door shut softly behind her before he even realized she was gone. By the time his right mind came back online and told his feet what to do, it was too late. He opened the door, poked his head out, and peered down the hallway, but it was empty. No doubt she was walled up in her own space, safely away from him ... which might not have been a bad outcome, considering he had no idea what more he would have said to her. *“Hey, great kissing you. When can we do that again? By the way, my roommate’s crushing on you, so don’t tell him. And yes, that makes me a complete and utter dickwad.”*

He closed his own door and slumped against it, mindful of the ache in his pants. What the fuck had just happened? His world had tilted, that’s what happened. It had just been rocked by a five-foot-nothing, curly-headed, silver-eyed woman he’d never seen coming. But Jesus, look what he would have missed! Which reminded him how wrong he’d been to kiss her in the first place. Guilt surged inside of him, and reflex sent his hand to his mouth, but he stopped himself before his fingers could swipe the taste of her off his lips. He wanted to savor that taste as long as it lasted.

Rocketing up to his feet, he let out a string of curses, asking himself one more time what he'd been thinking. He hadn't. Another part of his anatomy had done the thinking and yanked the rest of him right along with it in its single-minded quest.

For all his remorse and self-recrimination, though, he let out a laugh. "I don't need kissing lessons."

As he said the words aloud, his ego ballooned. He pumped his arm. "Yeah, you got this!" Now he could kiss indiscriminately without second-guessing himself—which struck him like a stick to the mouth. What if his kissing skills only applied to *her*? He'd been on sensory overload, the sweet taste of her, her fresh fragrance, the feel of her in his arms, of her mouth under his. His mind had blasted off into the clouds, and there had only been her and him ... and a kiss that had sent electrical current thrumming in his veins.

Had her world been rocked like his had?

*It's not like we're attracted to each other.* That *might* have been true before the kiss ... No, if he were being absolutely honest with himself, the attraction was there before. And he knew that because he'd been a little too eager to try out that kiss. Which made him a douche of epic proportions.

He shook his head. *I can't be attracted to her. Ferguson has dibs.* She wasn't even Blake's type, he told himself. Not that he had a type, but short and curly didn't do a thing for him. Nope, not a thing.

Jesus, what would Ferguson think if he knew?

*Wait.* Was the object of his roommate's attention in the habit of kissing guys she wasn't attracted to? If so, what did that number top out at? Guilt over the kiss loosened its stranglehold a fraction but roared right back when his mind zoomed to the solid fact that with or without glasses, curly hair or not, Michaela Wagner was hot as fuck and he wanted to know more about her. He gave himself an inner slap and got to work scouring the kitchen.

After slipping silently through her own door—as if she might wake someone who wasn't even there—Michaela made a beeline for the kitchen, deftly skirting a console table and the edge of an etched glass wall. Which was a minor miracle, considering her current lack of brainpower. Grabbing a drinking glass, she inserted it into the Sub-Zero's cold-water dispenser, filled it, and stared at it. Then she proceeded to pull her shirt away from her chest and tip the contents of the glass down her front, gasping when the icy water hit her skin. As water dribbled down her body and puddled at her feet, her brain snapped to. She blew out a breath.

"Oh. My. God!" Glancing at the empty glass, she pondered another dousing. "What the hell did you just do?" she admonished herself. "Kissed my neighbor. *After* telling him I wanted him for his bod," she answered herself in a feigned matter-of-fact tone. "And now you're talking to yourself, which proves you're losing your freaking mind." She shook her head and told herself to get a grip on her hormones.

With a wad of paper towels, she attacked the pooled water.

What, exactly, had she been trying to prove when she'd drawn Blake in for that kiss? *No idea.* If she had been trying to convince herself she wasn't attracted to him, she had failed miserably. Maybe she could have kept up a pretense before she locked lips with him, but there was no denying the pull once the deed was done. Remembering how his mouth had moved with hers, how he'd taken over the kiss and deepened it, caused her body to flush. She refilled her water glass.

After a restless sleep filled with alcohol-fueled dreams that were embarrassingly erotic, Michaela hauled her butt out of bed, intent on parking it at the office. She had a heap of work to make up, and submerging herself in it would help her erase one hunky, kissing-competent neighbor from her overactive imagination.

A shower later, followed by a few extra swipes at her wayward curls and a second dab of perfume—neither of which she *ever* did for a mere Sunday foray into the office—she tiptoed into the hallway. Shuffling past Blake's door, she prayed it wouldn't open and reveal his six-foot-whatever frame, blond hair, and green eyes. She also prayed it would. Luckily—or not—the door remained shut, and fifteen minutes later she was seated behind her desk, nose and eyes glued to her computer screen.

Shuffling in the hall grabbed her attention. She stood to find out what was making the noise and gasped when Mr. Steadman's white-haired head popped around her doorframe. "Why, Miss Wagner. It *is* you working on Sunday. Shouldn't you be home sleeping in or enjoying time with your boyfriend?" The glint in his eyes and his quirking smile told her she was right where he expected her to be—especially if she was going to pull ahead of the pack in the race for that coveted client. She chose to ignore his obvious fishing expedition to discover her single-or-not status.

"Mr. Steadman! I didn't realize you were in the office."

"Just stopped by to pick up a file."

Why did she get the impression he'd stopped by for more than a file? That maybe a quick tour to see who was putting in extra time had been his real motive? He had to be slick and sneaky to have ascended to his lawyerly pinnacle, after all.

She hesitated a beat before asking, "Is anyone else here? Just wondering so I know whether to lock up when I leave." She was being a little sneaky herself, harboring hope she could shine in his eyes by outshining the other juniors, who were probably having more fun than she was today.

He shook his head ruefully, and though it shouldn't have, her heart lifted. So did her shoulders. "No, Ms. Wagner, you are flying solo in the fort this fine Sunday morning."

*Oh yeah! Scoring some brownie points.* "Is it nice out? I've been so busy I hadn't noticed." *Okay, now you're just piling it on.*

"It's a lovely day. Hopefully, you will find time enough to enjoy it." He tapped her doorframe and looked at her as though adding sums in his head. "Ms. Wagner, my wife has decided it's high time we threw a dinner party for a select few of the newer associates and their significant others. Something about putting faces with names. At any rate, I do hope you can attend. I presume a pretty thing like you has a beau to bring along. If you don't, my wife has any number of friends with unattached sons. I'm sure one among them would prove a willing escort." The smile that followed this kernel of an inappropriate statement was of the fatherly variety, not that Michaela was one to borrow trouble and interpret it as something sexual harassment-worthy. Just a gentleman from a bygone era being complimentary. Probably.

In retrospect, she couldn't say which struck her dumber. That she was being singled out for dinner at the Steadmans'—along with other associates, of course—or that Mr. Steadman was offering for his wife to set her up with a date from among their lofty social circle. While the opportunity to hobnob in the vaunted Steadman mansion was too enticing to resist, she wasn't about to get sucked into a blind date that could easily go off the rails right before Steadman's very eyes. Even her closest friends' blind date choices had proved disastrous over the years, which was why she'd pretty much sworn them off. Well, except those she arranged herself through dating apps.

This thought process culminated in the ambitious devil on her shoulder blurting out for her, "I'd be delighted to come, Mr. Steadman, and so would my beau."

*Wait. What beau?*

His smile broadened. "Wonderful. I'll tell Francis to send you a formal invitation for two. I'm very much looking forward to meeting the man who has captured your attention."

"Of-of course, Mr. Steadman," she stammered.

"Have a pleasant Sunday, Ms. Wagner."

With that, he was gone, and Michaela stared at the open doorway where he'd just been. She blinked once, twice, suddenly aware she needed to go shopping ... for a date, and not just *any* date. He had to be someone well-mannered who could hold his own with the hoity-toity crowd—or who knew when to keep quiet. Who wouldn't embarrass her or blow her opportunity to cozy up to the Steadmans and, by default, the Fenton account.

Except she'd lied. Or had she? No, her statement could be massaged into something akin to a white lie by omission. If she *had* a boyfriend, he *would* be delighted to go because he'd be the supportive type. He could also be the type to come down with a last-minute illness and be too sick to accompany her, leaving her to attend without her nonexistent significant other. But that *would* be lying. Then again, if he didn't exist, would saying he couldn't make it truly be a lie?

Parsing could be so exhausting.

Nevertheless, she'd painted herself into a corner, and if she backpedaled now, her character might be called into question. And she might get stuck with a blind date she wanted no part of.

Heaving a breath, she picked up her phone and began scrolling through her contacts. Surely there was at least one man who could play the role.

Minutes after she'd launched her search—and repeated it twice—she put down the phone in defeat and thunked her forehead against her desktop. Her meager requirements meant 99.9 percent of the men in her phone didn't qualify, and the ones that did—like her father or her ex—were utterly unsuitable.

Her thought process spiraled in desperation, vaulting to various scenarios where she might find a solution. She could subject herself to another round of speed dating; maybe she'd been hasty in rejecting possible suitors that night. The hostess had begged her to give it another try and had even offered a free session. As she flicked through her mind's catalog of candidates from the event, though, she grimaced reflexively. *Nope, that's out.*

An idea winked on like the lights in a hockey arena. The newly single coach—Scott?—loomed in her future at Paige's party. If he was anything like Paige's husband, he could be her perfect stand-in. Michaela had been filled with dread at the prospect of going, churning through excuses to bow out. But now the thought of attending buoyed her spirits, and she hummed a tune as she sauntered into the break room to fix herself a cup of fuel, er, coffee.

"Half and half," she sang out, reaching for the creamy stuff in the fridge ... which she nearly dropped when she wheeled and found herself face-to-face with Brad Hewitt.

"Omigod!" she gasped and braced a hand on the counter. "I thought I was the only one working here today."

His wide eyes gave her chest a blatant and thorough sweep that had her stifling a shudder and sidestepping him.

"Sorry, Michaela. I thought you knew I was behind you."

*"No, you didn't,"* she wanted to fire back but didn't. Instead, she steadied the tremble in her hand and quickly prepped her cup. "What are you working on?" *And why do you always pop up during the same off-hours I'm here?*

"Just taking care of some loose ends before the work week." He crowded her, and she inched toward the fridge until she couldn't inch anymore. Brad wasn't scary, but he was verging on a creepiness she hadn't noticed before.

"So, ah, Michaela." She darted a look toward him. Moisture dotted his forehead, and his eyes shifted left to right. "What, um, about dinner when we're done here?"

She plucked her cup from the counter and wriggled away, heading for the door. "Oh, I can't. I have so much to do."

"But you have to eat sometime!" he whined, sounding as though he strained to come off as funny but not quite hitting the right note. Before she could conjure another flimsy reply, he was back in her bubble, a sweaty hand grasping her upper arm. Her alarm must have shown because he immediately dropped the hand.

"I just want to do s-something n-nice for you," he stammered. He looked so pathetic that she paused a second ... which offered him a chance to lean down to her.

She reared back in horror, bumping her cup and spilling half its contents on the counter. Had he meant to kiss her? No clue, but she tore off a few paper towels and tossed them at the mess before scurrying to her office, calling out, "Gotta get back to work," or something equally feeble over her shoulder. Inside her office, she locked her door and leaned against it until she got her runaway breathing under control.

He didn't follow her—that she could tell—and by the time she poked her head out hours later, he was gone and she'd convinced herself his clumsy lunge had been unintentional and she'd misread the entire situation.

# Chapter 8

# Mothers and Other Guilt-Inducing Anomalies

Blake was tossing spare rolls of tape into his gear bag when Owen sidled up beside him. "Good practice today, huh? You did okay, I thought."

Blake gave him a sidelong glance, chafed by Ferguson's unsolicited appraisal of him. And really, couldn't the guy give him a little more credit? Blake had done more than "okay," at least according to the coaches. Instead of voicing any of this, though, he merely grunted.

Fergs went on, apparently oblivious. "I was thinking about picking up some flowers on my way home and delivering them to our neighbor." His eyebrows bounced. "What do you think? Roses? Something more subtle?"

Why this irritated Blake so much, he couldn't say. "Does it matter?"

Ferguson leaned a shoulder against the stall. "Yeah, it matters. She's smart and classy. Sassy." He grinned. "I want to impress her, but I don't want to go overboard and chase her away. This girl's different."

*Yeah, she is.* "How so?"

"She's ... she's out of my league."

"Then maybe you should leave her alone," Blake huffed.

"Nah. I might be intimidated for now, but—"

"Listen up, boys," Coach LeBrun barked, and everyone's head swiveled in unison toward the locker room door. Beside the coach stood a familiar-looking guy, his face blank. Or was that surliness? "I want you to meet your new teammate, Cam Blue."

Whistles erupted throughout the locker room, punctuated by a few whoops. Their captain, Dave Grimson, pumped his fists in the air.

"Management figured you'd rather play *with* him than *against* him," Coach drawled. "So make him feel welcome."

Guys crowded around the newcomer, and Blake hung back with Fergs, waiting for their chance to say hello.

"Fuck me!" Fergs chuckled softly. "We just acquired the meanest, nastiest D-man in the league! God, I fucking love this club! They don't do anything half-assed."

Blake agreed wholeheartedly and was on the verge of saying so out loud when Coach, who had sidestepped the meet-and-greet mob, crooked his finger their way.

"Ferguson? Barrett? See you boys a minute?"

"Yep." Fergs pivoted to follow Coach out.

"Sure, Coach." When Blake looked down, he realized he'd crushed a roll of tape in his hand. He flung it into his bag and fell in line behind his coach and teammate. When he reached Coach's office, LeBrun instructed him to shut the door and take a seat beside Ferguson.

Coach dropped into the chair behind his desk and leaned forward, his elbows on his desktop. Marty LeBrun wasn't as big as Blake, but the force of his personality made up for it. All Blake had to do was look at the man's scarred hands and craggy face to understand what a total badass he'd been during his playing days. And if that wasn't proof enough, Blake had seen the video of Coach putting the hurt on guys from back in the day. No one to mess around with, and he had the respect of every member of the team. Somewhat soft-spoken, his even tone and spare words carried an undeniable impact. Like now.

"As you boys know, our chemistry's been off these last few games," he began. Blake nodded—they *had* been off, and their three-game losing streak proved it. Coach continued. "I've decided to mix things up for tomorrow night's game." His eyes shifted between them, finally landing on Blake. "Barrett, you're centering the first line. I'm moving Nelson to the second line."

Blake could practically hear Ferguson's eyes widen beside him. He *did* hear the edge in his voice when he said, "What about me, Coach?"

Coach's hawkeyed gaze focused on Ferguson. "You're on the fourth line. Depending on how the game goes, I might split you between third and fourth." Coach smacked his palm on the desk. "That's it. You boys can close the door on your way out."

Heart leaping in his chest, Blake stood. He reined in his excitement, though. Beside him, his mouth hanging open, Ferguson sat frozen in his chair as though his ass was superglued to the seat. Blake tapped his shoulder. "Let's go, Fergs."

Ferguson shot to his feet. When Blake closed Coach's door behind them, Ferguson still wore a stunned look. "You okay?" Blake asked his friend.

Ferguson rounded on him, his mouth a tight line, his eyes hard. "You asshole! What the fuck did you do?"

Blake took a step back. "What do you mean, what did I do? I didn't do anything. I'm as surprised as you."

"Bullshit!" Fergs snapped.

Blake laid his hand on Ferguson's arm. "Let's take this somewhere away from Coach's office." Blake had no idea what Ferguson had done to merit the demotion, but sounding off where Coach could hear wouldn't help his case. At. All. But Ferguson shrugged off his hold and stormed away. Blake sighed and hung his head for a beat. The surge of elation that had spiked in his system when he'd heard "first line" had been thoroughly tamped down.

His phone rang, and he pulled it from his pocket. He muttered a curse when he saw the caller ID. He picked up the call with a resigned, "Hi, Mom." His day was already in the crapper, so what difference would one more pile of shit make?

"Blake!" she shrieked. Her overenthusiastic greeting set his high-alert sirens screeching inside his head and his teeth on edge. She was drunk.

"Hey, uh, sorry I haven't called you. Amanda told me the bad news." Two days ago, when he'd called his sister back, she'd told him how their mom had left rehab—or had been kicked out. Amanda hadn't been sure of the real story because their mother wasn't exactly forthcoming, and Blake had called the rehab center. They'd nicely told him that because of HIPAA, it was none of his business. And while he should have called his mother right then—a good son would at least check on his mother's welfare, wouldn't he?—he simply hadn't been able to marshal the energy for it, telling himself he needed a few more days to build his reserves.

"What bad news?" The high, joyful pitch of her voice brought him back to the conversation and made him cringe.

"Mom, you left rehab again. Or did you get kicked out?"

"I didn't need to be there, so I checked myself out. And good riddance to them, those bunch of power-hungry, so-called medical professionals," she slurred. "Why did you make me go, Blake? Is that any way to treat your mother?"

He braced himself for the part about how she'd brought him into the world, and how she'd suffered doing it, but apparently she was sparing him that speech today.

Slowly, he ambled down the hall, looking for a private place to continue the conversation. "How have you been, Mom?"

"Terrible. Nobody cares about me, including my children." She sniffled on the other end, spurring a flood of emotions in him. Anger, pity, helplessness, guilt, and frustration coalesced into giant knots in his stomach and chest. He never knew how to respond, and in the silence she rushed on. "I might as well just get it over with."

He let himself into a deserted equipment room and sank to the floor. "Get what over with, Mom?"

"My life. What's the point? I'm just taking up space," she whined. "No one will miss me. Life will be easier for you and your sister if I'm gone."

"You know that's not true," he said gently. His head sagged, and he stared at the floor, noticing flecks in its pattern.

"If it's so true, then why aren't you here?"

"Mom, we've been through this. I have a job in Denver. That job is what keeps you in your house and Amanda in school."

Her sniffles amped up into soft sobs, and she sounded like she was starting to hyperventilate. "Why can't I come live with you?"

"Because I can't look after you, Mom."

"Why not?"

*I just can't.* "I'm gone most of the time. You'd be more alone here than you are in Oregon."

"I don't have any friends here. No one likes me. I'm a bad person. That's why you hate me, isn't it, Blake? Because I'm a bad person?"

His shoulders folded around his ears, and his head sank farther. He felt a familiar gash open up deep inside his soul, tearing him apart. "Mom, I don't hate you. But I hate your drinking. You need help, Mom, and I'm not the person to give it to you. Neither is Amanda. We need to find you someone who's a trained professional."

"You will not send me back to rehab," she suddenly snarled. He steeled his spine for the shift in her personality and what was coming.

"Mom, you need help," he repeated, keeping his voice as even as possible. "Help from people who understand what you're going through. I'll pay for it, whatever you need. You didn't like that rehab center, but there are others out there. I can make some calls—"

"Fuck you!" she lashed out. "There's nothing *wrong with me*! *You're* the reason I drink. This is *your* fault."

Every muscle in his body felt fatigued, wrung out, as if every ounce of energy had been drained. "I'm sorry, Mom. I can't do this."

"I love you, Blake," she whimpered, the evil mother supplanted by the pathetic one once more. "I know you hate me for what I did to your father."

Sadly, he knew too well there was no reasoning with her when she was like this. "Mom, I don't hate you. But I can't have this conversation with you when you've been drinking. When you sober up, call me back." Had he kept the harshness he felt from his voice? No idea, not that it mattered.

She spewed a string of vicious curses, telling him how worthless he was, how ungrateful he was, how he only cared about himself. When she stopped to pull in a breath—no doubt to ready her next salvo—he quickly interjected, "I love you, Mom, but I can't do this. I'm hanging up now." He cut off the call before any more spiteful words bombarded him, then turned his ringer to silent so he could keep his blood pressure from skyrocketing every time her number lit his screen. And she *would* call him back until she passed out. Last time, she'd left twenty-eight voicemails. After hearing the first one, he'd deleted the rest without listening.

He stowed his phone and looked around the darkened room, weighing his thoughts, pushing them through a sieve. What could he have said? What could he have done? How could he have handled the call differently? Even as anger heated his blood, he felt the cracks in his heart widen. She was his mother. It wasn't supposed to be like this. He started down the "if only" road ... If only he were a better son ... If only he could tolerate being around her for more than ten minutes ... If only ... "If only she wasn't a drunk," he said aloud, then immediately regretted it. A son shouldn't think such things about his mother, let alone voice them.

Dragging himself upright, he took heavy steps back to the locker room, lamenting how he should have been over the moon with his move to the first line. Problem was, the guy he'd have run to first with the good news was the best friend who had just lost out. Or was that *former* best friend? God, he hoped not. Besides Owen, Blake realized, he had no one to tell, not even family. Well, maybe Amanda, though she was caught up in her own world and disconnected from his by geography and general mindset. While they were siblings, they'd never grown up under the same roof and had only known about each other the last three years. Another uncomfortable chapter Blake would rather see torn out of the book that was his life. Because really, wasn't it at the root of his dysfunctional family?

When he entered the locker room, Fergs was waiting for him by his stall, a sour look on his face. *Go ahead. Pile it on.* In the next instant, Blake told himself to stop the pity party. His friend helped him do just that when he surprisingly said, "I'm sorry, Bear. I shouldn't have lost my cool. None of this is your fault. It's my shitty play that landed me on the fourth line." A ghost of a smile appeared, and he lifted his chin. "Good on you, man. You deserve it."

Blake nodded, masking his whirlpooling thoughts. "Thanks."

Suddenly looking all kinds of awkward, Ferguson scratched the back of his neck. "Well, I'm headed to Grandma's, so I won't be home for a while."

"She doing all right?"

"Yeah, she's great. Said she might have to go back and let the cute young doctor take care of her again," Fergs chuckled.

"Sounds like your grandma. Tell her hi for me. You around tonight?"

"Uh, don't know yet." Ferguson's familiar grin spread over his face. "If I'm lucky and Michaela jumps my bones after I give her the flowers, then no."

"Maybe I'll see you later," Blake grunted.

With a light "See ya later," Ferguson grabbed his gear bag and left as though nothing had happened. Blake leaned his head against his stall and blew out a long, lonely breath. Why couldn't the game be tonight? He could lose himself in hockey and forget this day ever happened.

A half hour later, he was back in his building, and the spot that normally held Ferguson's car was empty, not that he'd expected Fergs to beat him home. As Blake stood poised to unlock his condo, his eyes wandered to Michaela's door, pulling his mind back to the kiss. For a wistful moment, he wished he could knock on her door and repeat last night. If he couldn't lose himself in hockey, he could certainly lose himself in another electrifying kiss—and more.

Guilt once again bobbed to the surface. Admonishing himself with a headshake for his inappropriate thoughts, he opened his door and stepped inside. Time to ignore the rest of the world for a little while and give his heavy heart a time-out.

The time-out didn't last more than an hour because Fergs came home with an armload of roses in every color. "Three dozen," he announced happily. "'Course I bought two more besides to give Mom and Grandma, but it was worth it."

"Isn't three dozen overkill? You barely know the girl," Blake pointed out.

"You think it's too much?"

"Yeah ... maybe." *I have no idea.*

Ferguson tossed the flowers in the laundry room sink and headed off to shower. When he emerged, he smelled like he'd substituted cologne for water.

Blake pinched his nose. "Jesus! You trying to knock her out?"

"Oh, fuck you, Bear! Just because you can't get a date—"

A knock on the front door stopped Ferguson's rant. He threw it open and stuttered to a stop.

On the other side stood Michaela, all curls and smiles, holding a plate tented with foil. Her eyes darted to Blake, and he could have sworn they brightened. *Just your imagination, dumbass.* Her gaze swung back to the plate she held. "I brought you guys chocolate-chip cookies."

Ferguson stood stock-still, his mouth hanging open, so Blake stepped up. "Sweet! But what for?"

Her nose twitched, and she pressed her fingers to it. "For your help with the couch. Phoo! Did someone drop a bottle of cologne?"

Blake bit back his smirk while Fergs let out an embarrassed chuckle. "Guess I overdid it."

Michaela snorted. "Maybe just a little."

Fergs remained frozen, so Blake nudged him aside, lifted the cookies from Michaela's hold, and invited her to come in.

Her eyes took a tour around the entryway and the open living room. "Your place is a lot like mine. Except for the nudes, of course." Now her eyes danced from one overlarge painting to the next.

"Oh, those are Barrett's," Ferguson coughed.

*Liar!* Blake had stopped noticing them a week after Ferguson had had them hung up—okay, two weeks—but now they were blaring back into his consciousness, aided by the late afternoon sun lighting them up. He hadn't given them a second thought when Sherry had come over. It had been dark, but it struck him that even if she *had* seen them, any awkwardness he might have felt wouldn't have touched the awkwardness blazing his cheeks right now.

Two pairs of eyes rested on him. "Honestly, I don't even look at them," he said.

Michaela scoffed. "Right. You just read the ... signatures."

"No, seriously. Someone decorated this place for us, and—"

"I guess they thought hockey players like this kind of ... art," Ferguson added helpfully.

"Or at least naked women," Michaela tossed back.

"I'd much rather have hockey memorabilia on the wall," Blake blurted.

"Bet you say that to all the girls."

Ferguson closed the door behind her and pushed out a breath. "How about a drink?"

"No, thanks. I just wanted to drop off the cookies."

"You sure? I thought maybe we could go back to the Detour. I never got a chance to finish my beer, much less our conversation." Ferguson's voice straddled a curious linc between uninterested and pleading.

Michaela's eyes darted to Blake again. "Both of you?"

"Nah, Barrett's got a date tonight," Fergs rushed in to say. "But I'm free."

Blake was ready to lob a protest over the blatant lie when he noticed a flicker of something in her pretty gray eyes, but it was gone before he could begin decoding it. "Thanks, but I have a lot of work to catch up on, and I've already taken off too much time." She gave Fergs a warm smile. "Some other night."

"Uh, okay."

"Thanks for the cookies," Blake offered.

"Yeah, thanks," Fergs added, not hiding his disappointment.

After she left, Fergs pushed out another breath. "Well, that didn't turn out like I planned."

"Yeah, you weren't your smoothest."

Ferguson flew him double birds. "She's not easy to talk to," he groused.

*"She's* really *easy to talk to,"* Blake refrained from saying. In fact, she was easier to talk to than anyone he'd met lately.

Ferguson interrupted his thoughts. "I'm all dolled up with nowhere to go."

"Go to the Detour, like you planned."

"Wanna come with me?"

"Too tired. I'm gonna call our new defenseman and welcome him to Denver, then watch a movie and hit the sack." *Recharge.*

"Well, there's no point in wasting a sweet-smelling Fergs by cooping him up here." Ferguson's grin was back in place.

"Yeah," Blake replied dryly. "Where only the *nudes* can see you. Why the hell did you tell her they were mine, and why the hell are you talking about yourself in the third person?"

"Oh, shut it," Fergs grumbled.

Blake threw up his hands in surrender, breathing a sigh of relief when Ferguson finally left. He traipsed into the laundry room, and his eyes caught on the roses. Ferguson had completely forgotten them. After debating with himself about running them over to Michaela and telling her they were from Fergs, Blake decided to stick them in a bucket of water and let Fergs do it. They were *his* flowers, and he was better at sweeping women off their feet anyway. Not that Blake would dream of competing with his buddy. Nope. First of all, Michaela seemed to like Fergs, and second of all, if Ferguson thought she was out of his league, that placed her in an entirely different sport from Blake.

# *Chapter 9*

# Roses and Cookies

Five days after delivering the cookies, Michaela walked past the boys' door on her way to run errands. No need to slink. She hadn't run into either of them, partly because they'd been on the road. Were they back now? They'd played a West Coast game last night, but she had little idea how their travel schedules worked.

As if in answer to her silent question, their door swung open. There stood Blake, his tall frame blotting out the interior of his condo, his blond hair a bedhead mess, his green eyes wide with surprise. Her heart pounded a little harder. *Because I'm surprised, that's all.*

"Good morning. Where are you off to?" she chirped.

He closed his parted mouth and jabbed his thumb over his shoulder, stammering, "Practice. Except I forgot something and I need to get it because I need it for ... practice."

"Excuse me," a woman's voice called from behind him. He jumped out of the way as if he had no idea she was there. A mussed-up brunette in disheveled clothing squeezed past him, muttering about a walk of shame and needing to get home. Tempted though she was to bolt, Michaela held back, not wanting to climb aboard the elevator with the woman. The situation was sticky enough as it was.

"Is that what you left behind?" Michaela huffed, fully aware she had no huffing rights—unless her disgust was directed at herself for being such an idiot. *Doesn't know how to kiss, my ass.* She'd misjudged him, let herself get carried away, let that kiss dominate her thoughts for the past week. She'd let it move her world. *It's only because it's been so long.* The attraction she was feeling had to be cut off at the knees. The guy had a regular revolving door of women, and here she'd lost precious sleep over him that he hadn't deserved. Like his roommate, he was nothing more than a typical cocky jock—he simply hid the cocky part behind shyness that was an obvious act she'd bought into. It had been effective.

What a dummy! It wasn't that she wanted to spend the rest of her life with the guy, but she didn't want to go around kissing random playboys either. What if he had an STD? Could you catch STDs from kissing someone? She'd never felt a need to know before. It would be a helpful factoid to have on hand before she returned to dating sites. Remembering his penchant for trivia facts, she coughed out a laugh. *Bet he knows the answer to my question.*

"She's not ... We're not ..." he stammered.

"I suppose she's your roommate's date?" Michaela tossed out primly.

"Uh, not exactly. I mean, she's ... I don't know her," he blurted.

*Seriously?* Michaela withheld a comment about knowing her in the biblical sense and elbowed her qualms about sharing space with the woman. She hurried down the hall, only to have the elevator door slam in her face. *Stairs it is.*

As she hurled herself through the door that opened onto the stairwell, her phone pinged. She glanced down ... and groaned.

Brad Hewitt: *Morning, Michaela. Wondering if you'd care to meet me for lunch?*

Michaela: *Sorry, Brad. I have tons of errands to run.*

Brad Hewitt: *Perfect. I've got errands too. What if I pick you up and we combine efforts? Much more pleasant that way.*

Crap! Maybe she hadn't misread the awkward coffee-room incident. He had often hinted at an interest in her, but it had been mild at most. Seemingly, his interest was growing or his efforts were becoming bolder. How many nice ways could she say, "Not in your lifetime," before their working relationship became affected? There was an unfortunate chance she would soon find out, so she opted for another way out.

Michaela: *Very sweet of you, but I'm seeing someone and don't think he'd be too keen on it.*

She tucked her phone into her back pocket, where she wouldn't see Brad's reply if he sent one. As she stood on the stairwell landing, she told herself her excuse hadn't been a lie. She had literally just *seen someone*, and "seeing someone" was a simple matter of opening the door to the hallway and laying eyes on her playboy neighbor.

Not that she would ever want her "someone" to be him.

Two days later, April's black eyebrows wiggled as she stood in Michaela's office doorway. "Happy Monday. How are my favorite hot hockey players?"

"How about, 'How's my favorite boss?' instead?"

"Well, I can see that you're just fine, and while your neighbors are *mighty* fine, I can't see them. Of course, if you invited me over …"

"Don't waste your brain cells on those two yahoos," Michaela quickly retorted, ignoring the fact that she could still not get one of those yahoos out of her freaking mind. His warm, soft lips, his delectable mouth, those gorgeous green eyes—

"Yahoos is not what comes to mind when I think about ways to describe them." A salacious smile curved April's lips.

"You're incorrigible." Michaela shifted her gaze to her computer, pretending the land-sale contract was utterly absorbing.

"Maybe, but you gotta admit, they are *hot*!"

"And they know it," Michaela scoffed, eyes still focused on the black type against white, but none of it registered. What did register, sadly, was the redhead kissing Blake and the breathy brunette who'd pushed past him into the hallway. A rather uncomfortable, unrecognizable emotion spiked inside her. "Those guys have a door that revolves more than subway turnstiles at rush hour," Michaela grumbled. "I'll say it again. Men are overrated." Never mind that her neighbors were also alluringly cocksure and in jaw-dropping shape. "Sculpted" sparked to mind. Heat prickled Michaela's neck in irritating fashion.

"Neither of your neighbors is overrated. Since you don't want them, can I have at least one?"

Michaela rolled her eyes. "Remind me why haven't I fired you?"

"Because you love me too much. And you'd never figure out your schedule." Smug triumph overtook April's features.

Michaela lifted her head. "Watch me!"

Still standing in Michaela's doorway, April struck a thoughtful pose with her finger pressed against her chin. "I'm actually contemplating a career change."

Panic streaked through Michaela, and she raised wide eyes to her assistant. "What? Since when?"

April grinned. "See? I knew you loved me. But seriously, I think I should become a sports groupie."

"Technically, sports groupie isn't a profession because you don't get paid," Michaela countered dryly. "Scratch that. You might get paid, but that gets into illegal territory."

"It'd be totally worth it." April nodded to herself. "If you doubt what I'm saying, watch the Blizzard game tonight. And especially watch number twenty-one."

"Why? Who's that?" Michaela feigned innocence. She'd looked up the team roster for some unfathomable reason and knew *exactly* who wore twenty-one. "And what makes him so special?" Maybe she'd peeked at a few minutes here and there, but she'd never devoted precious time to an entire game.

"First of all, he's your neighbor Blake Barrett. Second of all, he doesn't wear an undershirt."

Michaela's brows knotted together in confusion. "And this is noteworthy why?"

April's grin broadened. "He sometimes wipes his face with the hem of his sweater, which means he lifts it up and shows off all those glorious muscles." She sighed dramatically.

Michaela swallowed, trying to coat her dry throat while she locked out a disturbing vision that did funny things to her baser side. "On purpose?" she blurted.

"No, not like he's showing off. At least I don't think so." April seemed to ponder, then she brightened. "Tell you what, you watch tonight, and if he does it, we'll compare notes tomorrow and vote on whether it's a deliberate move."

Refocusing on her computer screen, Michaela muttered, "I'm sure I'll be way too busy working to watch something as silly as a hockey game."

Hours later, she sat on her red couch, dinner perched on her lap, while she channel-surfed. "I need to catch up on *Bridgerton* ... or I've heard the *The Mandalorian* is good," she mumbled. She tried not to analyze the fact that she wound up on Altitude Sports and somehow got sucked into watching the Blizzard, her eyes riveted to number twenty-one, whose sweater—or was it a jersey?—stayed down, like it was supposed to.

When her phone chimed with a text, she jumped as if she'd been caught doing something naughty. Her shoulders eased when she saw who it was from.

Paige: *Still coming to the party?*

Michaela: *Wouldn't miss it.*

Paige: *Good! Scott will definitely be there. Can't wait for you to meet him.*

Michaela tapped out her reply: *Looking forward to it.* She set the phone down, wondering if she'd just lied. No. She *was* looking forward to meeting this Scott person. After all, she still needed a plus-one for the Steadman dinner, and he was the right candidate. She just knew it. Paige and Beckett wouldn't steer her wrong. As she stared at the players racing up and down the ice on her TV screen, her mind wandered to whether she should be formulating a Plan B.

Stomach fluttering, Michaela rang the doorbell and sucked in a calming breath. For an instant, she prayed Paige would open the door and tell her the party had been canceled. The door did open, but Beckett filled its frame. His face lit with a smile.

"Come on in." He stood aside and made a grand sweeping gesture with his hand. "Paige and I are really happy you could come," he said as he helped her off with her coat. She darted a quick look at herself in a mirror hanging above a console table, confirming she'd made the right choice in attire. A silky white V-neck top with bold black flowers skimmed the waist of her black skinny jeans. The blouse's long sleeves featured little peekaboo cutouts along the length of her arms to show off a little skin. Whimsical, but lawyer-appropriate. Her glasses were on her desk at home, and her curls were behaving themselves after being tamed with gel and a fat curling iron. Her high-heeled black booties gave her enough lift that she wouldn't break her neck looking up at Beckett. She gifted herself an inner nod of approval.

"Scott's running a little late," Beckett informed her as he hung up her coat, "but he should be here soon. In the meantime, let's get you something to drink and introduce you to the rest of the folks."

Head on a swivel, she gawked as he led her toward the back of the house and the family room, open kitchen, and a huge solarium. Though she'd been in the house several times, she couldn't help but admire the distinctive, beautiful Paige touches everywhere.

A burble of happy chatter grew louder as they neared the family room. Michaela drew in a breath and readied her so-nice-to-meet-you smile. Honestly, she didn't want to be here—a pile of work was likely reproducing on her desk at this very instant—but Paige was her client *and* friend. Michaela would stick around long enough to meet—and assess—Scott, then slip out while her hosts were busy entertaining other guests.

Beckett touched her arm, yanking her from her scheming, and winked. "Martinis are this way."

Warmth suffused her. "You remembered." *Why can't I find a guy like* him*?*

"Of course. You're my wife's attorney and a guest of honor. Hell, *you're* the reason Paige set up this martini station. Chopin, right?" He guided her toward a sharply dressed man in black who stood beside a makeshift bar filled with assorted vodkas, gins, chilled glasses, and every martini garnish imaginable.

She was both touched and dismayed—so much for sneaking out early tonight. "Yes. Thank you, Beckett."

He gave the martini-maker instructions while Michaela's eyes swept the room, looking for someone, anyone, she knew and could glom on to in order to hide her awkwardness—the awkwardness making her unsure what to do with her limbs. As host, Beckett wouldn't stick around much longer—in fact, someone else was already approaching him. Her attention was pulled to a group of tall, broad men clustered in a corner of the solarium with several pretty women. Something about them looked familiar, but before she could pin it down, Paige popped up and threw an arm around her shoulders.

"Micky, I'm so glad you're here! Love your top. Have you met everyone?"

Michaela squeezed her back, amused that Paige's free hand trailed behind her, clasped in her husband's, who faced away from her while talking to someone else. They never seemed able to keep their hands off each other—which explained the huge swell of Paige's tummy—and Michaela swallowed a pang of envy. "Thanks again for inviting me. And no, not yet. I'm still waiting for my martini."

On cue, the bartender flashed her a smile and handed her a frosty drink with a perfect lemon twist adorning its rim. Paige led her around the room, sweetly introducing her as the "best real estate attorney in Colorado." If Michaela played her cards right, maybe she'd pick up a date for the Steadman dinner *and* a few new clients. Paige left her with Katie, Paige's assistant and leasing agent. Katie brightened, her large brown eyes twinkling behind her round red rims. "Michaela, hi! Don't tell me you're flying solo too?"

"For now. I'm supposed to meet someone Beckett works with, but apparently he hasn't arrived yet."

Katie nodded knowingly. "Paige playing matchmaker again?"

"I guess so," Michaela laughed. "Is that something she does often?"

"With people she likes." Katie let out a wistful sigh. "I wish she liked me more."

Michaela raised her eyebrows. "Of course she likes you! She constantly sings your praises. You mean she won't set you up?"

Katie grinned. "She totally would. Problem is I know all the same people she knows."

Michaela waved her hand around herself. "So you know everyone here?"

"Almost. If they're Paige's clients, I've dealt with them. If they're Paige's employees, well, 'nuff said. And if they're Beckett's peeps, they're either guys he knows from Hockey World—and I avoid those guys like the plague—or they're Paige's clients. Or both. Which leaves me with a giant goose egg." Katie laughed.

"Why do you avoid guys Beckett knows?"

Katie's eyes widened as she seemed to realize what she'd said. "Oh, I'm sure whoever they want you to meet tonight is different from the usual ... uh, knuckleheads."

Michaela burst out with a laugh. "Knuckleheads?"

Katie's eyes lifted to somewhere over Michaela's shoulder, and she smirked. "Incoming." She abruptly jerked a thumb to her left. "Just saw some folks I need to talk to. I'll catch you later." As Katie turned to leave, Michaela heard a familiar voice behind her.

"Michaela?"

Unwanted chills danced along her spine, raising the tiny hairs on her arms. Michaela slowly turned to greet her neighbor.

# Chapter 10

# I Think Your Sun Is in My Moon

Blake's spirits unexpectedly rocketed when the curly-haired woman turned and confirmed his suspicions about her identity.

"Thought it was you." His lips twitched in a smile.

Silver eyes went round, though her half-smile told him she wasn't unhappy to see him. "What are *you* doing here?"

Unable to stop himself, he let his gaze sweep from her head to her pointed high-heeled boots before darting back up to her shimmering eyes. "So that's why you look taller." He groaned inwardly at his inane comment. He'd been trying to mask his blatant perusal, but which was worse? Having her think he was a perv or an idiot? With his luck, she probably thought he was both.

She perched a hand on her hip and smirked. "No short jokes."

"I promise."

Michaela peeped at him from over the rim of her martini glass. "So where's your sidekick?" Her eyes flicked over his shoulder as if looking for Ferguson.

"If you mean my roommate, he's not here tonight." Blake couldn't wait to tell Ferguson what he'd missed—it would serve the bastard right. Blake hadn't wanted to come tonight, but Ferguson had insisted. Like the dumbass he was, Blake had caved.

At the last minute, one mysterious text had Fergs bailing on the party. Blake suspected it was the girl Fergs had hooked up with the night he'd invited Michaela out to the Detour. As for the flowers, they'd gone to the cleaning lady, so Michaela was still in the dark about Ferguson's crush.

"You need to make an appearance for both of us," Fergs had insisted as he'd laid a too-tight palm on Blake's shoulder. Yeah, that had annoyed the hell out of Blake, but now he had something to rub in his roommate's face. He gave in to a smug smile.

"How about your date?"

Confusion wiped away some of his smugness. "My date?"

"The redhead? Or was it the brunette? Or maybe you're hoping to find someone here to practice your, um, skills on?" She leveled twinkling eyes on him, then took them for a tour around the room as though she was looking for someone.

"The brunette the other morning—" he began, prepared to spill the truth, but he bit it back, recalling Ferguson's wistful expression when he'd talked about Michaela. Of course, that was *before* the new girl, Tracy, but still, Tracy was just a momentary distraction—according to Fergs—while Michaela was the "real deal." Blake made little sense out of Ferguson's actions. Why get "distracted" when the "real deal" was in your line of sight? Then again, Fergs insisted he was "working up to" asking Michaela out again, and Blake decided to take him at his word. He wouldn't blow his friend's chances.

Delicate eyebrows arched above her eyes. "The brunette the other morning ..." she prompted.

"She, ah—"

"Michaela?" Paige appeared with a dark-haired guy in tow and sent Blake a rueful smile. "Sorry, Blake. I didn't mean to interrupt. There's someone I'd like Michaela to meet." Blake stepped to the side, making room for Paige and her belly. He'd stick around long enough to be polite, then make himself scarce.

Michaela's posture, which he just realized had been comfortably relaxed, suddenly snapped to as if a hockey stick had been shoved down her back. She smoothed her curls, and her expression morphed into marble coolness as she regarded first Paige, then the dude beside Paige.

"Scott Newburn, I'd like you to meet my attorney, Michaela Wagner." Paige's eyes sparkled with something Blake couldn't interpret. What he *could* interpret was the interest lighting up Scott's face as his eyes made a slow sweep of Michaela's … assets. Apparently, the guy liked what he saw—not that Blake could blame him because she looked … Wow! She'd been hot in workout clothes, but this was an entirely different side of her he wholly appreciated … or, more accurately, admired on Ferguson's behalf. Yeah, that was it. And now Blake would suss out the guy … for Ferguson, of course. It's what good wingmen did.

In the next instant, Paige was called away, and Scott turned his attention to Blake, sticking his hand out and giving him a curious once-over. Blake automatically responded in kind, offering his hand in a gripping handshake. Before he could introduce himself, Michaela laid her hand on his forearm. The light touch of her small fingers reminded him of feathers and sent tendrils of warmth snaking up to his shoulder.

"Scott, this is my neighbor Blake Barrett." She withdrew her hand, and his skin turned oddly cold.

Scott's face split into a shit-eating grin. "Center for the Blizzard, right?"

When Blake nodded, Scott ran on about a play Blake had made last week, ignoring Michaela and making Blake squirm with a mixture of pride and embarrassment. To her credit, Michaela gently interjected from time to time, trying to work her way into the conversation, but Scott ran over her like a motor grader would run over a bug. Even Blake couldn't get a word in edgewise, and while he loved geeking out on the sport himself, the guy was a little over the top.

Noticing her martini glass was empty, Blake held up his hand. "Can I get you a refill?" She handed it to him with a grateful nod.

Scott smacked his forehead and leveled his gaze at Michaela. "God, I am so sorry! I've been yammering on and on about hockey, and what I really want to talk about is you." He shrugged sheepishly. "Guess I'm a little nervous."

While Blake might have pegged the guy for a putz, his confession earned him a beaming smile from Michaela that curdled Blake's insides. What if she liked this guy? Fergs could miss out.

When he returned with her fresh cocktail, she and Scott seemed to be sharing an intimate conversation while being hemmed in by a press of guests. Scott's arm was parked on the wall above her head, and judging by Michaela's body language, she didn't mind the closeness.

Blake muscled his way in and handed her the drink. "Hey, Micky. Here's your martini. I asked him to make it just the way you like it." He had absolutely no clue how she liked it, but thank God the bartender remembered the "pretty lady with the curls" and was able to recreate whatever he'd mixed up for her before.

Her eyes widened, and a crease pinched her brows as her posture stiffened. Scott backed up. She flashed Blake a fake smile. "Thank you, Blakey. You always take such good care of me."

Scott gaped at her. "I didn't realize—Paige said you were single." He grimaced at Blake. "Sorry, man. Didn't mean to—"

"You didn't," Michaela piped up and waved a hand between her and Blake. "We're not ... He's just my neighbor."

*True, but ouch!* And why did it bother him to be referred to as "just my neighbor"?

Scott's shoulders seemed to ease, and he opened his mouth but quickly closed it when his phone rang. "Kids," he muttered and excused himself.

Her eyes followed his retreat, and Blake couldn't stop himself. "You like that guy?"

"He seems nice. He just became single, so it's got to be tough, especially when you're sharing a couple of kids. I bet he's lonely."

Blake frowned at her, though her eyes were still aimed in the direction Scott had gone. "So you feel sorry for him."

She puffed her cheeks and let out an extended exhale, then raised her eyes to his. "A little, yes."

Scott's sudden reappearance cut the conversation short.

"I'm so sorry," Scott said to Michaela. "I have the kids tonight, and one of them just started throwing up. I told the babysitter I'm on my way. Normally, I don't get sitters when it's my time with them, but Paige insisted I come. Now I understand why, and I'm glad she did." He flashed her a big smile. "Maybe I could take you out for coffee next week?"

Blake tried not to roll his eyes while Scott tapped Michaela's number into his phone. Why did he find this guy so irritating?

Scott took a few steps back and pointed at Blake. "Nice to meet you." He swung his finger to Michaela. "I'll text you next week." He sent her another huge smile, making Blake wonder if he was showing off new dental work.

A prickling sensation in the pit of Blake's stomach had him giving in to his dick side after Scott was gone. "There's probably a good reason he's single and lonely."

She shrugged. "Maybe. But I'm also feeling sorry for myself."

He didn't bother hiding his surprise. "Why?"

Her eyes shifted in the direction Scott had gone. "He was my best chance for the plus-one I need for an important event, and it turns out he's got his kids that night."

"So you asked him?" Blake spluttered.

"Mm-hmm." She raised her glass to her lips once more, and the holes in the sleeves of her shirt gave him a tantalizing peek at her flowery tattoo. His mind leapt to how far up that tattoo went, and what else it curled around.

He cleared his throat. "What kind of event?"

Her eyes locked on his. They were big, beautiful eyes that reminded him of liquid silver. Ferguson was a lucky man. "The big cheese of all cheeses in my firm is throwing a dinner party for us mini-cheeses and our dates. I, um, sorta led my boss to believe I had someone to bring."

"Seriously?" His spirits lifted a few feet.

"Unfortunately, yes."

"Did you know that cheese is the most stolen food item in the world?"

She gave him a very satisfactory eye-roll. “Maybe I can *steal* a date. Or a cheese. Maybe I should just hire an escort.”

“You mean, like ... an *escort* escort?”

She blinked at him and frowned in confusion.

“A gigolo?” he explained. A brilliant idea struck him, and without waiting for her answer, he ran on. “Ditch the gigolo idea. I have a better one.”

She cocked an expectant eyebrow and took another sip.

“What if one of us, let’s say Owen, was your date for the cheese wheel get-together?”

Her eyes rounded in mock surprise. “Are you guys even *old* enough to date?”

Wincing, he covered his heart with both hands. “Ouch! Wait. Let me dig out the arrow before I answer.” Was he insulted? He should have been, but talking to her was the most fun he’d had all night—all month, if he were being honest.

She beamed a self-satisfied smile that scrambled his brain. She was adorable. Wait. Were attorneys adorable? But she wasn’t just an attorney. No, she was way more than her job title, and he was intrigued by what else lay behind her façade.

*Christ! No, you’re not!* With an inner head slap, he barreled ahead.

“Yeah, pretty sure dating’s allowed now that I can grow a beard, Mom.”

Her dazzling smile turned embarrassed. “Come to think of it, after what I witnessed, I guess you *are* old enough. Or else you’re practicing the big-boy stuff and pulling it off.”

Casually propping his arm the same way Scott had, he frowned down at her. “Just how old do you think we are?”

“We?”

“Owen and me.” *Gotta keep Ferguson’s name front and center.*

A little shoulder shrug. “Nineteen? Twenty? Is that why you don’t drink?” Her expression telegraphed she was absolutely serious. Suddenly, he felt like a squirt again.

“Someday I’m going to take your guess as a compliment.”

"But not today, huh?" A little grimace of contrition decorated her full mouth, and his mind made the inconvenient leap to kissing her the previous week. Non-thinking parts of him wanted to start that session all over again.

He shook his head in answer to her question but more so to shake out the errant thoughts bombarding his brain. "But not today. As for my not drinking, age has nothing to do with it. For your information, I'll be twenty-five in about six weeks."

Her eyes startled wide. Maybe he *was* insulted after all. Did he really look that young?

"Oh! You look so ... so ... youthful," she stammered. "I just turned twenty-five a few weeks ago. October fourth."

Now it was his turn to be surprised. "No kidding? I thought you were—" She narrowed her eyes menacingly. He held up his free hand in surrender. "I wasn't going to say older. I was going to say ... never mind. Aren't attorneys ... Doesn't it take a long time to become an attorney? Or are you one of those super-achievers who was done with high school when you were eleven?"

She seemed to ease, and the twinkle returned to her eyes, which made him relax a tic too. "Nice recovery, ace."

"Honestly," he argued, "my assumption about your, uh, maturity had to do with your profession, not your appearance." Sensing he was losing ground, he fell back on his bag of trivia facts. "Did you know the age difference in thirty-four percent of heterosexual married couples in the US is only within one year?" Shit. And now he was blathering about marriage.

That cute little smirk of hers made another appearance, and the tiniest of dimples appeared on her right cheek. "I have a feeling it's time I saved you from yourself."

He hung his head dramatically. "Please. Someone has to."

Her eyes lifted to the ceiling as if she was looking for words up there, then leveled on his once more. "We've established there's a two-month age difference between us, and I'm the oldest." Her chin lifted a few inches, and her tone had taken on an appealing kind of brattiness. What was it Fergs had called her?

*Sassy*. Yeah, that. “We also established you’re a Sagittarius and I’m a Libra,” she added.

“We did? Wait. Is that a horoscope thing?” She nodded, and he jumped at the chance to steer the conversation in a different direction—hopefully one where he wasn’t so damn off balance and could bring the focus back to Fergs. “What sign is February fifth?”

“Aquarius. Why? Who’s that?”

“Owen, who’s older than me. Us. Are those signs compatible?”

“Which signs? Road work ahead? Stop? Merge with traffic?”

Chuckling, he barely avoided saying, “Yours and his,” going instead with, “Libra and Aquarius.”

“Supposedly, but personally I find Aquarius men pretty intolerable. Give me an air or fire sign any day.”

Something akin to disappointment—for Ferguson—and confusion welled inside him. “Intolerable how? And what’s a fire sign? And more importantly, how does a hardworking attorney know these things?”

“I used to do friends’ horoscopes in high school. Fire signs are Leo, Aries, and Sagittarius—like you. As for Aquarians of the male variety, they’re always right”—she put air quotes around the last two words—“and they know everything.” The last word she dragged out. “Just ask them, and they’ll tell you. They’re extremely smug in their self-righteousness. Plus, they’re aloof. Not affectionate at all.”

“So no PDA, I take it?” Come to think of it, he’d never seen Fergs slobber all over a girl like some of their teammates did. Then again, neither did Blake. He wasn’t anti-PDA; he’d just never been around anyone who made it hard to keep his hands to himself.

“No, but it’s not only public displays. It’s private ones too.” A faraway look passed through her eyes, like clouds silvered by moonlight.

“Speaking from experience?” Why had he asked? He didn’t want to know, and he sipped his club soda to mask his discomfort.

“Unfortunately, yes. But it was a long time ago, and water under the bridge and all that.”

Shifting uneasily, he blurted out the first thing to pop into his brain. "Did you know the idiom 'water under the bridge' derives from ancient Greece? It went something like 'you cannot step twice in the same river.'"

The bartender materialized from out of nowhere and offered her a fresh martini and a grin.

"What's this?" she said.

Bartender guy jerked his head toward somewhere behind him. "From the gentleman who had to leave, with his apologies." He lifted her nearly empty glass from her grasp and, with a wink, pivoted and marched back to his station.

"Thank you," she called after him. She took a tiny sip, then looked up at Blake. "See? Scott's a nice guy."

Blake glanced over his shoulder before looking back down at her. "About this date to your boss's dinner."

Her eyes shot to his, and mischief transformed her features. "Are you angling to be my date?"

Surprised for the umpteenth time that night, he jabbed his thumb against his chest. "Me? I was thinking Owen."

"Oh, right. I should have considered the fact you have a girlfriend ... er, girl*friends*. How's the kissing going, by the way?" Her eyes stay locked on his as she raised the rim of the glass to those lips he couldn't stop looking at.

"It's not going because I don't have any girlfriends," he huffed.

"Oh. You just ... get around a lot."

"No, I don't!" A few people nearby stopped talking and threw him a glance, so he dropped his voice and delved into her eyes, as if he could more forcefully convey what he wanted to say. Why her belief he was an indiscriminate manwhore bugged him, he had little clue, but there it was. "I can see where you might get that idea, but it's not true."

"So the redhead you were kissing stopped by to sell you Girl Scout cookies? Not that it's any of my business, of course." Her eyes sparkled like the frost on her glass.

"Are you always this ..."

"Annoying? Pretty much. Probably explains why I can't get a date."

He let loose a pent-up laugh. "I was going to say 'tenacious,' but 'annoying' works too." Silence ripened between them, and he rushed to fill it. "The thing is ... this is embarrassing."

"How so?"

"Because the redhead, Sherry, was ... I picked her up. Actually, I'm pretty sure it was the other way around." *Not that that makes it any better. And why in the hell am I telling you this in the first place?*

"Ah. So a one-nighter. Or were you planning on seeing her again, hence the kissing lessons?"

"Maybe. I don't know." But he *did* know. He just didn't want to admit what a bastard he was by admitting the truth that no, he didn't plan on seeing her again. That when she'd approached him with that wiggle walk of hers, he'd been caught in a particularly weak moment because he'd desperately needed the release, the connection to *someone*. But pursue her? A solid no. Matter of fact, he had yet to meet a woman he *wanted* to pursue. God, maybe he was more like Ferguson than he realized. Better that or be played like his dad had been? Of course, the very fact his dad had been worked so badly by his mom might explain why Blake hadn't found anyone worth pursuing—he hadn't looked. Survival kept him from repeating his father's mistakes and opening himself up to heartbroken misery.

"And the brunette?" Michaela's words jarred him back to the present.

He swallowed the truth dangling from the tip of his tongue. "She needed a place to crash, so she stayed over. Nothing happened between her and me." He winced inside. Michaela was a smart girl who could easily connect the dots and figure out Tracy was with Ferguson, which didn't paint his friend in the best light. Hell, neither of them was shining at their finest at the moment.

"Well, you're a hockey player. That explains it."

His defense mechanisms flared into action. "Explains what?"

She swept him with cool assessment. His defenses were locked and loaded.

Except a disarming gleam lit her pretty quicksilver eyes. “I was referring to ... You must get that a lot. You’re in good shape.”

His defensive systems collapsed. Not only had she noticed the body he worked on constantly, but she wasn’t judging him, and what he was sure was a goofy grin broke out. “Uh, yeah. I have to work out a lot.”

“I bet.” A cute smirk quirked her perfect bow mouth.

Was that a blush staining her freckled cheekbones? And why was he noticing every minute detail? Fuck. He was blowing it. He needed to get a grip. No, wait. He couldn’t blow anything because he had no intention of getting close to her. Unless it was on Ferguson’s behalf, of course. The fact he’d gotten himself tangled in the truth about the brunette was proof. But a little voice told him he needed to remind himself Michaela was in Ferguson’s crosshairs and was totally off-limits.

# Chapter 11
# Cheese and Martinis

Michaela should have been horrified by her behavior and her pushy pokes and prods—not to mention the BS about the astrology—but the little devil on her shoulder kept whispering in her ear, and she kept listening. She was having too much fun to stop, even if it was at this poor guy's expense. Besides, she always found the varied ways people handled pressure utterly fascinating. Blake Barrett was taking her ribbing with unexpected ease and grace, as he had with the embarrassingly forgettable pepper-spray incident.

"So. About Owen," he nudged. "He's single too."

Why, exactly, was he trying to foist his roommate on her? Then again, maybe he'd do for a one-off date, not that it would go beyond that. He was too cocky, too handsome, too impressed with his own charm. Not to mention she had little idea if he could carry on a conversation. But time was running out, and she was desperate.

She tilted her head. "Can he dress up? Hold his own in conversations?"

Blake's mouth opened and closed, and a calculating glint came into those pale green eyes of his. Whether it was amusement or irritation, she couldn't tell. "Yes and yes. Might be hard to believe for a smart attorney like yourself, but we jocks have to make appearances at all kinds of formal events and behave like real humans instead of the subspecies we come from."

*Irritation it is.* A frisson of guilt sped through her. She dipped her head and found refuge in her icy drink before meeting his cool gaze. "Touché, Mr. Renaissance Man. That was a poor attempt at a joke on my part, and I apologize."

He nodded, and her mind took another detour. While she wouldn't have pegged either man for dinner-party material, she was coming around to his suggestion—like a cruise ship making a turn in the ocean. Slow and ponderous at first but steady and sure.

"Okay. Why not? If your roommate's up for being my dinner date, then I'm up for it too."

Blake's eyes widened, which prompted her to say, "Oh. You were kidding."

"No, no. I meant it. When's the dinner? I'll check the schedule." He extracted his phone from his back pocket and started scrolling.

He managed Owen's schedule? He was Owen's own little April. "Less than a week away, on Halloween." Michaela paused to chuckle. "Maybe the dress-up part is the hostess's way of having us come in costume." To her relief, Blake's lips tipped up in a half-smile. Hopefully, he'd dismissed her jabs about his roommate.

His smile broadened as he stared at his phone. "Good news. We're in town, and we're not playing that night." He lifted his eyes to hers. "You've got a date."

"Don't you need to check with him first?"

"Nah. Trust me, he won't have made any plans. He probably has no idea he's free that night. You're good to go."

"So ... you'll set it up with him, then?" When he nodded again, she joked, "I feel like I'm working with a date broker."

One eyebrow kissed his hairline, and his smile transformed into a smirk. "Kinda like speed dating? Basically, isn't that what they are? Date brokers?"

"Possibly. I hadn't thought about it that way before." Crap, couldn't he just let the disastrous dating round-robin go already?

She masked her irritation. “Although I think you’re being generous.”

“How’s that?”

“Twenty-five four-minute conversations, and I didn’t connect with a soul. You’d think a date broker could at least have found one potential match.”

He surprised her when he cuffed her upper arm with a light touch. “Okay. As your *date broker*, I need to learn a little more about you so I can report to Owen and make the dinner go as smoothly as possible.”

“Oh, so you’re like a living, breathing dating app.”

He stared at her, mirth and surprise dancing in his eyes. “Don’t tell me you use those too.”

She shrugged. “Not very successfully.” When he quirked an eyebrow, she held up her hand. “Hey, eternal optimist here. I figure ‘the one’ has to be out there somewhere, and I’m trying to make it easier for him to find me.”

Tugging her behind him, he carved a path through clustered guests.

“Where are you taking me, date broker?”

Without answering, he stopped for a moment before guiding her to a private bistro table tucked in a corner of the solarium several yards from other partygoers.

“Someplace quieter.” He grinned as a thought seemed to occur. “That way I can conduct an interview. Consider me a living, breathing dating app questionnaire.” He pulled out a chair and motioned for her to sit.

Laughter bubbled up from her chest. “I think I need a fresh martini before we delve into twenty questions.” She eyeballed her mostly full glass of warming vodka. “You might get more honest answers from me that way.”

“Way ahead of you.” Blake raised his eyes above her head as he took the chair opposite her.

“Did someone at this table say ‘martini’?”

Michaela jerked in surprise as the accommodating bartender leaned down, handing her a fresh cocktail while he gently lifted the half-consumed one from her fingers. "Um, thank you," she said dumbly. He tilted his head, then strode away. She stared at Blake. "Are *you* responsible for that?"

"Yep. Gave him the signal as we were heading this way."

"Jeez, he's stealthy ... and fast! And wow! You've covered all the bases. That speed-dating coordinator could learn a thing or two from you." *How many drinks have I had now? I've lost count.* It occurred to her that while she'd intended to duck out quickly, she was enjoying herself all of a sudden. A whole lot. The thought of leaving got pushed to a back corner of her mind, though the little goody two-shoes on her *other* shoulder warned that she should ease up on the drinks. She reminded the conscience-wielder that she was using Lyfts tonight, then she narrowed her eyes at Blake. "You're not trying to get me drunk, are you?"

He appeared offended. "Wow. Suspicious much? No, I am definitely not trying to get you drunk. I just want to see you have a good time."

"Oh. Well, that's very considerate of you. But I need a promise from you."

"What's that?"

"You *will* tell me if I start to slur?"

He regarded her, seeming to fight a grin. "Yes, I will tell you if you slur ... or otherwise act like someone who's inhaled her weight in martinis."

"Hey! I have not."

"I didn't say you had ... yet. Nor am I encouraging you to. It's just ... I've seen it happen a few times." The grin bloomed on his handsome face.

*Wait. He's not handsome. He's just ... my kissable neighbor. Who's not as young as he used to be. Oh God, don't go there!* The martinis had her in their grip—again. This was only the second occurrence in the last year, and he was the sole witness both times. The guy was going to think she was a lush. "Before we begin, may I ask you a question?"

He leaned back in his chair and crossed his arms over his chest. "I'm not the one filling out the questionnaire, but ask away."

"Why don't you drink?"

The sudden tension in his body was unmistakable as he sat forward and carefully placed his forearms on the table. His deliberate movements had her guessing he was formulating his answer. Part of her was alarmed her question had turned him into a tightly wound coil, but another part registered his very masculine hands and wrists that disappeared into the cuffs of his charcoal button-down. His deep voice pulled her from her wayward thoughts. "I'm not an alcoholic, if that's what you're asking. I have a few reasons for not drinking. One, I'm an athlete who's constantly in training. Two, my family has ... issues. I stay away from the stuff out of principle."

"Doesn't every family have issues?" she replied.

His shoulders seemed to ease as he straightened, shrugged, and executed a drumroll on the tabletop with his index fingers. "I guess. But alcohol does funny things to people, like shutting down logic. I've seen drunk people do a lot of stupid things they would never even consider when they're sober. And unfortunately, I've also witnessed ordinarily decent human beings transform into very ugly ones."

"I completely agree. Sort of like the potion Dr. Jekyll drinks that turns him into Mr. Hyde." Lucky for her, she'd never had to deal with it personally, but she'd been witness to Fiona's anguish when dealing with her alcoholic father's behavior. Ugliness in spades. And though Michaela felt absolutely no judgment coming from Blake, she refrained from taking a sip of her as-yet untouched martini.

"Okay. No more distracting me with questions." His mouth quirked, and the tension seemed to dissolve. "Let's get this interview back on track. What kinds of issues does *your* family have?"

"Wow! You just go straight for the jugular, don't you?"

"May as well dig in."

She propped her elbow on the table and tapped her chin with her index finger. “Now let’s see.” She held up her finger in an “Aha!” gesture. “My father bakes.”

Blake gave her a bemused frown. “And that’s an issue why, exactly?”

“Because he’s a mad scientist, or more precisely, a mad chemist, who loves to put ingredients together and see what he can hatch.”

“Doesn’t sound so bad to me.”

Dropping her chin to her chest, she looked up at him through her lashes. “Have you ever eaten quiche made with olive loaf and maraschino cherries?”

His mouth dropped open.

“I know, right?”

“That sounds awful!” he spluttered.

“It *was* awful. And my mom and I had to eat it without gagging! Unfortunately, that was one of his more palatable experiments.”

Blake grimaced, then a more thoughtful look took over his features. “You get along with your parents?”

“I do. I had the rare upbringing that didn’t leave me damaged, like so many people I know. My parents are boringly normal and very sweet. A little overprotective, but I think it’s because I’m an only child and they’re a lot older. My mother was forty-one and my dad was forty-five when I was born. They’d given up trying to have a baby years before Mom got pregnant.”

“Were they happy when they found out?”

“Over the moon!” She threw her hand out. “Or so they tell me. Sometimes I wish I had siblings to pull some of their attention away from me, though.”

“Yeah, I know what you mean.”

“You’re an only child too?” She took a minuscule sip of her martini while he fidgeted.

“Not exactly, though my sister and I grew up in separate households, which left me smack in the center of my folks’ brutal tug-of-war.”

Sadness in his eyes plucked at her heartstrings. "I'm sorry to hear that. I take it your parents divorced."

"Not exactly." One of his powerful hands shot to the back of his head, smoothing his hair. "Let's put it this way. My dad *should* have divorced my mom, but he stuck it out because he was loyal that way. It is what it is ... or was. He's since passed."

"Oh no. That had to be really rough."

"It wasn't a day at the waterpark. But if it hadn't been for all the turmoil, I doubt I'd be where I am now. So there's that."

She cocked her head at him in question, and he went on. "Hockey was an outlet, a way for a little kid to blow off his pent-up emotions. We lived down the road from an ice rink, and that's where I went to escape. I could leave the arguing and nastiness behind and lose myself on the ice, so I became a rink rat." He paused to grin. "That's where I met Owen. He was better than I was, and he took me under his wing. We hung out at his house all the time, and being around him, around his family, gave me something solid to hang on to. It gave me a front-row seat to how a normal family acted."

He smiled wistfully, then let out a mild chuckle. "On the ice, we were always outdoing each other, skating faster than the other one, pushing the envelope. But when it came to sticking up for me, he was fearless. With the other kids, with his own family. Because I was there so much, his mother and even his grandma treated me like one of their own, which meant I got in trouble when I did something wrong. Owen, though, he'd deflect or try to take the blame himself. I guess he felt sorry for me because of my home life. His friendship was a lifeline that kept me from drowning." He stared at the tabletop as if seeing a film from his past there, then shook his head before reapplying his half-smile. "I guess I'm pretty competitive, so even after his family moved away, I kept at it, working my ass off as if Owen was right beside me, pushing me. In hindsight, I suppose I was trying to stay one stride ahead of the unpleasantness at home."

Her heart constricted, and she fought an odd urge to comfort the little boy he'd once been. "So, um, I take it you and Owen stayed connected all those years."

"Somehow we did, which is a miracle, considering we were a pair of prepubescent wing nuts." He huffed a laugh, and some of the melancholy slipped from his features. "We plotted and planned and ended up in juniors together. When that first day came, it was as if we'd never spent any time apart."

"How nice that you have each other."

"Yeah," he sighed, then suddenly brightened, as if waking up from a snooze. "I took us off track. This interview is about you, not me." He adjusted his too-tall frame in the too-small chair. "Who do you admire most in the world?"

"Perry Mason," she blurted without thinking.

He gave her a skeptical look. "The TV attorney?"

"You bet. He never lost a case. Well, there was one episode where he did, but then he worked everything out. Bet that was some trivia you didn't know."

Blake laughed, a warm, rumbly sound. "You're right. I'm not up on my Perry Mason trivia, but you can bet I'll get right on it and fill my head with even more useless facts. You do realize he's not real?"

"Doesn't mean he's not a stud. I mean, he *always* figures out who the true criminal is. Talk about a superhero crime-fighter. And your trivia is not useless. It's entertaining."

He shifted, as if the compliment sat awkwardly on his broad shoulders. "Do you think we should nominate him for a red cape with the letters PM on the back?"

A warm blanket of coziness wrapped around her, and she grinned at him. "Now you're talking. I like it." An image of *him* in a superhero cape with the words "Super Date" on it bobbed about in her brain. *Why can't I bring* you *with me to the Steadmans'?* Because he'd offered up his roommate instead.

After spending time with Blake, she found it hard to believe Owen was the older of the pair. Regardless, neither man was a candidate for the role of her future husband—only a guy poised enough to not make her look bad and possibly make her laugh at the dinner party. Blake definitely fit the bill; she hoped Owen would do the same.

She covertly scanned Blake's face, taking in features chiseled by more than mere years. Yep, he'd do in a pinch. It didn't hurt that he was easy on the eyes with his short blond hair and the way his cut body filled out his fitted shirt and slacks. Oh, and he smelled good too. Getting a whiff of his citrus-and-spice scent when he'd leaned in to talk to her, she'd struggled not to stick her nose in the air and inhale.

The devil on her shoulder had her mind leaping to places it shouldn't go, with her libido quickly falling in behind. *Down, girl!*

In her head, she began ticking off reasons why Blake would be the better fill-in. He had a relaxed confidence about him, he was intelligent, easy to talk to, and—bonus—something about him made her feel safe. But there was that one showstopper: he was a player, and not only at pro sports.

He snapped her out of her zigzagging musings when he said, "Okay. Your philosophy on ... relationships."

"Your point being ...?"

"I'm a dating app, remember? You still need to complete the questionnaire. Since this is about romance"—he executed an exaggerated air-quote thing, accompanied by an irreverent smirk and eye-roll—"therefore your input is required. The question is nonnegotiable."

"Wow," she laughed. "You even *sound* like a dating app."

He sat back, his light green eyes drilling into her while he waited. A cackle from the other side of the solarium reminded her revelers surrounded them, countering the feeling they'd been cocooned in their own little world.

"You do realize we're in the middle of a cocktail party, right?" she asked.

"You're good at throwing out diversionary tactics. Is that something they teach you in law school?"

Leveling her gaze at him, she took a long, slow sip of icy vodka. “And you’re good at being one-track-minded. Is that something they teach you in hockey school?”

He burst out with a laugh and leaned forward again. “Hockey school. That’s a good one.”

She grinned. “Well, what do you call it?”

“I think it’s called decades of playing. From the time you’re old enough to skate, you’re honing those skills. Ever read Malcolm Gladwell?”

“I love Malcolm Gladwell.” She held up her finger. “Wait. I think I know where you’re going with this. You need so many hours of doing something before you’re good at it. Ten thousand, right?”

He nodded, and a lazy smile curved his mouth. “Exactly. You need ten thousand hours of doing one thing before you’re proficient at it. You don’t go to ‘hockey school’ for that.”

She raised her glass to him again. “Just like you don’t go to tenacity school, right?”

He matched her, raising his mostly empty glass of club soda. “We’re on the same page.”

“You know, I wasn’t expecting to enjoy myself tonight, but thanks to your witty repartee, I’m having a blast.”

His eyebrows pulled together in a V. “Are you yanking my chain right now?”

“Not at all. I’m being very sincere. You’re fun to talk to. I’m having a good time hanging out with you.” The martinis might have nudged her into voicing the sentiment aloud, but she meant every single word.

# Chapter 12

# You Say Love, I Say Void

Blake told himself not to gawk at the woman sitting across from him—the one he was trying really, really hard to think of as just anyone else he might encounter in his life. A trainer, his housekeeper, a truck driver. Not that he encountered many truck drivers, but still. He needed all the backup he could get. Too bad nothing was working. Instead, what crowded his mind were the silky curls he longed to push back from her perfect, velvety skin ... plus, that taunting tattoo. And, of course, the smoking-hot kiss he couldn't forget.

And now she'd just leveled him by saying he was "fun to talk to" and that she was enjoying hanging with him. *What?* A beautiful, successful, intelligent woman like her? Must have been the martinis talking. Women didn't tell him stuff like that. Ever. In fact, the shit *they* normally focused on—which always centered on the money or fame—Michaela hadn't even brought up. The difference was refreshing, and his body was unfortunately taking note. He rolled his lips between his teeth and clamped down—hard—in a bid to get his libido under control. Usually not too difficult for him, but he was struggling with it tonight.

Not only was she turning out to be different than any other woman he'd met, she was different from the woman he'd assumed her to be; she was growing more attractive with every breath she took. And that was a problem.

He looked into her eyes, searching—practically praying—for a hint of deceit or her trying to stroke him, but all he saw looking back at him were those same eyes, big and clear, reminding him of a mountain lake shimmering with sunlight. Did the glasses normally obscure those liquid metal pools, the lush lashes, the—

*For fuck's sake! Knock it the hell off. You're not the one drinking, dumbass.*

"Okay," he practically shouted, instantly regretting his volume when he registered her flinch. "Uh, I mean, thank you. I'm, uh, enjoying hanging with you too." *And yes, I'm older than the thirteen-year-old I sound like.*

He offered her an awkward smile as an afterthought. Her gaze remained even, not giving away what thoughts lurked in her fascinating mind. *She thinks you're an idiot, and nothing you're doing will counteract that.* Ferguson was *way* better at this shit than Blake was. No wonder he could "close the deal" while Blake grappled with what the deal was.

Drumming his fingers on the edge of the tiny table to steady his jumpy nerves, he cleared his dry throat. "I believe there's a question that still needs to be answered."

"What was it again?"

What *had* he asked her? No idea. He was a transistor short of a full circuit. A chin strap short of a safely functioning helmet. A—

"I remember," she enthused, saving him from himself. "My philosophy on romance. Er, love. Or was it relationships?"

He flicked his hand at her, going for a casual demeanor he was incapable of mustering. "All of the above."

"Well, one might argue they're quite different ..." When he narrowed his eyes at her, she let out a very feminine, very pleasant giggle and kept going. "Message received. No attorney-speak." Her eyes traveled up to the glass ceiling and back. "In a nutshell, I bought into the fairy tales I heard as a little girl, and I believe there's someone out there who's my perfect complement ..."

*Oh God, don't say "the yin to my yang."* He found himself not wanting Michaela to be so ... easily hoodwinked, like his sister with her inane rom-coms. Or so predictable. So cliché. Because she was anything but, and her quirkiness delighted him. Mesmerized him.

"... the mustard to my ketchup, the salt to my pepper, the soy sauce to my rice." She paused and gave him a triumphant little grin. "How's that for philosophy?"

"That's ... it's brilliant!"

She blinked at him like a gnat had splattered itself against her eyeball. Not that he blamed her. He was acting certifiably idiotic.

"Which part?" she asked dubiously.

"The part about the mustard and ketchup pairing is my favorite."

"Huh. Okay. So nothing about the philosophy itself. Just the ... condiments?" Her grin turned impish. "Must be the food connection."

He laughed again. He found himself doing that a lot around her. "Yeah, food kinda makes my world go round. So we've established that you have an unrealistically idealistic view of romantic relationships."

"Wow. That's a pessimistic way of looking at it."

God, he *had* sounded pessimistic! It wasn't that he didn't believe in relationships, but he was skeptical one was in *his* future. The real deal, like what some of his teammates enjoyed. How would he find someone like they had when all he met were puck bunnies? A puck bunny *could* be the real deal, or she could be the woman who chased bragging rights or access to a player's bank account. Some guys he knew had attached themselves to those girls, and for some it hadn't ended well, while for others it had ended fine. But those guys had intentions shallower than those harbored by the girls they married: they'd been all about scoring trophy wives. His father had scored a trophy wife, except he'd deluded himself she was the real deal, gone all in, and had his heart ripped out.

"Frankly, I disagree that my view is unrealistic," Michaela continued. "I think it's a hopeful view. And if you aren't going for an ideal, aren't you setting the bar so low you're practically guaranteeing you'll never go higher? You didn't get where you are in your profession by setting low expectations for yourself, did you?"

"No, but that's different." *Isn't it?*

"How is it different? Don't you have a certain level of expectation for your personal life? Goals you're aiming for? So many points you want to rack up or retiring by a certain age, for instance?" She sat back, crossing her arms over her chest. The motion pulled her sleeve taut, exposing more delicately inked vines and flowers.

"No. Yes. Maybe." He dragged his hand across his chin. "I haven't really given it that much thought. It's been all about my career, which, by the way, is real. Tangible. And, unlike relationships where at least one other person is involved, it's within my control."

One eyebrow arched. "You sure about that? What if you're injured or you get traded?"

"Those possibilities are always there. Comes with the job. But in the meantime, how hard I push myself, how high I climb, is up to me, right? Yes, I'm part of a hockey team, but my individual effort is a solo journey. But that's not true in relationships. That's a team effort, and if the teammates don't agree on the vision for that team, any amount of pushing by one partner isn't going to work if the other isn't willing to get on board. And that's where the lack of control comes in."

She paused for a beat as if marshaling her next counter. "I see what you're saying, though I disagree on the lack of control. You always have control over yourself, and you shouldn't give that up to the other person." She raised her cocktail. "So you're a cynic when it comes to matters of the heart. Does that come from experience?" Glass at her lips, she took a deep sip.

*I'm a skeptic, and it comes from* lack *of experience.* With no past relationships of his own to call upon, and the volatile one modeled by his parents, how was he equipped to untangle the good from the bad?

He twirled his nearly empty glass between his hands on the tabletop, calculating how to answer. "I don't know that I'd classify myself as a cynic. I think I'm a realist, and yeah, that's based on observation."

"Okay. So what does a realist's philosophy look like?" Her bright eyes were trained on his, her look one of curiosity, nothing more, as if she really wanted to understand his take on this particular subject. He felt safe being up front with her.

"I think we get dazzled from time to time by someone we think is the so-called 'one,' but it's our minds and our libidos blowing smoke up our butts and letting the fantasies we've built up since childhood hack our common sense. Which blinds us to the pitfalls. I also believe we each have many possible partners, some better than others, and if we're lucky, we find the best match and build a decent life with that person." He shrugged.

She tilted her head to the side. "So tell me. Have you ever been dazzled, Blake Barrett?"

"Honestly? No." The admission brought a twinge of melancholy to his soul.

Nodding, she smiled knowingly. "Because you're a realist."

He nodded back, though inside he questioned what the hell he was agreeing to. No one had ever pushed him to delve inside and examine *these* beliefs, and he sure as hell hadn't pushed himself. Did he buy into the dry philosophy he had spewed? Love and happily-ever-afters had been vague ideas lurking in some musty back closet of his mind. Lofty, unattainable goals for a guy like him. And it was nothing he'd ever shared with anyone, nothing he'd ever put into words before. Now that he just had, he wasn't convinced they were true. He didn't want to ponder it, not now, so he put the irritating thought aside.

"That must get lonely." A hint of sadness flitted through her eyes. "You do realize you *might* change your tune if someone ... dazzling ... were to come along?"

Did he get lonely? Yeah, he did, which explained why he'd brought Sherry home the other night. While it might have let him lose himself for a few hours and scratch a very prickly itch, he was boggled by the fact that such an intimate act hadn't *filled* anything inside him. Which sounded weird as he turned it over in his head. "Anything's possible," he conceded at last.

"Just look at our host and hostess"—she glanced over her shoulder at a thinning crowd before turning back to him—"and I think they completely smoke your theory. And that's not all. I've met a handful of couples tonight who could give them a run for their money for Soul Mate Couple of the Year. And one of them is a teammate of yours."

He smirked, taking the bait. "Which teammate?"

She sat up brightly. "Mac. His fiancée, Mia, is the one who got me the couch you helped move into my apartment. Did you see the way they sort of orbited around each other all night? Even when they weren't 'together,' they were together, like some invisible rope bound them to one another."

"Rope. That's a good analogy. Makes me think of someone who's hog-tied."

She burst out with a mirthless laugh. "Wow, you *are* cynical. Seriously, I bet those two *like* being tied to one another. Keeps other people from trying to pull them apart, if nothing else. And if they aren't soul mates, I'll go on *Soul Train* and make a fool of myself dancing."

He raised his eyebrows. "*Soul Train*? Seriously? Didn't that die a long-overdue death a while ago?"

She wiggled her eyebrows. "My point exactly."

Though he didn't want it to, his mind detoured to the team goalie, Mac McPherson, whom Blake had partied with before the guy fell hard for Mia. No doubt about it, Mac was much happier since Mia had become a permanent—and the most central—fixture in his life.

"Come on. I'm sure you can think of at least *one* couple you couldn't imagine without each other," Michaela nudged so sweetly—dimple and all—that he found himself chuckling, and his mind vaulted to Dave Grimson.

When she raised an expectant brow, he elaborated. "Okay. Maybe one. Our team captain, Dave Grimson." Dropping his voice, he leaned across the table, and she leaned in too, the intoxicating perfume he recognized from before wreathing his head. It was a soft scent, like wildflowers or fresh laundry or rain or ... Shit! Now he was waxing poetic about perfume. He conjured the Grim Reaper's resting mad face, and it wrenched him back to reality. "The guy scares the crap out of me and nearly everyone else, but he's almost comical when his wife, Ellie, is around. His face transforms instantly"—he snapped his fingers for effect—"from fierce gladiator to melted butter the second his eyes land on her. I swear, he looks like badass Wade from *Dead Pool* with the cartoon bunnies and flowers tripping around his head." So yeah, anything was possible, even if growing up with his parents had convinced Blake otherwise. "You won't tell anyone, will you?"

"Tell them what?" Her eyes drifted to his mouth.

"That he scares the shit out of me." He forced himself to sit upright so he could put space between them, and she sat back too. "Wait. You *can't* tell anyone, right? Attorney-client privilege and all that?"

Her head wagged from side to side, causing her curls to bounce. "You're not my client, so I can pretty much tell whomever I want." She swiveled her head dramatically, as if looking for an audience to share the secret with, then her twinkling eyes landed back on him. "Except I won't. Your secret's safe with me, you cupid contrarian."

"Hey, wait a minute," he fake-protested. "I didn't say I hated hearts and flowers." *Or did I?* Thoughts were becoming more difficult to track. He decided to turn the tables on Michaela, whose expression had gone adorably mischievous again, though he wasn't certain he wanted to hear the answer to his next question. "How about you? Ever been 'dazzled'?" He bounced his eyebrows up and down in a bid to hide his uneasiness.

Her eyes circled the ceiling again. "Once. The guy I told you about," she admitted, and his heart sank for some strange reason.

"The guy who married someone else."

She nodded. "But now that I look back on it, I realize we were together because it was convenient." Her eyes stabbed his with an intensity that made him squirm. "Had we stuck it out, we both would have been settling, which would have been extremely sad."

"Do you still, ah, see him?"

"No, not for a long time. Which is as it should be."

A frisson of relief sped through him. He laced his fingers together and rested his forearms on the table. "I'm sorry. I didn't mean to stir up bad memories."

She gave him a warm smile. "You didn't. So what's your excuse for your world view? You sound like someone with firsthand knowledge in the broken-heart department."

Damn, he hated when those childhood memories bubbled up to the surface, jabbing at him. They were treading over rocky ground, and despite the discomfort he always felt when his thoughts turned to the mess that had been his parents' marriage, he found himself wanting to open up to Michaela. Well, not the *whole* ugly story—he'd never shared that—but some of it anyway.

"My parents met in college. He was from a small rural town in eastern Oregon, going to school on a scholarship, and she was a spoiled rich girl from an upper-class family in Lake Oswego. His world was hard work on a ranch, and hers was debutante balls and prom-queen parades. Talk about your opposites. The pictures of my mom from then ... She was gorgeous, a real looker, as my dad would say. He was so in love with her that he couldn't admit to himself what a piece of work she was. They got married right after Dad finished college. Apparently, she was a big party girl in school, and she never slowed down.

"My childhood memories of my mother aren't pleasant. She was a raging alcoholic with a quick, nasty temper who was a huge believer in corporal punishment. Sometimes she'd go off on benders and disappear for weeks at a time, which was a relief for me, but it left my dad juggling a little kid while holding down a full-time job. One time, when I was about five, she was gone for months, then just showed back up as if nothing had happened, and he took her back."

Michaela's mouth hinged open and quickly shut again. "How did he manage when she wasn't there?"

"His sister, my aunt, stepped in. My memories of her are a little sketchy, but I remember her smelling like garlic. Funny what you remember as a kid. I don't think she liked me much. Anyway, I always thought he'd get fed up and walk, but he didn't. Not even after I left to billet with another family. The only way he escaped his lousy marriage was by dying a few years ago."

Before his dad died, he'd taught Blake that women were to be protected, cherished—and forgiven for their sins. Blake had no problem with the first two, but swallowing the third one was like inhaling a thistle that clawed its way down his throat. That principle had destroyed his dad, but clinging to it as he had might also have allowed his father to justify what his mom had done.

"I am so sorry, Blake." Michaela reached out and traced his knuckles with soft fingertips.

"The thing is," he continued, not daring to move his hand, "they'd been crazy in love in the beginning ... not that I was there back then. How does something so good go so wrong?"

"I don't know, but it does, and it sounds like you witnessed only the crummy years." She let out a sad sigh. "It makes perfect sense to me now that you'd be cynical, skeptical—guarded might be the right word—about getting close to someone." Her hand closed around his. "He must have been very proud of you."

"Yeah, he was pretty pleased when I made it to The Show. That's a good memory." His dad—and mom—had been there draft day, and Blake would forever remember the tears spilling down his dad's cheeks. Blake's chest compressed with emotion as the vision came swimming back.

"What other good memories do you have of your dad?" Michaela murmured.

He choked out a laugh, breaking the bands loose. "He used to take me fishing, just the two of us. We had this little beat-up aluminum boat, and we'd spend the whole day on a lake chasing largemouth bass. He'd pack bologna-and-cheese sandwiches, and I swear they tasted like gourmet food. Fun times. And so damn peaceful being out there on the water." Blake's lips hitched up as scenes from his past danced through his head. *"Treasure those moments,"* his mother's voice hiccupped in his head, and the idyllic images dissolved. Such irony that those words came from *her*.

Michaela withdrew her hand and sat back.

Thankfully, the conversation steered itself in a different direction. His shoulders dropped a few inches, and laughter broke free more easily than it had moments before. From that point on, they got so lost in talking that the lessening din around them didn't register until Paige's voice rang out.

"Hey, you two. Beck and I are going to bed. Feel free to stay as long as you like. Just be sure you turn off the lights and lock up when you leave."

"What?" Blake and Michaela sang out at the same time.

Paige laughed. "I guess you're having a good conversation."

Michaela bolted upright, looking all kinds of flustered as she gathered up her empty glass and forgotten purse under the table. "Oh, Paige, I'm so sorry!"

Blake stood too as Paige flapped a hand. "Don't be! I'm thrilled when my guests enjoy themselves so much they forget about the time." She blew them a kiss. "Good night, you two. Blake, you're driving Micky home, I assume?"

Michaela fumbled with her phone. "No, I'll just call a Lyft. That was my plan anyway."

Paige's auburn eyebrows touched her hairline. "Even though you both live in the same building? On the same floor? Right next to each other?"

"I'll take her home," Blake immediately responded, telling himself it had everything to do with being a gentleman and absolutely nothing to do with wanting to spend more time talking to Michaela ... Micky. She looked more like an "M" to him. Had he earned the right to call her a nickname yet? Well, one besides "Curly," which she hadn't seemed to mind.

"No, no, you don't have to, Blake." Michaela continued wrestling her phone out of her tiny purse. Abruptly, she stopped and looked up at him. "Oh. Calling a Lyft would just be silly, wouldn't it?"

He offered her a cockeyed grin. “I’m not sure I’d put it quite that way, but yeah, it makes sense for both of us to share a ride. Save the planet and all that.”

“And bonus, you’re sober as a judge! Although I’ve met a few not-so-sober—whoops! TMI. Never mind.” Shaking her head, she tried to jam her partly liberated phone back into her purse, giving up with an exhale.

Cuffing her upper arm—while trying to ignore the feel of silky fabric over her warm skin—he steered her out of the solarium to where Paige stood grinning madly at them.

“Good. That’s more like it,” Paige said. She gave them a head bob to punctuate her statement. A disembodied male voice rose from somewhere in the house, asking why she wasn’t in bed. “Be right there, Beck,” she called, her eyes rising to the ceiling. “Just saying good-bye to our last guests.”

Blake picked up the words “guests” and “pregnant wife” sprinkled liberally with cursing, and he stepped up his pace. “Paige, I’m so sorry. We’ll let ourselves out so you can get to bed. Tell Beckett I’m sorry too.”

She shrugged a shoulder. “It’s all good. Honestly.” Gracious as ever, she led them to the front door—more like waddled—and, after giving them both their coats and an extra squeeze, ushered them out. The night was quiet, muffled by a light veil of snow sifting from the endless, inky vault above. Once they’d cleared the covered stoop, Michaela turned her face upward, opened her mouth, and stuck her tongue out. Yep, not attorney-like at all, and he stifled a laugh at her antics. The sidewalk was dusted in white, as though someone had sprinkled powdered sugar over its surface, and he felt rather than saw her leg shoot out from under her. He tightened his grip and yanked her against him before she could hit the concrete. For a stilted second, they stared at each other through clouds of exhaled steam. Her lips tipped up, and her eyes glittered like the snow crystals swirling around them.

*Ferguson. I need to tell Ferguson he has a date.*

“Thanks for saving me,” she said, breaking the spell as she tottered away from him and looked up and down the street. “Which one is your car?”

His eyes caught on her spiky heels. Jesus, no wonder she’d nearly fallen on her ass! They were dealing with strictly heavy-tread-footwear weather here. One quick stride and he caught her up, wrapping his hand around her small bicep buried inside her wool coat sleeve. “Hold on there, Micky Mouse, before those heels of yours land you on the sidewalk.” *Oh shit. Way to impress her, genius.*

Her eyes snapped to his and narrowed. “Did you say Micky? Mouse?”

“Sorry. After hearing other people call you Micky all night, it kinda slipped out.”

“Only special people call me Micky, and *no one* calls me Mouse.”

Unable to tell if she was truly offended, he marshaled on. “So even after tonight, I don’t rate high enough in the special category to call you Micky? Without the mouse part, of course,” he quickly qualified as he fought a telltale quirk of his lips. He nudged her along, and they trundled toward his blacked-out Range Rover SVAutobiography. “That’s my car,” he indicated with a chin lift.

She brought them to a stop a few feet from the front bumper and looked up at him. “Do you *want* to call me Micky?”

He shook his head. “Not really. You strike me as more of an ‘M.’”

Confusion drew her brows together. “‘M’? What’s that?”

*No idea.* He hustled her to the passenger door and opened it, urging her inside before her fingers turned to icicles. Where were her gloves? “*M* is the first initial of your name.” Giving himself an inner pat on the back for the nonsense that had sparked his brain, he got her situated, leaning over her to strap her in as though she were a little kid. She lifted her arms to accommodate him, seemingly unaware that he was practically lying across her lap.

As he pulled away, she surprised him by saying. “‘M.’ I kinda like it.”

With a chuckle and a headshake, he closed her door and rounded the hood.

"I like your car," she declared when he climbed inside.

"Thanks. Me too."

The drive went quickly—too quickly, if he were honest—because the population of Denver was way smarter than they were, with folks tucked in their warm homes instead of driving dark, icy streets. They talked the entire way, meandering from the topic of Range Rovers to cars in general to fast-food fare and what was really in those chicken sandwiches. Conversation with Michaela was easy, and it continually fueled his mind, making it vault from subject to subject. He was eager to find out what she thought, and the more they talked, the higher the well of possible topics filled. It seemed bottomless.

A quiet settled over them when they entered the building and climbed aboard the elevator. Only six inches separated them, and his index finger, as if controlled by some other being, sought her soft hand and stroked lightly. Coming to his senses, he pulled away. "Your fingers are cold," he murmured. She glanced up at him and hummed her agreement. All of him wanted to press his lips to hers, to feel their soft warmth once again, to feel that connection. Berating himself for being a lousy friend to Fergs, he dropped his gaze as he fought to keep his body in check. This had to be lust clouding his mind. Had to be.

His gaze took a tour of the elevator's dark interior, and he pondered whether he should take Sherry up on her offer to call. After all, he was no slouch in the kissing department, at least according to the woman currently sharing the elevator with him. However, the thought of kissing Sherry had him near hurling, and he ejected the idea from his head before it could grow legs. The only woman piquing his interest at the moment was the one beside him—an inconvenience he couldn't afford to indulge for so many reasons ... not the least of which was the guy who shared years of friendship and a condo with him.

Moments later, Blake stood at Michaela's door while she rummaged around in her purse for her key, his eyes wandering between the silky curls on her head and his own door. Was Ferguson home? The guy would be thrilled when Blake told him he had a date with her. Like weights on a scale, though, Blake's excitement would be inversely balanced with his roommate's, and it caused him to take a step back so he could preserve the modicum of loyalty he clung to.

When Michaela slid the key home and unlocked her door, she paused a moment and looked up at him. One step and she leaned into him, pushed up on one foot, and planted a kiss on his cheek. Despite his internal warning sirens, his knees instinctively bent so he could more easily accept the innocent kiss.

She pressed her hand against his chest for support. "Good night, Blake," she whispered. "Thank you for turning a very dull evening into a very enjoyable one."

He nodded, his tongue tied in knots that kept him from returning the sentiment flashing in his brain. Instead, he gave her a lame, "Good night, M." When he finally worked out the kinks, she'd disappeared behind her door and closed it.

# Chapter 13
## Twisted Wrister

"What do you mean, you can't go?" Blake gaped at his roommate, trying to focus on Denver traffic as he guided his Range Rover toward the arena. They were headed in for practice before hopping aboard a charter that would take them to Detroit for a game the following night. After Detroit came Chicago, followed by St. Paul. Three games in five days. Exhausting and exhilarating at the same time because Blake was slated to center the top line. Right now, though, he had other priorities.

"I can't go," Ferguson retorted. "I want to, but I can't. It's my grandma's birthday, and my family will string me up if I don't show. In fact, I think they're expecting you too."

"*What?* Since when?"

"Since Mom told me to invite you a few weeks ago."

"Fucking unbelievable," Blake muttered as he shook his head. "I play wingman for you, set you up with this girl you've been dying to get next to, and you can't go. And apparently, I'm headed to your grandma's on our one night off." He knew Ferguson's family, just like Fergs knew his mom and sister, and if they were expecting Blake, he was obligated to go. But that wasn't what was chafing at him like a too-small shin guard. Stopping at a red light, he swung his head toward Fergs and glared. At least his roommate had the decency to appear sheepish. “Do you want this girl or not?”

“Of course, I want her!”

“Yeah, you want her so bad that instead of asking her out, you’re dicking around with Tracy.” Blake puffed out an annoyed breath. *Get off your ass and go after her already! Before I do.*

Now where had *that* thought come from? Once again, Blake found himself stuffing down some damn uncomfortable notions swirling around in his brain, leaking all over his tidy life.

“I told you, Tracy’s an in-the-moment thing. For now, I like being around her. But it’ll fizzle when she wants to get serious, and by then I’ll be ready to ask Michaela out on a real date. Dinner, the works.”

*Un-fucking-believable.*

They drove in silence while Blake stewed in his aggravation. What the hell was he supposed to tell M? He’d as much as promised her an escort. How was she supposed to find a date at the eleventh hour? *Well, shit!*

“Look,” Fergs offered, “I appreciate what you did. I really do. And I appreciate you keeping an eye on her last night so guys didn’t hit on her. But why can’t she just go stag to this ... this whatever it is?” He twirled his hand in the air.

“Her boss’s dinner party, and it isn’t a *stag* kind of deal, Fergs, not when everyone else coming is a couple. Making the right appearance at this thing is really important for M’s career.”

Fergs turned in his seat and faced him. “‘M’? You’re calling her ‘M’ now?”

*Whoops.* Blake went on the defensive, which irritated him further. “It’s less of a mouthful than Michaela, and only special people get to call her Micky.” Which explained absolutely nothing.

“‘M’ sounds pretty fucking special to me. Look, instead of dinner, I’ll take her to the charity brunch fashion show event.”

“You don’t get it. Taking her to the charity brunch doesn’t solve *this* problem.”

“Maybe not, but the charity thing is the perfect way for Michaela to get to know me.” Fergs grinned. “With all the cameras and press and shit there, she'll be way more impressed than if I just take her to dinner."

Blake's head was about to explode as he pulled into the players' parking lot and coasted into a spot beside T.J. Shanstrom's Audi. He was so pissed off he hadn't realized the alternate captain was inside his car and on the verge of opening his door, and as T.J. unfolded himself from the driver's seat, he flipped Blake off. Another guy stepped out of the passenger side—Cam Blue, the new defenseman—and watched Blake and Fergs with curiosity from the sidewalk.

Before Blake could shout out an apology to T.J., Ferguson chortled, "I've got it!" He whacked Blake's shoulder a few times.

"You've got what?"

"I have a solution for the, ah, dating sitch." Ferguson's eyes were bright, and that stupid grin split his stupid face as he barreled on. "She likes you—it's obvious because she lets you call her a cute nickname—so *you* take her. For me. You can warm her up for me taking her to the charity gig."

Blake's mouth dropped open. "You're smoking crack."

"No, no, listen to this. I'll make an excuse that sounds legit so you can bow out of Grandma's party, no big deal, which frees you up to take M." Ferguson threw his hands in the air. "Problem solved! We're interchangeable. She's comfortable with you, and I trust you to keep your paws off her."

Of all the BS that came out of Ferguson's mouth, why did him calling Michaela "M" piss Blake off more than anything else? And why the fuck was his friend shoving him into this impossible situation?

Fergs gave Blake another whack. "I'd do it for you, man. All day long."

Oh, this had all the markings of a disaster rolling downhill fast, picking up more debris as it went, and causing even bigger disasters along the way, like fissures that spiderwebbed from an impact on ice. "No!"

Ferguson groaned. "Shit, Bear. Come on."

"What if *I'm* interested in her? Did you ever think of that?" Regretting the words as soon as they left his big mouth, Blake muttered a silent curse.

Now it was Ferguson's turn to go slack-jawed. A second later, he burst into laughter. "Good one, Bear!"

"What the fuck does *that* mean?"

"It means I've known you a long time, my man, and you don't know what to do with yourself when a hot little piece of ass wants in your pants—not that Michaela would ever want in your pants. That's *not* what I'm saying."

"Then what the hell *are* you saying? Enlighten me. Please," Blake growled.

"No way do I see you going after anyone, let alone someone your best bro wants. You're not *that* guy. That's just downright sleazy."

*Not helping*. "You're really going to ask Michaela to the gala?" Blake took pain to enunciate her full name.

Fergs shrugged. "Yeah. Sure. Even if she is a little intimidating, but like I told you, I'm working on that."

T.J. rapped his knuckles on the Range Rover's hood, making them both jump. *Speaking of intimidating*. "Are you assholes coming, or what?"

The big dude was *waiting* for them? Blake couldn't say whether he or Ferguson scrambled out of the vehicle faster, leaving their discussion in its leather interior. Even the new guy shook his head and smirked at them. *Dickwad.*

"So? Will you do it?" Fergs prodded as they stood by their tightly packed stalls in the Detroit visitors' locker room. They were cleaning up after a hard-fought victory against the Red Wings. "It's the least you can do after stealing my job, asshole." Though Fergs said it with a half-smile, there was a bite to those words Blake didn't like.

"Blake Barrett, game MVP," one of their teammates screeched from across the room. This was followed by several whoops, yeahs, and one eardrum-piercing, "Tah-wisted wrister, baby!" Blake ducked his head so he could avoid the look on his best friend's face. Blake had had a good game—an *awesome* game, if he'd been talking about someone besides himself—and his wrist shot had been lethal and unstoppable. Not too much flex, nor too little; just right. In the rarefied Goldilocks zone. He'd been working on it, perfecting it for years, and it seemed to finally be paying dividends ... which meant he was locked into the first-line center position as long as he kept up his play and Nelson's success continued on the second line.

Grimson shocked the hell out of Blake when he laid a big paw on his shoulder. "You should be proud of your play tonight. You won us a game. Bet your folks are busting at the seams."

"Thanks," was all Blake could muster. He *was* proud of his effort and was still riding enough of a high that his body hadn't started hurting yet. That would roar through his sleep at 2:00 a.m. or wake up with him the next morning. And yeah, his dad would definitely have been proud, but his lone remaining parent didn't have a clue. She was completely oblivious, lost in a bottle of Smirnoff.

Consequently, the pride that swelled his chest was all his, and God, he wanted to savor it, but when Grims left and Blake caught a glimpse of Ferguson, guilt quickly washed over him. If Blake's stellar play didn't mean Fergs was locked *out* of the position, he could have steeped in the sweet victory. And that's what led him to pivot on his refusal to take Ferguson's place as Michaela's escort to her boss's fancy dinner.

"I'll do it." He didn't miss how Ferguson's eyes lit up. "On one condition," Blake qualified.

Fergs rushed in with the eagerness of a dog about to get a slice of bacon. "Yeah, of course. Name it."

Blake wagged an index finger at him. "You call or text her and ask her first. She gets right of first refusal. If she's okay with it, I'll take her."

Ferguson's face split with an idiotic grin, and he clapped Blake on the shoulder. "Absolutely! Goes without saying!"

Blake's shoulders eased a bit, knowing that while he'd screwed up his friend's playing life, he'd brought some cheer to his personal one. Not to mention M wouldn't be left high and dry for this event that meant so much to her. Now he had to reconcile himself to spending an entire evening with a woman he hadn't been able to get out of his fricking mind since her soft lips had landed on his and who'd been haunting his dreams every night since. He'd need a boatload of liquid steel in his veins to resist the pull of those luminous gray eyes of hers.

Ferguson's hushed voice brought Blake back to the noise and tangy smell of the locker room. "Aren't you forgetting something?"

"What's that?"

"You haven't given me her number yet. I'll need it to contact her." Ferguson still sported the idiotic grin.

"Oh yeah. Right." How had Blake forgotten to pass along the number she'd given him at the Millers' party? It wasn't as if he'd done anything with it or had been hoarding it. Then again, as he picked up his phone to text it to his friend, his thumb hesitated. With a "For fuck's sake!" bellowing inside his head, he broke through his own barrier and hit "send." *There. Out of my hands now.* Now if he could only get the whole thing—and her—out of his head.

Hours later, they arrived at their hotel in Chicago. Blake was relieved to be bunking with their goalie, Mac, instead of Ferguson. Blake needed the break from Fergs, and Mac was chill, a good guy who would definitely *not* be riding him about taking away his job or dating a certain curly-haired attorney with a fascinating tattoo. Did Fergs even know she had a tattoo? Blake would relish keeping that little nugget to himself.

As he and Mac strode to the elevators with Cam Blue in tow, they passed the bar, where a few of their teammates were already mingling with a group of women. Ferguson was smack in the middle of their midst, chatting up a few of them, and judging by the way their eyes sparkled and followed his every word, he could get lucky tonight. But he wouldn't, would he? Not while he was still with Tracy and gunning for M.

That question was answered in the next second when Fergs slid his arm around one of the women and palmed her ass. She giggled and whispered something in his ear. Something inside Blake's stomach churned, but he couldn't put a name on it. Anger? Disgust? Whatever it was, it wasn't pleasant.

A woman at the back of the group looked up at Blake and gave him an inviting smile packed with promise. Her blond tresses, like her bare legs, were long. Thick, soft spirals were arranged just so over her stacked rack.

"You going to join them or head up to the room?" Mac, who stood at eye level with him, asked Blake and Cam nonchalantly.

Blake's brain came back on board in an instant. "Nope, I'm with you."

Cam was a man of few words, so his quiet rumble caught Blake off guard. "I'm too tired for this bullshit tonight. Besides, everything I see in that bar is fake."

Mac chuckled. "Yeah, I feel you. We all know how those conversations will go, and I'd rather spend time on the phone with my girl than watch those dumbasses play it up with the bunnies. Talking to Mia will be way more interesting ... and satisfying."

"You got a girl?" Blake asked Cam as they stepped on to the elevator.

"Fuck, no."

Mac jerked a thumb at Cam and snorted. "No one in her right mind wants to be with his grumpy ass."

Cam slid his middle finger along his nose, and Mac guffawed. "Yeah, fuck you very much too, bro."

Blake and Mac left Cam behind on the elevator—he was another floor up—and Blake shot Mac a questioning eyebrow as they made their way down the hall. "You guys know each other?"

"We played together in Philly for a hot minute. I give the guy as much grief as I can, but I love having him play in front of me. He's a beast who's in a constant state of being pissed off, and he likes to take it out on guys clogging up my net. Like Grimson, only faster and meaner."

"Hard to believe there's a nastier version of the Grim Reaper," Blake chuckled.

"Right?"

Mac had had to go back to square one and restart his career—no small feat in this business. Not only had he overcome a mountain of odds, but he'd become an integral part of the club through sheer determination and a gritty work ethic. Blake had looked up to him from the moment he'd met the goalie, and he couldn't imagine the team succeeding without him backstopping the net. At odds with his confident demeanor, Mac never hesitated exposing his soft underbelly when it came to Mia or his kids, which, oddly, didn't take away from his stature as a man's man. As for Mia, the fun, fiery brunette acted as crazy for Mac as he was about her. M had been right. They were a perfect match.

What did that feel like?

Blake had never had anyone like that in his life—he'd never even been in love—but he found himself wondering more and more what it would feel like knowing someone waited for him when he returned from a grueling road trip, someone soft and warm who threw her arms around his neck and told him how happy she was to see him.

Mac unlocked their door and entered a room with two queen beds. It was comfortable but identical to every other room they stayed in during their away games. Blake waited until Mac picked his bed, then dropped his bag at the foot of the other one. Goalies were a superstitious bunch, and he'd learned long ago to defer to their wishes; it could make the difference between winning and losing. If they believed sleeping in the hotel bed on the right meant a win, you didn't question it. Besides, at five years his senior, Mac was a veteran, and Blake respected the pecking order.

Mac shucked his coat and tie, and he parked his ass on the end of the bed to wrestle off his shoes. "Looked like your buddy Ferguson had his hands full down in that bar. But that's never been your thing, has it?"

"No, and as I seem to recall, it wasn't your thing much either before you and Mia got together." Blake pulled off his suit jacket and tossed it on the bed before loosening his tie.

"Yeah, well, I thought it was for a while, but I sucked at it. Maybe because I figured out it's not all about the sex. Not that there isn't a lot of that now—because there's *way* more than there used to be when I was single—and not that it isn't mind-blowing, because it is. On a whole other level and beyond anything with some random chick." He paused to waggle his eyebrows. "But it's only part of the picture."

Mind-blowing sex? Blake wasn't sure he'd ever had *that* either. And what was the rest of the picture? "You committed guys all sing the same tune," Blake retorted. "And, come to think of it, how come you all have brunettes who work with or for Paige Miller? What's up with that?"

Mac shrugged. "No idea. Maybe it's because that's where the good ones are at and we're all smart fuckers who pay attention." He chortled, then sobered. "They're definitely *not* in that bar downstairs or in any bars in any of the hotels we stay at, unless they're there for some other reason besides hooking up with a hockey player. And by the way, they're not all brunettes either. Grimson's wife is blond, and so is Nelson's. They're quality, but I'm sort of partial to brunettes myself."

*Apparently, so am I.* "Were you always partial to brunettes?"

"Nah, I was partial to opportunity. If the woman was willing, so was I. Didn't much matter beyond that. But then I married Becca, and when she died, I kind of went into a shell. I was just coming out of it when I met Mia, and ... I don't know. I was meeting a lot of women, but something about her just ... I couldn't get her out of my mind. She drove me insane, in good *and* bad ways." Smiling to himself, he tossed his shoe across the room.

A familiar chord struck somewhere deep down, and Blake nodded, locking out the cute, quirky brunette who'd moved into his consciousness.

Mac dropped his other shoe and glanced over at him. "So what do you say? Dinner out or room service?"

Blake didn't have to think about it. "Room service." More questions swirled in his head, and he wanted to extend this unexpected conversation.

After Mac placed their orders, he reclined on his bed. Blake picked up the thread. "Had you met Mia when we were in Toronto that one time? Those women at your table ... you looked downright annoyed." Blake was referring to a night in a Toronto club soon after their last season had started. They'd been celebrating Mac's first shutout of the season, and three smoking-hot women had practically begged Mac to fuck them; one had been grinding in his lap. He hadn't struck Blake as a man interested in opportunity. He'd looked miserable or mad or both.

Mac grinned. "Because I *was* annoyed. Yeah, I'd met Mia by then. I guess I was distracted and frustrated none of them were her. You, on the other hand, looked downright terrified."

That night, Blake felt like he'd fallen into some R-rated B movie about a man who crash-lands on an island populated by sex-starved women desperate to be fucked by him. Yeah, every guy's dream, except when he wakes up and discovers it's real.

"I wasn't sure what they wanted," he blurted. As soon as the comment left his mouth, he laughed aloud at his own stupidity.

"Looked pretty obvious what they wanted," Mac chortled. "I'm sure they would have been happy to show you if you were too big a dumbass to figure it out on your own."

Blake had been beyond uncomfortable, overwhelmed by the abundance of female attention and unsure how to handle it. *Fergs would have known exactly what to do.* "That's not what I meant. I mean, did they want *me* and why? Or was it the hockey player they wanted?"

Mac arched an eyebrow. "I think you already know the answer to that question. That's what we're talking about, isn't it? And it's one reason I was so damn annoyed that night. On the other hand, you have guys like Tompkins, who take advantage of every opportunity they can get their hands on and then some. And look how that worked out for him. Not that I'm complaining. I'd be out of a job otherwise, though I don't feel good that it happened the way it did."

Wyatt Tompkins had been the Blizzard goalie when Mac and Blake first joined the club. Tompkins apparently had been spiraling out of control since the team had won the Cup the prior year, believing he was entitled to whatever and whomever he wanted. Mostly, it had been true, but he'd been unable—or unwilling—to rein himself in and had gone off the deep end, eventually losing his job to Mac and getting shipped off to Buffalo, where it was cold as fuck and the team wasn't so great.

Before being traded, Tompkins had taken the club on a bumpy ride, and Mac had put the team on his shoulders and brought them through it admirably. Everyone knew bad blood simmered between the two goalies, but only because Tompkins whined about it. Mac, on the other hand, had been stoic and close-mouthed. Another reason Blake admired him. The man was a class act.

If Mac had found someone—*two* someones—and he hadn't settled, there could be someone out there for Blake too.

Maybe he had already met her.

Which brought him full-circle to Ferguson. He was seeing a side to his buddy he'd either never noticed or that was only now rearing its ugly head.

"What do you do if a Tompkins-esque character is aiming for a woman you know, and she has no idea he's a douchebag, and she deserves better? And just for fun, what if the douchebag is a friend of yours? Do you shut your mouth? Do you tip her off?"

Mac took a thoughtful pause. "My first question is if the guy's such a scum bucket, why's he your friend? But I get it. We all get into those situations where people who are our so-called friends do shit that make us go, 'What the fuck?' My second question is does the woman like the douchebag? Because if she does, you telling her he's a dick is only going to get her pissed off at *you*."

Blake pushed out an exhale. Nothing was simple, was it? "Yeah, but he talks out of both sides of his mouth." *And it rankles.* "He says he's crazy about one, that she's *it* for him, but then he's fucking someone else he says doesn't mean anything to him, and on top of that, now he acts like he's down to fuck every woman who'll drop her pants." *He's greedy. And it's plain wrong.* No other way to put it.

The thought struck that if Ferguson *did* get Michaela, he wouldn't treat her right. Blake barreled ahead. "This girl deserves to be treated like royalty—like you treat Mia and Grims treats Ellie and T.J. treats Natalie—not like she's another plaything in an already overflowing toybox."

Expressive quicksilver eyes and bouncy brown curls belonging to someone he'd known only a few short weeks popped into Blake's head. Like an army of white blood cells going to war inside his body to keep him safe, his brain cells were poised to march and shut the thought down before it could sprout roots.

*No, not M.*

He shot to his feet and paced.

Mac side-eyed him. "Know what I think?"

Blake shook his head.

"I think the friendship you're worried about isn't much of a friendship. I'm also thinking that this woman's kinda special and that you need to go after her yourself."

# Chapter 14

# That's Definitely a Buzz Saw Up Ahead

Michaela swallowed a frustrated curse aimed at the TV screen before she realized she was alone and her neighbors couldn't hear her ... because they were *on* the screen, playing the last of their away games. She let the curse fly, not exactly sure what she was cursing at, except the refs seemed to be calling everything in Minnesota's favor. What was up with that anyway? Although she'd told Blake she didn't have time to watch sports—and truthfully, she didn't—she had miraculously managed to carve out a few hours to watch the Blizzard's three road games.

Even though work was piling up on top of the existing towering heap, she was taking a much-needed breather, losing herself in the game, dazzled by the play of one blond, green-eyed center whom experts touted as having the best wrist shot in the league ... possibly ever. Michaela had never been into jocks, but she was finding she could be persuaded otherwise—specifically ones named Blake who wore the number twenty-one.

He was presently sitting on the bench, but on the ice one of the Minnesota players knocked down a Blizzard forward in front of the net.

"Hey, what was *that*? Damn mugging thugs on ice!" she shouted when the camera panned the Minnesota bench. This she followed up with a handful of trail mix she chucked at the TV.

"Shit! Now look what you made me do, you jackasses! I have to clean up the mess *you* made me make."

Yeah, she was being ridiculous, but it was sort of fun to scream about a game she suddenly cared a whole hell of a lot about, even if she didn't understand it completely. It popped the pressure valve on the steam that had been building inside her all week.

She trapped the breath rising in her throat as Blake prepared for the face-off. Gliding toward the face-off circle, he was all tics, twitches, and neck pops. Granted, she hadn't known him very long, but she'd been close enough to notice he didn't exhibit the nervous behavior anywhere but on the ice.

"Wonder if he knows he does that?" she asked herself aloud. "I'll have to ask Owen about it when we go to the Steadmans'." It could be a topic of conversation in case they ran out of subjects. While she could fall into a comfortable rhythm talking to Blake, she had no idea if his roommate was as easy to talk to, or if he'd just spend the entire evening trying to impress her with his pecs. She sighed. Oh well. At least she *had* a date.

As soon as Blake bent over and planted his stick on the ice, the twitching stopped. He was all business, his pale greens lasered to a fine point on the puck in the linesman's hand, as though he could drill right through its core. So intense, so focused, so ... *phew!*

She fanned herself with her hand. Without her permission, her mind leapt to whether he looked at his bedmates with the same intensity when he was about to—

*Whoa there, girl!*

She groaned aloud as the visual of him on top of the redhead shifted to him on top of *her*, stealing what little breath she had left in her lungs. She hurriedly banished the image. Where these thoughts were coming from, she had little idea, but they'd been making random appearances all week, driving her to distraction.

They had to stop. Good thing *he* wasn't taking her to the Steadmans'; she wasn't sure the little devil on her shoulder could be trusted not to jump him.

The puck dropped, pulling her from her fantasies—*thank God!*—as the announcers described the action. "Barrett has won *another* face-off, and big Dave Grimson's picked it up for a breakout pass. Oh, and now it's a three-on-two heading into the O-zone," the play-by-play guy exclaimed. "Barrett's got the puck again, and he's bringing it up the middle. Nice saucer pass to T.J. Shanstrom. And a one-timer, but the goalie made the stop ... and gave up a juicy rebound. Barrett's on it, crashing in front of the net and taking a beating from Minnesota's D-men, who are all over him."

One big guy cross-checked Blake in the back, and he jerked forward into the net and on top of the goalie. The announcer was drowned out by Michaela hollering at her TV. "Oh! Oh! Oh! No, no, no! You can't do that, mister! That's a penalty. Of some kind! That *has* to be a penalty!"

A whistle blew to stop the play. Blake pulled himself up and tapped the goalie on the helmet as if checking on him. *Oh, that's so sweet!* Then he spun and gave his tormentor a shove with his stick. *And that's so hot!* She let out a throaty growl.

The D-man's gloved hand shot out and landed on Blake's face before knocking his helmet back from his forehead. Then came some extracurricular face-washing, all delivered by the Minnesota asshole, before T.J. jumped in and pulled the guy back, giving him a friendly bear hug in the process.

"Yes, T.J.! You show him! C'mon, ref! Have you got a broken arm? Get that thing in the air already! You're letting these guys get away with *murder*!" She sat so far forward on her couch she nearly fell off.

Blake slashed at the guy's stick, and the ref's arm went up. He pointed at Blake first, then at the penalty box.

*"What?* You have *got* to be kidding me!"

Her phone rang, and when she saw Fiona's smiling face, she picked up. "What're you doing, Micky-Dub?"

"I'm watching hockey," Michaela snarled. "No, I'm watching a mugging on ice and refs who suck so much they've swallowed their whistles and gotten them stuck in their throats! The poor guy was getting beat up, and all he did was defend himself. So who do they send to the box? The guy defending himself! God, they are soooo lame!"

"Oh my," Fiona cackled. "Sounds like someone's a big fan all of a sudden. You even sound like you know what you're talking about."

"Oh. Well, they're my neighbors."

"Who? The refs?"

She let out an exasperated exhale. "No, the players. Did I not tell you this? I live next door to two hunky hockey players."

"Oh really," Fiona purred. "Do tell. Do we have some neighborly relations happening?"

"No, nothing like that. Well, that's not entirely true. I spent the night with the blond one at a friend's house—"

*"What?* You go, girl! Whoo! Love how you got right back on the horse. Way to overcome the speed-dating fiasco."

"No, Fi. We didn't *spend* the night. Just spent the entire time talking, and we went so late the hosts threw us out."

"Oh. Well, interesting, but not quite as exciting as I was picturing. So what's his name?"

"The blond one is Blake. I'm going on a date with his roommate, Owen." Funny, Michaela couldn't remember *his* eye color. Well, she'd discover it soon enough.

"Oh. My. God. Girl. You've been busy! When you said you were ready to put yourself back on the market, you weren't messing around!"

Michaela's eyes strayed toward the TV, and an unforeseen thrill raced through her. Blake sat in the box, rearranging his gear. Number twenty-one lifted his jersey, revealing a mouthwatering, muscled six-pack glistening with sweat as he wiped his forehead with the hem. April had called it. Yep, he was one of those rare players who didn't wear an undershirt, and Michaela's hormones cheered.

"Mick? You there?"

"Uh, yeah. Right here. What were we talking about?" *Got a little distracted.*

"The guy you're dating."

"We're not *dating*. He's simply acting as my escort to a *very* exciting event." Relief swept through Michaela when Blake exited the box. Minnesota hadn't scored on the power play, and the Blizzard still led by one goal. But soon the bad guys would pull their goalie; she wasn't sure her frayed nerves could take it.

"And that event would be?"

"A dinner at the Steadmans'!" Michaela squeed.

"Uh, yeah, Mick, that's exciting as hell." Fiona let out a strangled yippee that more closely resembled a deflating balloon than a cheer.

Michaela rushed headlong into an explanation of why this particular dinner was important.

"Good for you, Mick. It's about time they recognized what a treasure they have in you. Now tell me about this guy you're going to the party with. Have you seen him naked? If so, please describe all his parts in excruciating detail. I want to hear about every muscle on his body. *Every* muscle."

"Thanks for the rah-rah, Fi, and sorry to disappoint, but I have *not* seen him naked. Oh, wait. I have seen his naked torso. By the way, the body part your dirty mind thinks is a muscle is, in reality, an organ." *How's that for trivia, Blake Barrett?*

"Pfft. You say organ, I say muscle. What's the diff? It still works in wonderful and mysterious ways. Now about this torso. Nice pecs? Biceps? Any chest hair? Naughty tattoos? Ooh, and do *not* skimp on a single detail when it comes to his abs."

Michaela locked out the image of Blake's abs seared into her brain. "God, you're bad. Does your husband know about your interest in male torsos besides his?"

"No, but he doesn't look away when a fine female torso—besides mine—comes into his field of vision, so I think he and I are even on this one."

Michaela laughed, in no small part because the game was over, and the Blizzard had pulled out the win. Blake's team mug shot appeared on the screen as the first star of the game, and she heard background babble about his "wicked wrist shot." Her heart executed a quick little flip. "What were we talking about? Oh, right. Owen's torso. About what you'd expect for a professional athlete. In short, it's a fine torso, but he knows it and likes to show it off, which is a bit of a turnoff. To tell you the truth, if I had to pick one, I'd go with Blake."

"The blond?" Fiona squealed.

"Mm-hmm."

"And why's that?"

Michaela corralled a sigh. "Because he's got the most gorgeous green eyes I've ever seen, and he kisses really, really well."

"Wait. *What?* You've been holding out on your bestie! No fair! You're breaking the rules, Mick."

"They're more like guidelines." Michaela fizzed with laughter. God, she missed Fiona like a boat missed its rudder.

"When did you kiss him?"

"A few days after I met him. He said he needed kissing lessons."

"Are you shitting me? That's the oldest trick in the book!"

"It is? I'd never heard that one before. Besides, I'm the one who offered to, ah, teach him."

"Oh, you wicked woman! What's happened to you since I've been gone? You were so ... so serious! And boring. Seriously boring. How did the 'lessons' go?" Fiona's voice took on a salacious quality.

Michaela dropped her voice to match. "So well that he graduated with honors."

"Do you plan on 'teaching' him what else he can do with his mouth?"

"Only if he signs up for my advanced courses!"

They howled with laughter before the conversation moved on to what Michaela was wearing to the dinner, how Fiona's trip was going, and more excited chitchat that could have run on for hours had Fiona's husband, James, not interrupted with the reminder they needed to be somewhere.

"You have fun," Fiona said as they wrapped up, "and don't do anything I wouldn't do."

"Which means I have carte blanche to do anything my little heart desires?"

"Exactly!"

Michaela might be going to the dinner with the wrong guy, but she'd keep an open mind and enjoy hanging on the arm of the not-so-shabby wrong guy. And who knew? He had the potential to turn out better than his first impression.

Blake took the seat next to Ferguson on the plane. God, he was exhausted, crushed to the marrow. So crushed he could barely keep his eyes open. Right now his thoughts were wholly on his soft bed at home ... and one other small detail.

"Did you double-check that M's still cool with me taking her tomorrow night?"

Ferguson shifted in his seat. "Why do you keep asking? Nothing's changed, and it's not like I'm constantly checking with her. We've been a little busy," he grumped.

*Some of us busier than others.* Ferguson, he'd heard, had been out practically every night with a different bunny. Blake couldn't get a straight answer out of his friend, but the dark circles under his eyes and his shitty play were solid clues the rumors were true. He had little idea what had gotten into his friend, but he seemed to be finding a different gear with the ladies lately. Worse, he was verging on being a liability to the club—and he didn't seem to give a shit. Maybe it was time for a heart-to-heart.

As he'd been doing a lot this past week, Blake squirmed inside at the thought of Ferguson with M. It felt all wrong. She was a *nice* girl. Damn sexy, yeah, but also funny and sweet. The kind you took home to Mom—assuming Mom wasn't a raging alcoholic, of course, not that Owen's mom was. No, she was a "normal" mom, and Blake felt a familiar pang at what he'd missed during his screwed-up childhood.

Putting the self-pity away, he refocused on his moral dilemma with M. Mac had made his point, but it wasn't a point Blake could reconcile himself to yet. Maybe he would plant a seed when he took her to her big dinner so she'd have an inkling what she could be getting into with Fergs. Fuck, he hated to betray his best friend like that, but he felt an equally strong pull to protect Michaela—not only was that odd, but it was *at* odds to his friendship with Fergs. Hinting around without spilling the entire pot of beans couldn't be labeled disloyal—*could it?*—and M would have enough puzzle pieces to decide whether she wanted to get involved with the guy.

"The last thing I want to do is show up at her door when she's expecting *you*," Blake said. He'd been saying the same thing for days, and yeah, he should shut up, but the closer they got to Halloween, the more evasive Fergs became. That evasiveness sent Blake's spidey-senses into intense tingle mode.

"I told you, it'll be fine," Fergs said through clenched teeth.

Undaunted, Blake pressed forward. "Did you ask her to the charity brunch yet?"

"Yeah, and she said she'd love to go," Ferguson snapped. "Goddamn, you're worse at nagging than my mother."

"Sorry, dude. Just double-checking."

"You've double- and triple-checked. Now would you just shut the fuck up and let me get some sleep?" He turned his head to the side, facing away from Blake, crossed his arms over his chest, and shut his eyes. "And for fuck's sake, would you stop calling her 'M'?"

"Whatever your assholiness wants." Shaking his head, Blake stood and scanned the plane for a different seat. Spotting space beside Quinn Hadley, who was juggling little red beanbags as usual, Blake made a beeline toward the left winger. Quinn was always cheerful and quick with a joke—probably had something to do with the fact he'd scored one of those kick-ass brunettes and was heading home to her. Blake promised himself to stay away from the touchy-feely shit he and Mac had talked about. With any luck, Quinn's humor would keep Blake's mind off the impending feeling of doom he could not shake: that soon he would be walking into a buzz saw blindfolded with no way of avoiding it.

# Chapter 15
# The Substitute

Michaela hit the send button on her phone and held her breath. Moments later, as promised, Fiona's reply chimed. *You are stunning, Micky-Dub!*

Michaela released a puffed-cheek breath and typed, *So the silver jacket works?*

Fiona: *It's perfect! Hides the tats with stylish elegance and—bonus!—it brings out your gorgeous eyes. You will knock them dead, girlfriend!*

Unexpected tears stung Michaela's eyes, and she blinked them back furiously. "No time to reapply makeup, so knock it off, you ninny!" she softly told her reflection. The subtle smoky eyeliner and layers of mascara had taken nearly a half hour to perfect. She was not about to let a few happy tears ruin her hard work.

Michaela: *Thanks, Fi. Just what I needed to hear. Love you.*

Fiona: *Now go show that hockey player what a real woman is. And if you really love me, you'll send me pics if you *happen* to catch him in bare-torso mode again.*

Michaela laughed aloud, and the building reserve of tears evaporated. Taking one last look in the full-length bathroom mirror, she appraised her spruce-green dress. The body-hugging, halter-style bodice and swing skirt that brushed the tops of her knees was flattering, flirty, but classy. And Fiona was right: the simple open jacket covered the tattoos—a detail she always hid from her bosses and colleagues—but its shimmering material screamed "Grown-up!" along with the simple diamond pendant and diamond drop earrings. Just the effect she was going for.

As she plumped her curls and slid her glasses up the bridge of her nose, the doorbell bonged. *He's prompt.* Picking up her black-beaded evening bag, she flipped off the light, scooped up her coat, and headed for the front door, her black ankle-strap high heels click-clacking smartly across the wood-planked floor.

She pulled open the door and stopped short.

One arm casually resting against the doorjamb with his hand dangling in space, Blake Barrett practically filled the open doorway with his wide, squared-off frame. Dressed in an expensive black suit, crisp white button-down, and navy-blue silk tie, he looked like he'd just stepped out of a fashion magazine featuring men's formal wear. His short blond hair was neatly styled, his square jaw was clean-shaven, and his clear, fern-green eyes stood out, framed by lashes so long they verged on illegal.

A deep V creased the space between his brows. "You weren't expecting me." His voice—smooth and buttery, like pure sin—rolled over the statement.

Michaela's pulse took off at a gallop, and somewhere in the dim recesses of her mind, she registered he'd hadn't posed a question. Mentally, she checked her mouth—to be sure it hadn't dropped open like a sprung attic stairway—and composed herself. "No, I wasn't." *But I'm not complaining.* "What's ... what's going on?" She stood on tiptoe to peer over his shoulder, expecting to see his roommate in the hallway, but she couldn't see past the broad man in front of her.

He rolled his eyes to the ceiling as if praying for patience and ran a big hand over his smooth jaw. Leveling those eyes back on her, he let out a long sigh. "So Owen didn't tell you he couldn't make it and that he'd asked me to fill in for him?"

Words were beyond her grasp at the moment—whether from the shock of this new development or the mouthwatering man in front of her, she couldn't say—and she shook her head vigorously.

He muttered what she thought were a few colorful curses under his breath. “Shit, I am so sorry. He led me to believe ... He was supposed to get a hold of you last week, right after the Millers’ party, and let you know he couldn’t make it. He must have forgotten.”

“But apparently you could, and he strong-armed you into it.”

His mouth tipped up in a cute smirk, sending ripples of tingly star stuff through her body. “Trust me, it didn’t take much.”

*Oh. How ... nice.* Her hammering heart lifted a few inches. “So you’re okay with taking me?” She fought to keep the desperate hope from her tone.

He straightened, and though she wore four-inch heels, he towered over her. “No, I always deliver bad news dressed in formal wear.”

*I wouldn’t call this bad news.* She must have looked all kinds of confused because the next words out of his mouth were, “That was a joke.” His smile bloomed, brilliant white. “I’m more than okay with taking you. The real question is are *you* okay with me subbing for Owen tonight?”

She bit back the “Omigod, yes! I wanted you in the first place!” tap-dancing on the tip of her tongue, instead managing a demure, “Yes, I can live with that. Thank you.”

His big shoulders relaxed, and her mind leapt to hoping there would be dancing tonight so she’d have an excuse to run her hands all over their hard angles.

“I know how important this is to you, and I couldn’t leave you hanging.” He held out his hand for her coat.

The bristled edges of her heart melted. “Thank you,” she repeated as she spun in place and let him slide her coat up her arms and onto her shoulders.

“Shall we?” He offered his arm.

She slid her hand into the crook of his elbow and tugged the latch behind her. The door snicked closed with a dull thud, and they strolled down the hallway.

Her eyes shifted to Owen and Blake’s door. “So what’s he doing tonight? Or should I ask?” she whispered.

Blake led her into the elevator and punched the button for the lobby. "His family is throwing a birthday party for his grandma, who's turning eighty. I didn't know that when I committed him to take you, so that's on me."

"Sounds fun," she said absently. Suddenly, this evening had become much more interesting, and she was looking forward to the dinner far more than she had a mere fifteen minutes ago.

Now if her date could impress her bosses as much as he'd impressed her, she'd be on easy street.

*I am going to kill the bastard as soon as I get my hands on him. Break his toes, one by one, before I move on to his fingers.* Blake fumed inside, gathering all his willpower around him like a force field; he had to rein in his outrage over his buddy's callousness ... just as he needed to re-examine his minimum friendship requirements if this was the quality of "friend" he was getting. *How can such a selfish, lying jerkoff be my friend?* Because, Blake's conscience reminded him, he owed Ferguson a lot, that's why. As a ten-year-old, Ferguson had fearlessly stood up to Blake's mom when she'd been in one of her drunken rages and ready to take it out on Blake—and Ferguson had done it more than once. Not that Blake couldn't stick up for himself, but having your bigger buddy go to war for you against your *mother* meant a hell of a lot. It had earned Ferguson a lifetime of loyalty in Blake's book—or ledger, as M liked to say. Eventually, Mom backed way the hell off whenever Ferguson came to the house. The question was, though, did that same kid—the one Blake had pledged his loyalty to—still live inside Fergs?

As Blake walked M to his Range Rover in the underground garage, he turned over the conversations between Ferguson and himself ever since Ferguson had first hatched this scheme. Blake realized Ferguson had never actually stated he'd contacted her; then again, he hadn't denied it either. What the hell? Fergs had deceived him. Big-time. Wasn't loyalty a two-way street? It *had* to be at the top of the list of requirements for friends. Friendship—hell, *every* relationship—was based on loyalty. It was the foundation you built trust on.

M's heels clicked softly across the concrete garage floor, pulling him back to the here and now ... and her. He stole a glance—one of many since she'd opened the door and about knocked him on his ass. Good thing he'd been leaning against the doorframe so he could steady himself.

He rolled his lips between his teeth to stifle a private smile. Ferguson might be acting like a douche canoe of epic proportions, but Blake wasn't complaining about playing escort. Which led to another prickly problem: keeping his distance, physically and mentally, wouldn't be easy. But he had to do it.

A sharp voice sounded inside his head. "Why?"

Yeah, why indeed? Was Ferguson planning to hold M in reserve while he fucked his way through the northern hemisphere? That was wrong. There were lines friends didn't cross, though, even if they disagreed. Going after a girl your buddy liked was wrong too. It wasn't simply an uncrossable line: it was a metal barrier bolted into concrete.

After all, Fergs had bought her flowers—even if he hadn't given them to her—he'd asked her out, and he was taking her to the big-deal brunch. Maybe he'd stop screwing around once they got past that first date.

Which left Blake in the awkward position of being attracted to a woman he couldn't have.

*Your attraction is only lust talking. It'll pass.*

As he opened the car door and helped her inside, her dress hiked up her shapely thighs, and before she could wrestle it back into place, he caught a glimpse of black lace banding the top of her stockings. He squelched a groan rumbling in his chest.

*Lust, lust, lust. That's all.* Unfortunately, said lust was practically leaking from his pores, he had so much of it pent up. He rounded the back of the SUV, telling himself he could easily scratch that itch elsewhere. He had options. Lots of options. At the moment, though, *options* held little appeal.

As he slid behind the wheel, she gave him a shy smile. "Hi," she said softly. Two tiny letters and he was nearly undone.

"Hi," he replied stupidly, captured in her quicksilver gaze. She took his breath away. He could feel beads of sweat popping beneath his hairline, even though it was thirty fucking degrees outside. In that moment, every "option" was ejected from his brain until she was the only woman he saw. He had tunnel vision for her alone. Without even trying, she had all his attention, all his interest—and a few other parts of him he wasn't prepared to consider.

He was in deep, deep shit with little idea how to extricate himself.

*Just get through this dinner. That's all you need to do. After that, you can pretend you don't know her and avoid her until her time is up and she moves out in March or whenever the hell she said she was leaving.*

He plugged the address she gave him into the nav system and pulled out of the garage. As he drove through the darkness to her boss's house in Cherry Hills Village, she filled him in on the major players attending tonight. He listened with half a brain; the other half was busy helping him concoct more delusions that would create a life preserver to keep him afloat.

"So what do I call you at the dinner party?" he asked.

She shot him a curious look.

"I mean, should I stick to Michaela, or is it okay if I call you M in front of the muckety-mucks?" Since the night of the Millers' party, she'd transformed in his mind from Michaela the attorney to simply M, and he liked her that way. Somehow it made her more approachable and, if he were honest, made her a little bit of his with the special nickname.

Her impish grin was back. "You can call me whatever you like. M is fine. In fact, it'll sound more authentic ... you know, like we're a *real* couple."

*A real couple.* That sounded nice. *No, wait! It doesn't sound nice. At. All.*

They turned into a private drive flanked by two enormous metal scrollwork gates that stood open. As Blake followed the curving drive, a mansion blazing with light came into view.

"Oh my God!" she breathed. "We're having dinner at a castle!"

"Hang on to your slippers, Cinderella," he teased. He'd been in houses like this before, and while it seemed like no big deal to him, he was getting a kick out of the rapt expression on her pretty face. She reminded him of those fairy-tale characters she loved who were arriving at the prince's ball.

He pulled up to one of two valets and exchanged his keys for a "Good evening, sir." The other valet had M's door open and her hand in his before Blake could get there. Blake took over, tucking her hand in his arm, and looked down at her. "You ready, Curly?"

She inhaled a deep breath and beamed up at him. "I'm a little nervous. Do you have some trivia you can share? It might relax me."

His heart soared. She wanted trivia? That was something he could deliver. "Did you know that seventy-eight percent of valets are male? *And* did you know their average age is thirty-nine?"

"No! I had no idea."

"Yep. And did you know that some valets don't have licenses to drive?"

Her head jerked to the side as she peered over her shoulder.

"Your boss being an attorney, I'm pretty sure he hired qualified, *licensed* valets."

She glanced up at him. "They look like they're twenty years old."

"They balance out the octogenarian valets to get to the average age."

She laughed out loud, a delightful, musical sound that pulled at something in his chest.

As they approached two massive iron doors, he leaned down and whispered, "Ready now?"

"Yes," she whispered back. "Let's do this."

Foreign emotions overtook him as he stood at the front door with her on his arm. His chest ballooned, and he felt as though he'd grown a few inches taller, like he was some kind of big shot, a force to be reckoned with. *She* made him feel that way, and by God, he vowed to himself he would move the world for her tonight if she needed him to. Nowhere in his thoughts was Ferguson ... because he wasn't doing this for Ferguson. He was doing it for her and, truth be told, for himself.

They were let inside by a small, crisp man in tails and led to a formal living room, where a handful of guests stood, crystal wineglasses in hand.

A white-haired man of surprisingly large stature broke away and came toward them, a smile on his face and his hands extended. His eyes took in Blake for a nanosecond before zeroing in on M. "Ah," he exclaimed. She slid her hand from Blake's arm, and the man took it between his weathered ones. "There you are, my dear. I am delighted you came." A gleam shone in his eyes as they slid over her with masculine appreciation. It was subtle, but the move stirred a green beast Blake hadn't known existed deep in his gut. Boss or not, he didn't like the way the man's eyes moved over her.

Now they landed on Blake with hawkeyed interest. Michaela disentangled her hand and laid it on Blake's forearm. "Mr. Steadman, I'd like you to meet my ... special friend, Blake Barrett." They hadn't practiced this part—how she would introduce him—but Blake was okay with "special friend," and it seemed to satisfy the old geezer.

As they exchanged pleasantries, Blake felt eyes drilling into him, and he raised his gaze. A dark-haired dude with a soft, round face glowered at him from across the room. Beside him, an unremarkable young woman was talking, though the guy seemed unfazed by her presence. Moments later, they stood in front of the guy, and M was introducing them—Brad Hewitt, a colleague of M's—and while Brad's eyes softened noticeably when he looked at her, they hardened just as obviously when he stared at Blake.

A waiter appeared carrying a tray of wineglasses—some filled with red, some with white wine—and Blake leaned down, tucking his hand under Michaela's elbow while he pulled in the fresh fragrance floating from her hair. "Wine, M?"

"Oh yes, please."

"Red or white, sweetheart?" Shit! Where had *that* come from? He'd never called anyone "sweetheart" in his entire life, but it sure as hell rolled off his tongue easily—and sounded convincing to those observing them.

She gave him a sly little smirk, and the twinkle in her eyes said, *"You've slipped into character nicely."*

Reminding himself that's exactly what this night was about—him playing a character to help her out—he handed her a glass of white, and in another uncharacteristic move, he took a glass of red for himself. The first sip tasted good, the second one better. M's gaze moved from the glass to his face but otherwise telegraphed nothing beyond mild interest.

Conversation centered around M's law firm, and while Blake enjoyed learning more about her, he wound up learning way more about the windbags who commandeered the discussion. He didn't want to be "that" date—the one who couldn't function on his own—so he left her with her cohorts and drifted into a family room where a few older attorneys watched a basketball game flickering on a muted, wall-mounted big-screen TV. He ducked back and forth, checking that she had whatever she needed. Her eyes strayed to him frequently, as if she were checking on *him*—probably to be sure he didn't do anything to embarrass her. This was a foreign dynamic for him, so different from his world, but he was proud M had pulled him in and let him have a peek around *her* world. It felt intimate somehow, as though she was letting him into a private place few outsiders saw.

He also kept an eye on Steadman, and he couldn't decide if the guy was a dirty old man wanting in M's panties or if he was a patriarch with a soft spot for her. Could have gone either way, and Blake could understand both scenarios, though he found himself bristling at the first one.

The dark-haired guy with the soft features and softer body, Brad, was a different story altogether. No doubt the dude was crushing on M. Big-time. The eye-daggers he hurled Blake's way were only one slice of the proof pie. Other sure signs were the way he followed her around like a lost puppy, the way he hung on her every word and laughed louder than anyone else when something funny—or not so funny—tumbled from her lips, and the way his hands sort of fluttered around her when she wasn't looking. The guy looked as though he was dying to touch her but knew he couldn't. Or shouldn't. And Blake vowed to make sure he wouldn't.

At one point, he was so engrossed in watching Brad and Michaela that he didn't notice Brad's date sidle up next to him. He flinched involuntarily, nearly dumping his red wine on his white shirt. "Hey, hi," he laughed nervously. "Didn't see you there. I'm Blake."

She looked up at him. "I'm stealthy like that, and my name's Minerva." Her attention turned to Brad and Michaela. "Kinda pathetic, isn't it?"

"What's that?" Blake darted his gaze the same direction hers was pointed.

"The two people you're eyeing. Your date and mine." She lifted her chin toward them.

"What makes you say it's pathetic?" *Thank fuck I didn't ask if by pathetic she meant her old-timey name.*

She crossed her arms over her chest and smirked. "Because he's so obviously in love with her, and she's so obviously ... not." Her eyes swept Blake's body heatedly, uncomfortably, as if she were inspecting a juicy T-bone she planned on having for dinner. "And honestly, why *would* she be interested in him when she's got such an attractive alternative?" Her smirk transformed into a knowing smile that made Blake's skin crawl, but he felt sorry for the woman, so he suppressed his urge to sprint and decided instead to talk to her for a few minutes. Her date had completely abandoned her after all.

"Uh, how long have you and Brad known each other?"

She shrugged. “Our whole lives.”

“Really? What, are you guys like childhood sweethearts or something?”

“Oh hell no! He’s my cousin.” Minerva pulled a face that had Blake concerned she might hurl.

“Sorry. Didn’t know. I just assumed ... I mean, he’s your date ... or you’re *his* date.”

She nodded. “Yeah, we help each other out from time to time when one of us needs a plus-one since we’re both single.” Her sizable eyebrows bounced suggestively. Blake’s face remained a blank mask, and she sighed. “He said he needed a date in order to wrangle an invitation to this swanky dinner.”

Whoa! Had Brad wormed his way in? Why? Now it was Blake’s turn to get in some eyebrow action. “No kidding. He really wanted to be here, huh?”

“No kidding, and Brad doesn’t like being left out of *anything*. I’m sure he would have preferred bringing *her*, but the firm is pretty strict about office romances.”

“Huh. But didn’t Mr. Steadman know ... I mean, Brad isn’t married and doesn’t have a girlfriend, does he?” Yeah, he was fishing, but sometimes you got lucky when you dropped bait in the water.

“No, but when my clever cousin got wind of the dinner, he weaseled his way in. I swear, he’s got something on the boss.”

Minerva suddenly had all of Blake’s attention. “You sound like you don’t like him very much. Your cousin, not the boss.”

Another shrug. “Brad? He’s family.” Her unsaid “but” hung heavy in the air. “Let’s just say he found his calling as a slimy attorney. He was a sneaky little kid. You never knew until it was too late that he’d set himself up for the extra piece of cake or the shiny new toy the rest of us were clamoring for. Or worse, that he’d set you up to take the fall for something you didn’t do. Not much has changed, except the stakes are higher. Your Michaela would be smart to watch out for him.”

*Your Michaela.* Blake got so distracted by Minerva's words he nearly missed the giant red-flag warning she had just planted in the sand.

At that moment, M turned and flashed him a dazzling smile. She pulled away from Brad and started toward Blake and Minerva.

"I'll let you get back to Michaela. Nice chatting with you." Minerva turned on her heel and gave Blake a little finger wave at the same time Brad shot him another glare. Blake tucked away the interesting tidbit, his focus shifting to the breathtaking woman sashaying toward him. He grinned to himself. *Yes, indeed, M is killing it in the sashaying department.* He promptly reminded himself—again—tonight was only playacting.

Fortunately, he was seated beside M at dinner so he wasn't bored the entire time. They sat toward the end of a table large enough to seat sixteen, opposite the head, where Steadman and his wife held court. After dinner, as a server handed Blake another glass of red wine, M looked at him, her lips quirking. Despite the sexy smart-girl glasses, the mischievous gleam in her eyes was easy to spot. She dropped her voice and leaned into him, and he filled his nose with the scent of fresh flowers. "How many have you had?"

He lowered his head to hers and whispered back, "Me? About a third of one. I didn't finish the first glass. I think I lost it in the TV room. And just so you know, I'm a total lightweight, a really cheap date. In fact, after I knock this one back, you'll be able to take me home and do whatever you want with me."

Her mouth dropped open, and he grinned at her, gauging her reaction. It wasn't good. *So much for flirting.* He'd never been very adept at that particular art anyway.

"You're my DD!" she hissed.

"I agreed to be your date, not your DD. That requires a whole different kind of payment."

She swiveled her head, obviously checking to see if anyone was paying attention before leaning back into him. "Payment? I'm not paying you!"

"Of course not. Not in money." He waggled his eyebrows, and she gave him an astonished look.

He patted her arm. "Calm down. I'm just entertaining myself at your expense. I may be a cheap date, but not that cheap. And I am perfectly capable of driving you home." *Or of calling an Uber.* Since he rarely drank, alcohol had a way of rocketing straight to his brain, but he didn't plan to have that much.

She gave him something completely unexpected: a rueful smile. "I'm sorry. This has gone on longer than I expected, and it has to be boring you to tears. Maybe we should scoot as soon as everyone finishes dessert?"

Dessert had been served fifteen minutes ago. *God, yes, please!* He nodded politely, reining in the desire to leave that instant and drag her behind him. It struck him that if tonight wasn't fake and he had a real relationship with this woman, it would never work … not if she expected him at these sorts of suffocating social events. He'd always heard attorneys cut loose, but maybe this crowd hadn't gotten the memo. Then again, wasn't this whole dinner sort of an elaborate interview for a special account? He lifted his eyes to Brad, seated across the table a few chairs down.

The guy had been glaring at him all night, and now was no different. He met Blake's gaze in a near-challenge. "What do *you* do, um … Drake, is it?"

Before Blake could answer, Minerva—who was a fan, apparently—piped up from beside him, "He plays for the Blizzard."

Brad looked between his cousin and Blake. "What's a blizzard? Besides a snowstorm, that is?"

"Seriously?" Minerva chuffed. "Denver's NHL team. You know, big-league hockey? The pros? *Sports?*"

Brad sat back dramatically as if he'd been shoved. "Really," he exclaimed. "Well, that explains it. Michaela!" he snapped like he was fucking royalty. His haughty tone set Blake's teeth on edge.

M, who had been talking to the woman seated next to her, jerked her head up and narrowed her eyes. "What is it, Brad?"

The edge in her voice seemed to take Brad down a few needed notches. *Way to drop some sass on him, M!* Pride surged in Blake. A strange reaction, and one he decided not to deliberate.

Brad's takedown didn't last long, though. He waved a dismissive hand Blake's way while aiming a question at Michaela. "So. Your *special date*." The last two words grated, like he'd chewed glass when he spat them out. "Since when are you into jocks? Thought you liked mature men, men smart enough to hold up their end of a conversation." He hadn't said it very loud, but loud enough that a few people around him seemed to inhale and hold their collective breath. A snide look slid across his face, like he'd won some fucking ribbon at a state fair and no one was going to take it away from him. Minerva's descriptor "sneaky" popped into Blake's consciousness. Yeah, he could totally see it now, along with a few other choice adjectives, but for M's sake, he kept his temper in check and swallowed his tongue.

Though he hated to admit it, two things Brad said had touched a nerve: mature and smart. That yappy little voice inside Blake's head reminded him he didn't have enough of either trait to win someone like M.

When no one within earshot laughed or otherwise uttered a peep, Brad turned his attention back to M and raised a pointed eyebrow. M shot Blake a worried glance before opening her mouth to—Blake assumed—defend him. He didn't need defending—not by T.J. or Grimson on the ice, and certainly not by her here. He'd been playing placid and polite, and while he didn't care what people said about him, he *did* care that this guy had crossed the line where M was concerned. Brad was begging to have a whole new asshole ripped for him, and Blake nominated himself for the job.

Placing a calming hand on her forearm, he murmured for her ears only, "I got this." Then he rose from his chair—not entirely, just enough to turn his body toward Brad and plant his fists on the fine linen tablecloth, lending his already broad frame a little more girth. He drilled a look he normally reserved for opponents into Brad's face.

“Yes, she’s into jocks now. One in particular.” He kept his voice low, even. “If you’ve got a problem with that, I’d be happy to step outside and do some parsing with you.”

A few jaws dropped, and eyes went round. Beside him, the faintest of gasps escaped M’s mouth. But the reaction he most cared about was the one that had replaced the smug look on Brad’s face only seconds before. To Blake’s great satisfaction, the guy looked like he was about to shit his pants. *Message delivered.* Eyes still fastened on the toad’s face, Blake slowly lowered himself back into his chair, cracking first his neck and then his knuckles for effect. “Not interested? Let me know if you change your mind,” he tossed out for good measure before taking another sip of wine.

M gripped his arm, and he turned to her, bracing himself for a sound tongue-lashing. These were *her* people, and he’d given in to an inner caveman he hadn’t known lived inside him. He hadn’t been loud or violent, but he’d brought a warrior’s coarseness to a refined table, and he already regretted it. Though Steadman had been oblivious to the drama, others had gotten an eyeful. But M about knocked him on his butt—for such a small woman, she had a knack for doing that—when she leaned into him and whispered, “Some trivia about dessert. Quick!”

Conversation close to them had completely died away when Blake had pulled his imitation of a rabid guard dog, and silence still hung heavy at their end of the table. “What, *here*? Now?”

“Yes, now,” she insisted. One corner of her mouth twitched.

She’d completely thrown him off balance—again—which was probably what she’d meant to do.

He pulled in an extended breath and pushed it out in one long, cleansing exhale while he rummaged around in his brain for trivia facts. “Uh, let me see. Okay, here we go. Women in the seventeenth century slept with a piece of cake under their pillows so they would dream about their future husbands.”

“Ew, I bet that was messy,” Minerva offered. Her face split with a grin that seemed to break the ice. “Then again, I bet those future husbands were messy too.” A few relieved laughs erupted around them.

Impressed as hell at how easily M had defused the situation, he got on board and threw out another factoid. "Did you know that Beverly Hills has an ATM that dispenses cupcakes twenty-four-seven?"

M gave him a brilliant smile. "I want to go there. And that's two facts."

"Correct, Ms. Wagner. Do you need more?"

"No, I think we're good." Her hand slid over his and squeezed lightly, and she mouthed, "Thank you." For what, he had no clue; after all, he'd acted like the very Neanderthal he's professed *not* to be. When conversation began buzzing around them again, Brad scraped his chair back and stormed away.

Blake's eyes scanned Michaela's, looking for any sign of anger or some other emotion that might fill him with more remorse. "I'm sorry for acting like an asshole," he whispered to her.

Ignoring his statement, she pushed on. "Are you adding that extra trivia to my ledger, by the way?"

"No, I'm throwing that in as a freebie. Do I beg your forgiveness now or later?"

"No begging. Ready to get out of here?"

Caught off guard, he blurted, "Where do you want to go?" Never did he assume she wanted to go straight home ... maybe because he had not a shred of desire to take her there.

# *Chapter 16*

# Brooding Is Hot

*Omigod, that was so hot!*

Michaela resisted the urge to fan herself. *Never have I ever had a man go all alpha for me like that!* He'd practically bared dripping fangs, yet he'd pulled it off in such a way that Steadman hadn't noticed. The independent woman in Michaela should have been as affronted by Blake's behavior as she was by Brad's—for entirely different reasons—but another side of her, one she wasn't too familiar with, wanted a grunting Blake to drag her back to his cave by her hair, lose the loincloth, and make her his. And judging by the reactions of the witnesses who'd watched the whole scene, her reputation hadn't been damaged. If anything, it had been elevated among her peers. Truth be told, she'd sweated an eensy-weensy bit about how he'd conduct himself with the partners, but she needn't have worried. He'd been more engaging than any real date she could remember, talking *just* enough and encouraging them, through thoughtful questions, to talk about their favorite subject: themselves. And he'd even acted interested.

Blake was a delightful surprise.

Yes, she would have fences to mend with Brad come Monday morning, but he'd been a jerk and deserved what he got. Right now, though, she didn't give a damn. *Never mess with a hockey player!*

In answer to her suggestion they leave, her defender's green eyes took on a gleam. "Where do you want to go?"

In that moment, she wanted to launch herself at him and cover his handsome face with kisses. Somehow he got her. Without her saying a word to him, he knew she didn't want to go home. Not yet.

"I don't know. It's Halloween. People are celebrating somewhere, right?"

"Everywhere," he chuckled. "Let's go have some fun."

After they said their starchy good-byes and were safely within the confines of his Range Rover, she exhaled and felt her shoulders drop a few inches. Had the oppressive dinner party been a glimpse into the life of a senior partner? If so, was it really the life she wanted? Doubt, like a weed in the crack of a sidewalk, began to take root.

She side-eyed him. "Thank you for tonight."

"My pleasure," he replied. "It was fun."

She let loose a laugh. "No, it wasn't!"

"No, it wasn't," he agreed with a lopsided grin. "But we'll change that. What do you want to do?"

"Take me to your favorite club."

Something akin to panic overtook his features. "What?"

"I want to dance. Take me someplace you usually go."

"I don't really hang out at clubs. Not in Denver. I mean, I don't hang in clubs anywhere, except sometimes, you know, on the road," he stammered. "With the guys."

*And lots of pretty girls, no doubt.* Why did that tug at something toothy inside her? She certainly had no claim on this man.

He hung his head briefly, looking extremely uncomfortable, then leveled an even gaze at her. "Look, I'll take you to a club. But let me text one of my teammates and find out the best place to go around here. You good with that?"

"Yeah, I'm good with that." Okay, so he wanted to find the right place to go. He wasn't worried about running into a woman—women—he'd slept with. Maybe. Michaela wasn't experienced at this sort of thing. The men she dated were ... they didn't attract the same level of attention Blake did. Her mind unfortunately shot to the damn redhead again. Michaela's eyes wandered to his squared-off frame as he sat behind the wheel thumbing a text. Had Red downgraded his performance in ... other areas? Maybe Michaela was just the woman to help him with *that* too, not that she was any expert. But if he did other things the way he kissed, she would happily help boost his confidence and wipe some more of that red ink off the ledger. But what if they ran into the redhead tonight? Or the mussed-up brunette? Michaela bit down on a nail, frustrated that her own confidence seemed to be leaking out of her, drop by drop.

As if he'd read her mind, he gave her a pained look. "Really, I'm not that familiar with the clubbing scene. You already caught me with Sherry, so you know I'm not exactly a choir boy, but going to clubs and picking up girls isn't something I normally do, so it's not like I'm worried about running into anyone."

The elephant in the room had just been exposed, and she drew in a grateful breath.

"For the record, I'm a big girl and we're only neighbors, so it doesn't really concern me. You don't owe me a thing," she said, sounding way more grown-up than she felt.

"Hopefully, we're more than neighbors," he said quietly. "I'd like to think we're friends too." He stared out the window and exhaled, sounding deflated. "But you get it. The women I meet ... there aren't many I spend time with, and we don't normally cross paths again." He swung his eyes back to hers. "And now you know my dark, dirty secret."

"That's all you've got? Pfft." She offered him a dismissive wave and a half-smile.

His green eyes shone in the dark. "Pretty much. Well, when it comes to stuff like that. Hockey doesn't leave time for much else."

She let his confession—and the fact that it was obviously bothering him—sink in for a beat. It didn't escape her attention that he seemed embarrassed and wanted her to see him in a less sleazy light. Then again, a guy who devoted himself to his profession and shied away from long-term probably lived a fairly lonely life. Giving in to urges was a stopgap, a way to blow off some testosterone and connect for a little while, shallow as it was. She got it. Hadn't she been guilty of the same thing from time to time? Her heart even ached for him a tiny bit, but in an unexpected dichotomy, it also lifted a few rungs. "I guess it's similar to what I've been doing with the stupid dating apps and speed dating."

"But you're not ... it's not like you're on Tinder looking to hook up." His eyes narrowed and flashed flinty and cold. "Are you?"

*What was* that*?* A flicker of jealousy? "No. Are *you*?" she tossed back, feeling an odd little pull of possessiveness herself.

"Not at all."

*No, you don't need Tinder. Your app is live.* "Because you won't fill out the questionnaires," she quipped.

He smirked. "What would I put on there? 'Trivia nerd slash asshole seeks someone who doesn't exist'?"

His buzzing phone made them both jerk in their seats. Eyes scanning whatever message he was reading, a slow smile spread over his face. He looked up at her, excitement dancing in his eyes. "What would you think of joining one of my teammates and his wife? I think you met them at the Millers' party. Quinn Hadley and Sarah Nelson? They're headed to a new place I haven't been before. You up for that?"

He wanted to bring her along for a night out with a teammate and his wife? Like ... a real date? Michaela vaguely remembered meeting a good-looking guy with longish, dark hair whose hand seemed to be glued to a very pretty, spunky brunette that she'd felt a kinship with. Simpatico. *Or is it simpatica?* Didn't matter because something warm and tingly filled her belly, filing down her jagged edges.

She let out a tiny breath she hadn't realized she'd trapped in her chest. "That sounds fun."

He pumped his arm. "Yes!"

She laughed out loud at his overzealous reaction. The air in the SUV's cabin suddenly lightened and became easier to breathe.

This would be good, Blake told himself. They'd meet up with Quinn and Sarah and have fun, use up some of this crackling energy in a place where the music was so loud they couldn't carry on a conversation. No conversation meant no skating onto thin ice made up of the unfamiliar and uncomfortable. A prickliness had crawled under his skin tonight and traveled at will throughout his body like tiny flares. Flares ready to detonate and unleash the threat simmering just below the surface of his calm demeanor—a surface of smoke and mirrors hiding the sexual storm fomenting inside of him.

What the fuck was wrong with him? He couldn't remember feeling this way before, as if every nerve was raw and exposed and vulnerable yet vibrating with so much energy he thought he might burst out of his skin. What the hell *was* that? It had to do with her. It absolutely did. Normally when he spent time with a woman, it was beneath a veneer that dulled his insides. But this was *intense*, the complete opposite of what he was familiar with. *Electrifying*. He hated it; he loved it. He had no idea what to *do* with it. And then there was the Ferguson factor unfurling a black shroud over emotions Blake couldn't corral for much longer. But he *had* to.

They reached the club—a place called Vinyl—without pushing any more of each other's buttons, good or bad. A pulsing beat spilled out onto the pavement, and Blake was surprised when they were ushered inside. Costumed people crowded every space, and they were led to a low, oval table where Quinn and Sarah were waiting. The table sat in a private top-floor balcony that overlooked the main dance floor. Sarah, dressed in all black, sported some painted-on cat whiskers and a nose for the occasion.

As they were about to reach the table, M gushed, "Ooh, I've always wanted to sit at this table. It's the best seat in the house!"

"Wait. What? You've been here before?" *What the hell?*

She nodded, but the conversation halted because they were at the table where Quinn stood, greeting them with a ready hand and a grin. “What do you think? Sometimes it pays to have people recognize you.”

“Nice setup,” Blake agreed. A little off-kilter, he pulled out the empty chair to Sarah’s right for M before taking the empty chair beside Quinn himself. Sarah meowed, and M meowed back as though they’d rehearsed the exchange.

*Cute.*

“Where are your costumes?” Sarah asked.

M took off her brainiac glasses and stashed them in her purse. “There!” They laughed and bent their heads together and stayed that way while he and Quinn talked hockey, even after the drinks arrived—martini for M, bourbon for him. Blake tuned one ear to the girls’ conversation, wishing he could hear what they were saying over the noise. He had been on a few double dates before, but this felt ... different. Technically, it *wasn’t* a double date. Wasn’t a date at all.

When Sarah and M looked over at him and giggled, he *really* wished he could hear.

“What?” he yelled, trying to out-volume the music.

M straightened, tilted her head to the side, and mouthed, “Dance?”

He nodded, and she slid off the slinky silver jacket she’d worn all night. He did a double-take. Not only was he treated to a better look at the dress she was wearing and the curves it hugged, but he got an eyeful of smooth, pale shoulders and the stunning tattoo he’d been dreaming about. Graceful green vines curled around her right arm, beginning just above her wrist. Entwined with them were vibrant red flowers in various stages of opening. The vines wove a sinuous path up to a fully open red bloom capping her delicate shoulder, then dove to her upper back and disappeared beneath her dress. The intricacy of the artwork was jaw-dropping, and M’s skin was the perfect canvas to display the ink. He’d never been with anyone with an elaborate tattoo—not that he was going to be with *her*—but damn, it was hot! The movie screen in his mind flashed a scene where she lay beside him in bed, naked, and his fingers traced every flower, every line, followed by his lips, his tongue. Yeah, his libido could totally get behind the idea. Maybe he needed to tamp it down with another bourbon ... or three.

M waved her hand in front of his face. "Ready?"

He lurched to his feet, grateful for the dark suit pants hiding his semi. She dragged him toward a small dance floor off to one side, and his eyes traced her tattoo the entire way.

One fast song after another played, and he was disappointed when a slow one finally came on and she opted to take a break. *Probably for the best.*

The rest of the night was spent with the four of them dancing, talking, and laughing—and drinking—and he marveled at how seamlessly M fit into *his* world. The unpleasantness from earlier had completely drained from him by the time 2:00 a.m. rolled around.

Quinn tapped his chest with the back of his hand. "Hey, Sarah and I took a Lyft. Why don't you let us drop you and Michaela off and you can pick up your ride tomorrow?"

Feeling a touch of belligerence, Blake smirked at him. "What, you think I can't drive?"

"I don't know if you can drive or not, but I've never seen you drink, and you were doing a good job putting way that bourbon."

He opened his mouth to protest, but M's eyes landed on him, soft and searching, without a hint of judgment, before sparking with mischief. "I hope being out with me tonight isn't driving you to drink."

"In a way, it is," he laughed. She frowned. "Not the way you're thinking. What I meant was that I'm having a good time." *And yeah, I sound like a total dipstick. Probably* shouldn't *drive.* No reason to push his—and her luck by climbing behind the wheel. "Yeah, okay. We'll ride with you."

"I don't know about you all," M said after they were settled in the Lyft, "but I haven't closed a place down in a long time." Quinn and Sarah, who shared the backseat with her, agreed they hadn't either.

Blake's mind leapt to M going to Vinyl before. Who had she gone with? An app date? None of his damn business. Still, the question sat in his stomach like a handful of nails. Spiky and steely.

Sarah leaned forward and tapped Blake on the shoulder, pulling him from his prickly thoughts. "You should bring Michaela to the charity brunch."

"She's already going," he shot back.

"I am?" M piped up. "What's the charity brunch?"

While Sarah explained the event, Blake's bourbon-soaked brain wrestled with Ferguson's words. *Didn't he say he invited her and she accepted? Then again, he also lied about filling her in on the switch tonight.*

"So?" Sarah chirped, and he realized she was chirping at *him*. He swung his gaze to her. "Why not take M?" she persisted. God, the woman was pushy!

When Blake snuck a look at Quinn, he was staring out the window, his hand covering his mouth like he was holding back a laugh. Sarah elbowed him, and he dropped the hand. "Uh, yeah, sweetheart. Sounds like a great idea. But what if Michaela's busy?"

"What if someone else is taking her?" Blake offered.

"Have you two not been listening?" Sarah squawked. "She just said she's free. She said—"

"Sarah," M interrupted quietly, placing a light hand on Sarah's arm, "maybe we shouldn't put him on the spot? He might have already invited someone." She flicked her gaze to Blake, looking all kinds of embarrassed, looking like she wanted to rescue him from Sarah's mission, and he felt a tug to save *her* instead. But how could he do that without shining an unflattering spotlight on her? He'd have to reveal that Ferguson was *supposed* to ask her to the brunch but hadn't. M didn't know Fergs had lied about that too, and Blake didn't want to be the one to heap that humiliation onto tonight's switcheroo. Talk about making her feel like crap. *"Hey, you're not worth the two seconds of brainpower it would take to ask if you want to go to this important thing with me."*

His gaze skipped to M. "Has Owen called or texted you? Ever?"

The confusion on M's face told him all he needed to know. No, Ferguson hadn't said a damn thing. The urge to throttle Fergs made a violent resurgence. Blake couldn't think of anyone he'd rather have on his arm than the smart, sexy attorney in the backseat.

Silence settled like a soggy blanket over the car's interior. At least Sarah had dropped her needling, pressing her lips between her teeth.

About two blocks from their building, barricades blocked the way and construction lights blinked yellow. "What's going on?" Quinn asked.

"They shut down the street to do some overnight roadwork," the Lyft driver replied.

M peered at Blake. "I don't mind walking. Is that okay with you?"

*Abso-fucking-lutely.* Hopefully, the icy air would clear the colliding thoughts from his head.

They said their good-byes, and he wrapped his hand around her upper arm to guide her down the street. She canted her head to the side. "I'm sorry about Sarah pushing back there. I had no idea she—"

"No worries. I know you didn't. Speaking of Sarah, I've been wondering."

Up went a questioning eyebrow.

"When we first sat down, you two had your heads stuck together, then you looked at me and started laughing. Maybe my ego can't take it, but what were you guys saying?"

An adorable giggle-snort escaped her. "We were looking for a word to describe you."

A silent puff of relief escaped him. "And 'handsome' made you laugh?" he teased.

"No. We did use that word, but it's not the one that made us laugh. We used 'hot' and a few others along those lines, but they didn't make us laugh either. Wanna know what it was?" Those mischievous gray eyes fastened on him.

Flustered, he directed her around a crack in the sidewalk. "I think so?"

"The word was 'broody.'"

"'Broody'? What the hell is 'broody'?"

"Broody is ... hmm, how to describe it. It's someone who's always caught up in thought, who's serious. Intense."

"You think I'm intense?" *And handsome? And hot?* Distracted as hell, he pulled her up at a red light—even though there was no traffic—and glanced down at her.

She rolled her eyes, "Oh hell yes! Look up 'intense' in the dictionary, and you'll find your picture there."

"Is that ... is it a bad thing?"

"What? No! It's part of your hotness factor." She grinned at him, and her teeth shone white. "Green light."

"What?"

She flicked her finger toward the other side of the street. "The light. It's green. That means 'go.'"

*Go.* Stepping off the curb with her in tow, he chuckled in spite of himself. "Did you know that the yellow light didn't exist until the twenties?"

"Nope, did not know that."

"Did you know you can see the red light sooner than you can see the green light?"

She frowned. "I think I suspected that."

"Do you know what one word I think describes you?"

"That was sneaky!" She wagged her finger at him. "But let me think ... no. I have no idea. Tell me."

"Sassy." *And fun and gorgeous and sexy and smart and breathtaking*, his alcohol-fueled brain shouted. *Shit! I need to stop thinking about her like this.* He reminded himself that "sassy" was Ferguson's word for her.

Ferguson, the motherfucking douche canoe who was leading her on and lying to her.

"Sassy?" she giggled. "I don't think I've ever been called that before. My mom used to call her little sister, 'sass-mouth.'"

*Sass-mouth. Yeah, I'd like to kiss the sass right out of your mouth. Suck it out.* He let out an inadvertent groan.

"Are you feeling all right?"

*No.* He dragged his hand over his chin. "I'm fine. Look, about Ferguson—"

She flapped a hand. "I don't know what happened, but I'm guessing a puck got dropped or a play was lost in translation somewhere, and he's not on the same page as you ... or me, apparently. Let's just let whatever it is—or whatever it was supposed to be—go. Oh, look. We're here."

*Thank God!* He slipped out his key card and swiped it over the electronic lock to the building's glass door.

*Almost there. All I have to do is get her to her door. I can do this. I can do this without touching her. Without kissing her. I can do this.*

On the elevator, he took pains to stand as far away from her as he could. Unfortunately, it afforded him an even better view of her. She slid off her coat, and he fought the natural urge to help her. He didn't trust himself that close. When the coat came off, so did the silver jacket—briefly—and her tantalizing tattoo teased him before she covered it up. Her lips curving in a sexy little half-smile, she eyed him curiously. Did she have any idea what pervy thoughts were crowding his brain? Because of her? When the doors opened, he practically ran into their hallway to stand at her door.

She unlocked it, which was his signal to take off. His duty was fulfilled. "Well, good night. I hope everything works out with your boss." His words were so abrupt she probably thought he had a full bladder to empty.

Tilting her head, she bit her bottom lip. "Do you want to come in for a few minutes? Join me for a nightcap?"

"No, I'm good."

Her delicate brows drew together. No doubt she was trying to figure out why the hell he was acting like such an idiot; he wasn't sure he had the answer. "Well, thank you again for playing escort tonight. I appreciate you putting up with the whole work thing." She rolled her eyes to the ceiling and twirled her hand in the air. "And thanks for taking me out afterward. I still wish you had let me pay my way." Before he could respond that hell no, letting her pay had never been an option, she placed her hand lightly on his chest and pushed up on her toes. She was going for his cheek, like the last time, but for some insane reason, instead of offering it to her, he turned into the kiss and brushed her lips awkwardly with his own.

"Oh, whoops!" she giggled. "I didn't mean to do that."

"Sorry. That was my bad." His voice cracked, making him sound like the thirteen-year-old he was imitating.

Her warm fingers continued pressing against his chest, and she was up on tiptoe, her mouth mere inches from his. "Are you sure you're sorry?" she whispered in an irresistibly sultry tone, her beautiful eyes scanning his face.

*Oh. Fuck.*

*Fuck, fuck, fuck!*

She smelled so damn good. *Looked* so damn good. His eyes strayed from her face to his own door. Ferguson wasn't home—he said he'd be spending the night at his mom's—but he was there in spirit, and Blake should *not* be making a move on M, no matter how big a nutsack Fergs was.

Eyes ticking back to hers, Blake gently removed her hand from his chest and took a step back. She sank back, her heels hitting the floor, a hurt look etched on her face.

*Killing me here.*

Shoving his hands into his front pockets to keep them from going where they wanted to go, he cleared his throat. "M, there's something you should know."

# Chapter 17
# Practice Makes Perfect

Confusion, hurt, anger. And those were only the emotions Michaela recognized. There were a boatload of others churning away in her gut, causing a swell of nausea. What an idiot she was! How could she have been so off? *Because I was having a good time, and I deluded myself into reading his signals all wrong. Or his signals aren't straight because he's been drinking. He can't even recognize green lights!* Then again, if he was into women like the redhead, Michaela hadn't stood a chance in the first place.

Well, no matter what, Blake didn't get to call her "M." She took a few steps back so she could shake off the intoxicating citrusy-spicy man scent she'd been inhaling all night, and she folded her arms over her chest like armor protecting her heart.

"M, I—"

"Please don't call me that." Her voice dripped with icicles. She wasn't used to rejection—hell, she wasn't used to coming on to a man in the first place—and she wasn't quite sure what to do with it. Its sharpness hurt. It stung. Humiliated, she wanted to lash out.

The goody two-shoes perched on her shoulder told her to take the high road, but the devil girl wanted to kick him in the balls, which meant it was probably best to straddle a line somewhere between her careening thoughts.

"I'm sorry. Michaela," he stammered. He'd dropped his voice to a hush, and his eyes kept dashing down to his own door. Apparently, he was dying to escape. She'd make this easy on him. Gripping the edge of her door, she wound up for an epically satisfying slam, but the door stopped mid-swing. Blake had caught it with his forearm without so much as a wince. With a huff and a puff, she pushed against it in vain.

"Look," he said, "I know you're pissed, and I get it. But you have to understand this isn't about you."

"Oh, here we go! Please spare me the 'it's not about you, it's about me' speech." *I've seen what kinds of women you like, and it's clear I don't fit the type.* "Just go away!" *And leave me to lick my wounds.* She gave the door one more useless shove.

His face pinched as though he was in pain, but it wasn't from her weak door action. "That couldn't be farther from the truth."

"Then what the hell *is* the truth, Blake?"

His forearm still braced the door when he blurted, "Owen really likes you."

*What?* "Excuse me? What does that even mean, and what does it have to do with … this?" She waved her hand between them.

"He's been crushing on you since you first moved in, which is why I was trying so hard to set him up for tonight, but he really *did* have to be at his grandma's birthday party. He asked me to take you so you wouldn't be left without a date, and I agreed. He also told me he plans to ask you to the charity brunch." His breathing was a little on the heavy side, as if he'd run up the stairs.

"Wait. Did he *pay* you for tonight or something?"

Horror flashed in his eyes. "Fuck no! I was happy to take his place … a little too happy, and that's the problem."

Michaela paused to draw in a long, slow breath as she pushed his words through her brain's screen, sorting the nuggets from the clods of dirt. She felt like the kid who was blindfolded, spun in circles on the playground, and suddenly had to walk toward a target: off balance, wobbly kneed, and unable to hold a straight line.

The only thing certain in that moment was the earnest expression on Blake's handsome face. He wanted her to believe him. Tidbits from the night floated back to her: his arm around her chair, hand on the small of her back, how he'd smiled at her, and how his eyes had tracked her every move. Signals. He'd seemed relaxed, warm, attentive. He couldn't have faked wanting to be with her, could he?

"What if I don't like Owen?" she snapped.

"You just haven't gotten to know him yet. What you need is to spend time with him."

"No, what I *need* is a man who's willing to step up and go after what he wants. Not someone who hides behind his friend like Cyrano De Bergerac."

Blake looked to the ceiling, seeming to stifle a smile. "Technically, Cyrano was the front man with the smooth words. His buddy did the hiding."

She gave him an epic eye-roll and made a strangled sort of scoffing noise, and the smile he'd been fighting disappeared. "Honestly, I don't think Owen deserves you—"

"I'm not *Owen's* to deserve!"

"—but I can't ... I will not, go after what *I* want." He ran right over her without listening to a word she'd uttered. "Not as long as he has his eye on the same prize. He's my best friend." Worry lines creased his forehead.

"I give up," she muttered. Wait. Had he just called her a "prize"?

A few silent beats passed as they held a staring standoff. "So how does that work in hockey?" she finally posed.

"Excuse me?"

"April told me you and Owen sort of switched spots—or lines—and it translates to a promotion for you, a demotion for him."

Head tipped back, he puffed out a lungful of air and leveled his gaze back at her. "That was Coach's choice, not mine."

"Are you saying if it were up to you, you'd give up the juicier role to Owen without a fight merely based on the fact that he's your best friend?"

He barked a laugh. "Damn, you like to argue!"

"Not really. I'm trying to make a point."

"I'm too tired to spar."

*And I'm utterly exhausted trying to follow the bouncing ball.* "Then go home." She hooked a thumb toward his door.

His chest deflating, he pulled his forearm from the door. "Okay. I'm sorry about all this. Really sorry."

"Good night, Blake." She shoved the door closed. It didn't give her the satisfaction she'd been seeking before, but at least she was alone and could review her twisted feelings and stomp around for a bit to let steam escape the pressure valve of her emotions.

With a tired sigh, she wandered to the red couch and perched on the edge, where she slipped off her jacket. She pulled the heels from her sore feet, then rolled down the stockings and flopped back. She let go a mirthless laugh. The guy she liked liked her back but had some loyalty clause he wouldn't break for the other guy who liked her that she didn't like back.

Talk about convoluted!

She needed to call Fiona. What time was it in Europe anyway? Where exactly in Europe was Fi? Michaela fetched her phone and texted. *You able to talk? I need you.*

Seconds later, her phone rang, and the emotions washed over her, bringing tears to her eyes. "Hey, Fi," she choked.

"Micky-Dub, what on earth is going on? Did the dinner go that badly? Did you lose out?"

"I lost out, but not the way you think. Where are you?"

"Floating down the Seine."

"Oh shit, I'm sorry. I didn't mean to disturb—" Banging on her door interrupted her.

"What was that?"

"My front door. Hang on."

"Don't open it, Micky! It could be a slasher!"

"I'm in a secured building, Fi." Michaela did open it ... and blinked. On the other end of the phone, Fiona was screeching about finding her dead, mutilated body. "Fi, it's not a slasher. It's only my neighbor."

"Chad Michael Murray? The guy making out with some chick in your hallway? The one you almost pepper-sprayed?"

Michaela sighed. "Yes, that one. I'll call you later." She ended the call and looked up. "Why are you back here, Blake?"

"Since you won't let me call you M anymore, can I call you Micky?" His hair was mussed, sticking out at funny angles, and his eyebrows were two angry slashes over his green eyes. The expression and the nonsensical question did not match up.

God, this guy confused the hell out of her! Or was it the cocktails talking? For both of them? "That's it? You're pounding on my door at 3:00 a.m. to discuss name choices?"

"No, that's not it." Moving into her foyer, he closed the door behind him. He paced a few steps, back and forth, looking all kinds of agitated. Should she be scared? No. Whatever this was, it wasn't directed at her, and even if it was, he didn't strike her as the kind of guy who'd lay a hand on her. She almost let out a laugh. He wouldn't lay a hand on her even if she wanted him to.

"I don't understand what you're doing here, Blake."

"I came to ask you to the charity brunch."

Her eyebrows shot to her hairline. "At 3:00 a.m."

"At 3:00 a.m."

She crossed her arms over her chest. "What about your precious Owen? I don't understand the dynamic between you, and you probably don't want to hear this, but I'm going to say it anyway: I'm not attracted to him. Physically *or* mentally. Are you able to get that through your thick man skull?"

Nodding, he paused to face her, hands on his hips. "You've just given me permission to say what's on my mind." He hung his head for a beat and raked his fingers through his hair. *Ah. That explains the hair.*

She tapped her foot expectantly.

"Fuck Owen," he huffed. "Let me rephrase that. Don't fuck him. Fuck me instead. Shit! That didn't come out right either." A pained expression twisted his gorgeous face.

Her mouth dropped open. She couldn't help it. *Maybe it came out wrong, but it sounded pretty damn honest.* Pixels were filling in, a complete picture coming into focus. He liked her, and he was torn because his best friend did too. A thrill raced through her veins, and needy parts of her neglected for far too long cheered.

His eyes bored into hers. "Things could get ugly between him and me, and I want you to know that before ... You might want to think twice about letting me in. I wouldn't blame you for telling me to get the fuck out."

"I'm not sure I know what you're talking about, but if it has anything to do with you taking me up on that nightcap, then come in."

He stared at her a few beats, deliberating, his chest moving in and out. Muscles that had been bunching his jaw eased, and one corner of his mouth hitched. "Technically, I'm already in."

"You sure like getting technical."

He opened his mouth as if to say something but seemed to change his mind, returning to the smirk instead.

She quirked an eyebrow at him. "What's so funny?"

He shook his head. "Nothing."

"That's not 'nothing' written all over your face. Let me in on the joke." Now that he'd relaxed a bit, shadows played over the angles of his chiseled face, sharpening them, and he looked even more handsome than he had before. Her knees dipped a fraction, feeling as though they were turning to jelly.

"I was just remembering earlier, when you were mad. You're kinda cute when you're riled up, you know that?"

She jabbed her finger at his face, trying for all the world to muster anger when all she wanted to do was start giggling like a preteen. "Don't you go there. *Not* funny. I am *not* cute."

He threw up his hands in surrender. "I stand corrected. You're not cute." His voice went low and gravelly, and a predatory gleam simmered in his eyes that was different from anything she'd ever seen in him. "You're beautiful. And the sexiest damn thing I've ever seen in my life."

His words snatched the wind from her sails. "Um, oh." Maybe she shouldn't have called him "hot" and "handsome"—except it was true. Maybe it was time for that drink—ice water for her so she could pour it over her chest and let the cold dampen some of this charged space between them. Suddenly very self-conscious, she scampered to the open kitchen.

Yanking down a glass and a bottle of Breckenridge Reserve Blend bourbon, she shoved them at him and pointed at the Sub-Zero. "Ice is in that dispenser." As he ignored the liquor and prepared a drink of water, she pulled a frosted shot glass and an iced bottle of Chopin from the freezer, resisting the urge to rub them against her heated face. Her fingers trembled, but the trembling wasn't out of fear. No, it was all about the hot blond hockey player whose presence seemed to suck air from the room. She trusted him, felt safe with him, but she stood on the precipice of a deep abyss and had no idea what sort of void she might be leaping into. Whatever it was, it felt dangerous. She might get pulled up short, she might smash into bits when she hit bottom, or she might fall forever and ever.

She poured a measure of vodka into the shot glass, feeling the unrelenting weight of his gaze on her. The silence that hung between them was thick, ripe with sexual energy. Deafening. The only sound was the pounding pulse of blood whooshing through her ears.

Pulling in a breath, she turned and clinked her glass against his before gulping half her drink.

She jerked her chin at his drink. "Is your water okay?" Her voice came out in a squeak.

"Perfect." Calculations seemed to race at warp speed behind the eyes he trained on her with intensity. He reminded her of someone computing the number of stars in the Milky Way or who was waging war inside himself.

"I'm still not sure why you came back," she ventured in a softened tone, "unless it really is about the brunch thingie."

Appearing as though he'd answered some great mystery for himself, he set down the drink and closed the distance between them. She craned her head back to look up at him. "Michaela," he began, "much as I want to take you to the charity brunch, that's not why I came back. And tasty as your water is, I can get that anywhere."

She blinked, her only thought that the way "M" rolled off his tongue in that deep timbre was so much nicer than when he used her full name. He reached out a finger and began tracing her tattoo from her shoulder down, his touch deliberate and featherlight, his gaze following the trail. Shivers chased one another down her spine and radiated outward, puckering her skin with tiny goose bumps.

"What I can't get anywhere else is this," he murmured. He raised heated, haunted eyes to hers. Light green had shifted to verdelite, so deep and spellbinding she thought she might drown in them.

"A-a tattoo?" she stuttered.

His lips curved. "No, not the tattoo." His hand dropped to hers. Weaving his long, thick fingers with her small ones, he tugged her toward him until her hip brushed his thigh. Her mind was blowing circuits left and right, and she couldn't have stopped him if she'd wanted to. And she didn't want to. The clenching she'd felt in her stomach minutes before was replaced with cottonwood fluff floating, floating, and other parts of her began to blaze. With his free hand, he lifted her drink from her grasp and placed it on the island behind her, then cradled her cheek. He lowered his head, hovering his mouth just above hers. "I might need more lessons."

"Haven't you been practicing?" she whispered against his lips.

"No. Didn't want to practice with anyone but you." His thumb stroked her cheek softly while his eyes searched hers. His reassuring words scattered her doubts like dry leaves in a stiff wind. Mesmerized, like a deer caught in a beam, she couldn't move. His lips brushed hers, so warm, so soft, so tantalizing. "Tell me to stop, M. Tell me to go home."

Her head was reeling, and she couldn't hold on to more than a few tangible thoughts. Not with his moist breath caressing her lips or his heady smell swirling around her or his body so close his heat seeped into her dress. His hard planes angled toward her, and a single-purposed gleam in his eyes broadcast she was a morsel he wanted to consume. Hunger from deep inside her rose up, overtaking her, and she let herself sink against that powerful, masculine frame. "I don't want you to go home," she breathed.

*Kiss me, kiss me. Then take me to bed.*

# *Chapter 18*
# Storms and Other Electrical Phenomena

Blake was on fire. And it wasn't because of the unexpected, stomach-turning sight of Ferguson and Tracy that greeted him when he'd walked into the condo. No, this was akin to a scorching *wild*fire that took hold as soon as M opened her door after his dumbass retreat, making the anger that had spiked inside him disappear in a puff of smoke. She was so ... sinfully adorable. Innocent and worldly and hot as hell at the same time. How did she do that? Looking at her made him ache to tell Ferguson and Brad Hewitt and every man whose eyes had caressed her tonight to back the fuck off. Not that he deserved to claim her any more than they did, but he was here and they weren't. Wasn't that nine-tenths of the law or some BS he couldn't reconcile at the moment?

He also had no ability to analyze the complicated intricacies—or the ramifications—of the foreign feelings invading him. One goal—that was his only focus in that moment, and it had absolutely zilch to do with a puck and a net. He was starved for her, as if the air had been vacuumed from the sliver of space separating them and she was his next inhale, his only way to continue breathing.

By some miracle, she had let him in. Well, she'd let him *barge* his way in. When she told him she didn't want him to leave, desire and need and want had pinned him in place. Right now, with her soft, warm curves nestled against him, her lips parting as he lowered his mouth to hers, his world contracted to her and him. All other thought was sent skittering to a dimly lit corner of his mind.

Tonight she was his, if she'd have him. No more deferring to someone who wasn't worthy of her. Not that he was any worthier than Ferguson, but at least he knew what he wanted and was willing to lay it all on the line for this one chance. He'd deal with the consequences later.

When he finally took her mouth, he took it hard, banding his arms around her, letting his pent-up desire spill over.

Pushing against his chest, she drew back and placed a staying finger against his lips. "Take it slow," she whispered. "We have all night to explore."

His breathing was ragged, his heart a runaway freight train trying to escape his chest. "Is that part of the lesson?" *Don't devour the mouth you've been dreaming about?* Equal parts embarrassed and hoping he could rein in his overzealous libido, he eased his hold on her and waited for her lead. He didn't have to wait long.

"Something like that." A small smile curved her generous lips. Fisting his shirt in her hands, she pulled him to her and softly pressed those full lips to his, sucking lightly, nibbling, tasting him languidly, her body molding to his. Her dress made a crinkly noise where it brushed against him. Telling himself to take it easy, he ran the tip of his tongue gently along the open seam of her mouth before slipping it inside. She tasted like vodka and sweetness and Michaela, and a primal switch flipped on inside of him when she lightly sucked on his tongue, inviting him deeper, inviting him to explore. Her hands twined around his neck, and her fingertips dug into his shoulders. A low groan he couldn't corral rose in his throat, and she responded with a surrendering mewl of her own. With insatiable hunger swelling inside of him, the soft, slow, sensuous kiss quickly transformed into a decadent plunge, and he feasted on her mouth, her tongue, and her lips while his hands roamed over her back, her arms, twisting in her hair, delighting in the feel of her.

She broke the kiss once more, her breathing uneven, and slid her hands to his chest. One of his hands was buried in her silky curls, the other skimming the small of her back, ready to snake down and cup her ass. Silver eyes peeked up at him through long, inky lashes.

"Do I need to slow down again?" he near-gasped.

She shook her head. "No, that was perfect. You sure you haven't been practicing?"

He let out a chuckle of relief—and pride. "Positive."

"You're a quick learner," she murmured as she pushed up on her toes and landed her lips on his throat. Hands wrapping around his neck, she plowed her fingers through his hair. Her mouth began moving across his skin, and she laid down wet, soft kisses followed by the scraping of her teeth, and his eyes rolled back in his head. *Jesuuuus, that feels good!* Hot chills shot though his blood, lighting it ablaze. Soon her mouth was back on his, sucking and nipping at his bottom lip, and he responded greedily, spearing her mouth with his tongue. The little mewling sighs that came from her spurred him into a fervor he'd never experienced before.

While their tongues danced and sparred, his fingers fumbled with the zipper at her nape and slowly released the teeth as far as they would go, only midway down her back. He slid his hand inside, relishing the feel of her smooth back crisscrossed by bra straps. She moaned into his mouth. Her hands swept over his shoulders, down his back, gliding over his ass. His hips rocked against her flagrantly, his rock-hard shaft surging, anxious to grind against her softness, but all he got were the multilayered folds of her skirt.

This time he broke the kiss, his fingers splaying the opening wide at the back of her dress. "How does this thing come off?" he panted. Shit. Was he letting his impatient libido gallop ahead again?

Her head swiveled to a row of windows, blackened by the night beyond but softly reflecting their intertwined bodies in the kitchen's ambient light. Wriggling from his embrace, she took a half-dozen graceful steps and flipped a switch beside the sink. Pendants that had illuminated the island were suddenly doused, leaving only the golden glow of under-cabinet lights. She executed a graceful pirouette and spun right into his waiting arms.

Tracing her fingertips over his pecs in tiny circles, she purred, "No peep shows for the neighbors."

While he tried to get his breathing—and himself—under control, he caressed her upper arms, marveling at how big his hands looked against her delicate, pale skin. "What about me? Do I get a peep show?" He waggled his eyebrows in an attempt to keep things light, to hide the maelstrom of want swirling inside him. To forget his dick was straining against his fly, begging to be released.

Her swollen lips tipped up in a coy smile, the little tease. "If you want."

"I want," he practically shouted. "All night, I've been imagining what you look like under that dress," he confessed. "I bet you look great naked." *Fuck! I couldn't sound any more like a fifteen-year-old if I tried!*

She burst out with a nervous laugh. "Trust me. I look much better with the dress on."

"I'd really like to test that theory out for myself," his fifteen-year-old, bourbon-emboldened self persisted.

Biting her lower lip, she caught his gaze with hers, looking as though she wanted to say something. She was probably weighing the merit of letting him into her bed. After all, what the hell would a girl like her—correction, a *woman*—want with an unseasoned idiot like him?

"Sorry," he mumbled. His fingers stroked her neck. The skin was so soft, so inviting, and he fought the urge to sink his teeth into it. "That was a totally inappropriate thing for me to say."

Her eyes swept from his chin up to his hairline, landing back on his mouth. His dick jumped. "Not really. A girl likes to know she can drive a man crazy."

"Then you should be ecstatic because I'm verging on certifiable right now."

She laughed softly and once more stepped out of his grasp. Hypnotized, he watched as she gripped the hem of her skirt and tugged it up. For the instant her head was stuck in the dress, he brazenly ran his gaze over her body, from her painted toes to the flare of her hips, stuttering on tiny black panties, over her trim waist, up to her chest, lingering on full, creamy breasts cresting the cups of a black satin bra. It revealed nothing more than the promise of what lay underneath, but it was the sexiest damn thing he'd ever seen, and his mouth practically watered.

An inner beast he wasn't acquainted with roared to the fore. He leashed it long enough to help her extricate herself from the tangle of material, and before it had completely slid off her arms, his hands were on her, skimming over her sides, gliding over all that gorgeous skin.

"Turn around," he croaked.

She did as he asked, glancing at him over her shoulder with a shy smile. With his index finger, he traced the rest of the tattoo that had been hidden from his sight. The vines curled around her right shoulder blade, ending in another full-bloomed red flower. He leaned forward, resting his hands on her small waist as he dipped his head and planted his lips on the flower, kissing it reverently. Then he dragged the tip of his tongue along the vines, up to her shoulder. Her skin tasted like salt and honey and heaven. He spread his fingers across her flat stomach and pulled her against his hardness so she had no doubt what she was doing to him.

She laid her head on his shoulder and melted against him with a sigh, then lifted her arms, hooking them around his neck and pressing her ass to his groin. *Fuck yeah!* He took his time laying a kiss on the bloom on her shoulder before working his way up her neck. Pushing her curls aside, he ran his tongue along the shell of her ear and whispered, “The dress looks beautiful on you, but I like you this way much, much better. You are breathtaking, M. Flawless. Everywhere.” And he meant every word. He wasn’t one for false compliments or talking before, during, or after sex, but this didn’t feel like ... sex. Well, it did, but everything with her was different, went deeper, pulled at different cords inside of him as though she was playing a line of chorusing bells. He rang with his desire for her, but all he could think was how he wanted to make *her* feel, how he wanted to be the best she’d ever had. And how the hell he was going to make that happen.

Her foot came up and began stroking his calf as he nibbled her ear. His hands fanned over her stomach, nearly covering it, then slid up her sides until they reached her bra. He unhooked it and felt the weight of her breasts pull the bra forward as it released. Eagerly, he abandoned the confounding crisscrossing straps and swept his hands to her front, pushing the bra out of his way, cupping her soft, full mounds. A moan escaped her, and she arched into his touch as if offering herself to him. His hands barely contained all of her. Massaging and kneading, he pinched her nipples into tight pebbles, aching to get his mouth on them, to bury his face between her breasts.

“My God, you feel so damn good in my hands,” he breathed.

Her soft mewls about had him letting go of his load right there. Unable to take much more, he spun her around, picked her up, and plopped her butt on the countertop. Wedging himself between her legs, he slowed a moment to take her in while she lifted the bra over her head and flung it to the floor. Her eyes were glazed with want, and her beautiful, round breasts swayed sinfully with her movements. He dropped his head and latched on to one of her nipples. His hand toyed with the other one while his tongue stroked and flicked and laved the bead he held in his mouth. He suckled and bit down softly, then pulled in as much of her breast as he could, his teeth scraping the skin, his tongue relentlessly working over her flesh. She dug her fingers into his scalp as if to hold him in place while she moaned and gasped and bucked softly against nothingness, only releasing her hold long enough for him to switch and lavish the same attention on the other side.

That primal being inside of him purred its pleasure at pleasuring *her*.

He straightened, pulling away from her, and a little growl of disappointment rose in her throat, making him chuckle. "Greedy girl." *I love it.* She seemed to want him as much as he wanted her, and the knowledge was more intoxicating than the cocktails he'd consumed. Hooking his fingers into her panties, he leaned in to kiss her. "Lift up for me." Holding on to his shoulders, she raised her ass, and as he slipped her panties off her hips and down her legs, she showed him just how greedy she could be with the kiss she took and returned. He didn't want to break it off. Deepened it as he scooted her ass to the edge of the counter and spread her thighs farther apart. Wrapping an arm around her, bracing her, he slid a finger inside her wet heat. *So wet.*

She gasped into his mouth.

He began a slow pump. "I hope that's a good gasp," he murmured against her lips.

"Mm-hmm," she hummed as he kissed her. She made a halfhearted attempt to undo one of his shirt buttons but abandoned the effort when he slid in a second finger and increased the tempo. Grinding against his hand, she wound her arms around his shoulders and sank her nails into his shirt and into the muscle beneath. Her mouth slid from his and came to rest against his neck, where she part-sucked, part-licked his skin between shuddering intakes of breath.

"Show me what you like and how you like it," he whispered against her ear.

She hooked a heel around his thigh. "Mmm, this is good." She dragged out the last word.

Could he make her come like this? Women didn't always react the same way to his touch, and the effect his ministrations had on their bodies was somewhat of a mystery. He'd never put in the time to get to know one particular body, but he found himself desperate to learn what would send *this* body zooming over the edge.

He kissed her neck, her shoulders, her mouth—whatever he could reach—as his fingers stroked in and out of her. Every move, every kiss, every touch elicited an extra buck, a louder gasp, or a longer string of mewling. A wildness danced just below her surface, and he grew impatient to discover how to unfetter it, putting aside his own burgeoning need as his cock throbbed heavily inside his pants. He became lost in her soft, sensual noises and her undulations, his focus narrowing on bringing her closer to the edge.

He'd never been big on going down on women, but the urge to taste her, to bury his tongue inside of her, was too powerful to resist. Withdrawing his fingers, he dropped his head and clamped his hands over her thighs, pinning her in place. He ran his nose along her seam, pulling in her scent before running his tongue along the same path and tasting her. She jerked and let out a long, wobbly breath. He did it again, pausing to flick and suck, loving how she tasted and how her body moved. He repeated the motion over and over again, spiraling into his own carnal cloud with the sensation of her writhing against his mouth. Suddenly, his shoulders locked up from being bent over, and he struggled to straighten.

Her eyes fluttered open.

Pushing her hair from her face, he licked his lips and rasped, "You taste amazing, M, and I want more, but this position is killing me. Where's your bedroom?" Without waiting for an answer, he scooped her up, and she wrapped her legs around him and pointed toward the hallway that, he dimly registered, mirrored his own. Once inside, he laid her out on the bed and began removing his clothes, frustrated by buttons and a belt that took more concentration than he had in his arsenal. He was so ready to crawl up her body, skin to skin, and slide inside. Pulling in a deep breath, he told himself to slow down. Again.

In one corner of the room, a lamp stoop beside an overstuffed armchair, and it suffused the space in soft amber, mingling with dark-shadowed pools. Michaela's soft frame was outlined in a golden glow. Her arms lay gracefully over her head, and she drew up one knee, her body rocking beguilingly, slowly, side to side as she watched him through half-lidded eyes. She oozed sex. She was a wet dream. A fucking centerfold, with her full breasts and her creamy skin. He branded the image in his brain so he could conjure it in the future. *This*, right here—her splayed out and ready for him—was what he would see every time he took himself in hand.

Losing the shirt, he dropped on the edge of the mattress beside her and yanked off his socks, his shoes, his pants and boxers until he was as naked as she was. His palms and eyes roved over her supple form, and she rose to meet his touch, sensual sighs tumbling from her lips. Though she didn't say it aloud, he heard her call with every look she gave him, every ripple of her body. Because of *him*, she was purring for him to take her, to fuck her, this instant.

He swallowed hard, his Adam's apple a fist lodged in his throat. Shit. This was the part he hated. He leaned over, forearms planted on either side of her shoulders, and her arms encircled his neck. "What about birth control?" The excruciatingly practical question could wield a sledgehammer against the velvet-cloaked ambience dripping with sexual anticipation. Passion temporarily iced, spontaneity suspended.

Her arms slid from him, and she rose up on her elbows, tilting her head in confusion. "I'm on the pill, but don't you use condoms?"

"Normally." He hesitated a beat, toying with blurting out what was running through his mind. *Always, but I don't want any barriers with you. I want to feel* all *of you surrounding me.* "I'm clean, but I'll use a condom if that's what you want." He held his breath. He'd never given anyone the option before.

Her cheeks pinked, and she gave a slight nod. He tamped down his disappointment. Whatever she wanted, he'd give her in any way she wanted it. Swinging his legs off the mattress, he folded over his knees, fumbling until he found his pants. He pulled a few packets from his wallet, tossing one beside her and the others on her nightstand. Judging by the cute little smirk on her face, she was pondering whether he could use them all. He didn't know if he could either. At least she wasn't laughing him out of her bedroom.

He leaned over her again, letting his skin slide against hers. She was all heat and silk, and his body was electrified wherever they touched. His mouth found hers, teasing it with his tongue while her arms wound around his shoulders and her taut nipples brushed his chest. A languid dance, he struggled to keep his hands splayed on either side of her, touching with mouths and skin, savoring the taste and feel of her in slow, steady strokes. But her hands weren't so idle, and when she glided one palm down his chest and over his abs, his muscles contracted and his skin blazed in tiny pinpricks of fire. Her hand closed around his engorged shaft, and slow and sensual gave way to urgency, like a dam bursting inside him. His arms slid under her back, scooping her up, crushing her against him while he plundered her mouth. She ran her fingertips along his length, around it, squeezing lightly, exploring it. Dropping to his balls and exploring those too while breath rattled in his chest.

Moaning filled his ears—his, as she tormented him, and hers echoing his. She pulled away from his mouth to kiss and lick his jaw and neck hungrily. "I want to taste you," she murmured, and his cock jumped in her hand.

"Not tonight." He didn't want to come in her mouth, not for their first time, and that was exactly what he'd do as soon as her lips wrapped around his dick. He'd never been so on edge, clinging to control by one taut thread.

"But you tasted me," she insisted as she worked over his neck. God, if having her mouth on his neck felt this good, sliding his dick into her mouth would be heaven. But it was something he could hold out for, something to look forward to.

*There will be more than just tonight, if I have a choice.*

"Hmm?" she hummed and pulled away, her lips curled in that half-smile.

Had he said that out loud? He stared at her, stroking her hair, wrapping a curl around his finger. "I did taste you, but I wasn't quite done yet." Before she could react, he maneuvered her on her back, tossed her legs over each of his shoulders, splitting her wide, and pinned her pelvis down to the mattress. "I want more," he rumbled right before he dropped his open mouth on her. Nose nuzzling her, he used his tongue to flick and lick and probe, his teeth to scrape and nibble, and his lips to suck and sip and lap and lave relentlessly. Her whimpers, wails, and gasps fueled him. Hands fisting the bedcovers, she alternated between bucking to escape the sensual torture and pressing into his mouth with wanton abandon.

And he loved it. Loved watching her throw her head side to side, her chest heaving and her beautiful breasts bouncing. Loved every fucking second he drove her body through the wild, to the edge, until her muscles seized and shuddered, and he tasted her orgasm on his tongue.

He'd never known eating someone out could be such an aphrodisiac. That pleasing *her*, that having the power to strum her body until it shattered would make him want to beat his chest and howl. And he would have continued the onslaught too—could have gone on for days—but she pried his hands from her hips and panted, "I want you inside me. Now." The demand held no bossiness, nor was it a plea. Simply her honest, uninhibited way of saying she wanted him. So different and so fucking hot. Damn if his ego wasn't cartwheeling around his hammering heart.

His own inhibitions uncoiled, and his cock practically yanked him forward in its impatience to get to her, to bury itself deep inside the wet seam he'd been bestowing with unbridled devotion. Yeah, he wanted in. So damn much. Wanted to seat himself to the hilt and lose himself inside her. Join with her in a primal dance.

Her flailing hand on the bedcover snapped him to. She was searching for the condom, but before her fingers could locate it, he surged to his knees and snatched it up, tore it open with his teeth, and nearly botched getting it on as desire flooded his body and brain.

Her hands on his arms and the sweet moans rising in her throat urged him on her, in her, but he needed to slow down or risk firing off all his bottle rockets at once. In a bid to distract himself, he zeroed in on the crimson flower adorning her shoulder. From there, his eyes traced the vines and were quickly snagged by her luscious breasts—breasts that beckoned and begged him to fondle and lick one more time. Dipping his head to suckle each one, he lingered a few more moments before settling between her welcoming thighs. He bracketed her arms, his weight spanning his forearms. Clawing for control, he breached her tight entrance, sinking in slowly, his eyes squeezed shut as the feel of her core cradling his cock overtook him. He found himself oddly grateful for the condom dulling the sensation. Going bare, feeling her moist heat pulling him in, might be more than he could take. Beneath him, she whimpered and gripped his biceps while she tilted her hips to take all of him in. When he was fully seated, he stilled and snapped his eyes open to find her staring at him, though he had no idea what played in her silver orbs.

"Is this all right? Are *you* all right?" He sounded ridiculous, but a frisson of alarm jolted him. He'd been so focused on the intense pleasure pulsing from his cock that his brain had switched off for a beat, leaving her in the dust.

Her fingertips danced over his shoulders and into his hair, then cupped his jaw. She regarded him with a tenderness he'd never seen and wasn't sure he deserved. "I'm wonderful. Just enjoying ... this ... you," she murmured.

He pushed the curls off her face, raking his fingers through her hair. "Yeah, I'm enjoying you too." *You* are *wonderful. Never felt anything like you.* He covered her mouth with his and began moving inside of her, slow and steady, matching the strokes of his tongue inside her delectable mouth. He didn't get far before the heat coursing through him cranked up to full flame. He flexed his hips, driving in and out of her, and his mouth and tongue dueled hers in deep, wet kisses. Her hips rose to meet him thrust for thrust. His heart pounded, his breathing grew labored, and he felt the familiar sensation at the base of his spine that he wasn't ready to give in to. A groan tore from his lungs.

Boldness flared inside him, and he stopped and pulled out. Her lashes fluttered, and a little frown creased her brows. Her chest was stained raspberry-red, and her breaths came in short bursts. "What is it?"

Without answering—not in words anyway—he rolled them both over and pulled himself upright so he sat with his back against the headboard. Dragging her up his body, he placed her hands on his shoulders and lifted her until she straddled him, her heat snugging against his shaft jutting between them. He ran his hands along her neck, over her shoulder, down her arms, cupping her forearms and pulling her closer.

Tilting her head, she pulled her bottom lip between her teeth and sawed on it while she considered him. "What are we doing?"

"I want you to ride me," he said. *I want to watch your gorgeous tits bounce while you're fucking me, and I want to watch your beautiful face when you come.* Holding her gaze, he caressed her breasts and gently rolled her nipples between his thumbs and fingers until they turned into tight beads. He leaned forward and gave each one a flick of his tongue, then repositioned her so she was poised above his cock. Eyes locked on his, she wrapped her fingers around him and lined him up with her entrance, then lowered her body, impaling herself in one go. Eyes wide, she gasped, and air left his lungs in a whoosh.

*Jesuuuuus!*

Arching her back, she dropped her head back and began to move, sheathing and unsheathing him as she worked her body up and down his steely length in long strokes. Fascinated, he watched her mouth part while a series of low moans rolled from her.

My God, she was the most fucking erotic, most beautiful sight he'd ever seen.

Hands gripping her hips, he fought to let her set the tempo, arm-wrestling the beast rearing up inside of him, the one that wanted to own her and fuck her mercilessly. These feelings were new to him. He loved them, but they twisted him inside. They exhilarated him yet terrified him. They made him woozy, yet he felt more alive than he'd ever been. She was addictive; he already ached for the next fix without getting his first one.

And God, while he loved watching her body sway in its sensual dance in front of him, loved gliding his hands over her hips, her ribs, palming her breasts at will, the visuals overwhelmed him.

Lust scrambling his brains, he surrendered to his inner beast, and with a grunt, he rolled them back over without breaking the connection. He yanked her to him roughly, their pubic bones grinding together. Then he bent her legs, slotting his hands at the backs of her knees, and pushed her thighs apart, opening her completely. Eyes closed, her hands reached above her head and grasped the bars of her headboard as if bracing herself for a wild ride, and she pulsed her pelvis against him, egging him on.

He withdrew, only to plow into her harder, in and out, over and over, again and again, flexing his hips, driving, drilling, as she squirmed and moaned and whimpered and writhed underneath him. He pounded her with a fierceness he didn't know he had. And the harder he went, the louder she got, the more animated her body grew, until she shouted out incoherent words and came to shuddering halt. A few more hammering strokes, and all of him let loose in a blinding flash as he followed her over the edge of ecstasy, the earth crumbling away below him.

# Chapter 19
# The Good, The Bad, and the Ugly

Michaela's heart jackhammered in her chest as all the little shattered pieces of herself drew back together again, like shards of a broken mirror reassembling themselves. Spread over top of her was one large man, his smooth skin slicked in sweat, his sandpaper jaw smashed against her left breast. Whenever he drew in a breath—which was frequently, considering he was panting like he'd just completed multiple laps around the ice—his sexy stubble that hadn't been there at the start of the evening scraped her tender flesh. It tickled but didn't, the sensation dancing a fine line along a razor's edge between pleasant and prickly.

He raised his head and peered at her with a hesitant smile curving his oh-so-kissable lips. "I'm crushing you, aren't I?"

"No. I just sank a little deeper in the mattress is all." *And you feel really good right where you are, so don't you dare move.* She smoothed his hair back, and he leaned into her touch with a contented sigh. Something warm and fuzzy bloomed in her heart.

Heaving himself up on a forearm, he dipped his head and gave her nipple a light suck. "Wouldn't want to crush these." Then he gave the other one the same treatment. "Or make this one jealous." He waggled his eyebrows at her.

She laughed, and her muscles clenched and pushed him out.

"Damn, woman. You just spat me out. I didn't think the joke was *that* bad," he mock-protested, his grin broad. "I get the hint. Guess I should clean up anyway." He ran the back of his finger along her cheek, and his expression shifted to something far more serious and tender. "So beautiful," he murmured. Then he hoisted himself off of her with a grunt.

*You make me feel beautiful.* Like no one ever had.

Rolling to her side, she admired his squared-off man butt as he sauntered toward the bathroom like he owned the place. "Are you checking out my ass?" he called over his shoulder.

"No more than you've been checking out my boobs." Maybe she needed to show his cheeks as much attention as he'd shown her breasts. *Lick and suck and bite. Repeat.*

"Which is code for you're *totally* checking it out." He shot her another playful look before closing the door behind him.

Giggles percolated inside of her as she flopped onto her back. *Oh my!* Just like his kissing, very few improvements were warranted in the bedroom. Her body was suspended, floating atop a cloud, and she fluttered her hand over her belly, her chest, lingering a beat on each hypersensitive breast. She'd never felt quite so ... worshipped before. She was pretty damn sure she glowed all over, and she reveled in the feeling.

When he emerged from the bathroom, she remembered herself and snatched her hand away. Heat crept over her already flushed skin.

"Your bathroom has the same layout as—hey, those are mine. But go ahead and play with them if you like, as long as I get to watch." He gave her a ridiculous leer, then dropped his big frame on the mattress beside her, making it dip under his weight as he stretched out on his side. Elbow bent, head resting on the heel of his hand, he trailed the calloused tip of his finger from her breast bone to her belly button.

"Do that again." His voice came out thick and rough.

"Do what again?" She injected innocence into her tone.

"Cute, but I'm not buying it." He dropped his mouth to her ear and whispered, "I saw you touching yourself." When he pulled back, smugness was etched in his features. Suddenly, his face fell and his mouth formed an O.

"What?" *You realized you said, "Those are mine"*?

"Nothing."

She poked his hard chest. "Ooh, about broke my finger." She grinned when his lips quirked. "Tell me what's bugging you. It's not like we have a lot to hide here."

"It's just that ... if you were doing what I'm pretty sure you were doing"—he waved a hand vaguely over her chest— "it means *I* didn't do a good job."

Was this his male ego asking to be stroked? No, he looked devastatingly sincere—worried, even. She ran the back of her hand along his powerful jaw, and he caught her hand and kissed her palm before returning her hand to his face. "No, it means you did a great job, and I was testing to see if I could duplicate the sensation. For the record, it feels *way* better when you do it." She bounced her eyebrows a few times. Sure, she was indulging him—he had a few well-earned attaboys coming his way—but she couldn't hold back the laughter bubbling inside her when his face lit up like a little kid's at the sight of a table full of birthday presents.

"Yeah?" He splayed his big hand over her belly, warming it.

"Yeah. Kinda rocked my world there, big guy, but don't let it go to your head."

He chuckled. "Duly noted." Then his light green gaze began roaming over her body, scalding her skin wherever it lit.

A zing vibrated her core, and chills raced to her extremities, raising her skin into goose bumps and hardening her achy nipples—a reaction he did not seem to miss, judging by the flare of appreciation in those eyes. Self-conscious, she craned her head to better look at him. "Are you ogling me?"

His gaze met hers squarely. "Every chance I get. I really like your girlie parts, by the way. All of them." Before she could toss out a rejoinder, his mouth returned to hers, tasting of the smoke and vanilla that lingered from the bourbon. He kissed her long and wet and sweet. Unmistakable hunger surged, though he seemed to hold it in check before his kiss grew demanding, his tongue probing and possessive, making her toes curl.

She turned into him, molding her curves against all that smooth, heated skin stretched over hard muscle. The feel of his angled body set her belly to quivering. His arms encircled her and tightened, his embrace like a boa constrictor, pressing her abdomen to something unexpectedly hard. *No, can't be.* As if he'd read her mind, his hands dropped to her ass and yanked her against his steely shaft. He began a slow grind against her.

*Whoa!* She broke the kiss and stared at him. *He's ready to go again?*

His chest heaved against hers. "What's wrong?"

"N-nothing ... I'm just surprised ... I mean ..." *Come on, word wizard. Spit it out already!* She couldn't for some reason, so she slid her hand between them, her fingers skipping over the defined blocks of his abdomen she longed to explore, opting for the tip of his taut, satiny knob instead. "Didn't you, you know, when we ...?" *Oh, for God's sake!*

Thank God he possessed the ability to read between her stammers. "Yes, I did." A cocky grin tugged his mouth. "But I have this theory that it wasn't a one-off, and I want to test out that theory by duplicating what we just did." His eyebrow dipped with concern. "You okay with that?"

*God, yes!* "I think I could be persuaded."

He nipped at her bottom lip, pulling it between his teeth and tugging gently. "Let me get right to work on that." He moved his soft mouth over her jaw, along her neck, and she stretched her head to the side to give him better access.

"Ooh, right there," she moaned shamelessly. *Feels soooo good.* Her goose bumps grew goose bumps. "Can I ask you a trivia question?" Now her voice was harsh and gravelly, like a woman who'd been smoking and throwing back whiskey her entire life.

He didn't slow down, mumbling, "Now?"

"Mm-hmm. What's the average recovery time for a man after sex?"

This time he did stop, one green eye peering at her as he raised his mouth from her throat. "Refractory time?"

"Yes, that."

His lips landed back on her neck, nibbling and sucking a path to her ear. "No idea. Just know mine, and that's typically about an hour."

She blinked. "Really? So how do you explain ..."

He teased her earlobe with the tip of his tongue. "I'm inspired. Now be quiet and enjoy the ride, unless you're trying to sidetrack me."

"Oh no, I *definitely* wouldn't want to do that." She yielded to his ministrations with an extended sigh.

Their second round was much less frenzied, fingers and tongues exploring in languid strokes, learning what elicited goose bumps, moans, and gasps. Blake was especially intent on pleasing her, which in *itself* pleased her. She couldn't recall a more unselfish lover. By the third round, her brazen side wanted to grab the reins of control and return the favor. No lie, she got a charge out of knowing she could bend this big, bad hockey player to her will. Not that he put up much of a fight, or that she didn't enjoy herself. But still ...

When they finally flopped back in exhaustion, he pulled her against him, kissed the top of her head, and promptly drifted off. One arm cradled her, and the other was bent across his chest, his hand clamped around her forearm as if he wanted to be sure she stayed put. Every muscle in her body was spent, and she slung a noodle leg over his thick thighs, snuggling close, savoring his musky, masculine scent and the delicious soreness between her legs.

She should have immediately tumbled after him into sleep, and while her eyelids were droopy, her mind was restless, replaying the unexpected night ... the unexpected man next to her. She barely knew him, yet she felt safer, more relaxed, more herself with him than she'd ever felt with Anders in five years. How was that possible? Hadn't she known Anders inside and out? What he liked, what he thought before he said it aloud? Looking back, it struck her that what she'd had with him merely bobbed on the surface of a fathoms-deep ocean. Only a few weeks with Blake—with no intimacy until these past few hours—and she felt a connection like a live wire tethering her to him, resonating inside her, making her thrum with a vitality so big she wanted to burst with it, let it spill out and touch everything around her with light.

What *was* that?

Maybe *it* was exhaustion and vodka skewing her thoughts.

Tilting her head back, she peeped up at his strong profile and smiled. No, she really shouldn't be having these thoughts about him, her logical mind trumpeted. But here, in the dark, while he slept, she could safely let her mind wander along a path of what-ifs. He was a mix of sharp edges and tenderness, with just enough hesitancy to make her want to trust him and enough swagger to make her want to follow him. He hit all the notes that made her insides sing. A diamond in the rough, but buff his facets and you uncovered one magical layer after another. It was about how he made her laugh, how exceptional he made her feel, and what was between his ears. And there was so much more to discover beneath his strata.

She ran a lusty gaze over his very fine bod, appreciating the physical side of the equation too. He knew how to use that very fine bod to coax and wheedle passions living deep inside her. The benefits of having a younger, anaerobically fine-tuned athlete for a bed partner were undeniable. Tonight he'd been a determined Jacques Cousteau exploring her depths.

*Oh God, I'm waxing sexually poetic now—and it's all his fault. He's doing this to me.* No one had ever stirred this fervor in her before, and it occurred to her—vaguely—that no one might ever again.

Maybe it was time to pitch the dating apps.

Blake awoke in a fog. Piercing that fog, though, was an acute awareness of silken curls and a sweet feminine fragrance tickling his nose. Nestled against him were plush forever curves that had about driven him out of his fucking mind last night, curves he'd needed all his willpower to resist when he'd left her at her door, and curves he probably shouldn't have touched when he'd returned to apologize—or whatever the hell had been rattling around his agitated brain.

But touched them he had—and then some—and the harsh daylight leaking through shaded windows reminded him he had the piper to pay. Blake covered his eyes with his free hand while his drowsy mind began a sluggish inventory, wandering through the events of last night. The good, the bad, and the ugly.

He lay on his back, his arm slung around M, his shoulder numb from her using it as a pillow. He raised his head ... and winced. His brain thudded against his skull, and his mouth was sour with last night's brown liquid overkill. Shit. This was why he shouldn't drink ... or why he should drink all the time so his body knew what to do with the stuff. The in-between shit didn't work.

Drinking to excess brought other consequences, like stripping away the inhibitions that had been holding desire in check for weeks. Fuck! What had he done?

He'd been mad as a swatted hornet when he'd walked in on Ferguson fucking Tracy in *his* living room, on *his* couch. Jesus! Ferguson wasn't even supposed to be home, but there he'd been, treating Blake to a scene he wasn't sure he could scour from his brain. That was the ugly.

And then Blake had taken it to the next level of stupid by hauling his pissed-off ass to M's, where he'd taken it out on her ... by fucking her all night. *We used all the condoms. Yay, me.* That was the bad ... but it was also the good. The so-good-he-ached-for-more. *The best.*

A memory streaked through his mind, paralyzing his ability to reason as it played out. His mother, in a drunken rage for reasons his ten-year-old self couldn't fathom, running at him with a pair of heavy-duty tongs one day when he'd come home from school to pick up his gear. The memory unfurled, and he could hear her shrieking in his head, hear every name she called him, names he *shouldn't* have known but did because he'd heard them so many times before. Ferguson had been with him, had been waiting for him by the front door, and had *sprinted*, arms flailing, yelling "No!" as he hurled himself between Blake and his mom, taking the crack of the tongs on the forearm shielding his head. Horror had passed through Mom's eyes as what she'd done seemed to register in her stewed brain. Blake had been rooted to the floor in shock, and Ferguson had grabbed his hand and wrenched him away. The memory dimmed after that, but from that day forward, Blake had kept his gear at Ferguson's—hell, he'd kept *himself* there too—not daring to go home until dinnertime when he knew his dad would be there. The dynamic between his folks had been a whole different sort of fun as his mom took out her wrath on his dad, letting Blake slink off and out of harm's way.

*Coward.* Why had he never stuck up for his dad like Fergs had stuck up for him? He'd been in awe of Fergs after that. Ferguson had always been full of bluster, but that day he'd backed it up, and Blake had been trying to make it up to him ever since.

Until lately.

Blake's cheeks heated with guilt as he recalled how much his friend had roughened up his nerves lately. Was Blake only now taking off his rose-colored glasses and *really* looking at his friend? Was he *envious* of Ferguson? Or did it have something to do with the woman he held in his arms? Was it possible he'd used M to get back at Ferguson?

A shout of *No!* ricocheted inside his head. Still, Fergs might see it that way. Fuck, he'd ramped up the complications—all because he hadn't been able to keep his hands and lips off of her.

Waking up beside someone—with dawn chasing away the dark—wasn't something he normally did. Not just spending the night, but wanting to stay right where he was instead of craning for the closest exit. Falling asleep with M had seemed so natural he hadn't given it a passing thought last night. *Pretty sure that wasn't just the alcohol talking*. And right now he didn't want to move because it meant surrendering the soft, warm weight he held. But he needed to let her go ... at least until he could figure out what the hell to do.

Letting out an errant grunt, he gingerly disentangled himself and sat up, rubbing the circulation back into his shoulder while reluctantly putting space between himself and the heat radiating from her. For a woman, and such a small one at that, she threw off some mighty big BTUs. *Take her camping in the winter and you'll never get cold.*

Furnace Girl let out a few mewling sighs and burrowed into the mattress, wiggling that luscious ass of hers. It might have been hidden under the covers and out of his sight, but it sure as hell was front and center in his mind, where it would occupy space for a long while. The image made his dick harden to full mast. He whacked the damn thing in a futile attempt to get it to calm the fuck down, but it bobbed to the side, as if seeking her welcoming body, where it wanted to bury itself one more time.

Fuck! He needed to get out of here, tell Ferguson he was out of the picture, and neutralize any awkwardness for M. And he needed to do it *now* before his baser side could outmuscle his less-baser side. As he retrieved his clothes, his mind zoomed back to lurching in here fully dressed, with her naked body wrapped around him. God, that had felt good. The memory didn't do a thing to soften his dick.

His meandering thoughts took a detour to leaving her a note so she didn't wake up to nothing. *Hey, sleeping with you last night was mind-blowing, the highlight of my life, the best sex I've ever had. Bar none. Can we do it again tonight?* Too eager, he told himself. And what if it hadn't been mind-blowing for her? He'd felt like a fucking god in her bed, but what if he was the only one who thought so? *Shit*. Was this temporary? Would she still want to keep the dating apps alive? Was she still planning to have coffee with Scott? *Double shit.*

Doubt clawed its way into his chest.

As he pulled on his shirt and began buttoning it, his gaze ran over the riot of curls surrounding her head like a lion's mane, then traced the tattoo from her wrist up her arm, finally landing on her smooth, pale back that flared and dipped below the blankets. He'd had his fingers and tongue all over that tattoo, and the memory of how she'd tasted had him swelling even more. When had he ever pulled a marathon like the one he'd pulled with her last night? Never. Had never had the desire the way he had with her. And even now he wanted—needed—more.

He paused his buttoning to stare for long, awestruck moments, committing every curve and valley to memory. She was perfect. Better than perfect, and something warm and sticky bloomed inside him only to congeal with the thought of *anyone* else laying his eyes on her the way Blake was right now. Red bursts exploded in his head, and his gut twisted into knots. His swollen dick deflated, so there was that.

He finished dressing, and with one last longing look, he closed the door silently, feeling like he was leaving a piece of himself behind. In the kitchen, he found pen and paper, and his brain froze. *Can I take you to breakfast?* was the first thing that popped into his head, followed unhelpfully by *Can I spend the day with you? Take you to dinner? Curl up with you tonight? Just be with you?*

God, he was pathetic.

With a sigh, he forced himself to scrawl, "Sorry, had to leave—team stuff to take care of. Had a great time. Hope your head doesn't hurt too much." Like his head did … like his heart did.

Letting himself out of her condo, he stood in front of his own door and fought down the tangle of emotions colliding inside of him. He was pissed at Ferguson but guilty over the friendship he was about to detonate. And if M didn't want to see Blake again, had he just sacrificed that friendship for nothing? It hadn't been nothing, though. He missed her already, though she was mere feet away. At the center of his jumbled thoughts pulsed desire and need and want for her.

He pushed a series of breaths through his lungs, then opened his door and walked in, braced for a sight that, thank fuck, wasn't there. His couch was empty now, but he wasn't sure he'd ever be able to sit on it again without first scrubbing it with a gallon of bleach. Renewed anger at Ferguson's faithlessness bristled inside him—except Ferguson wasn't *with* M to have betrayed her in the first place. Blake was. Maybe. Hopefully.

How would he tell his friend he'd gotten there first?

Filling a glass of water and chugging it down in one pass, he pondered his next move. If Tracy was still there, the brewing shit-show would have to wait. In the meantime, Blake could escape to his safe haven: the rink.

In his bedroom, he swapped his nice clothes for jeans, a T-shirt, and a hoodie. M's fresh scent wreathed him as he hung up his suit. Or maybe her smell was on his skin, which meant it would be gone with his next shower. *Not showering until I can rub her all over me again.*

He strode to the laundry room, where he kept his gear stowed in a closet. As he hoisted the bag over his shoulder, it struck him that he didn't have his car. Heaving a frustrated sigh, he pulled out his phone and pulled up the Lyft app. Wait. It was only 7:00 a.m. Did they run that early? Before he could give it much thought, a familiar voice sidetracked him.

"No sleeping in for you this morning, Bear? Where you off to anyway?" Ferguson stood in a pair of gym shorts—nothing else—yawning so wide all he needed was a black hood and his imitation of the *Scream* mask would be complete.

"Gonna go work on my wrist shot," Blake grunted.

Fergs chuffed derisively. "What? Perfect isn't good enough for you?"

And just like that, anger elbowed guilt out of the way, tearing through Blake like a wildfire through dry grass, though he managed to keep his voice even. "I can't tell if you're complimenting me on my shot or if you're just being your usual dick self."

Ferguson's mouth snapped open. "What the hell crawled up your ass this morning?" Some kind of realization dawned in his eyes, and he tossed his head back, laughing, and gave Blake a knowing smile. "I got it. It's because you walked in on Tracy and me, and you're jealous."

*"Jealous?"* Blake gawked at him. *Is he serious?*

"You're jealous of the fact I'm dipping my wick on the regular and you're not." Ferguson's lips curled, adding an extra dose of smug to his already intolerable self-satisfaction. "By the way, I saw Sherry the other night, and she asked about you. Maybe you should hit that again. I'll bet she could help you work some of those kinks out of your attitude." His eyebrows bounced, and Blake choked back a retort.

The thought of ever being with Sherry, especially after what he'd shared with M, made his insides recoil. Worse, M seeing him with Sherry ... it hadn't bothered him when he hadn't known M, but now guilt washed over him. And she'd seen Tracy stumble out that morning, but he'd never explained because he'd been protecting Fergs. *Well, shit!* Why hadn't she told him to fuck off? *She still might.* And he wouldn't blame her.

A muscle in his jaw jumped. "About last night," he said instead, "I thought you were spending the night at your mom's."

"Yeah, well, Tracy needed the high hard one, and I couldn't leave the poor girl hanging. She's addicted to the Fergs. I'm the drug she needs, know what I'm saying?" He chortled.

*Do you even hear yourself?* Blake corralled his disgust by muttering a curse under his breath. He looked at Ferguson expectantly, but Ferguson didn't mention word one about Michaela or Blake's stand-in date with her last night. Had he even given her a passing thought? One thing was certain: Fergs *sure* as hell didn't deserve her. He'd transformed into a complete and utter dick, and Blake had blinded himself to it. Now was the time to yank those blinders off.

"Well, next time you're giving Tracy the *high hard one*, do us all a favor and keep it on your own damn sheets instead of messing up my couch, huh?"

Fergs shrugged. "Sure. As long as she doesn't do what she did last night and rip off my clothes before I can get her into the bedroom. I tell ya, Bear, this girl can't wait to get her lips around my—"

Blake threw up a hand. "Spare me the visual. My stomach can't take it."

"What, you don't want the *blow-by-blow*? At the rate you're going, having me describe it is the closest you're gonna get to having your dick in a chick's mouth."

Blake asked the question whirring in his head. "Have you always been this big of a prick?"

Ferguson chortled. "Ha! Knew it. You *are* jealous!"

Blake stormed to the front door, slamming it behind him. He paused in the hallway to catch his breath. The click of a door jerked his attention to the *other* door. M's head poked out, her hair a sex-tousled mass of curls he had an overwhelming urge to tangle his fingers in. Again. The look on her face was part-sleepy, part-tentative, and it strained at something in his chest. In that moment, all he wanted was to climb back into bed with her and hit "reset." His mind began running through the possibilities—

"Escaped in kind of a hurry, big guy. Something I said?" A frown creased her forehead, and thunderclouds rolled through her gray eyes.

"No! Don't even think that. You were—are—perfect. Just me trying to be a gentleman and let you get some sleep. I figured you didn't need me pawing at you again." God, he was an idiot. What had he been thinking when he'd left? Either he hadn't been thinking or he'd been thinking too much. Here he could have drifted back to sleep with her in his arms instead of trying to fix what couldn't be fixed between him and Ferguson.

His feet—which were apparently smarter than he was—turned and paced off the few steps to her door. When he looked down at her, his pulse leapt into overdrive. Her head had been craned around the doorframe, so he hadn't seen at first, but she only wore a towel she held to her front. The towel wasn't covering her back worth a damn. A pretty blush pinked her cheeks. "I was in the bathroom when I thought I heard your door, and I didn't want to miss you, so I grabbed whatever I could. So, um, you were contemplating pawing me this morning before you left?"

*Always*. He fought the first smile that had cracked his lips all morning. "M," he rasped, "with you dressed like that—or not dressed—it's all I *can* contemplate. You shouldn't be hanging out in doorways without clothes on." His eyes darted to his door, willing Ferguson to stay put. No way was his roommate laying eyes on a naked M. No, that was for Blake alone.

She opened her mouth to say something, but he nudged her inside before she could speak. In one swift motion, he dropped his bag, closed the door, and swept his arms around her, grabbing her bare ass and hauling her against his stiffening cock. Crashing his lips against hers, he swallowed whatever had been on the tip of her delicious tongue. Body and mouth yielding to his demand, she wound her arms around his neck, welcoming his touch, his probing tongue. The towel slid between them to the floor. He spun in place, tucking one of her legs around his hips, and had her back against the wall in a heartbeat, his pulse and breathing accelerating like a top fuel dragster off the starting line.

When they finally pulled apart, her pretty silver eyes scanned his face. "Well, good morning. And here I thought you snuck out because you had second thoughts about last night."

Her words thunked him hard in the solar plexus, and he pulled in a sharp breath. What the hell had he been thinking, giving up what he wanted out of loyalty to Ferguson? Forget that shit. No more Mr. Nice Guy.

"Never." He pecked her lips twice. "And there's something you need to know. The brunette the other morning you assumed was with me? She's with Ferguson."

M blinked. "You mean, like right now?"

He nodded.

“Is she the reason he couldn’t take me last night?” She quickly shook her head. “Never mind. I don’t need to know. It doesn’t matter because I like the way it ended.”

His heart ballooned, and he kissed her again. “I’m heading to the rink. Come with me. In fact, you can help me get my wheels. Take some of that red ink off your ledger since you’re part of the reason I left my SUV behind last night.”

“To the *rink*? I was going to go into the office.”

“To the *office*?” he mimicked. “Why? Wasn’t last night’s appearance at your boss’s enough for the weekend? Don’t you get a day off?” Still holding her up, he dropped his head and began trailing kisses along her shoulder to the base of her neck, where he paused to suck softly and tease with his tongue, just the way she’d shown him she liked it last night. He loved how she’d boldly taught him what did and didn’t turn her on. No other woman had ever done that, and the thought crossed his mind his technique had been flawed for years.

Oh well. As long as he could get it right with her, that was all he cared about.

“Mmm, I love your skin,” he murmured. *The texture and the way you taste. So damn good.* As if her skin had been created for his taste buds alone.

She let the back of her head fall against the wall and hummed, “Maybe ...”

“Better make up your mind quick, or I’ll have you flat on your back again,” he mumbled against her jaw.

“If you meant that as a threat, it’s not working. It’s more of an incentive.” She let out a throaty laugh, then gave him a heated gaze. “Why is it I’m always naked and you’re fully dressed?”

He lifted his head and offered her a salacious smile as he dipped his gaze to her chest and squeezed her ass. Suddenly, he was feeling a whole helluva lot better than he had a mere five minutes ago. “You’re *always* naked and I’m not? Sounds like my fantasy come true. Is that a promise?”

"No," she scoffed. "And speaking of being naked, I'd prefer it if we were equally undressed at the same time because your belt is ... uh—"

"Oh shit! Sorry!" He set her back on her feet, and she plucked the towel from the floor and wrapped it around herself before he could get much of a look—not that he needed it because his dick was about to unzip his fly. "So. Are you in?"

"Do I have time for a shower?"

He waggled his eyebrows. "As long as you take me with you." She turned, but he caught the towel and tugged it from her before she escaped. With a squeal, she took off for the bedroom, and he followed just close enough to get an eyeful.

The rink wasn't going anywhere. He'd get there sometime today. Maybe.

# Chapter 20

# I Am So Pucked

Michaela sat in the stands of a practice rink, hugging her knees, enthralled by the gorgeous man slapping one puck after another from different angles and different areas of the ice. Watching him glide over the slick surface as he expertly maneuvered stick and puck made her heart flutter. She could do this for days and never get sick of the sight of him, all fluid grace and effortless speed.

The worst hockey-isms ran through her dirty mind like hamsters on a wheel. *Puck me. I like your big stick. Shoot from the high slot.* Yep, she was growing to like this sport.

Every time he looked up at her—like now—the determination in his knotted brows eased and he sent her a grin or a wink or a wave, making her tingle all over.

Her phone vibrated in the back pocket of her jeans, and she answered as soon as she saw Fiona's tongue-sticking-out goofy face on her screen.

"Hey, Fi."

"Oh. My. God!" she shrieked. "You *are* alive! Why didn't you call me back? I've been sick with worry!"

"So sick with worry you're just now calling me," Michaela replied dryly. "What happened? Were you getting ready for bed when it dawned on you to follow up?"

"Okay. So not that worried after you told me you were with Chad, although... tell me you didn't have to whip out the pepper spray again."

Michaela laughed. "No, the pepper spray stayed in my purse." *I wanted him closer, not running away.*

"So where are you? It sounds like ... slapping noises?"

"I'm at the rink with Chad, er, Blake, and I'm watching him practice."

"Okay, Micky-Dub. Spill. Now."

Michaela squirmed on the cold metal bench. "There's nothing to spill. We sort of went out last night, had fun, and he invited me to tag along today."

"Mick. This is Fi you're talking to, so cut the crap. I want all the blanks filled in between going out last night, opening your door to him at 3:00 a.m., and coming to his practice." She paused for breath, and her voice grew gleeful. "Oh God. You had sex with him, didn't you? Oh Jesus, and I bet it was scorching hot! Can you walk? Those guys are built for endurance."

"Fi—"

"You *did*!" Fiona squealed so loud Michaela was sure Blake could hear her over the booming echoes. Heat bloomed on Michaela's face, and she cast her eyes the other away.

Fiona sniggered. "So what's he *practicing* right now? Wink, wink, nudge, nudge."

"Fi, we're not in middle school anymore." Still, Michaela couldn't help the smile quirking her lips. "He's practicing his *wrist shot*. He's got a wicked wrister, and he wants to make it even better so he's the best in the league." Why did hockey terms sound so ... dirty?

"Ooh, so *more* wicked? And listen to you going all hockey on me. What's his last name? I wanna look him up."

"Why?"

"Just curious," Fiona singsonged.

"Fi, this is nothing serious. Just a little fun with a hot guy."

"Hmm ... Mick, are you capable of 'just a little fun with a hot guy' without falling?"

Michaela blew out a breath. "I don't know where this is going"—*or if it's going*—"but I plan to enjoy the ride as long as it lasts." She sounded more resolute than she felt. Last night had been ... She couldn't remember feeling like that before, and it wasn't the sex. Okay. So the sex had been spectacular, but how much of that had been because of the way he'd touched her emotionally? Made her come alive like she'd only been sleep-walking before?

Miss Goody Two-Shoes whispered a warning that Michaela was drifting into dangerous territory, but she virtually flicked the cautious one from her shoulder and fist-bumped the devil girl.

"And I'll bet you're really, ahem, enjoying the kind of ride he's giving you. So hot sex it is, girlfriend. But still, I want his last name."

Fiona's protective side was one of the many traits Michaela loved about her, even though it was annoying at times—like now. From experience, though, she knew holding out did no good. With a defeated sigh, she said, "It's Barrett. Blake Barrett."

What Michaela didn't tell her best friend was that when she'd awakened in an empty bed this morning, her heart had fallen. After reading his scrawled note, it had dropped a few more inches—especially on the heels of his one-hundred-and-eighty-degree about-face last night. One minute he'd been fleeing her, and the next he'd been breaking down her door. Regret tended to rise right along with the morning sun, and she'd figured their night of passion had been a one-and-done for him. Hadn't he said he didn't hook up often, or words to that effect? She hadn't dared hope she was an exception, that she wasn't simply the next redhead or brunette or blond who'd blipped on his radar. Yet somewhere along the line she *had* hoped, which was why she'd opened her front door like a fangirl when she thought she'd heard the thud of his door this morning. She'd been semi-stalking him, hadn't she? But with one look and a few words, he'd eased the worst of her doubts, giving her heart a helium lift. And now she was all giggly and giddy and goose-bumpy. *Ugh!*

"Hey, Curly!" the object of her fangirling yelled from the ice.

She held the phone to her chest. "What?"

He'd gathered the pucks around him and was casually leaning on his stick, smirking, looking all hot and muscly and mouthwatering. God, did he have any idea how gorgeous he was? *Don't think so.* "Get your cute little ass down here." When she scrunched up her eyebrows in question, he added, "Let's see you hit a few pucks."

"I can't even skate!" she squawked.

"Can't skate?" His eyes widened in mock surprise. "I know someone who's happy to fix that, but it'll take lots of lessons. Maybe we can work out a trade." He waggled his eyebrows. "Right now, though, you don't need to skate. We're just hitting pucks. So come on."

Teach her to skate? Oh, this had the ring of something beyond one night ... and one morning. Not that she was expecting anything permanent from him. *Just enjoy the ride while it lasts,* she reminded herself. "Fi, I gotta go. Blake's going to teach me how to hit pucks."

"What on earth has this man done to my serious, stuffy attorney best friend? Oh. He's returned her to her former fun self. I think I like him already. Do I get to meet him at Thanksgiving?"

"Oh, Fi, I don't know. Probably not. Maybe. It's way too early for that."

They exchanged I-love-yous and hung up. Her stomach full of fizzies, Michaela wound her way down the stairs to the open door where Blake waited for her, stick in hand. He cocked his chin toward the phone still in her hand. "Everything okay?"

She shoved it back in her pocket. "What? Yes, everything's fine. Well, except I'm going to face-plant on the ice and make a total fool of myself."

He canted his body and held out his arm. "No, you're not. Just hang on to me. I won't let you fall."

She glanced up at him, clamping down on the thought that popped into her head. *Might be too late for that.* "Promise?"

"Yeah. Promise." The warmth in his green eyes conveyed there was more to that promise.

He guided her to where the pucks awaited. “Before we get started, I need to ask you something.”

She smirked. “Must be bad if you brought me out here on slippery ice where I can’t run away.”

He let out a mild laugh. “Hopefully, you won’t want to run away.” His eyes captured hers. “You never said yes when I asked you to go to the charity brunch.”

“Oh. I didn’t realize you were serious.”

He winked. “Probably because it sounded as if Sarah was asking you instead of me.” After explaining his reluctance last night was due to Owen’s intention to ask her—*God, it all makes sense now!*—he pushed on. “So will you go? With me?”

Bubbles popped in her tummy. “I’d like that.”

“One more thing ...” He faltered, and she cocked an eyebrow at him. “You’re not going to see that guy from the party, are you? Scott?”

Her eyes darted to the stands before coming back to his. “I kind of already did.”

His face dropped, and she rushed on. “What I mean is we were going to go for coffee, but our schedules didn’t match up, so we talked for a bit on the phone. After that conversation, we sort of agreed there wasn’t much clicking between us.” Though Scott had seemed interested in taking a next step, absolutely no buzz existed for Michaela—certainly nothing like the electricity that crackled whenever she was with Blake. “The other thing”—which she hadn’t told Scott—“is he’s just coming off a breakup after being married ten years, and I’m not interested in being the rebound relationship.” She tilted her head. “Make sense?”

Blake’s shoulders seemed to relax, as did his features, and her heart flipped over. He gave her a casual nod. “Yep, totally. Now let’s shoot some pucks.”

After handing her the too-long stick, he grasped her hips to position her, his warm hands lingering longer than necessary—not that she was complaining. “Are you a golfer?”

“Not really. The firm encourages us to take out clients, but my biggest client doesn’t golf, and it feels downright weird when I tag along with other attorneys and their clients. Besides, it's hard to find the time. You?"

"Not much of one, but I enjoy getting out with the guys and seeing the views. Golf courses are like manicured parks dropped in the choicest places." He leaned into her, his front to her back, his arms surrounding her. His hands covered hers where they gripped the stick. "The stick's too long, but we can work with it."

"I think we proved that last night," she giggle-snorted.

He let out a snort of his own.

She wiggled her butt against him. "Are you going to show me your twisted wrister?"

A groan escaped him. "Not if you keep doing that. I might have to show you the dark corners of a locker room instead. Now behave and pay attention. We're going to tap pucks in first, so you can get a feel for the motion."

"Ooh, there you go, talking dirty again."

"Killing me here, woman," he growled.

The banter continued throughout the exercise, which Michaela was convinced was an elaborate ruse for him to pull her against his body and caress her arms and hips with his big, warm hands, using covert methods that weren't so ... covert. Not that she minded. The feel of his hard planes and the heat radiating at her back were exhilarating, and she spent most of their touch-time squelching the quivers swimming at high speed through her bloodstream. If he'd *asked* for permission to touch without boundaries, she'd have given it to him in a heartbeat, accompanied by a "Yes, please touch!"

Through their flirty game, she glimpsed his world and the sport he loved. Sprinkled throughout his teaching, his ridiculous trivia and relaxed humor kept her laughing, making it hard to concentrate on connecting the stick with the puck.

Though they'd been at their excuse-for-PDA exercise for over an hour, the end came too soon when he breathed in her ear, "It's almost time for the mites' practice, and we need to clear out so the Zamboni can resurface the ice." He lifted his chin toward the glass where little faces were pressed, displaying gap-toothed smiles.

How had she missed them? Or the open gate where a flat-fronted Zamboni stood ready to rumble onto the rink?

After depositing the pucks in a bag, Blake handed her his stick and helped her shuffle off the ice. Eager little kids swarmed him as soon as he stepped out of the rink with her in tow. She slipped from his grasp and stood back, fascinated by the spectacle. Her heart melted when he got down on one knee to be at the kids' eye level, then puddled as he talked to them, smiling easily, answering their exuberant questions, asking them questions in return. A few parents thrust things at him, and he signed them all without losing sight of his miniature fans.

He rose to his full height, head on a swivel until his gaze landed on her. A grin split his face, and his eyes lit up like polished gemstones. She hadn't imagined this. Nor had she imagined him holding out his hand to her in front of his audience and pulling her with him as he headed toward a bench in front of a bank of lockers. She plopped down beside him, fascinated as his strong hands swiftly undid his skate laces.

"You seemed to enjoy being mobbed by munchkins," she posed.

"The kids make it fun. I love seeing their faces light up when you talk to them about hockey. They absolutely love the game."

"Almost as much as they love you."

He yanked off a boot. "Nah. To them, I *am* the game. If I were on the street in regular clothes and they didn't recognize me—or their parents didn't recognize me—they wouldn't look at me twice. But the connection, that's all about hockey."

"I think you're being humble. You're underestimating your impact."

He glanced at her as he pulled off the second skate. "On them? I beg to differ. Hopefully I'm underestimating my impact on you, though." His boyish grin widened, and a sudden shyness overcame her even as tingles raced along her spine and her limbs.

"You'll make a good dad," she blurted out in her fluster. "If you want to be a dad someday. Do you? Want to be a dad?" A flush shot up her neck, engulfing her face. How had the errant thought slipped in and taken control of her mouth? She needed to keep a tighter lid on her musings before they pulled her too far out on a branch that could break under her hopeful weight.

Putting the skates aside, he bent over and pulled on hiking shoes he began lacing. When he looked up at her, a frown had replaced the grin. “Can’t say I’ve ever thought about it much.”

“Right. When you don’t believe happily-ever-after is in your future, it’s probably hard to imagine parenthood in the mix.”

“Not necessarily. Lots of people have kids together without love being part of the equation. My parents are a great example.” The words came out as though they left a bitter taste in his mouth, and a pang stabbed her heart. Before she had time to cobble together a soothing speech, his sunny smile made a sudden reappearance. “C’mon, Curly. Let’s get out of here before my pint-sized fan club mobs me again.”

She let out a relieved laugh. “All those knee-biters hanging on your legs could be dangerous for your health.”

As they stood, he wrapped an arm around her waist and drew her in, dropping a kiss on top of her head. “Hungry? Want to grab a bite somewhere?” He nudged her toward the entrance of the facility.

She smirked up at him. “Is that wise? Don’t you get mobbed in restaurants too?” An image of pretty women lining up for “autographs” flashed in her brain. Did he like that kind of attention? Weeks ago, she’d have answered her own question in the affirmative. But now that she’d had a peek behind the celebrity façade? The answer was much murkier, and she found herself thirsty to learn more about this man walking her toward his SUV.

A sigh escaped him. “Yeah, sometimes eating out can be a pain in the ass.”

“You could always cook for me.” She wiggled her eyebrows.

His smile dropped. “Not at my place.”

*Oh shoot. The Ferguson factor?* “Um, okay. My place, then? I don’t have much food, though.”

Whatever cloud had come over him quickly vanished, and a laugh rumbled through his chest. “No, you certainly don’t.”

"Wait. How do you know?"

"Because when you opened your fridge last night, I only saw clear shelves. No wonder you're so skinny."

She stopped mid-walk to gape at him. *"Skinny? Me?"*

He reached the passenger side and opened the door. "*Not* skinny in all the right places." His voice came out low and husky, like a man with sex on the brain. As if to back up his words, he made a slow, assessing sweep of her body, heating her skin wherever his gaze landed. It lingered for several beats on her chest, as if he could see through her jacket, her sweater, her bra, to her bare breasts. As if he were fondling them right there in the parking lot with his eyes. Her mind zoomed back to his mouth and fingers on them, manipulating them the way she'd shown him she liked. Her nipples perked right the hell up.

The spell was suspended when she took a step forward. As he helped her into her seat, she murmured, "A boob man if I ever saw one." How many other boobs had he admired?

He leaned in, his face so close his warm breath fell on her mouth. His light green eyes were dusky and glazed as they took in her face, her mouth. Her lips parted on instinct, inviting him to kiss her. Instead of granting her wish, he whispered back, "Never was a boob man before. And just for the record, with you I'm also an ass man and a leg man. Pretty much an any-part-that-belongs-to-M man."

*Then* he kissed her, taking his time, playing and probing and plunging, exquisitely torturing her by touching her with only his lips and tongue. Wanting all of him in contact with all of her, she grasped his biceps and arched her back, pulling him to her, but he didn't budge. Instead, he pulled away and gave her a cocky grin. "Is that your way of saying I passed the kissing class, teach?"

She blinked, unable to form a coherent thought. He'd left her speechless, breathless, and unsure of her own name. And she loved it.

*Damn. I am in so much pucking trouble.*

# Chapter 21
# Zigging Instead of Zagging

After the fun at the rink, they had returned to M's place, where Blake had made himself at home.

"How did you end up in this place again?" he called out to her as he perused shelves of law books in the hallway built-ins outside her office door.

"Paige Miller arranged it," she sang from the kitchen, where she was putting away the leftovers from their Thai takeout. Normally, he didn't leave any food, but he'd ordered extra tonight. All part of his diabolical plan where he'd convince her to let him stay over, in which case there'd be something to eat if hunger struck him in the middle of the night. "She has a client on a six-month assignment in Australia, and I'm covering his HOA dues and utilities in exchange for staying here."

Stuffing his hands in his front pockets, he sauntered toward her. "Where do you go when he comes back?"

Wiping her hands on a towel, she shot him an impish grin and shrugged. "Who knows? Maybe by then, she'll have another uber-rich client whose place I can house-sit for a while."

"Seriously? You're okay with moving from place to place?"

"I don't know. This is my first time doing it. So far, it's worked out well." She patted his pec.

He trapped M's hand against his chest, reeled her in, and encircled her in his arms. "Can't argue with that. Thank you, Paige Miller." The move soothed a burgeoning need to have his hands on her, though it didn't go far enough. He'd been hungry for her touch all day, chasing it like a fox chasing a rabbit.

Tilting her head, she slid her hands to his shoulders, her eyes twinkling like starlight. "Did you want something from me?"

He drew in a hissing breath and tightened his hold. "Now that's a loaded question." *I want everything.*

She tapped his bottom lip with her forefinger. "Maybe you were looking for more kissing lessons?" He tried to bite her finger or suck it into his mouth, but she was too quick and pulled it away with a laugh. Then it was back, smoothing his lower lip in a way that made his dick twitch. "Or maybe you're looking for some *other* kind of lesson?" Her voice was soft and smoky, like aged whiskey, and she arched an eyebrow.

"Anything you want to teach me, Curly, I'm willing to learn." He dropped his head to the spot where her neck met her shoulder and sucked so she wouldn't see his tongue lolling as though he were an eager dog.

She canted her head to give him better access. "Bet you say that to all the girls," she murmured.

The thought of kissing someone besides her popped into his head, leaving him a little tepid. His head whipped up, and he looked her square in the eye. "No, I don't." His voice came out harsher than he'd intended, and she flinched in his arms. *I've never acted this way with anyone else. You're special, M, and I'm not sure what to do about it.* She was coaxing emotions from him he hadn't processed and didn't understand. The pace at which this thing between them was moving spun his head, but the feel of her body pressed against his distracted him, flinging his apprehension into a remote corner of his brain.

Her eyes widened. "I didn't mean—"

"Then kiss me, woman. Show me what you got." He pushed a curl behind her ear.

A giggle-snort escaped her. "I thought that was *my* line? And I also thought I'd already shown you everything I've got?"

"Mm-hmm, but it was dark, and I didn't get a good look." A total lie. "I'll need to see it again. All of it. In the light." When had he become so damn bold? She brought it out in him, for better or worse, and he liked it. Liked how complete he felt with her, as though some missing piece of himself had been returned and woven back into his psyche. Is this how his dad had felt when he'd met his mom?

*Shit! Where did that come from?*

Her hands curled into his T-shirt. "*All* of it?" she teased, pulling him back to the present.

He nodded, but his mind zigged when it should have zagged. As he stared into the depths of M's eyes, he contemplated whether this thing between them would turn into something more—he wanted it to—and if it did, whether it would endure. He wanted that too. His words about his parents' relationship floated back to him. *"How does something so good go so wrong?"*

M's expression transformed from seductive to concerned, her eyebrows knotting. "Hey, big guy, where did you go?" She brushed her soft fingers over his jaw.

He straightened and loosened his grip on her. "Nowhere. Just zoned out for a sec."

Something unreadable flashed in her eyes. "You're probably tired from last night." Her fingers continued their gentle caress, and he closed his eyes and leaned into her touch. "Why don't we relax and watch a movie?"

He snapped his eyes open. "Yeah, okay." Maybe a movie would hold his heart-constricting brain-churn at bay. With any luck, he'd drift off in her arms.

They sat on her red couch, and she fiddled with the remote. "My parents did pizza and movie night every Friday, and the three of us would curl up on the couch together," she said. *"Raiders of the Lost Ark* was one of their favorites."

"Sounds nice," he offered. *Wonder what growing up like that would have been like?*

"I haven't seen any of the other ones, though. Isn't the second one *Temple of Doom*?"

"Yeah, but it's terrible. The chick screams the entire time, like this one scene where they're in some palace and they serve her monkey brains." At odds with the subject, his stomach began to uncoil.

"Ew! Well, we're not watching that one, then." She clicked some more.

He dropped his head against the top of the couch and rolled it toward her. Her face was scrunched up, her tongue poking out at the TV. She looked ridiculous and adorable, and his emotions climbed a roller coaster. A laugh burst from him, and he couldn't stop. Dipping one eyebrow, she gave him a look that telegraphed she thought he was nuts. Her expression shifted, and she joined him, laughing along with him. Every time they got their laughter under control, one shared look sent them into hysterics ... over absolutely nothing. Jesus, it felt good! Being with *her* felt good, he mused as he wiped tears from his cheeks.

They settled in to watch *Vertigo*, but Blake barely paid the suspenseful film any mind because his attention was riveted to M. She was all heart, sunshine, and flowers, bringing lightness into his rain-cloud-covered life. If a few days was all he could get from her, he was richer for it, but God, he longed to turn a few days into weeks ... months ... years.

Awestruck, he stole glances at her while her focus was glued to the screen. A good and bad thing. Good because he could fill his inner photo album with her upturned nose, her pinked cheekbones, her perfect peachy skin without her thinking he was a creeper. Bad because ... well, her attention wasn't on *him*. Which was where he wanted it to be, he realized.

He lifted his arm and rested it on the back of the couch. Her sweater had slipped from her un-inked shoulder, and his fingers inched toward it. It was sprinkled lightly with freckles he wanted to count. If he connected the dots, what picture would emerge? His fingers stretched involuntarily.

"Oh my God, did you see that?" She turned, and he jerked his hand away like a kid caught sneaking a nip of Grandma's bourbon. Her eyes skated to his hand, and he patted the back of the couch a little too vigorously. The casualness he feigned was nothing close to the vibe rolling off of him in waves. Jesus! What was the matter with him?

He knew *exactly* what was the matter with him. M made his mind race in all directions until those directions got all twisted up and he had no idea whether he was coming or going. She tied his tongue. Knotted his insides. Gave him whiplash. Made him uncomfortably hot. Filled his eyes with stardust. She was so far out of his class she may as well have been in college and he in kindergarten. They may have been the same age, but this girl—this *woman*—was light years beyond his dumbass jock self.

But he was damned if he'd let that stop him from trying to win her.

She turned toward him. "You're not watching the movie, are you?"

He shook his head.

"Should I find something else?"

"It doesn't matter what you put on. I'm too busy watching you." *Oh, smooth! Now she has no doubt what a numbnut you are.* He wasn't good at lines and hadn't meant it that way in the first place—it was simply a slice of unadorned truth. But something flared in her pretty eyes, and soon she was tucked against him, kissing his neck, shooting chills along his scalp and down his spine, her small fingers roaming over his chest, snaking under his T-shirt, outlining his abs while he fought the gasps rising in his throat from her light, ticklish touch. Then those fingers went to work on his belt, the button on his jeans, his fly, slipping nimbly beneath his boxers. When she took him in hand, he couldn't hold back *that* gasp.

He dropped his head back on the couch with a strangled sigh. A smile tugged at his mouth. *Yeah, the only vertigo happening is right here on this couch. Bring it, Curly.*

And she did.

Even his pinging phone and clouded conscience couldn't pull him away from M's expert hands on him and her even wickeder mouth. He shoved the question of how she acquired those skills to the back porch of his mind, letting himself get carried away in the sensations.

When he woke the next morning, he was curled around her small form, his chest to her back, his knees tucked behind hers, her bare, silky skin caressing his with each slow breath moving through her. Her furnace heat wasn't blasting him today. Nuzzling her hair, he pulled in the scent of soap and flowers and her, and his cock swelled. They'd gone at it pretty good last night, but he found himself wanting more—from her, with her—despite a gratifyingly deep ache in a few muscles that had gotten one hell of a workout.

Jesus! It was probably a good thing he was leaving on a road trip this afternoon. One part of him registered relief to escape the dizzying emotions being close to her stirred up, but the other part missed her already. Not merely her hot little body, but her sharp mind and her twinkling smile. How easily she laughed at his stupid jokes and even stupider trivia. How she saw into the heart of a thing or a person. Her warmth, her kindness. Her ability to live life out loud. He admired all of it. Craved all of it for himself. Was he good enough for her, though? Would she leave him with a wrecked heart that would never heal? What if he fell hard, like some guys he knew who weren't only whipped but lost their minds and their game? What if he lost himself to the mercy of a woman like his father had? Ultimately, his father hadn't been good enough for his mother.

The realization sent a shiver rippling through his body.

*Don't end up like Dad.*

Maybe if he didn't get too close ... Trouble was that train had already left the station, a fact made abundantly clear when M sighed in his arms and nestled a little closer. God, she felt good. He could die like this and have no regrets. She was the polar opposite of his mother, he assured himself. Right now, his biggest regret was that he had to leave her bed. Wanting his fill before the inevitable, he rolled her onto her back, interlaced his fingers with hers, and stretched her arms above her head. Eyes closed, a sleepy smile twitching her lips, she arched her warm body into him, purring, “Good morning, handsome.”

It was a good morning now.

# Chapter 22

# MYSTERY WOMAN

"Where the hell were you? And why the hell don't you answer your phone?"

"Jesus, Ferguson, you sound like my wife—if I had one. Only she'd be a whole hell of a lot prettier and way more fuckable," Blake snapped as he dropped his packed duffel by the door. Ferguson had blown up his phone when Blake had been burning up the sheets with M, asking where he was and if they were riding to the arena together. By the time Blake saw the messages, it was time to leave M's scorched bed and traipse the few feet to his own place.

"So what the hell kept you so fucking busy?" Ferguson grumbled as they headed out the door.

Blake shrugged. "Little of this, little of that."

In the hallway, his eyes strayed to M's front door, and he pictured her where he'd left her, dozing in bed on her stomach, naked except for a swath of ivory sheet covering most of her butt. The image wasn't one he'd have to carry in his head, he thought to himself sheepishly. Not when he'd captured it in his phone.

Call him dishonorable, call him a perv, but he wanted to take beautifully bare M with him on this extended road trip. Besides, no one else would ever see it.

When he and Fergs climbed into Blake's Range Rover, what used to be a comfortable ride to the arena was suddenly awkward as hell. Fifteen minutes seemed to triple in the charged silence.

Ferguson stared out the window as Blake pulled into the players' parking lot. "If it makes you feel any better, Tracy and I are done."

Blake turned off the engine and looked at his friend. "Why would that make me feel better? And why are you done?"

Fergs shrugged. "Yeah, well, she was a fun fuck and all, but it ran its course."

"Just like you predicted it would." Blake pulled in a breath and puffed it out. "Who ended it?"

"Why does it freaking matter?"

Blake had no idea why, but it did. Maybe it struck a little too close to home. His mind whirled, pondering whether M would still want him when he returned in ten days. Or a month from now. Six months. A year. Why his mind fixated on the end of something that was just getting off the ground confounded him.

"I don't know. Just wondering if you're okay with it, that's all."

Fergs snorted. "I'm fine with it. It was only about the sex anyway, and that's easy enough to find anywhere. Just watch me on this trip." He threw open his door and hopped out, peering in at Blake.

"What, you planning to fuck your way up the West Coast?"

Fergs grinned. "I can throw a little action your way if you're up for it. Ha! Get it? Up for it."

Huh. Was that a white flag Fergs was extending? Blake offered him a half-smile. "Thanks. I'll let you know if I'm interested." *Not gonna happen.* He was already impatient to get home—and he hadn't even left yet.

On the plane, while half of his teammates slept around him, he pulled out his phone and scrolled until he landed on the picture he'd taken of M this morning. She'd kill him if she knew, but he hadn't been able to stop himself. Her head was turned toward the camera, her sex-tousled curls tumbling over her closed eyes. Her pretty pink lips were parted, and he stiffened thinking about sliding his tongue—and other body parts—between them. The sheet covered her ass below the dimples on her lower back, hinting at her cheeks where they kissed her thighs, leaving her legs and the smooth skin on her back completely exposed. The girl thrashed in her sleep, and the covers paid the price. Blake had seen this pose before; it was one of his favorites, second only to her on her back.

From this angle, her tattoo was on full display, and his eyes traced the vines snaking along her delicate bent arm. His mind filled in blanks—the tip of his tongue on those vines and other parts of her—and all that came before she'd passed out in the pose he'd captured. The pleasant memories made his dick throb painfully behind his zipper. Good thing he sat in his own row. With one last longing look, he stowed the phone before he could really embarrass himself, promising to spend time with her later when he was alone.

Like Fergs, Blake told himself it was about the sex, and his borderline obsession was because the sex was beyond incredible. *Mind-blowing. A whole other level.* But he wasn't sure he bought his own story. He had a bad case of M; hopefully, he wouldn't need a cure.

When they reached the hotel, Blake followed Mac up to their room and called her while Mac used the bathroom. "Hey, just got here. What are you doing?"

"Cleaning up last night's mess." He could hear the cute little smirk in her voice.

"I hope it brings back good memories."

"Mm-hmm, that and the sore muscles you left me with."

"Hey, mine are sore too."

She laughed. "Well, good. At least I'm not suffering alone. So a game tomorrow afternoon, then where to?"

"We're headed to Vegas for a few days. From there, it's southern California, and we work our way north to Vancouver. When we're done there, we head home." *And I can't wait.* "How about you? What are your big plans for the week?"

"My usual sixteen-hour days at the office, where I'll hopefully slay a few dragons and earn a shiny golden penny."

"I have a feeling that whatever you set your mind to chase, you'll catch. Look what you've accomplished already." No doubt he was awestruck by her, but he meant every damn word. "You'll get that account you want so badly."

"Thanks," she sighed. "Not sure how bad I want it anymore, though, and that worries me."

Mac walked out of the bathroom, threw himself on the bed, and started playing with his phone.

Blake turned his back on the goalie and dropped his voice, a few alarm bells ringing in his head over what M had said. "Why? I mean, why wouldn't you want it anymore?"

"I don't know. Being at Steadman's opened my eyes a little, and I'm not sure I like what I saw."

This was a surprise. "What did you see?"

"My future?" It came out as a question.

Concern and intrigue twined inside of him. Concern because he detected vulnerability in her voice, and intrigue because he wanted to learn what she thought and why. He realized he wanted her to run to him with her problems. "What's in that future?" he prodded.

She let out a long exhale. "Very little control over my own life. A lot of bowing and scraping, long hours doing other people's bidding while I sacrifice my personal time. And after I've paid my dues, I earn a partnership in a giant wheel and become part of what perpetuates it. I thought that's what I wanted. It's what I've worked so hard for. But now? The blinders are slipping. I'm seeing it up close, and I'm not so sure it's for me." She paused for breath. "I'm sorry. I didn't mean to get all maudlin on you. I just ... I guess you're my Fiona substitute."

Ranking the same status as M's best friend swelled his chest with something warm, fuzzy, and prideful. "Hmm ... so does this mean I have to wear heels and talk in a high, squeaky voice?" He glanced over his shoulder at Mac, who seemed to be ignoring him, though a telltale quirk at one corner of his mouth told a different story. *Bastard.*

M burst into a fit of giggles, and Blake's chest ballooned a little more. He'd made her laugh, and he'd pulled her from a bleak place. "That's my girl," he murmured, unsure she could hear him.

"First of all, you goof, Fiona doesn't talk in a high, squeaky voice, and second of all, she only wears heels for special occasions. She'll be here for Thanksgiving, and you can see for yourself if ... if you want to. No pressure, though."

He chuckled. "Okay. No heels and no high-pitching. And yeah, I want to." *And I want you to meet Amanda.* Not his mom so much. His mom might send M running for the nearest exit.

"Phew!" she mocked. "Glad to hear you won't go changing that voice." Her own tone dropped into the smoky range. "I like it just the way it is. Kinda low and sexy. That rumble does funny things to certain parts of me."

*Oh Jesus!* His cock jumped, and he bent at the waist, placing his elbows on his knees to hide his growing problem. "Really? I'd like to hear more about that, but right now I'm—"

"Oh shit! You're sharing a room with someone, aren't you?"

"Yep."

She giggled. "Okay. No more sexy talk for you, big guy. Don't want to embarrass you."

"Might be too late for that." He grinned like an idiot. He'd never had anyone to call before, and he liked it. A lot. Liked the idea that someone who gave a shit might be waiting for him to come home. A curly-haired, silver-eyed someone that he gave a shit about in return. A hell of a lot. "But maybe save it for later?"

"I can do that. Is it okay to say I miss you?"

*Hell yeah.* "Why wouldn't it be?"

"We haven't known each other very long, and things feel like they might be moving a little ... fast."

"Not sure the time matters as long as we're both on the same page. For what it's worth, I feel the same way."

A pillow sailed from the other bed and pegged Blake in the head. "Oh, for fuck's sake, stop talking in code and get it over with already!" Mac grumbled. "Pansy-ass."

"What was that?" M asked.

Blake glanced over his shoulder. "*That* was my roommate. Bit of a jackass, if you ask me. But all goalies are weird."

"Oh! You're rooming with Dana McPherson?" He could pick out the pretty blush in her voice and wished he could see it in her cheeks. "I'll let you go."

"Okay. Call or text me if you need anything." *What the hell does* that *mean?* He had no idea why he said it, only that it felt natural coming out of his mouth.

When he hung up, Mac cocked an eyebrow at him. "Can I assume you took my advice and decided to go after the girl? Or was that a guy? You *were* talking about high heels and shit I don't wanna know about. Next time take it out in the hall or the bathroom, dude."

Blake chucked the pillow back at him. "Asshole. None of your business, but it was a ... woman." *Not a girl. A very hot woman.*

"Yeah? Do I know the unlucky lady?"

"Yeah, I think you do. Mia knows her for sure."

"Mia? Oh Christ. Please tell me it's not her crazy mind-fuck sister."

Blake snickered. "Nah, I think you've told us all enough scary stories that no one would go near her." His dick back under control, Blake reclined, lacing his hands under his head as he stared at the popcorn ceiling. "So when did you first know Mia was, you know, the right one?"

"Shit, I don't know. Never really thought about it." Mac turned on the TV and lowered the volume on a basketball game. "Maybe when she was the only woman I could think about? Like I said before, I couldn't get her out of my mind—like a damn tune that gets stuck in your head. Pleasant, but it doesn't go away, and it's distracting as hell." Mac chuckled, a knowing gleam in his eye. "When I met Mia, I wasn't looking for anything beyond a little fun. But when you least expect it ... Let's just say I was smart enough to realize women like her are rare. I mean, she was someone I could really talk to, be myself with, let down my guard. But first I had to convince myself she was the one, *then* I had to convince *her*. *That*, bro, took some dedication." He shook his head, though his grin remained intact. "Totally worth it. Wish I'd met her sooner." His eyes glazed over for a split second before he asked, "So who is she?"

"Paige Miller's attorney."

"Michaela? That cute little thing with the dark fuzzy hair?"

Something toothy roared inside of Blake, and he went into defender mode, something he'd only ever done on a smaller scale with Amanda. "It's not fuzzy. It's curly," he bit. *Asshole.*

"Sorry, dude," Mac chuckled. "Guess I didn't look that closely."

Blake's mind landed back in M's bed, her tight curls wound around his fingers. Normally, he'd be thinking about the upcoming game, what opposing D-men he'd go up against and their goalie's weaknesses. Instead, he was totally distracted with thoughts of her.

Yeah, he got it now.

Blake braced his stick against his knees, poised, ready for the linesman to drop the puck so he could beat the son of a bitch facing him and explode toward the net. They needed a goal. Bad. Then they needed a few more. Irritation rocketed through his veins, not helped at all by lack of sleep from his late night at a Vegas nightclub. He'd attended a buddy's bachelor party he hadn't wanted to go to in the first place, and the fatigue was catching up with him at the worst time. Plus, he hadn't talked to M for three days. He ground his back molars, ready to take out his frustration on Anaheim.

The puck finally hit the ice, and Blake crossed sticks with the other guy, battling for it, pulling it toward his wingers. Not a clean win, but Quinn managed to corral it and head toward the O-zone. He passed it back to Blake, who dished it off to T.J. T.J. one-timed it, but the goalie smothered it. *Damn it!*

Another face-off, in their zone this time, and the Anaheim center won. But Blake shoved him off the puck and stole it. Fired it. Missed wide. One of their defensemen slashed his calf, and Blake jabbed his stick into him without looking. A modicum of satisfaction spiked inside of him when he felt the impact and heard a grunt ... without the ref seeing the obvious spearing penalty.

The puck came off the boards, and Blake dashed to it. It fluttered against his blade, and he shoveled it toward the net. Somehow the damn thing snuck between a few skates and the goalie's pads and went in. A dribbler, an ugly goal, but it counted. His teammates mobbed him, and he ran the gauntlet of fist bumps along his team's bench.

"All right, boys," T.J. growled. "Let's get back to work and show Mac he doesn't have to fucking stand on his head for every win. Let's get this one for him."

They were behind three-to-two, and the clock was winding down. Coach LeBrun kept Blake's line out, and Blake leaned over for the next face-off. Eyes riveted to the ice in front of him, he whispered to the Anaheim player, "Hey, dickhead, your laces are untied."

"Fuck off, asshole. That's mites crap."

It might have been mites crap, but Blake threw him off just enough to win the draw and fire the puck at the net. The goalie smothered it again, unwilling to give up the rebound. LeBrun gave them the signal to stay out. Blake faced a different Anaheim player this time.

"Hey, Barrett," the jerk said. "Your girlfriend sucked my dick the other night."

One corner of Blake's mouth curled wickedly. "Yeah? Guess a pencil dick is a welcome change once in a while. No choke hazard," Blake fired back. He'd heard the chirping, the trash talk, his entire career. Nothing fazed him anymore. But until now, he hadn't had a *girlfriend* to get riled up about. Not that he had one now, but he was closer than he'd ever been, and the thought of M on her knees with someone else—

He understood how guys got thrown off their game. Not that it mattered because he won the face-off. And carried the puck to the net, squaring himself up to the goalie, *looking* at the goalie, like he was going to shoot it himself, only to pass it to Quinn, who one-timed it. Before the netminder could react to the pass, the puck was in the back of the net.

*Yes!*

In the end, the Blizzard squeaked out a win in an overtime shootout, with Blake scoring a perfectly placed shot top-shelf, earning him the number-one star of the game. Nice, but earning the two points was what really counted. Come tomorrow, everyone would forget, including him. Jubilation from the locker room extended to the plane, where teammates slapped Blake's back repeatedly—even Gage Nelson, who'd given up his spot on the first line and might not be able to take it back for a while. He seemed to have no hard feelings, though it had to be tough. No, Gage, one of the alternate captains, was all about the team, which was why he was a locker room leader.

The only guy who didn't show enthusiasm was Fergs, sulking in a seat a few rows back. He'd only seen five minutes of ice time on the fourth line, but Blake couldn't be bothered trying to soothe the guy's ego. It was his own damn fault he was playing like he was ten strides behind.

When Blake finally got a few moments to himself, he plunked down in a seat and checked his phone. His heart kicked up when he read a text from M. *First star! Good job, big guy. You put the team on your back tonight. Very impressive.*

Wow. The fact she had not only watched but was making something out of his effort added an extra slap to his happy.

Blake: *You still awake, Curvy?*

MW: *For a few more minutes. Thought I was Curly?*

Blake: *Curvy and curly. Best of both worlds.* He couldn't stop himself and added, *You were impressed, huh?*

MW: *Very impressed. No lie, that was kinda hot.*

Blake: *Do I get a special prize when I get home?*

MW: *Could be.*

The little tease. But he loved it.

Blake: *We still have a few games to go. What do I get if I score a hat trick?*

MW: *How about me in your jersey? And nothing else?*

A groan rumbled in his chest. Shit. Now he was as hard as the metal struts holding the plane's wheels. At this rate, he'd either wind up with blue balls or he'd have to head straight to the shower as soon as they reached their hotel room in San Jose.

Blake: *Tempting as that is, how about you in those heels you wore to your boss's dinner ... and nothing else?*

MW: *You're a better hockey player than you are a negotiator.*

Blake: *???*

MW: *A hat trick is three goals. If I were in your skates, I'd be bargaining for the jersey, the heels, AND a third fantasy.*;-D

Fuck yes! His giddy mind raced with the possibilities. *M in nothing but whipped cream. In nothing but a chain belt. In nothing but a leather thong. Do they make leather thongs?* He was so intent on those possibilities and the ache in his pants that he paid no attention to what was going on around him. As he prepared to tap out a response from the depths of his dirty mind, his phone was swiped from his hand.

"What do we have here?" Ferguson sniggered. "Sexting? No wonder I couldn't get ahold of you! You were busy banging someone."

"Give me that!" Blake bellowed, flailing at Ferguson's arm, but Ferguson easily stepped out of his reach.

His eyes scrolled over the screen, his smirk growing. "Cute. Maybe I should send this chick a message for you, Bear. Who is this anyway? Who's MW?"

Panic welled inside of Blake, and he coiled, ready to launch himself over the back of his seat. He stopped mid-spring when the phone was wrested from Ferguson's grip.

"MW stands for 'Mystery Woman,' dickhead," Dave Grimson snapped. Stormy eyes drilled enough holes through Ferguson to turn him into a slice of Swiss cheese. Their captain tossed the phone back to Blake.

Blake gulped. "Thanks, man."

"Protect that shit, rookie. Good game, by the way." Grimson gave him a nod and sat back down in his seat.

Blake wasn't sure if protecting that shit meant the phone, M's identity, or the relationship. And the fact he hadn't been a rookie for years wasn't a point he was about to argue with the guy who'd not only thrown him another compliment but who'd saved his—or M's—ass.

The announcement to turn off their electronics came over the speakers, and Blake quickly typed one last message to her: *Too many fantasies where you're concerned. Picking one takes a lot more thought. Gotta turn off our phones, but you can bet your beautiful ass I'll be contemplating this all the way to San Jose. 'Night, Curvy.*

Blake shuddered at the close call, and a fresh wave of panic rose up inside him. Mac knew who M was. He needed to talk to him, tonight, and ask him to keep quiet until Blake could finally tell Ferguson. And that confession had to happen very soon.

# Chapter 23

# HAT TRICK

Michaela checked her watch. God, she was exhausted. Her bed called to her, but at 10:00 p.m., she still had loose ends to tie up—loose ends that were the remnants from the disaster that had blown up before her shuttered eyes this morning.

For weeks, nothing had gone right at work. Misdirected emails, computer glitches, and a variety of inexplicable oddities had plagued her and left her with egg on her face she couldn't even explain. For instance, sending a contract meant for one client to a different client. Only April's anal meticulousness had prevented the contract, and all its confidential details, from actually going out.

But this morning's disaster du jour? Neither she nor April had seen it coming, but how could they have? That question had been rolling around in her head since the debacle. Things had been tilting out of control beyond her line of sight, like two stars colliding in the universe. How would you know doom was on your doorstep until long after the actual explosion? And these weren't errors she could blame on solar flares or other astrological anomalies.

Her phone pinged, and her heart beat a little faster only to plummet to its regular rhythm when she saw it was April, not Blake. He'd been gone seven days, and while they communicated here and there, she missed the hell out of him. His smile. His intent look when she confided in him. His silly trivia. His deep timbre. His hands. His mouth on hers. His way of making her feel safe, which was weird after only knowing him a month.

Maybe it was better he was on the road. Him being down the hall would have been a distraction, and she wouldn't have been able to see him anyway—not with the ridiculous workload that had increased tenfold in the past week. At times it felt as though she was being set up for failure. Was it humanly possible to juggle all the plates they kept tossing at her? Whoever "they" were. No one seemed to know how the assignments wound up in *her* lap, and the other oddity was that she seemed to be the only one in the firm experiencing the inexplicable string of bad luck.

She read April's text: *I'm calling it a night. You need to do the same, boss. You're no good to anyone when you're running on fumes.*

April was right, but Michaela didn't have the luxury of indulging her need for sleep. A familiar push-pull twanged deep inside her chest. April had been her rock, and Michaela was beyond grateful. At the same time, April was being lashed by the squalls that Michaela had been riding simply by being her assistant. Guilt by association, though April insisted it was her choice to see it through.

Another text chimed, and her heart lifted. Instead of replying, she tapped the phone icon and Fiona picked up on the first ring. "Oh good, you *are* awake! I was hoping I'd catch you before you turned in."

"Not turning in anytime soon, Fi. But you're a lovely reason to take a break."

"Where are you?"

"I'm at home."

"What's going on, Micky-Dub? You sound ... not good."

Michaela cocked an elbow on her desk and dropped her forehead in her palm. "I wish I knew. This morning one of the partners came roaring into my office demanding to know why I wasn't at some deposition that'd been scheduled months ago.

Problem was no one told me, and it's not even in my wheelhouse. It was a family law case."

"The whoever did the scheduling screwed up, right?"

"That's what I thought too, but when April checked, not only was it on the schedule, but there was a stack of other deadlines I'd been assigned that I had no clue about. April spent the morning rearranging and trying to figure out how everything got so twisted, but she hasn't been able to unravel the mess yet."

Fiona's voice to a whisper. "Are you in danger of losing your job?"

"I'm on shaky ground, but I don't think so—not yet—but getting the Fenton account is looking more like a pipe dream. Not only does this disaster give the firm a big black eye, but I can't help but feel guilty about these poor clients who got shafted."

"But it doesn't sound like you had anything to do with it. It sounds more like gremlins in the scheduling system to me."

"I'm not so sure, Fi. One woman called and chewed me out, then started bawling about losing custody of her kids. It wasn't even my case, but then April checked, and the file was in my cabinet. How did it get there? I swear, I'd never seen it before." Michaela blew out an exasperated breath. "Maybe I'm losing my mind."

"Gaslight."

"What?"

"The movie *Gaslight*, where the husband—I think it was Charles Boyer—poisons Ingrid Bergman and stages these scenes to make her think she's lost it. Watch it. It's a great movie."

"Um, okay." *Not that watching a movie is going to help me right now, Fi.*

"Not that watching the movie is going to help you right now, Mick."

Michaela stifled a laugh. "So Thanksgiving. You and James are still staying here, right?"

"That's the plan. Do we get to meet the hot hockey player?"

"I think so. I hope so."

"Is everything all right on that end?"

"Yes, I guess so. I mean, it feels like everything else in my life right now. Temporary. Just like my job, just like this apartment. It's a blip on the racetrack of life."

"What makes you say it's temporary?"

Though her friend couldn't see her, Michaela shook her head. "I don't know. Maybe it's just that it's too new and shiny. Our relationship, if you can call it that, consists of a month of knowing each other, some phone calls and texts, and a few sessions of really hot sex."

"No long conversations or laughter?"

"Oh. Lots of that too."

"Apparently, the sex made you forget. How hot is it?"

Michaela fanned herself with her hand, and her parts south contracted. "So hot the sheets not only went up in flames, but all my leg hairs were singed off."

"Ooh, better than shaving."

Michaela burst out with a laugh. "Thanks for making me laugh, Fi."

"Always, Micky-Dub. I can't wait to meet this guy. Hot sex or not, I am dying to find out if he's good enough for you. If he's not, he's out."

"Do I have any say?"

"Nope. You don't always have the best judgment when it comes to men. I mean, c'mon. Five years with Anders? No one else would have put up with him that long."

"Except his wife," Michaela huffed. The words didn't sound as bitter as they once had.

"Not so fast. They haven't been married that long yet."

"True. Okay, you can interrogate Blake. Just leave me the option of using him as a boy toy if you decide he can't have the job of being my soul mate, deal?"

"He's that good?"

"Let's just say he's eager to please, and something about him brings out the teacher in me."

"Ooh, naughty girl!"

"The role reversal feels pretty damn good after letting Anders run our sex life all those years."

"I love it! I think I'm gonna like this guy for you."

"Here's a piece of trivia for you, Fi. Did you know the average man lasts less than six minutes from penetration to ejaculation?"

"I did not know that. But I'm guessing the average man believes that time is closer to thirty minutes."

"Actually, the average man self-reports it as two times longer than it actually takes. The average woman, by contrast, needs thirteen minutes to orgasm."

"Sounds like a mismatch to me."

"Sounds like a damn good reason for foreplay to me," Michaela chuckled.

"So your hockey player ... is he *average*?"

"No, I'd say he was one of those optimistic types—only he can back it up." *And he can go again and again and again.* Michaela suddenly felt light-headed.

"Okay. I'll go easy on him so I can give him the Fiona seal of approval."

A beep interrupted the conversation. "He's calling me now, Fi. Gotta run! Love you!"

"Love you too, Mick."

Michaela hit the green button. "Blake?"

"Hey, M. Did I wake you?"

"No, I was just finishing a call with Fiona." *Were your ears burning?*

"Oh good. I wanted to catch you while I have a few minutes to myself. What did you think of the game?"

Oh crap. With everything else going on, she hadn't watched it. "I didn't catch it all. It's ... it's really stressful when you have a friend playing." She palmed her forehead. When he didn't answer right away, she said, "You still there?"

"Uh, yeah. Sorry, brain fart." He cleared his throat. "I'm a *friend*?"

A flush heated her cheeks as the incredulity in his tone registered. "Well, yeah. What would you call you?" Again, he didn't answer, so she rushed into the silence. "You're the guy with the jaded view of the, shall we say, long game, aren't you?"

He dropped his voice to a near whisper. "You might be changing my mind about that."

Her belly did a few flips. "Really?"

"Yeah, really. I—shit." Muffled noises came from the other end, as though he'd covered the mouthpiece and was talking to someone else. Then he was back. "Hey, uh, the guys are heading out, and I—"

"Oh. You're going out?"

"Yeah, well, they want to celebrate my... You didn't watch at all, did you?"

She hung her head and shook it. "I'm sorry, Blake. Work has been a bitch, and I—"

"You're not still *working*, are you?"

A defeated sigh whooshed out, and her shoulders folded in around her. "I am." Tempting as it was to explain why—and unload some of her worries at the same time—she bit back the impulse. He would either try to shoulder her load, solve her troubles, or both. Which was kinda sweet, but he had something to celebrate, and she didn't want to dampen his mood.

"Well, you'd better finish it up because I scored a hatter tonight, and you're going to need to take some time off to deliver on those promises. I'm bringing you a jersey. You supply the rest."

*Ooh, he's taking charge!* She could practically *hear* his eyebrows waggle, and her insides puddled liked melted candle wax. "Oh, I'll supply the rest all right." *Whatever that is.* "You best be ready, big guy." She hoped her voice carried the sultriness she was going for and not the squeak her ears picked up.

"No, M," he rumbled. "*You* be ready. I'm bringing my A-game. Bank on it. And part of what you're supplying is the canned whipped cream. I hear Costco sells a three-pack. Might want to get a couple of those." And then he was gone.

Tingles of anticipation rippled through her body, zinging every finger and toe, making her feel lighter than she had since he'd left. Only three more days until she'd see him again. They promised to be the longest three days of her life.

Blake stretched his legs under the table and slouched in his seat, making his lap a smaller target. Maybe he could disappear and the girls would leave him alone. Except Ferguson kept sending them over, telling them to "put a smile on my buddy's face." It had been borderline annoying before, but now it was fucking obnoxious. And he couldn't say a damn thing because Coach LeBrun had just delivered the bad news after tonight's game that Ferguson was a healthy scratch for the rest of the road trip. Fergs needed this celebration more than Blake did. If this party hadn't been in his honor, Blake would have been back in his hotel room by now, visualizing everything he planned to do to M when he got home. He'd thrown a lot of bravado her way, and he intended to back it up. A smile twitched his lips.

A meaty hand grabbed him by the nape, yanking him out of his pleasant fantasy. That hand belonged to Fergs, who slid in beside him. "'Bout fucking time you cracked a smile! Did that pink-haired hottie help you get rid of your surly attitude? I heard she can suck the chrome off a bumper."

"No, and I wouldn't know. I was just thinking about something else." Blake slugged down some of his club soda.

Ferguson's eyebrows bounced. "Or some*one* else. You've got it bad for this mystery woman of yours. You ever going to tell me who she is?"

Blake stared at him for a beat, tempted to come clean, but this wasn't the time or place. The news about M would wait. "I don't know if it's going anywhere, so there's no point in revealing any names just yet."

A pretty brunette in a micro dress climbed onto Ferguson's lap. "Who's your friend, Owen?"

Ferguson slid an arm around her waist and clamped his other hand on her bare thigh. “He’s why we’re here, but forget him, baby. He gave his balls to a woman to hold for him.”

A salacious smile curved her overdone lips. “Lucky her. I wouldn’t mind holding his balls for a while.” Staring pointedly at Blake, she twirled a straw in her pink drink and sucked it hard enough to hollow her cheeks before making a big show of licking her lips.

Ferguson chuckled and arched his eyebrows at Blake as if to say, “We got ourselves a live wire here.” He wiggled his finger at her in a come-here motion, and when she leaned down, he whispered something in her ear and kissed her.

“Okay.” She giggled and slid off his lap, and he handed her a couple of twenties.

Ferguson watched her ass sway until his view was blocked. “She’s hot. Kinda reminds me of Michaela.”

*What? Oh hell no.* “She’s *nothing* like Michaela!” Blake pointed in the direction the girl had gone. “She’s a bitch in heat, and she’d let herself be fucked by anything resembling a dick.” His pulse pounded, and he began drumming the table.

Ferguson looked from Blake’s tapping fingers to his face and frowned. “What the fuck is eating you? I don’t get it. You’re a first-line center on one of the best damn teams in the league, you’re on pace to put up the best numbers of your career, and you’ve got your panties in a wad because some chick thinks you’re hot shit and wants to suck your cock? Loosen up, bro! Life’s pretty fucking spectacular for you right now. Enjoy the ride.” He shook his head, tilted his beer bottle to his lips, and chugged its contents.

Blake dragged a hand across his jaw and exhaled. “Hey, I’m sorry. You’re right. Guess I’m a little tired.”

Before long, the skanky brunette was back with a few beers for Fergs, another club soda for Blake, and a tall blue drink for herself. *Pink and blue. She’s got the baby drinks going.* She slid back into Ferguson’s lap and dropped her arms around his shoulders. They went at each other’s mouths, all tongue and teeth.

Ferguson slipped his hand in the V of her low-cut neckline, and she moaned.

*Jesuuuus!* Blake dropped his head and pulled out his phone. Scrolled to his favorite picture of M. *Yeah, gorgeous. You, me, and my hand have a date back in my hotel room as soon as I can get out of here.* He caressed the image on the screen with his thumb. He felt eyes on him, and when he looked up, Ferguson had both hands inside the brunette's dress, one squeezing her tit, and the other one up her skirt. She was grinding against his hand, and they were still sucking face, but Ferguson's eyes were on Blake's phone.

Blake's absurd thought process leapt from *great multitasker* to *bastard.* He placed the phone facedown on the table, and when he looked up again, all Ferguson's attention seemed to be on getting the girl off. *His eyes just strayed for a moment. He didn't see it.*

Blake sipped at his drink, locking out the show to his left that was making him squirm in his seat. Sometimes he wished he *did* drink regularly.

Maybe looking at M's picture had put him in this state. To distract himself, he turned to thoughts of his best friend. When had Ferguson become so careless and cavalier? Yes, this girl wanted it, but did Ferguson's ego trump everyday decorum? *He should have taken her someplace private.* When had he transformed into the second coming of Wyatt Tompkins?

Mercifully, the brunette seemed to get what she needed, and she stood, rearranged her clothing, and sauntered away, shooting Fergs a coy look over her shoulder. He made a jacking-off motion above his groin, and she giggled and blew him a kiss.

His eyes darted to Blake. "Don't worry. She's coming back to take care of me."

"Wasn't worried," Blake mumbled.

"You enjoy the show?"

"Not particularly."

"Some girls get off on doing it in public. I'm merely obliging a fantasy. You could join the party, you know, instead of sitting over there with a stick up your ass. I don't mind sharing, and I'm sure she wouldn't complain."

Blake's stomach rolled over, and he made a scoffing noise. "No, thanks."

Ferguson leaned back in his chair. "When did you become such a prude?"

Blake looked him square in the eye. "I haven't changed. When did you become such an asshole?"

Ferguson broke out a smirk Blake wanted to knock off his mug. Just then, T.J. caught his eye and motioned him over. Blake needed to get away from the stench, and he stood to join T.J. and a few other guys who were laughing at something on someone's phone.

T.J. pointed. "Check this out, dude. You're all over the air. ESPN, *NHL Tonight*, fucking everywhere!"

"Must be a slow news night," Blake replied dryly. He watched the replay a few times and grinned in spite of himself. Had M at least caught the replays? God, he hoped so. Maybe he could send her a link. He reached for his phone, but it wasn't in his back pocket. His eyes dashed to the table where Fergs still sat, alone, and he breathed a sigh of relief. He ambled back over, picked up the device, and slid it into his back pocket before casually taking a sip of his soda. The bubbles scraped his parched throat.

Fergs flicked his eyes up to him. "You got it bad. You're infected with it." He huffed a mirthless laugh. "Not that I can blame you."

Sirens started up in Blake's head. When he didn't rise to the bait, Fergs continued. "If I didn't know any better, I'd say you've either designated yourself M's personal bodyguard or you've got a serious hard-on for her. 'Course with as fine as she is, she gives me a hard-on too."

Blake's head jerked like he'd been slapped, and he clenched his fists at his sides, his whole body vibrating.

"Yeah, like that," Ferguson drawled. "It's like I hit a hot button every time I mention her." Ferguson stared at him for long beats. "You don't, do you?"

"I don't what?"

Ferguson didn't break his gaze, but his eyes narrowed. "Have a hard-on for M? Because that would not be cool."

*Fuck, I hate it when he calls her 'M'!* Blake tipped his glass back, but it was empty. "No? And why's that?" he near-growled.

"You know why, asshole. I saw her first." Ferguson leaned back in his chair, pursing his lips.

"And did squat about it," Blake tossed back. "Well, nothing except lie, that is."

"About what?" Ferguson demanded.

"About me taking your place the night of her work dinner. I guess technically you didn't lie to her because you never *told her*! But you sure as shit lied to me when you said you'd told her I was her date that night, *and* you lied to me about asking her to the brunch."

"You were all over my ass, and I was sick of it." An audience of their teammates began closing in. "So I haven't asked her to the brunch yet. I'll do it right now." He started scrolling through his contacts while the statement hung there, loaded and heavy.

Blake's back molars ground against one another. "You might have seen her first, but you switched to team Tracy. Which made *Michaela* fair game. And she's already got a date for the brunch—me." He jabbed his thumb against his chest.

Ferguson abruptly stood, facing Blake, a look of disbelief on his face. "Fuck me, you cocksucker! I told you I was working my way up to it. So while I'm doing that, you roll in like a fucking red tide and steal her away."

Blake squared himself up. "I didn't steal her away. You've been nothing but *working your way up to it* ever since you met her. I guess she decided she wanted the guy who actually made a move."

"*You?* You're a fucking joke," Ferguson chuffed. "She's your mystery woman, isn't she?" As if a light had winked on, he let out a wild, high-pitched laugh. "MW doesn't stand for 'Mystery Woman.' It stands for 'Michaela Wagner.' And here I thought you had my back." He shook his head. "I don't fucking believe it. What the hell could she possibly see in you anyway?"

Blake got his breathing under control and braced himself for the next buffeting. This storm had been a long time brewing. "Let's just get this over with."

Ferguson turned his head to him, venom in his eyes and his voice. "What makes her different from the pink-haired bitch or that girl in my lap who wants to go down on you so bad she's practically drooling? What is so fucking special about *M* that you betrayed a bro, huh? She suck your dick better than it's ever been sucked before? Or is it the way her ass looks with the sheet draped over it? It's a mighty fine ass, I'll grant you that."

Blake was on the verge of exploding, and he held himself back by a razor-thin margin. This was neither the time nor the place.

But Ferguson wasn't done.

"I get it. No man could keep a sane thought with those sweet tits of hers; they're some of the finest I've seen. But I don't want your—"

Blake's fist crashed into Ferguson's jaw, knocking him backward on his ass. He didn't remember making a conscious decision to hit Ferguson, didn't remember cocking his fist. He was only aware of the angry buzz in his head, the veil of red clouding his vision, and the overwhelming tsunami of fury swamping him, urging him to hit Ferguson again and again and again.

Fist primed for another hit, he became aware of loud voices around him, of someone pulling his arm back, of people gasping—and of Ferguson turtled on the floor, arms covering his head.

A hand wrapped around Blake's neck, dragging him backward, and T.J.'s commanding voice in his ear said, "I can think of better ways to celebrate a hat trick, Barrett. Now chill the fuck out. I'm getting you the hell out of here."

Blake hunched forward in his chair, locking out the stark office. The waiting was agony, though when Coach LeBrun finally walked in and took a seat across the desk from him, Blake wasn't sure getting it over with was any better.

Behind him, like sentinels, stood the captains: Grimson, T.J., and Nelson. LeBrun seemed to take for-fucking-ever to lower himself into his seat. He leaned forward, elbows on the desk, his hands steepled in front of him.

"Want to tell me what happened last night?"

*No, not really*. "Ferguson and I had a disagreement."

"About what?"

Blake's jaw tightened. When he didn't respond, LeBrun straightened and let out a long exhalation. "You two have been friends a long time, so I don't think it's about your changing roles in hockey. Friends usually work that stuff out without having to throw punches. It wasn't alcohol since you're no drinker, so that leaves one possibility: you fought over a woman."

*How the fuck does he know?*

As if Coach had read Blake's inner thoughts, he said, "I can't think of anything else that would make you lose your mind the way I hear you did. You have an edge when you play, but you keep it on a tight leash. Women ... they have a way of snapping that leash and laughing at us idiots as the leash goes sailing into a bottomless pit. I gather it was one of the ladies at the club?"

Blake shook his head.

"Oh fuck. That's even worse."

Coach hadn't been there, but Grimson and T.J. had. If they'd been paying attention, they still wouldn't have known who the catalyst was at the center of this shit-show, and Blake was not about to reveal her identity. That was between him and Ferguson.

But he *had* snapped. Like he'd never snapped before. Like he'd never imagined himself capable of snapping. The thing of it was Ferguson could have said whatever the hell he wanted about Blake or about the chick he'd been finger-fucking last night—none of that mattered. But he'd had M's name on his filthy tongue, and goddamn it, he'd seen her picture. The intimate portrait Blake never should never have taken in the first place, meant for his greedy eyes only. No! Ferguson thinking about M, seeing M ... Blake's guts were bunched in an ungainly wad.

"This thing between you and Ferguson"—Coach's words jerked Blake from his whirlwind of miserable thoughts—"cannot bleed over to your team. It will not be tolerated. You're a hell of a center, Barrett, and because you've never done anything like this before, I'm not suspending you, but do *not* push me."

"But Coach, you don't understand." God, Blake sounded pathetic, even to his own ears. Had he become one of those whipped dudes who'd turned over his man card? *"He gave his balls to a woman to hold for him."*

Coach dropped a hand to the desk and began drumming with his fingers. "That's just it, Barrett. I *do* understand because I've been in those skates." He straightened and cleared his throat as if suddenly uncomfortable he'd revealed too much. "Any damages sustained by the club last night will come out of *your* paycheck. Now get out of here."

Blake tucked his tail between his legs and scrambled from the office. When he walked into the hotel room, Mac looked up at him from where he reclined on his bed. "You still on this road trip?"

Blake sank onto his mattress and released a long exhale. "Yep." He flopped back on his bed, holding back a humorless laugh. At least it was out in the open now.

Three days later, Blake walked into the condo on Ferguson's heels. The tension filling the Range Rover on the ride home from the arena had been so thick Blake could have practically chewed it. Ferguson had yet to apologize for the crude way he'd talked about M, and Blake hadn't uttered a single "sorry" for the black eye, split lip, and lacerated cheek he'd given his ex-buddy.

Fergs stormed to his side of the condo, and before Blake could retreat to his, he was back, crashing through the great room with a big-ass suitcase.

"What are you doing?" Blake huffed.

"What does it look I'm doing, asswipe?" Ferguson didn't stop, just barreled into the laundry room, where he made all kinds of racket.

Arms crossed, Blake leaned against the doorframe and watched as his roommate—correction: soon-to-be *ex*-roommate—stuffed the suitcase with laundry. Clean or dirty, Blake hadn't a clue. Fergs probably didn't either.

"Looks like you're packing the contents of the laundry room," Blake replied blandly.

Ferguson, who was stooped over the bag, shot him a glare over his shoulder. "Guess you're not as stupid as you look, genius. For your information, this is *my* shit I'm packing."

"Did I say it wasn't?"

Ferguson stood upright and crossed his arms, mirroring Blake's stance. He flexed his chest. "Don't you have something better to do than stand there and harass me? Haven't you fucking done enough?" He pointed to his face.

Blake ignored the questions. "Where are you going?"

Fergs went back to packing. "Anywhere but here. And before you start in on the rent, I've got it covered through the end of December. After that, you'll need to find yourself a new punching bag."

Blake rolled his eyes. "For fuck's sake, stop acting like a prima donna. We've had plenty of go-rounds where I ended up with a face like yours."

Ferguson straightened again and turned, his index finger cocked. "One major difference: they were *fair* fights, not unprovoked, blindside hits in the middle of a fucking nightclub where people are drinking and having a good time. Except you, because you're too fucking perfect to drink. Maybe if you let loose once in a while, you wouldn't walk around with your nose in the air and a stick up your ass."

Blake pushed from the doorframe, fists clenched at his sides. "Unprovoked? You were begging to be hit, and you know it. You must be out of your fucking mind if you think anyone would walk away from the shit you threw down about M. You were so far out of line you were in the next county. Say anything you want about me, but you leave her out of it." Blake's temper, held in check at a simmer for the better part of three days, heated to a rolling boil as if his burner had just been cranked.

"Who's the real prima donna, Mr. Twisted Fucking Wrister? You're so in love with your own press you can't pull your head out of your ass long enough to recognize you got where you are by sheer luck." He jabbed his thumb into his chest "And because you had—*had*—a friend willing to stick up for your ass when you were too big a pussy to do it yourself. You wouldn't be where you are if I hadn't fought your battles as a kid. Christ, you make me sick."

Blake's brain streamed but didn't process all Ferguson's words, and he stood rooted where he was as Ferguson returned to chucking clothes into the suitcase. Fury and misery and shame brewed inside of him, a toxic sludge that blunted his ability to think or move.

"Something else you want?" Ferguson snarled from where he was, bent over his task. "Because if you don't mind, I'd rather do my business without an audience."

Blake snapped out of his fog. "Knock yourself out. See you at practice."

"Actually, you won't."

*What?*

As if he'd heard Blake's silent question, Fergs continued. "Coach informed me he's shipping me down to the minors for what he affectionately calls a little R&R. It'll officially be called a reconditioning stint, but you and I both know what it really is," Ferguson said bitterly.

An arrow of sympathy struck Blake, but it quickly passed through him. Ferguson had sabotaged himself. For whatever reason, he hadn't kept his head in the game, and ultimately that's what a pro did. He locked out the other bullshit and kept his focus on his club and on winning. Period. No gray area.

"Good luck with that," Blake said as he retreated to his bedroom, Ferguson's grunt chasing him.

An hour or so later, when he heard the front door close, Blake exited his room, where he'd paced the entire time. He was exhausted yet keyed up. When he ducked his head into Ferguson's bedroom and bath, he noted their empty contents. Not that Fergs had weighed himself down with a lot of stuff to begin with, and not that he'd packed any furniture in his suitcase, but the family pictures and bits of his hockey past were gone. So were Ferguson's pillows and the quilt his grandma had made for him. The necessities that turned a space into home.

Ambling into the kitchen, Blake spotted an unopened bottle of bourbon sitting on top of a note. Ferguson had scrawled, "Take a swig once in a while and learn to be human again."

Blake scoffed and crumpled the note, lobbing it into the trash. *Asshole. You didn't fight all my battles for me. Jerk. And I don't need alcohol to loosen up.*

He slid onto a barstool and stared at the bottle, turning over questions in his head. Was he a prima donna? A perfectionist? A pussy? No. Ferguson had been lashing out, out of his mind. Did Blake deserve some blame? Maybe, but Ferguson was jealous, and he had pushed too far, damn it. He was always pushing too far, and Blake had tolerated it all these years out of some sense of loyalty. Except that loyalty had been deserved once upon a time, and things had changed. People changed, and not always for the better.

His ponderings twisted in on themselves, and his temper spiked again.

"Christ, I'm never getting to sleep." His eyes strayed in the general direction of M's condo. Would she answer if he knocked on her door? Even if she did, it was after midnight, she was probably asleep, and he was in a foul mood. Not a winning combination.

Instead, he studied the bottle. He *liked* the taste of good bourbon. He liked beer and wine too. What was wrong with that? Enjoying the stuff didn't make him a drunk, though it often made him sleepy. He could use a little bit of sleepy right about now.

He stood, plucked out a glass, opened the bottle, and poured a measure of bourbon. A small sip first, then he threw the rest back, letting the liquid burn a satisfying path down his throat. His sore muscles began to let go. Yeah, alcohol definitely had its purposes.

After consuming a second pour, his spiraling thoughts stopped their tight tailspin, taking on a less frenzied pace—like a lazy whirlpool—that made them easier to examine one by one ... or put aside altogether.

Yeah, he was feeling better now. The grip on his anger wasn't exactly loosening, but the anger itself was a dull thud. Why didn't he drink more often? Because his mom did. Because he wanted to maintain control. But wasn't he actually *giving up* control by molding his actions around hers? Lots of people drank, and it didn't mess them up. Case in point: Michaela. Considering her size and how much vodka he'd seen her consume, she held her own just fine. Then again, maybe she was used to it. Shit, maybe she was a functioning alcoholic, and he hadn't seen it before. Tinny alarm bells clanged with the echoes of his mom. No, his mom was a *non*-functioning alcoholic. Big difference. The alarms quieted.

More brown liquid splashed into his glass, and he downed a few gulps. What had he been thinking about? Oh yeah. Michaela. He thought about M all. The. Time. What had he filled his mind with before it had been filled with her? No idea.

He had also been thinking about functioning alcoholics. Being an attorney, she had a lot of schmoozing to do, and that usually involved some form of alcohol. How many attorneys battled alcoholism? *I bet a lot of them function just fine.* Simply because a person didn't rage at others like his mom didn't mean they weren't as addicted as she was.

Time passed, and Blake sat in his dark living room, every muscle taut as he moved between philosophical discussions in his head to solutions to humanity's problems to the bad shit that had gone down between him and Ferguson. The harder he thought, the more he drank, and by 2:00 a.m., he was fucking tired and more wound up than ever. But it wasn't the bourbon.

It was because M was only a few feet down the hall, and every molecule in his body screamed for her. The bourbon should have dulled the ache, but like the rest of his emotions, it only seemed to sharpen it. He told himself he shouldn't wake her up. Besides, she'd ask about the trip, and he couldn't talk about Fergs yet. So he drank a little more, trying to declaw the pain digging into him.

# Chapter 24

# How Think Do You Drunk I Am?

Pounding on her door brought Michaela out of a deep sleep. *What the hell?*

She'd fallen asleep on her couch clothed in her jeans and sweater. Staggering to her stockinged feet, she crept toward the racket.

"M, lemme in!"

"Blake?" she hissed. "Are you drunk?"

He bellowed, "You know I don't do that shit. Now lemme in, woman!" His voice became a plea. "I miss you."

Opening the door, she ushered his staggering frame inside. He reeked of distillery fumes, and his white button-down shirt was partially undone and untucked. One sleeve was cuffed at his elbow, revealing his corded forearm. His dark dress pants were intact, but he wore only socks. His normally neat blond hair stuck out in asymmetrical tufts. In short, he resembled a bed that had been slept in for weeks without being made.

She grasped a steely bicep and, unable to get her hand around its circumference, wrapped both hands around it and pointed him toward her couch. He plopped down heavily and looked up at her with a lopsided grin plastered on his handsome face.

"When did you get home?"

"A few hours ago. Didn't want to wake you up."

"Did you go out with the boys or something before you came home?"

He shook his head slowly.

*Then why are you shit-faced?* "So you sat at your place and *drank*?" She tried, and failed, to keep the incredulity from her voice.

He did this hiss-cringe thing. "Don't tell my mom."

"You're a mess." Reaching down to stack pillows behind his back, she murmured, "Men. Why do we women put up with your nonsense?" She straightened and looked down at him, perching her hands on her hips.

He let out a high-pitched chuckle—the man equivalent of a giggle—and tossed the pillows aside. "Because you want what's between our legs. That's what Ferguson says anyway." The smile dropped from his face the moment his friend's name tumbled off his tongue, and a spectacular set of storm clouds took over his expression.

*Huh. What's that about?* He appeared to be in the advanced stages of inebriation, so chances were his signals were misfiring.

"Ferguson, Schmerguson," she scoffed. "Don't kid yourself, stud. First of all, I'd beg to differ that it's what's between *our* legs that *men* can't live without. And that thing"—she twirled her finger in a circle and pointed at his crotch—"controls what you do *way* too much. When it does your thinking for you, it gets you men in a hell of a lot of trouble."

His lips curved up in a lazy, cocksure smile. "Did you just call me a stud?"

She rolled her eyes. "That's what you got out of that?"

In a surprise move, he lunged for her, and one big hand caught her thigh, making her squeak. "C'mere, M. Wanna show you how much I missed you," he mumbled.

She broke his grasp and gave his shoulder a little shove. He sank slowly against the back of the couch and listed to the side. "I doubt you could even get it up right now," she muttered to herself.

"Stay right there," she instructed. "I'm going to get you some water." *Gallons and gallons. I'd better brew up some coffee too. I have a feeling this is going to be a long night.*

Wide awake, she moved about the kitchen, filling a huge cup with water and firing up the coffee machine.

"Oh, I can get it up all right. Wanna know why?" His deep rumble caught her by surprise, and she whirled to face him leaning against a cabinet. Apparently, he had heard her muttering.

"Don't think so, no."

He barreled on anyway. "Because you're in the room, that's why. My dick knows. He has M radar, and he stands up whenever you're within sight ... or smell range. Come a little closer, and I'll show you."

Without her permission, her eyes strayed to his groin. *Oh my.* The long, thick bulge was proof he wasn't kidding. Her eyes zoomed to his. His brows waggled over evergreen eyes and a cocky smirk. Damn, he'd caught her looking, and the flush heating her cheeks broadcast her guilt.

Barely propped up, he cupped himself and executed a Michael Jackson thrust. "Don't be shy. You know you want it, babygirl."

She cinched her arms over her chest. "I am *not* your babygirl. And you need to sober up before you even *think* about pulling that thing out." How could someone so damn annoying be so cute at the same time? More importantly, why had he gotten so wasted?

"Okay, your hotness. I apologize for my poor word choice, but being around you does that to me. You scramble my brain." He exhaled a noisy breath. "Just ... lead me to your bedroom, take off your clothes, and sit on my dick. Or my face. Lady's choice. Either way, I promise I'll make you feel good."

"Gee, how's a girl to pass on a great come-on like that?" she said dryly. "Oh, I know. *Pass.*"

The smugness slid from his face. "M, I know I'm not smooth, but I've been dreaming about you all week. Just put me out of my misery. Please." His head lolled, and for an instant she thought he might fall over.

"Water first." Not that she was going to lead him anywhere but back to the couch and let him sleep it off.

After he'd chugged half his body weight in water, she did just that, tucking a pillow under his head as he flopped onto his stomach. Perched on the edge of the couch, she smoothed his hair, and he let out a long, happy sigh. She rubbed his scalp, his neck, his shoulders, and his back and chuckled at the little moans and mumbles of "so good" he emitted. Soon the only noise was his soft snoring, and she got up, poured herself a mug of coffee, and watched him from across the room, contemplating what had made him reach for the bottle. Her worry had her parking her own troubles on the back burner of her mind.

He was an enigma, and she wanted to tease out all his puzzle pieces because the mere sight of this hot mess of a man on her couch made her heart swell like it never had before. God help her, she'd only known him a month and she was in love with him.

Michaela had no idea how much time had passed when she startled awake. She was curled up in the armchair, and it was still dark out. A lone table lamp glowed, and two gleaming eyes peered at her from the couch.

Blake sat forward. "I'm sorry, I didn't mean to wake you up. I didn't even know you were there until I stumbled back to the couch."

She unfurled her body and rolled her sore neck from side to side. "Stumbled back to the couch? Where did you come from?"

"The bathroom. Someone made me drink a few gallons of water, and my bladder was ready to burst."

"Hopefully, it flushed some of that alcohol out of your system."

He nodded. "It did, but there's still a lot more in there."

"Why were you drinking?"

"I missed you. Now why don't you get your ass over here so I can stop missing you?"

Stifling a laugh, she sauntered to where he sat, bumping her knee against his thigh. He reached up, the muscles along his forearm flexing as he tugged at her. God, she loved watching all that beautiful power stretch and bunch. "I need you, M," he whispered.

She threw a leg over his lap and settled against his hard length, grinding lightly, teasingly, pushing her fingers through his mussed-up hair. She hovered her mouth over his. "Is this what you want?"

He stared into her eyes through his hooded ones. "Yeah, just like that. Except your clothes are still on." He might have looked dazed, but his hands were on full alert and they went to work, lifting the hem of her top and pulling her bra cups up in one fluid move. Fingertips dancing over her skin, he held her gaze as he hissed a breath. "So beautiful."

Was he talking about her or her breasts? Not that it mattered when a second later his tongue swiped the underside of each breast, followed by the scrape of his teeth. Meanwhile, his fingers lightly pinched and twisted and pulled at her nipples. A gasp flew from her mouth, and he raised his head to smile at her drunkenly while his fingers continued their pleasantly rough assault.

"Do you like that? I learned that in Vegas." His eyebrows bounced.

She stiffened and pushed against his shoulders to get away, but he was too quick, too strong, and he clamped down on her hips, pinning her to his hard, bulky legs before pulling her to his chest. While images of him screwing other women in a Las Vegas hotel room invaded her brain, he stroked her curls and dropped soothing kisses on her head. "Shh. That didn't come out right. It's not what you think."

Wiggling, she managed to sit somewhat upright, but there were his strong fingers on her breasts again, kneading, fondling. She pushed his hands down, off of her and onto his stomach, where they stayed. "If it's not what I think, then what exactly is it?" she snapped. "Were you getting *lessons*? Watching some sex show at a strip club? Or at one of the whorehouses?" And here she'd just admitted she loved this jackass.

His Adam's apple bobbed in his muscular neck. "Don't be like that. I only went to a strip club once with the boys, and they don't do shit like that there."

His eyes widened as he seemed to realize what he'd confessed, not that she could hold a strip club against him. He was a good-looking single guy with gobs of money, and she had no strings on him. *Oh God, strippers have strings. Did he stuff bills into their G-strings? Did his fingers graze unblemished skin? Did he buy a lap dance?* With his intense, brooding ways, he didn't strike her as the type, but she'd been proven wrong too many times before to rely on instinct.

He seemed to read her racing mind. "M, I only went because one of the guys I know from a different team is getting married. It was sort of an early bachelor party, and I couldn't not go. But nothing happened. Yeah, it was a late night, but I stuck to club soda, and I didn't touch anyone. Had absolutely no desire to. As for whorehouses, I've never been to one, never been tempted to go, and I sure as hell wasn't tempted on this trip. Some of the guys at the bachelor party, after a few drinks ... they were talking about what women like, so I paid attention." His expression was pure earnestness with a dash of dejection coloring it. He swallowed. "I wanted to surprise you, to show you I had a few moves that maybe you ... I wanted to please you in ways you might not have been pleased before."

The look on his face about broke her heart. She'd been bossy in the bedroom, hadn't she? She'd basked in the power she held over this gorgeous, powerful man and had wielded it like a conductor wielded a baton to direct the orchestra the way *he*—or she—saw fit. Maybe he wanted to claim some of that control; maybe she should let him. Maybe he had a thing or two to teach *her*. Her tummy fluttered at the thought of him taking complete charge. "So you weren't with anyone else?"

A little storm erupted on his face, like a two-year-old winding up for a tantrum. “Fuck no!”

God, she felt stupid. They hadn’t talked about exclusivity, but his words flooded sweet relief through her, and her body softened against him. One thing she understood about this man was he gave his loyalty unflinchingly.

His hands remained where they were, resting idly on his stomach. “I don’t ever want you having doubts, M. Do you believe me?” His voice was quiet, tentative. One finger traced a path from her shoulder to her wrist.

Desire kindled and caught hold, overtaking her doubts. She slid her hands into his warm calloused ones and drew them under her sweater, placing them back on her breasts. “I believe you. Now what was it you wanted to show me?”

One corner of his mouth twitched. He dragged his eyes over her, a dark glimmer lighting them with wildness. His hands slid to her hem, where he tugged.

“This is pretty, but it’s gotta go,” he said hoarsely.

She whipped the top off. Her chest was heaving, her pulse galloping. The bra was still askew, and she felt a flush of embarrassment racing up her neck as he took stock of her exposed flesh, licking his lips. His eyes flicked up to hers. “The bra too. I want to see all of you, M. Now. I’ve missed seeing you.” His voice was low and gruff, not quite a demand but a growl nonetheless.

Without a stitch of hesitation, she flung the bra over her shoulder in an act of false sexual bravado. Beneath her, his cock jumped, but he didn’t touch her; he just looked, making her blood sizzle with lust. “Yeah, like that,” he murmured.

In a surprise move that stole her breath, he flipped her on her back, his heavy body sinking atop hers as he pinned her to the couch. “Let’s christen this couch.” He hauled her hands above her head, trapping them in one of his big fists. “I want to mark you, M. Mark you with my mouth.” Eyes clouded with thunderstorms searched hers, seeking permission. Though unsure exactly what he sought permission for, she trusted him wholly. And while he wasn’t fully sober, she didn’t care. She gave him a nod, captivated by this alpha side he'd been hiding and that she desperately wanted more of.

His meaning became clear when he dropped his mouth to her breast. He began gently by licking the underside once more, and the sensation along her sensitive skin made her squirm. He nibbled lightly, then sucked hard, soothing the spot with the tip of his tongue before sucking her skin again. Her nipple furled into a tight bead, and he showed it some attention with a flick of his tongue.

"I can tell you like this," he growled. He bit down, sawing the nipple between his teeth, before returning to the hard-suck-nibble-lick action around her breast. While he tortured one breast with lips, tongue, and teeth, his free hand tormented the other one with calloused fingers, a sort of gentle-rough push-pull.

As his mouth traced a circle around her breast, he drove her to the outer reaches of pleasure where she hadn't been before. Unable to hold back her moans, she let them warble in her chest unchecked, her hips bucking as much as they could with his weight pressed against them—her silent plea for him to enter her.

He popped his head up and inspected his work. "Mmm, missed a spot, but I'll come back to it." Her thighs clenched in anticipation. His eyes grazed her chest, lifting lazily to hers. "I want you naked under me. I'm going to let your hands go so you can take off your pants, your panties, everything. But be quick about it. Then you're going to give your hands back to me. Got it?"

She nodded. He released her hands and lifted himself in a plank so she could squirm out of her bottoms under him, but her trembling hands fumbled. He didn't seem to notice—or care—because his attention was back on taking care of that spot he'd missed.

"Is this something you learned from the guys?" she rasped.

"No, this is all me. Told you, you inspire me. Now settle down. This is going to take a while."

He moved to the other breast and gave it the same tortuous treatment. Weren't his lips worn out? When he was done and she thought he might finally take off his pants and send her crashing over the edge where he'd kept her dangling, he released her hands. He used both of his to push her thighs apart and wedge his broad shoulders between them.

"Gonna mark you here too," he murmured. Then his mouth was on the tender flesh of her inner thigh, clamping down, his tongue swirling, sucking the blood to the surface, and her hips rose off the couch. *Oh God!*

She'd lost count of how many hickeys he'd put on her, though he didn't leave as many marks between her legs. No, he became distracted and moved to her center, rumbling against her. "Fuck, you are so damn wet!" One long lick along her entire length released even more wetness. Soon he was using that suck-nibble-lick technique along her seam, and her entire body seized, muscles clenched, fists bunched, and his name tore from her lungs as she flew over the edge.

The laving gentled but didn't stop, and her path back to earth stuttered along rough-hewn stairsteps. "Blake!" she gasped when she was finally back.

He raised his head. "Mmm? Ready to see?"

She wasn't sure she could stand, but she nodded anyway. He helped her up, and she leaned on him with wobbly legs as he guided her to the guest bathroom. Flipping on the vanity light, he stood behind her and turned her to face the mirror. She blinked. And blinked again. His big hands had been holding her hips, but he swept them up her sides and cupped her breasts gently. He seemed to wince. "Uh, does that hurt?"

She shook her head, staring at marks that circled each breast like a string of large purple beads. The decorations disappeared beneath her breasts, but when he lifted them, she could see that the circle continued, unbroken, on the undersides.

He dropped a kiss on her shoulder and caught her gaze in the mirror. "Think I might have overdone it."

"Doesn't your mouth hurt?"

"No. Can't feel it, though."

*No surprise there.* "What did you leave between my legs?"

"Besides an orgasm, you mean?" His lips quirked, and he slid one large hand behind her knee, lifting her leg, spreading it wide while the other hand steadied her other side. She looked like a ballet dancer in this pose, except that she was completely nude and could count three purple ovals high on her inner thigh.

Her legs trembled, and he placed her toes on the covered toilet while he kept her splayed open. His chin rested on her shoulder. "What do you think?"

A giggle escaped her. "I'm not sure. I'm just glad I don't have an appointment with my OB-GYN anytime soon. I'd be too embarrassed to explain how I got these marks."

He pulled her tighter against him. One hand cupped her mound while the other moved to a breast. He kissed her shoulder, along her neck, moving upward. He ran the tip of his tongue along the shell of her ear and whispered, "You're beautiful. You're probably sick of hearing me say that."

Before she could respond that no, she wasn't tired of hearing it, his gaze returned to hers, holding it captive while one thick finger pushed inside her. She gasped.

"Does that feel good, M?" His voice was edgy and deep, with smoke threaded through it. The one hand took turns massaging her breasts, his thumb and finger brushing her sensitive nipples over and over, alternating with pinching and rolling. Without waiting for her answer, he slipped in a second finger, his dark eyes watching her reflection. "Talk to me, M. I want to make this good for you." Behind her, his shaft dug into her ass. At least she wasn't the only one about to combust here.

He bit her neck softly. "You like my fingers fucking you?"

*God, yes!* "Mm-hmm..."

"And when I fuck you with my tongue? You like that too?"

"Yessss," she breathed, reaching her arms behind herself to cradle his head. Her eyes fluttered closed, and she let the sensations wash over her. She didn't care that he was watching her hump his hand, didn't care that she was fully exposed, didn't care that he could see how his every word and every movement affected her. Didn't care that, in this moment, he owned her.

He added a third finger, curling it, hitting that just-right spot, and she bit her lower lip to keep from crying out. He shifted behind her, his hips rocking his erection against her ass. "This is what I'm going to see next time I stroke myself. I'm going to imagine your gorgeous tits swaying and your perfect naked body squirming because my fingers are inside you. I'll picture the way your face looks when you're chasing the orgasm I'm giving you, and I'm gonna come so fucking hard."

Her heart beat double-time, pumping hot lava through her veins, but with his shockingly filthy words dancing in her sex-dazed brain, that flow became a torrent, an out-of-control, rushing river of fire.

He sank his teeth into her shoulder, and she bucked against his hand, matching each urgent thrust of his fingers. Her head rolled against his shoulder side to side, and she couldn't contain the mewling noises rising in her chest, clawing in her throat, or the orgasm blooming in her body, ready to release liquid heat.

"Never seen anything as incredibly beautiful as you," he purred against her neck. "That's it. I want you coming all over my hand, then I want you riding my swollen cock. It's so damn ready for you."

A shout, followed by an incoherent string of noises, burst from her, and her muscles contracted around his fingers, squeezing them until they stopped moving. Her mind blanked, and her body let go, folding like a wet noodle while he held her up. "I got you," he soothed against her temple. "I got you."

Then he spun her in place, and his mouth crashed down on hers before she could catch her breath. He scooped her up in his arms and carried her to the bedroom. The tenderness he showed when he laid her down on the bed was at complete odds with the frantic way he tore off his clothes and heaped them on the floor. He climbed up her body, his engorged cock blazing a trail to her entrance. Gathering up her legs on either side of his hips, he lined himself up and plunged inside her hard.

"Oh fuck!" tore from his chest, followed by a low, long, hissing growl as he drove in deeper, seating himself to the hilt. When she opened her eyes, he wasn't moving, his mouth parted and his face contorted in an intriguing mix of ecstasy and agony. His eyelids lifted, revealing deep emerald orbs swirling with fever and fire. He began moving again, his hips flexing slow and steady, but his rhythm soon grew punishing and relentless. He held her gaze without wavering, his eyes locked onto hers like magnets to steel.

Ricocheting through her head was how vulnerable she was, with his eyes mining hers as he pounded into her over and over again at a ruthless rate. It was as though he'd snagged a grappling hook deep in her soul and was using it climb inside her. Totally bared to him, she had never experienced anything like it, and her body buzzed with the carnal energy flowing through him into her.

When she finally shattered into a million shards of pleasure, he followed her, releasing himself inside her with a primal groan that seemed to move through his entire frame like an earthquake moving through solid ground.

As she lay under the warm blanket that was his big body, her even breathing and her sanity returned. She stifled a giggle. She'd made no note, but she was pretty damn sure it took far less than thirteen minutes for her to soar to her peak and less than the "average man" for him to hit his. But oh, how beautifully those glorious minutes had filled space and time. Until this moment, she hadn't even realized they'd forgotten a condom.

# Chapter 25

# A Chalk Outline of the Heart

Blake didn't possess enough swear words in his arsenal to articulate the explosion that had rocked his mind and his body. He'd gone nuclear, melted down, leaving nothing but a useless heap of radioactive ash.

M's chest moved at a normal tempo, so he hadn't killed her, but all his weight was pressed on her. Reluctant to pull himself from his post-sex dream state, he slid off nonetheless and rolled onto his back to keep from crushing her. It was then he realized his mistake. He turned his head toward her. Half-lidded, soft gray eyes peered at him.

"I forgot the condom," he blurted. Was it because he'd still been half-drunk? One mistake compounding another.

"We both did," she said in a drowsy voice.

"You said you were on birth control. That hasn't changed, has it?"

"No."

"I'm clean. I promise." He caressed her hair and dropped a kiss on her forehead. "I'll get tested and show you the results if you want."

She tipped onto her side, propped up an elbow, and cradled her head in her palm, her eyes never leaving his.

"Is that a smirk?" His own smile formed.

"It sure is. Does it occur to you that *I* might not be clean? Why wouldn't you want to see *my* test results?"

A frisson of discomfort jolted him, but it had nothing to do with STDs. It was because she could have been with someone. Recently. He laced his hands over his chest uneasily. They hadn't talked exclusivity, but he'd assumed it anyway. "Are you trying to tell me something?"

The smirk widened. "Yes. I'm trying to tell you to be careful and not trust everything women tell you when you're taking them to bed. You'd be a great catch for someone."

"I don't plan on being anyone's 'catch.'" *Unless it's you.* "I also don't plan on taking any women to bed. Present company excepted."

"Just saying." Her fingertip traced a path down his nose and along his jaw, and he closed his eyes. "You're very trusting."

"Not really." He opened his eyes and caught her gaze in his. "That's the only time I've gone bare since my *first* time. My horny teenage self got lucky. Despite my raging hormones, I wised up real quick and never played Russian Roulette again."

"And started using condoms from that day forward," she finished for him.

"Didn't work exactly that way," he chuckled. "I kept it simple and stayed away from girls. Channeled all my energy into hockey, which worked out for the best."

She tossed her head back and let out a throaty laugh. "I take it that first time wasn't enough to convince you it was worth the trouble of messing with protection, huh?"

Shaking his head, he wrapped a coil of her soft hair around his finger. "Honestly, I was terrified."

"Of what?"

"Of everything! I was terrified I wouldn't find the right hole, terrified I'd come *before* getting it in, terrified I'd get it in and come on the first stroke, terrified she wouldn't like it, terrified she'd get pregnant, terrified her parents would find out. All that shit was going through my mind at once. I don't even remember the actual screwing part."

Giggles shook M's shoulders. "You were afraid you wouldn't find the *right hole*?"

"Hey, getting to third base a few times was the only experience I had. It's one thing to look at porn, but it's a whole different hockey game when it's show time. There's a lot of pressure on us guys. All you women have to do is lie back."

She dropped her head on his shoulder, and the giggles escalated. "Is that what she did? Lie back?"

He chuckled. "Pretty much, although she did help guide me to the right spot. I appreciated that. And she didn't laugh at me, which was helpful too."

"I'm sorry," she snickered.

"You should be," he teased. "Guess you'll have to make it up to me."

After she stopped laughing, M placed her small hand on his chest, tracing his pecs and playing with his nipples. Tiny shivers ran up his neck. "Hey, that feels kinda good," he murmured.

"Probably nowhere near as good as when you do it to me." She leaned in and nibbled his bottom lip, whispering, "I, for one, am very glad you learned your way around a woman's body."

This surprised him—and puffed his chest with pride. "Yeah? I always feel clumsy, like I don't know what the hell I'm doing, and some of those same old thoughts take over."

Her eyes popped wide in mock surprise. "That you won't be able to find the right hole?"

He pulled her to his chest and grinned. "Don't be a sass mouth. No, not that part. Mostly, the part about whether she'll enjoy it."

She raised her head, propped her chin on his chest, and looked straight into his eyes, all traces of teasing gone. "Speaking from personal experience, you don't need to worry about that. Just like you didn't need to worry about your kissing skills."

*That's just with you.* He raked his fingers through her hair. "It's because you're a very patient teacher."

"About that."

"About what?"

"Have I been bossy in bed?"

He started to laugh, but one look at her furrowed brows and her lower lip caught between her teeth made him hold back. "I don't think you're bossy. I think you're ... into it. Adventurous. Fun. I like it. I think it's hot. Incredible. Incredibly hot. I think I need a new vocabulary." The relieved look on her pretty face lifted his heart into his throat.

M was the first woman he could remember really letting himself go with, which, he realized, was one reason sex was so spectacular with her. No little voices telling him she wouldn't enjoy it or otherwise crushing his confidence. She was *very* clear at communicating what she liked and how much, and if she didn't like it, or liked something else better, she didn't hesitate letting him know in such a way that coddled his ego. They worked like a team, and when he got it right—when he scored—she rewarded him with fireworks. He'd never felt connected that way before, and tonight, when he needed it most, she'd been there and he'd lost himself with her ... and found himself in a wholly better place. Why had he convinced himself alcohol held the escape he'd craved? Right now he was just sober enough to admit drinking had spiraled him in the wrong direction, and he shuddered at how easy it had been to kid himself he could maintain control.

"Your vocabulary is just fine." She let out a lilting laugh, yanking him back to the bed, and thank fuck because he didn't want to be in his own mind examining his actions.

"I think I need one that's less juvenile."

He melted into the mattress, loving her soft curves caressing him and the way her fingers floated over his skin. Being with her felt so right. He closed his eyes, ready to drift, when she suddenly pulled in a shaky breath. "Speaking of horny teenagers and other things juvenile, tell me about growing up. I don't know anything about your family. Your sister, Amanda, for instance. Are you close?"

Before he could check himself, his muscles tensed and his eyes snapped open.

She must have felt the shift. "I'm sorry," she soothed. Her fingers continued their lazy circles over his chest, inching up to stroke his jaw. "I just want to know more about little boy Blake."

"Uh ..." Damn. The post-sex glow was gone, swallowed up by a few words.

M climbed up his body a little higher so their heads were close. His arm cradled her, and without thinking, he swept his hand down her back and fondled her ass. "You can play with my ass if that helps," she teased, "but I'd really like to know. Doesn't have to be tonight. How about we play a little game of truth or dare with only the truth part?"

He tilted his head to look at her.

"You can go first," she offered. "Ask me anything. Well, except about my clients. That's confidential." Her lips quirked, and she was so adorable that in that moment he ached to give her whatever her heart desired. And it wasn't the bourbon talking.

*I am so fucked.*

All his circuits fired up at once, and he dragged his hand over his jaw. Shit. He needed to shave. Had he shredded her tender skin? He blinked, staring at the shadows on the ceiling. "Did you know that couples who use terms of endearment have a higher level of satisfaction in their relationships? And that 'sweetheart,' 'honey,' and 'darling' have been around for centuries? 'Babygirl' is a millennial thing."

She chuckled, and her warm body jiggled against him, scrambling those circuits. "Is this your 'truth' question? Not exactly what I had in mind, but thanks for educating me on pet names." She snuggled a little closer. "Let's try that again. I love your trivia, but I've noticed you sometimes use it like a shield, which tells me that right now, in this bed, there's something you want to ask me, some truth that's making you uncomfortable. Just spit it out."

For hours, Ferguson's words had been festering inside Blake. *"Does she suck your dick better than ..."* She did, in fact—not that he'd ever admit it to Ferguson—but that wasn't why he wanted to be with her. The way she worked her talented tongue and mouth on him was merely a very delightful perk. But it did stir up thoughts he didn't like entertaining.

He cleared his throat and braced himself. "When we're in bed, you seem to know how to push all the right buttons for me. *You* know *your* way around a man's body, and I've been wondering how..." God, he didn't want to know about past lovers or how many. Why had he started down this path ripe with insecurity?

"You want to know if I've been with lots of men?" she said softly. "Is that the question?"

He nodded, his mind a twister of emotions dominated by dread.

"No, I haven't. But I was with one man for a long time, an older man, who had very specific ideas about what he liked and didn't like in bed. I wanted to please him, like people do for their partners when they're in love, so I learned to do what he liked. It wasn't abusive, though toward the end, it always seemed to be about him, you know? The last year we were together, we didn't have real sex. The only intimacy we shared ... we only had oral sex. His. I guess I worked at it extra hard to try and ... entice him to do more." She pushed out an extended breath. "I can't believe I'm telling you this. Only Fiona knows. It's so ... humiliating. Like my body was dirty somehow, and he couldn't stand to touch me."

Anger flared inside of Blake, and he arrowed some of that anger at himself for putting her through the gut-wrenching memory—all to smooth over his own fucking insecurities. *Selfish much?*

"Shh ... that was him, M, never you. I can't fathom anyone not wanting to touch you." *Because that's all I can think about; it's all I want to do. I've never been with anyone like you.*

He tightened his hold on her, pulling her close, rubbing his cheek against the top of her head, hoping to comfort her, to give her strength to draw on so she could wrap it around herself and ward off the jerk from her past. Her intimate confession, her faith in him to hold her secret, touched him deep inside his chest, plucking at his newfound heartstrings. He bit his tongue, fighting the urge to feed her platitudes she'd probably see right the hell through. He hadn't had much practice acting the supportive whatever—beyond the little he'd shown Amanda since she'd come into his life—and the impotence was suddenly overwhelming.

M sniffled against his chest. "That's what Fiona said." A laugh lifted from her. "Not the part about touching me, but that it was his hang-up and had nothing to do with me. I know that. I get it, I do. But sometimes it still stings." She raised her head to look at him, her eyes shimmering silver. "Maybe that's why I'm a little bossy. I feel safe being that way with you. And just so you know, when I'm with you, I'm not thinking about what to do. I just ... feel you. You let me know, without out-and-out telling me, what you want, and my body and mind simply respond to you. I can let myself go. And when I know you're enjoying it, it feeds something in my soul. Does that make sense?"

He nodded, his throat sticky, unable to do much beyond grunting, "Yeah," because her words left him humbled and speechless. As he tightened his hold on her, he knew in that instant that he might have only known her a month, but it was too late to keep himself from falling because he'd already splatted on the pavement. Time to outline him in chalk. He was a goner.

Rolling onto her side, she tucked herself against him, her hand idly doing its lazy circles on his skin. Her curls tickled him, and he buried his nose in her hair to pull in her fragrance. "Your turn to answer," she whispered. "Should I repeat the question?"

"You lying next to me like this turns me on." He took her hand in his and skimmed it down his chest, over his abs, and placed it on his sleepy cock that was waking right the hell up. Yeah, he was totally going off topic.

She began drawing the same lazy circles along his length and over his crown. "Hmm. I can tell. Is this your way of distracting me so you can avoid answering?"

He turned on his side and faced her, caressing her back languidly, exploring the dimples above her ass. "No, I'll answer—but this here feels so damn good, and going back to little boy Blake doesn't. I want to wait a while." He nuzzled her neck. "Is that okay?" *There's other stuff I'd rather do right now.* It wasn't so much the question he was avoiding—well, okay, he was—but rather he was feeding the need to stake his claim, to erase the memories of her past lovers.

She trailed soft, sucking kisses along the base of his neck. "Of course, it's okay. And if you never want to answer, that's okay too. I don't want to stir up anything unpleasant for you."

With an abruptness that stirred him from his path down Sexy Lane, she sat up beside him. Her thigh touching his, she sank back on her heels, offering him a view that turned him ridiculously hard. There was no hiding the flagpole jutting from his crotch, and he glanced from her to it and back again, pretty sure "Help me out here" was written all over his face.

"If we're going for round number two, I need food." With an impish grin and an arch of her eyebrow, she swung her legs over the side of the bed.

Confused, he spluttered, "What? Right *now*?"

"Yes, right now. Care to join me?" She slid off the bed and swayed to the bathroom.

"Join you for a shower?" he asked hopefully.

She wheeled, perching a hand on her hip, and leaned her tattooed arm against the doorframe like she was posing for a picture. An X-rated picture. "A shower sounds nice, but not right now. Maybe later. I'm talking about *food*. Grilled cheese, omelets, sustenance, which I need because I've got Captain One-Track Mind in my bed." She reached behind the door and pulled down a slinky robe she wrapped around herself.

A moment later, the playful look slid from her face, replaced by shock, when he blurted, "My mother made my father kill himself."

# Chapter 26
# DEBRIS HAPPENS

Michaela blinked furiously. *What?* She hadn't been trying to coax him into telling her; no, she'd been willing to let it drop—she really *was* hungry and had wanted a break before they mauled each other again. Correction: *had been* hungry.

Blake was on his side, looking like a male model posing for an underwear ad—sans the underwear—as he watched her hawkishly. She pushed the absurd model thought from her mind and, a heartbeat later, dropped beside him on the mattress. Her gut corkscrewed while she found her voice. "What happened?"

Eyes still glued to hers, he dragged a hand over his stubbled jaw, then sat up beside her. "I need—" Without finishing his sentence, he leaned forward and started rummaging through his scattered clothing. No surprise, all traces of his arousal were gone.

He slid on his underwear, then his pants, though he left them undone as he leaned forward, elbows on his trousered knees. "You know I have a sister named Amanda."

Nodding, Michaela stared at his strong profile and wrapped her arms around herself. He kept his focus straight ahead, as if studying a piece of art on her blank wall. "She's my half sister," he continued. "I didn't know she existed until three years ago."

*His father had an affair.*

Blake side-eyed her. “You’re probably thinking Amanda is my dad’s daughter, but she’s not. She’s my mom’s.”

*Wait. What?* “Isn’t she younger than you?”

He turned his gaze back to the blank wall. “Yep. By five years. Remember me telling you about how my mom would take off, and that once she was gone for a really long time? The reason she was gone so long was she stayed with relatives, where she gave birth to my sister. Then my big-hearted mother put her up for adoption and came home like she’d been off on an extended cruise.” His voice was laced with sarcasm and icicles.

Various scenarios rapid-fired through Michaela’s mind, but she struggled to pull apart the tentacles and turn the circumstances into a story that made sense.

“My father would have raised her as his own,” he murmured, almost as if to himself, “but my mother refused.”

“What happened to Amanda’s biological father?”

Blake shrugged. “No idea, and my parents never mentioned him. I’ve only got bits and pieces of the story because my father took the rest of it to his grave, and my mother is such a wet-brained mess that I can’t believe anything she tells me. She’s confused most of the time—and that’s when she’s sober, which is rare.” He chuffed a mirthless laugh.

Like cracks on an iced-over pond, fissures spiderwebbed through Michaela’s heart for the little boy trapped in a tragedy beyond his control. Missing pieces clicked into place. She hovered her hand over his back, unsure whether her touch would soothe or annoy. Tentatively, she brushed her fingertips over his shoulder, and he latched on to her hand, pressing it to his skin and gripping it like a lifeline. Scooting a little closer, she leaned her head against his upper arm.

He pulled in a sharp breath. “I used to hear them arguing through the walls,” he continued in a voice laden with tangled emotions. “She’d be falling-down drunk, and she’d call him all kinds of shit. Tell him how much she hated him for ‘what he’d done’ to her. Imagine that: she hated the man who worked his ass off to support her, who wanted her to stay home with him and her kid instead of leaving them to go screw other men. And during those arguments, while she was flaying him alive with her words, he never raised his voice. Not once. Just sat there and took it." He paused to pull in a shaky breath.

"When I left home, I left it all behind me and never went back. It must have killed my dad, but there was nothing I could do for him and I just wanted the hell away from that toxic mess. He wouldn't leave her, no matter how much I pleaded.

"When I was twenty-one, I quit college to enter the draft. I got picked up, and I was set—enough to have him come with me anyway. Hell, I offered to put him up in his own place as long he got away from *her*. But he'd just smile and give me some line about getting what he deserved. *Nobody* deserves the way she treated him. The last time I talked to him, he made me promise to look after her. A day later, he was dead."

Strong fingers nearly crushed hers as they clung to her hand. "He knew, M," Blake said in a voice so low she barely heard. "He had it planned. A day after that conversation, he was dead. The only explanation that makes sense is that once he knew I'd made it, he didn't have to worry about me anymore. Ironically, my success freed him." She felt him shake his head. "He shot himself in his workshop—so she wouldn't have a mess to clean up in the house. Even when he killed himself, he put her first. Loving her brought him nothing but a boatload of misery." His voice cracked.

Michaela didn't realize she'd been crying until she stroked Blake's arm and her fingers came away wet—from *her* tears. She sniffled softly. "It also brought him you, Blake, but I am so, so sorry you were caught up in their volatile dynamic."

He patted her hand and, in a voice suddenly devoid of emotion, said, "Don't be. It's over."

Straightening, she blinked away tears and peered at him. He turned, meeting her gaze with hooded eyes. "Thank you for telling me," she murmured. "I feel like I understand you a little better now, and for that I'm truly grateful."

Light flickered in his orbs, and he brushed a thumb over her jaw. His fingers unfurled, and he stroked her cheek. "I've never told anyone. Even Amanda doesn't know the whole story."

Michaela leaned into his touch. "I'm honored you trusted me, and I'll keep your story safe. It makes so much sense now why you don't talk about your mother."

Dropping his hand, he sat upright and pushed out an extended exhale. "Yeah. And she's going to be here in a few weeks." Dread was carved into every line on his face.

"I have another question for you, but only if you're up for it."

"Yeah. Go."

"Does any of this have anything to do with why you got drunk tonight?"

His face froze. A beat later, he broke into a lopsided grin. "No, that was me wanting to see you and stupidly thinking a few hits of bourbon could cure me." Running a calloused hand up her thigh, he teased it higher, sending tingles to all the best places. "Guess that bright idea was a fail. Instead of taking the edge off, it sharpened it, and I nearly crashed down your door, I wanted to see you so badly." His grin turned wicked.

She arched an eyebrow at him. "That was your whole reason for drinking tonight? You were horny?" She couldn't muster indignation—he was too damn handsome and sexy, sitting there casually with his chiseled torso on display—though she hoped she had been the only scratch he considered for his itch.

A disturbing thought surfaced, tamping down the small fires he'd lit inside her only seconds earlier with his adorably sinful smile. Everything she was showing him she liked, that he was learning so quickly and enthusiastically, would someday be applied to someone else he took to bed. Possibly *many* someone else's. Shaping him into a better lover for her would also turn him into a dynamite lover for them.

With an inner headshake, she dragged herself back to the conversation.

He winced. "It sounds bad when you put it that way. I mean, I guess I was, but I was horny-specific." His big hand squeezed her thigh, then worked its way up, his pinkie idly stroking the dip where her thigh and pelvis met. “It’s been ten days, M, and I missed you. And not just because of ... this.” With his free hand, he waved between them. “I like talking to you. Just being with you.”

Her heart melted, making her speechless. When she recovered her voice, it quavered a bit. “And you say you’re not smooth?”

Surprise popped his eyes wide. “You’re saying I am?”

“You sounded pretty damn smooth to me just then.” She leaned in and bit his earlobe. “Not to mention you’re also damn gorgeous.”

“I *am*? Now who’s being smooth, little Miss Blow-Smoke-Up-My-Ass?”

She began to protest, but he cut her off, whispering, “You’re the gorgeous one, and you make me fucking crazy. I can’t stop thinking about you.” He sealed her mouth with another searing kiss. Breathless, she pulled away to sort herself before he could distract her into losing her robe and pulling him back on top of her. Willpower fizzled when he kissed her like that.

“I make you crazy?” she croaked.

He chuckled. “In a good way.”

Oh. That was hard to find fault with. Without her permission, her insides cartwheeled over and around her puddled heart. Feeling so desirable was intoxicating. Addictive.

The practical little angel reminded her—again—of the danger she was placing herself in. And once again, she flicked her off her shoulder, handing the reins to the devil girl.

*Dear God, please don’t let this be an epic mistake.*

M stood at the kitchen island, surveying the omelet fixings she’d pulled from the fridge while Blake sprawled on one of her stools, more relaxed than he’d been in a long, long time. Sure, the post-sex high and regretful booze buzz hadn't completely waned, but he suspected it had more to do with getting the one-ton concrete block from his past lifted from his chest. In fact, it nearly offset the guilt eating at him over getting hammered. He'd resisted confiding in her, but she'd made it so damn easy that the story had just poured out of him, and now his spirit floated like a fluttering puck finding the back of the net.

She looked up at him and smiled. "Peppers and onions okay? I have mushrooms too."

"Your choice. I'll eat anything."

Vaguely aware of his empty stomach, he was more interested in the way her silky robe molded to her perfect curves, showcasing the evidence that the kitchen was nippy where the fabric draped her chest. He shifted on his stool, rearranging himself. Again.

Entranced, he watched her graceful movements and the way the robe shimmied over her small form. It struck him that somewhere along the line his hyperfocus had shifted from hockey to her. She was the latest shiny piece of hockey gear he wanted to inspect, fondle, and take for a spin. And while he wanted to understand the deepest inner workings of her mind, he couldn't stop his mind wandering to what he wanted to do with that body. His screwed-up family aside, every time he looked at her, all he could think about was getting her naked and under him ... over him ... on her knees in front of him. Trying every damn position in the Kama Sutra. Hell, she didn't even need to be in his line of sight to conjure the dirty thoughts. What the hell was wrong with him? God, was it normal to be so obsessed with someone? Had their sexcapades kindled something twisted inside of him? He was an unhinged Pandora's box. And while part of him reveled in the sweet wickedness, another part pushed against it. Was this like the spell his dad had been under when he'd sacrificed his life at the altar of his mom?

Blake stuffed the bothersome thought down, letting his dick take over the conversation in his head. He slid off the stool and sauntered up behind her while she stirred milk into the eggs. Gliding his hands over the satiny fabric, he quickly dipped them inside the opening barely held together with a tie, working it loose as he went. In short order, the robe gaped wide.

"Are you trying to distract me again?" The whip she was using on the egg mixture faltered, and he broke out in a smug smile. *No trying about it.*

He nipped her neck, and she paused to lean back against him, humming as his hands moved over her skin. "Now that you've dragged my deepest secrets from me, I have to know if you use the same interrogation tactics on your clients when you're getting them to cough up information. Because I'm here to tell ya, it's effective as hell."

She turned in his hold and looped her arms around his neck, her breasts swaying, her taut nipples grazing his chest. He moved his hands to her ass, cupping it. "First of all, I don't interrogate anyone. Second of all, you're the only one who sees me naked. Well, except my doctor. Third, I might have to reconsider how I interview clients from now on."

Crushing her to him, he growled, "Nuh-uh. Don't even think about it." He lowered his head to her neck and sucked. *Mine.*

She pulled away, squealing. "No hickeys in places where my bosses can see!"

He eyed her breasts. "Which means I can put hickeys in other places?"

"Pretty sure you already covered that. Besides, your lips must be ready to fall off."

He grasped the lapels of her robe and slipped it off her shoulders. "I see a lot of white here. And my lips aren't even tired. Lip push-ups. It's part of my workout routine."

"No, Captain One-Track Mind." Giggling, she snatched the robe from his grasp and had it tied before he could utter a protest. Then she pushed up on her toes, gripped his shoulders, and latched on to his neck, the little vampire. He threw his head back with a grin. *Wonder if it'll show up on TV?*

Three hickeys later, she lowered herself to her heels. His eyes fluttered open in time to see her inspect her work and give a self-satisfied nod. He'd been grinding against her the entire time she'd sucked him purple, but apparently to little avail because she stepped from his embrace and turned back to her eggs. “Now I’m *really* hungry,” she enthused.

“What, sucking my blood didn’t fill you up?” Grabbing her hips, he spun her to face him again and gave her his best eyebrow waggle. “I’ve got something else you can suck on.”

She rolled her eyes. “I’m sure you do.”

In a total perv move, he dropped his underwear, laced his hands behind his head, and gyrated his hips like his three-year-old self used to before bath time. But the fun he was having was unwinding his knots, especially when he caught her surveying him from head to toe, her gray eyes sparkling with mischief and interest. God, he loved that look on her.

“Much as I hate to spoil my view,” she drawled, “the neighbors *can* see in. You might want to corral that thing.” Her eyes landed—and blatantly lingered—on his steel-hard erection.

He pulled her against him, wrapping her up in his arms. “They can’t see if we do this.”

“Okay, big guy, but if the goods end up on the Internet, don’t say I didn’t warn you. Bet you’d get a lot of views, though.” She pecked his lips and broke from his grasp.

His chest deflated with a sigh, and he bent to swipe his boxers off the floor. “Gonna have to work on my *Magic Mike* moves.”

She bubbled with laughter. “Your routine is fine. No complaints here.”

He slid on his boxers, tucking his length in as best he could before retaking his seat. “I know. You need *food*.”

“So do you, big guy. Gotta keep your strength up so you can show me *all* your moves.” She threw him a wink that left him feeling slightly less foolish.

“Happy to.” Grinning, he leaned his elbow on the island and cupped his chin in his palm. “Speaking of food, what are you doing for Thanksgiving?”

“Fiona and James will be here most of the week, and I planned on cooking us a turkey. I invited April too; she doesn’t have family close by." She looked up from the mushrooms she was slicing. "You?"

"I'm cooking too. Amanda and Mom will be here through Sunday."

She poured the ingredients into a hot skillet and seemed to get lost in her cooking while he pondered the looming holiday with his mom and sister. At least Amanda was arriving the weekend before—probably so she'd have an excuse not to stop in Oregon and pick up their mother—and he'd get to spend some time with her before their mom got there and fucked up everyone's holiday.

"How about Owen?"

He jerked his head up, but she wasn't looking at him. "No, uh, Owen won't be here for Thanksgiving."

"Oh, right. He's probably spending it with his family."

He'd have to tell Amanda about Ferguson. Part of the reason she was coming early was to "spend time with Owen too." On second thought, why not wait until she got there to say, "Ferguson doesn't live here anymore because I hit him"? Cowardly, but practical.

A band tightened around his chest.

"Man, that smells good," he said to put his thoughts on a different track. The aroma of onions and peppers cooking hit him square in the olfactory receptors, and his stomach rumbled with anticipation. Apparently, he *was* hungry.

M maneuvered a perfect yellow omelet onto a plate and slid it in front of him, along with utensils and a napkin. He picked up his fork, poised to attack the steaming food when she wiggled her eyebrows at him. "What would you think of combining our cooking duties and our guests? We could turn two mini-feasts into one big one here, or at your place."

He paused midway to his first bite, panic growing inside him. He loved the idea of introducing M to his sister, but his mother could send her running. "It means meeting my mom and sister," he said as he shoveled food into his mouth.

M expertly slid a second omelet onto a plate, her eyes flitting to his. "We don't have to, Blake. I just thought it might be fun to have a bigger group. When I was a kid, my parents used to invite lots of people: neighbors, co-workers, the mechanic down the street. Our house overflowed on Thanksgiving. They always said, 'The more, the merrier,' and I guess that philosophy and the happy memories stuck with me." She let out a wistful sigh. "I wish they could come this year, but they're on some Elder Hostel trip they booked eons ago."

She took the seat beside him. "If we combine our groups, having more people could also diffuse some of the ... angst."

Swallowing his bite, he studied her profile as she nibbled at her food, and his heart expanded. His first instinct had been to say no, but as he turned over her suggestion, something warm that smelled of family blossomed inside his chest. It was a foreign feeling, one he hadn't experienced since he'd been in elementary school at Christmastime. All of him wanted to sweep her up and hold her to him, but he reined himself in and planted a sloppy kiss on her cheek instead.

Her pretty eyes lit up. "Is that a yes?"

Stuffing another bite in his mouth, he nodded. "Yep, but we're gonna have to figure out the sleeping-together thing. Can't do it at my place."

Michaela released a laugh. "With Fi and James staying *here*, I guess we'll have to put the sleeping-together thing on hold or limit it to whenever they aren't around. 'Course, then *you* might not be around."

He straightened and rolled his eyes dramatically. "Killing me, woman. I don't think I can be in the same building as you and hold it together that long. We'd better call off Thanksgiving."

When she scoffed, he continued. "Or we'd better get in as much as we can now." He pointed his fork at the food she was pushing around her plate. "You gonna eat that?"

"Why?"

"Since we're starting *now*, I need my strength to show you my moves." He wiggled his eyebrows, and a pretty blush pinked her cheeks. He nudged her with his elbow. “Hurry up and eat, or pass it over to me. I’ve got big plans that involve you out of that robe, and we haven’t got all night. Remember, you still owe me for my hat trick.”

She took a prim bite of her omelet and casually said, “Whipped cream’s in the fridge.” Then she turned toward him, her eyes smoldering as they locked on his. “I went to Costco.”

He flipped his fork on his plate, landing it with a clatter. “I’m done. Time for dessert.”

# Chapter 27

# A Bad Day for Turkeys

April stuck her head into Michaela's office as Michaela was closing up the last file on her desk.

"Why are you still here?" she asked her assistant good-naturedly.

"Uh, because *you're* still here?"

"But I told you to go home hours ago, when everybody else left. It's Thanksgiving Eve, for heaven's sake, and we deserve some time off. Are we the last two manning the fort?"

"You're the one who's been burning the midnight oil, boss, not me. And yes, I think we're the only ones stupid enough to still be here."

Michaela stood to adjust her blinds; night was closing in already. "It's not stupidity that's kept us busy, girl." No, it had been the need to tie up loose ends that seemed to become untied on their own and spread endless mayhem. Why it was always her, she had no idea. She'd barely been home in the last two weeks, and she was giddy at the prospect of having a few days *away* from Steadman, Hart & Fast.

"I'll walk out with you," April offered.

"No, you get going. I still have a few things to tidy up. Besides, you need to get cracking on that yummy marshmallow salad you're bringing tomorrow." Michaela darted April a look, expecting the eye-roll she was rewarded with.

"I keep telling you, I'm bringing a traditional Korean—" April's head whipped to the side. "Oh, hi, Brad. Didn't realize you were still here." She parked a hand on her hip and gave him a dismissive once-over. Although he'd finally stopped asking Michaela out, he still seemed to work late whenever she did, and he came around more frequently than the rest of her colleagues put together.

Completely dismissing April, he filled the doorway and smirked at Michaela. "Still here, just like me, huh? I swear you're competing with me for longest hours."

Tiny hackles rose along Michaela's neck. "I'm not competing against you for anything, Brad. I just have a lot of things on my plate to deal with."

"Yeah, fixing errors can be so time-consuming," he tsked.

A spritz of relief cooled her frustration; she wasn't the only one dealing with gremlins after all! "Oh. So you're having to put out fires too?"

"Oh, not at all. I'm just handling a heavier workload. From Mr. Steadman himself. I guess the guy trusts me more than any other associates here." He shrugged, but nothing was self-deprecating about the move, and Michaela stifled the urge to gag.

"I heard through the grapevine that your workload's been cut, though," he drawled, pursing his lips with fake sympathy. "Must be tough spending time fixing all those mistakes without being able to bill time. Doesn't seem fair, but Steadman, Fast & Hart isn't fond of carelessness." He wagged his chinless head side to side. "Maybe if you iced that hockey player, you wouldn't be so distracted. The quality of your work might improve."

*Omigod, what a jerk!* Those tiny hackles sprouted into thick ones, and she readied to bare her teeth, opening her mouth to take off Brad's head. April seemed to be gearing up to do the same.

Brad swiftly moved out of the doorway, his head swiveling in a different direction. "Well, good afternoon, Mr. Steadman. I was just telling Michaela that only the most dedicated among us are still here, sir." He stood slightly behind April and swept his gaze over her with a sneer, as if to say, "Except *her*, of course."

Michaela was half out of her seat to throttle the toady prick, but Steadman's frame replaced Brad's in the doorway, and she stood fully before freezing. The older man bestowed polite smiles on Brad and April. "I just wanted a few words with Ms. Wagner before the holiday. Enjoy your Thanksgiving, Ms. Joon, Mr. Hewitt."

April shot Michaela an apologetic look before saying goodbye. She'd been dismissed by the grand master, and she scurried away.

Brad, on the other hand, gave Steadman a bow of his head, wishing Steadman and his family Happy Thanksgiving. As he withdrew, Michaela could have sworn he quirked a smug smile at her only she could see.

Steadman stepped into Michaela's office and shut the door. "Sit, Ms. Wagner. Please." The smile was gone.

Michaela's heart sank. She was already late getting home to meet Blake's mother and be at his side, offering moral support before he left for the arena. His teeth had been on edge over his mom's arrival and because Amanda, who'd been staying with him the last few days, relentlessly harped on him about seeing Owen. Owen was staying an hour away in Greeley, and something about that whole situation was contributing to Blake's irritability. Not helping was her crazy calendar and Blake's in-and-out-of-town game schedule, meaning that since he'd pounded on her door in the middle of the night a week ago, they'd only managed to snatch a few hours together.

Tonight she was attending Blake's game with Amanda and his mother, DeeAnn, whose looming arrival had Michaela's belly ratcheting into all sizes of knots—especially after she glanced at her watch. How long would this impromptu meeting with Steadman last?

The senior attorney took a seat across from her and steepled his fingers, propping his chin thoughtfully on them. Something felt off, and Michaela's tummy doubled down on the knot-making. His eyes drifted over her bookshelf, and she pushed her glasses high on the bridge of her nose, then clasped her hands in her lap as she sat forward on the edge of her seat.

At last, he swung his gaze to her. "Ms. Wagner, I'm sure you have family to get to, as do I, so I'll come straight to the point. You have been an exemplary employee, one of our best ... that is, up until a few weeks ago." He paused as if gauging her reaction. Thankfully, he couldn't see the nausea rippling through her. "I'm not sure what's happening, but your little team has been riddled with mistakes this firm cannot afford to continue covering up." Their *little team* consisted of her and April.

Shocked, numb, she stared at him stupidly before making her tongue work. "But, Mr. Steadman, sir, I respectfully—"

He held up a weathered hand and lowered his lids as if he were drained. "Save it for another time, Ms. Wagner." There was steel in his tone that she'd rarely heard from him. "You might think I'm not involved in the day-to-day, but I assure you I have been kept abreast of every misstep, every folly that has taken place in this very office. Missing files, missed appointments, clients left flapping in the wind, and now ... irregularities, shall we say, in your billing hours."

His eyes hard, icy, bored into her, while she tried to make sense of what he was saying. *Billing irregularities?*

"I am granting you a three-week leave of absence so we can sort your mess," he continued, "contain any damage, and get to the bottom of what is really going on. Meanwhile, you can sort ... your life. You may leave your desk as it is, but I ask that you relinquish all keys in your possession, including those to your desk, your filing cabinets, and the front door."

*What?* Was she in the throes of a nightmare? Dwelling in an alternate universe?

What he *wasn't* saying finally pierced the mists of disbelief. He suspected her of duplicity. But why the hell would she sabotage herself? Did they think she was that stupid? Or maybe they thought she was an inexperienced blunderer.

A flame of outrage ignited inside her and rose from her center to her scalp, making her cheeks blaze. "Why would I—" He cut her off before she could defend herself.

"Ms. Wagner, I suggest you save your energy for other things, such as examining whether Steadman, Hart & Fast is the right fit for you. We, in turn, will do the same during your absence."

With that, he stood and held out his hand, palm up. "Your keys? I will lock up once you depart."

*I need to keep my mouth shut. I'm not rational right now, and anything I say can and will be used against me.* Her hands trembled as she gathered her keys under his flinty gaze. When she finally placed them in his open palm, he strode to the door, wheeling as he opened it. "Do not trouble yourself over Ms. Joon. She has been assigned to a different attorney beginning Monday."

"Does she know this?" Michaela blurted.

One side of his mouth lifted in a knowing smile—or was it mocking? "She will before morning. You have precisely five minutes to gather up what you need. I will wait right here."

Though Michaela's mind raced in opposite directions like spokes on a wheel, it also stood frozen, unable to tell her what she needed to "gather up." Did she take her plant? Her diplomas? Her coffee mug? She pulled in a cleansing breath and locked out the white-haired man watching from the doorway as she scanned the space and evaluated each item in turn. Anger swirled with bile, and hot tears threatened to fill her eyes. *I will not cry. I will keep my big-girl panties on, get my shit, and get out of here with dignity. I'll fall apart when I get home.*

Somehow she made it home without shedding a tear and, even more miraculously, without throwing up. She hadn't checked her phone, and as she opened her door, her eyes dashed to Blake's condo. He had to have left already, and that was probably for the best. If she saw him now, she was likely to dissolve into tears before he could introduce his mother. She told herself to get inside and have a good cry, get it out of her system, then pack her emotions away.

If only Fi were on the other side of this door, but she and James had basically dropped their bags and headed out to visit other friends.

A clicking latch had Michaela fumbling with her lock. Too late. Amanda, her long blond tresses swinging, stuck her head out the door, a smile lighting her face. "There you are! We were getting worried." She stepped out into the hallway before Michaela could put on her game face. Amanda was abuzz with orders to text Blake *right away*, to get dressed because they were leaving for dinner in ten minutes—*Really?*—and a string of other instructions Michaela couldn't fit in her brain. Not with the other baggage taking up space. Amanda jerked her head and pressed her lips together. "We've got to go. Soon!"

"Is she here?" a feminine voice called from behind Amanda, and the poor girl's shoulders sagged.

Michaela straightened hers. *Showtime.*

A statuesque woman with shoulder-length, honey-blond hair and a tentative smile peered over Amanda's shoulder. She stood a half-head taller, which placed her in the five-ten range. Since Michaela had never seen a picture of Blake's mother, she hadn't known what to expect, and she'd missed the mark. Blake's green eyes blinked from a once-beautiful face that was lined with age and marked with fine red spiderwebs on her cheeks and nose.

"You must be Blake's Michaela." Her voice was like sandpaper, huskier than Michaela would have guessed.

Michaela gave herself an inner kick to get in gear. "Yes, and you must be Mrs. Barrett."

Amanda's mother sailed past her daughter and grasped Michaela's free hand with her own. The sour smell of alcohol rolled off her as she drew near, and Michaela noticed her eyes were watery and rimmed in red. The woman studied Michaela's face with something akin to wonder. "You are very lovely. I can see why Blake is so taken with you."

*He is?* "I ... Thank you, Mrs. Barrett."

She shook her head. "No, no. You must call me DeeAnn. I insist."

"Of course ... DeeAnn."

The older woman broke out in a smile that lit her entire face, erasing her years. With a warmth that wrapped around Michaela, she said, "I can't wait to get to know the woman Blake's going to marry."

Michaela spluttered. Had Blake said something to his mom? *No! We haven't known each other that long*. Maybe DeeAnn was sauced and the alcohol was talking. Before Michaela could marshal a denial, the woman had already retreated back into the condo, leaving Michaela with her mouth hanging open.

Early the next morning, Michaela was finishing up the stuffing when a yawning Fiona wandered into the kitchen in a cozy robe. Michaela bobbed her head toward the counter. "Coffee's over there, Fi. The good stuff."

"Oh, thank God!"

"Late night, huh? And here I thought *I* was out late." Michaela refrained from thanking her friend for inadvertently giving Michaela and Blake an hour to themselves so Michaela could properly show him how sorry she was about standing him up. Passions had ignited quickly, and she had been spared going into details about *why* she hadn't made it. The little talking they'd done had been focused on the game—a blur of speed and dazzle, with Blake putting on a show that pulled oohs and aahs from everyone in the packed arena—and his gratitude for her staying with his sister and mom. Not that it had been a chore. Other than a pouting bout over Owen's absence, Amanda had chattered nearly the entire game, sparing Michaela the need to talk much herself. DeeAnn had been on her best behavior, and Michaela had enjoyed stories of Blake playing hockey as a kid.

Fiona parked her hands on her hips and stared at the cabinets. "Okay. Where are the mugs? This mini-mansion has so many cabinets it might take me an hour to find them."

"In the cabinet to the right of the microwave. James still sleeping?"

Fiona selected a mug and began pouring. "Mm-hmm. We're still jet-lagged, and while my husband refuses to stay up and reset his body clock, I will slog on as long as I have plenty of this." She held up her mug. "This place is gorgeous, Mick. Will you miss it?"

Michaela shrugged. "Maybe. I think I'll miss the guy next door more."

Fiona settled herself on a stool, her eyebrows bouncing. "Why not just move next door, then?"

"We hardly know each other. Besides, it's not that easy."

"Mm-hmm. I can't wait to meet Mr. Hot Body."

A light tap on the front door had Michaela's pulse racing. "Open the door and you can meet him right now."

Fiona's eyes popped wide as she stood. "An early bird, huh? Thought those guys stayed up late, like on swing-shift hours?"

Michaela laughed. "They do, but he promised to help get the turkey ready."

Fiona padded to the front door, her voice floating when she opened it. "You must be Blake."

"And you must be Fiona. I'm glad to finally meet M's best bud."

When the pair came into Michaela's line of sight, Fiona was hanging on his arm. Hanging from his other arm were a few bags of groceries. "You didn't tell me how tall"—she squeezed his bicep—"and muscular he is, *M*." She winked and released him. "May I get you a cup of coffee, Blake?" She batted her eyes comically.

Michaela dismissed her antics because breath stuttered in her chest. Blake's hair was mussy and wet, as though he'd just showered, and his green eyes flashed dark when they landed on her. He wore sweats that hung low on his hips, and an old, well-loved, too-tight T-shirt with the Oregon Ducks' logo on the front. It molded itself to his carved chest, squared-off shoulders, and sculpted biceps. Her eyes were drawn to his mouthwatering forearms and those powerful hands that worked not only wicked magic with a stick but on her body as well. The man didn't have an ounce of fat on him, and everything was beautifully defined. She pressed her lips together to keep drool from leaking from her mouth.

He dropped the groceries on the island, leaned down, and sniffed her hair, murmuring so only she could hear, "Hey, gorgeous. Your banging body's mighty bite-worthy this morning." He kissed her cheek and tweaked her ass.

"You're not so bad yourself, sailor." She hip-bumped him, and he laughed. "What's in the bags?"

"I was in the grocery store picking up a few things for our dinner, and I, uh, found some stuff I knew you liked, so I grabbed that too."

She peered into the bag and stifled a squeal when she saw a pack of cashew balls, yogurt-covered raisins, Korean-style beef jerky, and a pack of Milano cookies. No way was she sharing with her houseguests. Blake seemed to understand and swiped the bag off the counter. "Want this in your office?"

"Yes, but first ..." With her tummy full of flapping butterflies, she pulled him close and wound her arms around his neck. She kissed him with a fervor that let him know how thankful she was. If the hard length pressing into her abdomen was any indication, her nonverbal message had struck the right chord.

"All right, you two. Either knock it off or get a room," Fiona fake-grumbled before sipping her brew.

Blake pulled away with a wink and traipsed down the hall with the bag of goodies. When he returned, things seemed to have settled down in his pants, and he filled his mug and leaned back against the counter, ankles casually crossed. He shot Michaela a heated glance. "I like the idea of getting a room, M. Know where there's one around here we could use for an hour or so?"

"Nuh-uh, Captain One-Track. We have a dinner to cook."

Soon they were working side-by-side, trading barbs and stories with Fiona and James—when he finally drifted out to join them. It felt so natural, so comfortable, and Michaela stowed away her bleak yesterday and rode the wave of fun.

James found football on TV, and Fiona curled up beside him on the couch. Blake's attention was torn between the game and chopping sweet potatoes for some uber-healthy dish he was concocting. When Amanda popped by, he'd succeeded in prepping exactly one potato.

He handed her a mug, which she accepted. "Thanks, bro. Hey, you look like you know your way around this kitchen. Been spending all your spare time here?"

He started on potato number two. "If you paid attention, nosy, you'd notice the units are mirror images."

"Yeah, but that doesn't mean the dishes are in the same cupboards." Her eyebrows wiggled with mischief.

Seemingly ignoring her comment, he tossed back, "What's Mom doing?"

Amanda splashed creamer into her cup. "Working on her pumpkin pies."

Michaela's eyes darted around the room before giving Blake a suggestive look meant for him alone. "Does your mom know we have plenty of whipped cream?"

The look he returned could have ignited a forest fire. "Thought it got used up."

"I got more when I was at Costco two days ago."

He quirked a devilish eyebrow, matched by an equally devilish grin that held all sorts of tummy-fluttering promise. "Tell me you set some aside."

Amanda fake-gagged. "Please! Keep your coded messages to yourselves. I don't want to know what they mean because ew! Just ew!"

"Those two are pretty obvious, huh?" Fiona called from where she rested against James's shoulder.

"Obviously disgusting," Amanda groused.

"Shouldn't you be next door *helping* Mom?" Blake scoffed.

*Helping*, Michaela was pretty damn sure, meant *supervising*, but she stayed out of it. Not her family, not her fight. Lord knew she had plenty of ... *Nope, not thinking about work. Not today.*

Amanda shrugged just as a knock sounded at the front door. "Probably her now."

It turned out to be April instead, with a covered baking sheet and an insulated bag strapped over her shoulder. Amanda took the pan from her while Michaela took the bag and her coat. "What did you end up bringing? It smells wonderful! And how'd you get into the lobby?"

"I brought Korean barbecue short ribs—for those who want something besides turkey—and someone was leaving as I was coming in and held the door for me. Thanksgiving cheer and all that." April grinned.

Michaela introduced her around until April's eyes landed on Blake and bugged out. Michaela had warned her he'd be here—in case she needed a drool bib—but hadn't mentioned anything about their ... whatever it was. *It's a relationship. We have a relationship, even if it's not of the long-lasting variety, with him being skeptical of romance and all. And damn it, I'm going to enjoy it while it lasts.*

She plunked April's heavy bag on the counter with an oomph. "What's in the bag? Rocks?"

April reached inside and pulled out two bottles of Veuve Clicquot. "There're two more."

Michaela's eyes widened. "Oh wow! Kinda fancy for a throw-together Thanksgiving meal, isn't it?"

"Hey!" Blake grumbled. "There's nothing 'throw-together' about this meal—at least not my portion."

"Didn't mean to ruffle those man feathers of yours, big guy." Michaela went up on tiptoe to kiss Blake's cheek, and he leaned down to accept it, his gorgeous mouth curling up. While April busied herself hauling out the other bottles, she shot her a questioning side-eye.

Michaela had Amanda help her pull down champagne glasses while James sauntered over to open a bottle and pour it out in equal measures.

Michaela handed glasses around and turned to April. "Do you always serve good champagne with ribs?"

"Definitely not, but I figured we needed a special bubbly today so we could make an extra-special fuck-you toast to the bastards at Steadman, Hart & Fast." April raised her glass, and Michaela nearly choked. After taking a sip, she gave Michaela sad eyes. "HR contacted me yesterday after Steadman had his little chat with you. I'm so sorry, Miss Micky."

Blake's glass was poised mid-lift, but he looked all kinds of confused—for good reason. "Sorry for what, and who are we telling to fuck themselves and why?" While others laughed—though they didn't know exactly what they were laughing at—and tipped their glasses back, he set his down, untouched, and frowned. "M? What's going on?"

Just then, DeeAnn pushed through the front door, her watery eyes zeroing in on the bottles like a missile on its target. "Ooh, I got here just in time! I *love* champagne!"

Michaela felt Blake's body tauten like a steel cable ratcheted up to maximum tension. The day had just jumped the track from homespun fun to double disaster.

# Chapter 28

# These Rails Lead to Crazy Town

M did a spectacular job avoiding Blake's gaze—and his touch—for the next hour while they finished preparing the meal. Truth be told, he wasn't trying to pin her down as much as he would have liked because he was busy running interference between his mom and her next drink. He even tried watering down her champagne with some of the sparkling apple juice M had bought just for him, but it didn't seem to prevent her careening into drunk-as-a-skunk territory.

Amanda had been of little help, finding various excuses to duck back into his condo alone, and he was torn. One part of him wanted to shield his sister from their mom's unpredictable behavior, while another part longed to turn over babysitting long enough to take a calming breath and find out what had happened to M. His mother's over-the-top outbursts of laughter signaled her level of intoxication and had him grinding his molars so hard he thought he might crack one. He was wobbling along a tightrope twenty feet above jagged rocks.

One of his wishes was granted when M and Fiona moved off to set the large dining table beside a wall of floor-to-ceiling windows.

"Micky, it's all going to get cleared up," he overheard Fiona say as he ambled over. "In the meantime, enjoy this unexpected vacation. Think what all you can get done. Get your Christmas shopping out of the way early, for instance."

"Vacation?" Blake parroted.

Apparently, neither woman had known he was there because their heads turned in unison, their eyes saucer-wide.

Fiona shoved the rest of the cutlery she held into his hand and mumbled, "You're up," before hurrying away. M stood across the table, staring at him with an unreadable expression.

He frowned. "What's going on, M?"

The utensils she held slid from her hand to the tabletop. She crossed her arms and pressed fingers from one hand against her forehead. Her curls bobbed, and her shoulders shook. Alarms blared inside of him. Was she crying? He dropped what he held and rounded the table to pull her against him. "You're freaking me out here," he confessed as he laid a kiss on her hair.

Hands curled against his chest, she looked up at him with eyes brimming with tears. "I'm sorry," she choked. "I was trying to forget what happened and enjoy Thanksgiving. I didn't mean to mess up anyone's day with my problems."

The condo was an open concept, but where they stood offered a sliver of privacy from their friends and family, so he pulled out a chair and sat, tugging her into his lap. One hand cupped her head while the other wrapped around her waist.

"I *want* to know, M. Please tell me." A warrior surged inside him, ready to slay any demons or dragons threatening to hurt her. He tucked her close, as if his embrace could protect her from any volleys headed her way. In that moment, he realized he would put himself in harm's way without a second thought in order to save her, and though he'd never felt that way about anyone before, it all came so naturally with her.

She sniffled, then, in a voice muffled by his shirt, said, "Mr. Steadman put me on a three-week unpaid leave yesterday and reassigned April to a different attorney."

*What?* He cradled her head in his hands and tipped it up so he could see her eyes. "The fuck? Why?"

"For the past few weeks," she stuttered as though fighting tears, "it seems everything I touch at work blows up, and it's causing the firm a lot of problems."

"Like *what*?"

A screech reached his ears, and he cringed when he recognized his mother's voice.

"How could you have voted for him?" she screamed. "The man's a Communist! He's the worst fucking president we've ever had! Thanks to idiots like you, we'll all become Chinese citizens!"

"Oh shit," he and M chorused. She scrambled from his lap and followed him as he headed into the fray. His heart executed a cliff-dive when his eyes landed on his mother. Her arms flailed and spittle flew as she stood over a seated James and Fiona and continued her rant. In one hand, she gripped a beer bottle with just enough liquid that drops flew as she swung her arm. Though he couldn't see their faces, he didn't need to. April and Amanda shrank back against the kitchen cabinets as if they could fold themselves into them, their faces twin expressions of horror, mirroring the way James and Fiona must have looked—and the way *he* felt.

"Mom!" he barked. When she didn't acknowledge him and barreled ahead, he repeated himself with a sharpness that got everyone's attention.

She narrowed her eyes at him, and if looks could have been daggers, he'd have been sliced to ribbons. "How dare you take that tone with me! You think you're some fucking hot shot? Well, you're not! You're nothing but a spoiled, ungrateful bastard who always took your father's side, and you did it without knowing the whole story!" The last five words came out in a vicious snarl. "You need to show me some respect, Blake!"

Horror, embarrassment, and anger, along with a healthy dose of hurt, collided inside him as he fought to keep his bearings and box up his roiling emotions. He dragged a hand over his jaw, his adrenalin pumping, his mind ricocheting as he tried to grasp for the quickest solution to end this shit-show. To his utter surprise, while everyone stood mute and frozen, M stepped forward, took his mother's arm, and said something in a voice too low for him to hear. His mother blinked, then turned her gaze to M. Her body seemed to sag. Speaking in soothing tones, M removed the beer bottle and handed it off to Amanda, then guided his mother toward the other end of the condo where M's office and the master bedroom lay.

As soon as his mom disappeared from sight, they all let out a collective breath. James and Fiona popped up, looking all kinds of apologetic.

"Blake," Fiona blurted, "I'm so sorry. We didn't mean to upset her."

He put aside his own mortification to reassure her they'd done nothing wrong, that they weren't responsible for his mother going ballistic. He looked around at four shell-shocked faces. "I don't know what to say except Christ, I am so sorry. She can be volatile when she drinks, and I thought"—he darted his eyes to his astonished sister—"we had her under control. Obviously, I was wrong."

Of the people gathered around him, he'd wanted to impress Fiona most, and he hadn't even recognized that desire until this moment. He'd wanted to measure up in her eyes and show her he was worthy of her best friend. Well, that dandy plan had just gone up in an epic fireball.

He pushed out a long, deflating exhale. "I'd better go see ..." he said lamely, flicking his index finger in the direction M and his mom had gone. Within a few strides, he heard their soft voices coming from M's office. "I have it right here," M was saying.

His mother clapped. "Oh, I can't wait!"

Hanging on to the doorframe, he peeked in. His mother sat in front of M's desk, and M was running her fingers over a row of books on a tall shelf. She glanced over her shoulder at him and smiled. "We're having some girl time. Maybe you and Fi can finish setting the table and get everything ready?"

His mother followed M's gaze, turning slowly in her seat until her eyes found Blake's. Her face positively lit up. "Michaela's going to read my horoscope! Isn't that fun?" Her pendulum had swung from one side to the other.

His mouth dropped open.

"We'll be out in a little bit," M assured him. Then she gave him a tiny nod as if to say, *"I got this."*

But for how long? They were on borrowed time, and he nodded back and returned to the kitchen with urgency. "Hey, can I get some help here? The sooner we get food into my mom, the sooner I can get her home."

Everyone sprang into action ... everyone except Amanda, who was nowhere to be seen.

Fiona seemed to read his mind. "Your sister said she needed to grab something from your place. She'll be back soon."

He didn't know how much time passed before Amanda reappeared, or until his mother and M emerged from the shadowed hallway, arm in arm. His mother spoke to M in whispered tones like she was a teenage girl sharing a secret with her bestie. M wore a patient half-smile as she listened to whatever the hell his mom was saying. If he hadn't fallen under M's spell before, he certainly was wholly captivated now.

By the time they sat down to dinner, his mom was as docile as a newborn kitten, but Blake still sat on pins and needles—and judging by their expressions, so did their guests—waiting for the powder keg that was her personality to detonate once more. M seemed to make it her personal mission to ensure that didn't happen, and as he watched her wheedle his mother, gratitude and pride swelled inside him. He didn't even care that her wheedling skills might extend to him. She could maneuver him all she wanted, and he'd happily follow her anywhere.

Ferguson had been right about one thing: Blake had it bad—real bad. And he was okay with that.

“I’m going out at eight,” Amanda announced as she helped James clean up the dishes. The oven clock read 5:30. Blake was seated on the couch, splitting his attention between the muted football game and Fiona, who stood to one side chatting about the destinations she and her husband had visited. The tension that had shrouded them throughout dinner had hitched a ride right out the door with his mother when M took her back to his place to put her to bed … like a child. April had cleared out not long after, leaving the four of them, and Blake was ready to swap Amanda to get M back.

He arched an eyebrow at his sister. “On Thanksgiving?”

“Yeah. A little post-turkey celebration before we hit the stores at midnight for Black Friday.

“Are you serious?” he retorted.

“Dead serious. So don’t worry if I’m not back by the time you get up tomorrow morning.”

He must have looked confused because Fiona patted his hand. “It’s a real thing. Not my cup of tea, but lots of people enjoy it.”

“Would you at least go stay with Mom before you go so Michaela can get back to her guests?” *And spend a little time with me instead of babysitting Mom?* “I’ll take over when you’re ready to go.”

He sipped his club soda, his strongest drink of the entire day—actually, since the night he’d gotten sickeningly plastered. After a series of self-inflicted lectures, he hadn’t touched a drop of alcohol, nor had he been tempted. Watching his mom today was a sobering reminder he was better off without the stuff.

Amanda snapped a kitchen towel on the counter. “You got it, bro.” After saying her good nights to James and Fiona, she headed out the door.

James joined him in front of the TV, and Fiona tilted her head as though contemplating him. Her focus shifted to Blake, and she sprouted a little half-smile that made him nervous.

"I feel like I'm being evaluated for something," he finally said.

"No, I did that hours ago."

His eyebrows shot to his hairline. "For what?"

James put his hand to one side of his mouth and whisper-shouted, "For Michaela. Haven't you heard? Those two are Siamese twins." He chuckled lightly as he turned back to the TV screen.

Blake swallowed, his throat dry, and awaited his verdict. Fiona broke out in a big grin. "You pass."

Shoulders he didn't know he'd tensed eased a few inches.

"You more than pass," she continued. "I'll tell you what I told Micky-Dub: she done good."

Her stamp of approval nearly wiped out the bad taste his mom had left. He'd apologized a dozen times, but they'd shushed him and compared stories about their drunk uncles or cousins or grandmas.

"Everyone's got an alcoholic in their family," James had declared. Some of his stories had been almost—*almost*—worse than DeeAnn's meltdown today.

Blake dipped his head and thanked Fiona, unsure what to add, when M waltzed back through the door. Every nerve in his body came alive, and he launched himself from the couch to pull her into an embrace.

Looping her arms around his shoulders, she laughed. "What's that for?"

He nuzzled her neck and trailed kisses over her soft skin. "Thank you."

"For what?"

He pulled back to look into her sparkling eyes. "For what? For being wonderful. For doing what you did for my mom. You saved the holiday for Amanda and me, and I suspect for everyone else too." He bobbed his head toward Fiona and James.

Her gray eyes turned smoky. “Yeah? Maybe you can show me how thankful you are by getting me a vodka.”

“Haven’t you had a few martinis already?” He cringed inside at the accusation in his voice.

“I have, but now I want another one.” Her eyes drifted toward the Sub-Zero, where the vodka was chilling. “If you don’t want to get me one, that’s fine. You can show me how thankful you are ... later.”

He dropped his forehead against hers and sighed. “I have to be in by eight.”

She dug her fingertips into the muscles spanning his upper back. “Because it’s a school night?” Her voice was low and sultry.

“No. Because Amanda’s going out, and someone has to stay with Mom.”

“Want me to stay with you?”

*Absolutely. Yes.* “You should stay here with your guests.”

A throat clear had them both turning toward James and Fiona. “Your *guests* are going to watch TV in their bedroom. Guess that means the place is all yours for at least a few hours.” She stood and held her hand out to her husband.

Confusion crowded his features. “We are? But there’s no big screen—”

She leaned down and bit his earlobe. “I’ll make it worth your while,” she whispered loud enough for everyone to hear.

James let the remote drop from his hand onto the couch. He hopped up, turned, and waved, a shit-eating grin all over his face. “Guess the missus and I are watching in the bedroom. Keep the noise down, children.”

“We might say the same thing to you,” M threw back.

After they were gone, she ran her hands over Blake’s pecs, and his dick stirred. “Gee. I wonder what there is for us to do?” She gave him an innocent look that was anything but, and the stirring transformed into a full-on stiffening.

He wanted to ask her about Steadman, about this unpaid leave she was on, about why she hadn’t confided in him about her problems at work. But as soon as her tight little body slid against his, undulating like she was doing the dance of the seven veils, coherent thought evaporated.

He tightened his grip on her waist. "I have a few ideas. But we need to get started. I'm a pumpkin at eight."

She hooked a finger through his belt loop and tugged him after her as she retreated to her bedroom. "Then what are we waiting for?"

He followed like a bear cub needing its next meal.

M snuggled close, her head pillowed on his chest, humming her contentment over the fireworks they'd just set off in her bed. Her body radiated heat like a boiler. "I like your ideas." Her voice was thick with sex and sleep.

While he roved one hand over her bare ass and back, the other one toyed with her hair, wrapping curls around his fingers. "I like that you like my ideas." He wanted to stay like this for the rest of the night, but it wouldn't be long before he had to spell Amanda at home, so he fought the urge to doze.

"Did you know the average person has 48.6 thoughts per minute? That's somewhere between twenty-five and thirty-three hundred thoughts per *hour*." He chuckled, recognizing he sounded like a complete moron and not giving a shit because she chuckled too.

"I love that you have a big brain to go with this big body," she murmured. Her soft lips pressed a kiss to his pec.

He craned his head to look down at her face. "You think I have a big brain? And you *like* my trivia?"

Her eyelids fluttered open, then closed again. "Mm-hmm. Your brain is one of my favorite things about you."

"One of. Does that mean you have other favorite things?" He dropped a kiss on her crown.

"Of course, but don't ask me to name them all. There're too many." She burrowed into his side, mumbling, "That's why I like being with you."

Emotion welled and overwhelmed him ... that this gorgeous, intelligent, vibrant woman wanted to be with *him*. That she could be *his*. He'd always carried a vague notion of the woman he'd eventually end up with, but he'd given it—her—little thought. Veiled in the mists of his mind, she'd been more of an outline, her feminine contours the only features that distinguished her as female. Lately, though, the image had sharpened into this curly-haired, raincloud-gray-eyed woman. The one who now lay beside him, her creamy curves he wanted to touch forever molded against him like she fit him. He'd never wanted anyone as much as he wanted her. Unbelievably, she'd hip-checked hockey right out of its reigning number-one spot on his priority list. In that moment, twirling her silky curls around his fingers, he would give up everything to be with her—even the sport he loved. Hands down.

Jesus, when had she so fully filled the chinks in his heart he hadn't even known he had? When had she become the perfect woman he hadn't even known he'd been looking for? When had he fallen in love with her?

And how the hell was he going to convince her to let him take care of her?

Questions that had been buzzing in his head all afternoon returned with a vengeance. "M, these problems at work—what kind are they and how long have they been going on?"

She nipped his chest, chasing it with a lick. Her head lolled back, and her gaze met his. "They're lots of mysterious little fires I've had to put out, and they started about the same time as Steadman's dinner."

"That was weeks ago." He tried to block the hurt from his voice. "Why didn't you tell me?"

A sigh escaped her. "We've had so little time alone together lately, and I didn't want to spend it talking about work. You're my safe harbor, Blake. I feel like I can park my worries and drift for a while."

Warmth bloomed in his chest. "You're my safe harbor too, M," he murmured in the dimness of her room.

She parked her chin on his chest. "I'll be okay. I have savings to fall back on while they—"

"M, what if ..." He traced the side of her face with his fingertips. "Don't take this the wrong way—for the record, I think they're a bunch of fucking idiots—but what if they don't bring you back when your leave is up? What then?"

"I don't know," she breathed. "I haven't gotten that far. I'm still reeling from yesterday. Guess I should start worrying." She let out a mirthless laugh and flopped on her back.

Bands tightened around his chest. He drew in a sharp breath. "What if you *don't* worry about it? What if I took care of you during those three weeks, or however long it ends up being?"

She raised her torso off the bed, propping herself on her elbows, and peered at him, her eyes glinting like hard diamonds. *"What?"*

*Yep, there it is.*

"I'll take care of your expenses. You can bake me cookies if that makes you feel better ... among other things." He wiggled his eyebrows. Even in the gloom, he saw hers drop into spectacular slashes.

"I'm not going to be your ... your ..."

"Kept woman? Why not? The duties are pretty damn light," he teased. "Easiest job you'll ever have."

She stiffened beside him, and he turned on his side and hoisted himself onto an elbow. With his free hand, he stroked the sex-tousled curls from her face and ran the back of his hand along her soft cheek. "I'm kidding about the duties, M. There are none. No obligations whatsoever. And I don't want to take away your independence. I just want to take care of you. Is that so wrong?"

She blinked. And blinked again. "Not wrong, but kinda unexpected." She scrunched her cute little nose.

"How so?"

"I-I'm not sure I can explain. I've just always seen myself as being completely self-sufficient."

"Well, you've nailed that in spades. Maybe it's time to entertain some alternatives."

She seemed to gulp, and while all of him wanted to push the subject further, he sensed he'd only succeed in pushing her away. He rolled his head to the side to check the time. Shit. Babysitting duty was less than an hour away; he needed to capitalize on the moments they had left.

Flopping onto his back, he tucked his hands under his head. "Where are your glasses?"

"Um, why?"

"Because I've always wanted to fuck a schoolteacher ... or a librarian. With you in your glasses, I get both fantasies." He rotated his head toward her and offered her a salacious smile.

She batted her eyes coyly, and relief rippled through him. They were back on solid ground. "So you never wanted to fuck an attorney?"

"Not until I met you. Now it's all I can think about," he laughed. *Truth. But only one attorney.*

She swung her legs over the side of the bed. Oh shit. Had he pissed her off with the coarse language? He'd have to bite it back—though it didn't stop him from admiring her ass as she headed to the bathroom. As he lay there, tapping out a beat on his chest, he considered various apologies, considered she might never emerge. But then she turned all his thoughts upside down when she appeared in the doorframe and leaned against it, doing a little shimmy thing like a cat rubbing its back.

*Fuck. Me!*

She pulled her black glasses down her nose and shot him a sultry look over the top of them. Besides the rims and a pair of conservative black pumps, she wore nothing else. "Is this what you had in mind, sailor? Will this satisfy your fantasies?"

Heat prickled every inch of his skin, and his cock grew rock-hard as he fought for control. "Get your cute little ass over here," he croaked, "and I'll show you just how much you satisfy my fantasies."

"Uh-uh." Wagging a teasing finger at him, she sauntered to the door leading to her office. Because of the heels, her ass swayed more than usual, and he about sprang out of bed to pull her down on his lap and have her grind that ass against him. Hand on the doorknob, she paused, giving him another fuck-me look that had him checking for drool. "I think for this fantasy to be just right," she purred, "you need to bend me over my desk." Her knees dipped, and she covered her mouth delicately with her fingers, reminding him of a naked Betty Boop. "There's a ruler in the drawer, if you think I've been naughty." Her voice was breathy, husky. "Ready to play, big guy?"

*Oh hell yes!* He was so fucking ready he lurched from the bed in his eagerness to reach her, tangling himself in the sheets and narrowly missing spraining his wood by landing on it. In a heartbeat, he recovered his footing and followed her into her office, where he braced his arms on either side of her, pinning her to her desk.

"Ready to play, sexpot."

As she wound her arms around his neck and pulled him to her, he answered by wrapping her in a tight embrace. This girl was never getting away from him.

# Chapter 29
# Reunions and Other Disasters

Michaela sat at a table in the Cherry Creek Grill, her eyes flicking nervously to the door every time it opened. It was Monday after Thanksgiving and the first day that had been the closest to normal since she'd been "put on leave" five days ago. Blake had gone back on the road after a matinee game on Saturday, but DeeAnn and Amanda hadn't flown home until yesterday. Consequently, Michaela had spent half the weekend catering to the two women. Well, more like just his mom because Amanda had been gone most of the time visiting friends. Not that Michaela minded, really, but she'd walked on eggshells, worried the slightest misstep would trigger DeeAnn's evil twin. Blake had stashed the alcohol, and though it seemed DeeAnn hadn't left the condo, her speech was often slurred and she smelled like she'd just rolled out of a distillery.

"Why are *you* watching my mother?" Blake had asked when he'd called her Saturday night.

*Because Amanda's not here, and I'm a little worried about her staying alone*, she wanted to say. Instead, she'd said, "Because she loves the horoscope stuff and wanted me to teach her." And she'd done just that, showing DeeAnn what she knew—well, as much as she could remember. The rest she faked, and

DeeAnn sponged it all up. In exchange, Michaela had learned about DeeAnn as a young woman. While Michaela had hoped to glean more about her son, the woman basked in memories of debutante balls, coming-out parties, and summer days spent boating from estate to estate on Lake Oswego. Foreign and fascinating, Michaela became caught up in a world more aligned with the stately Steadmans and nothing like her own modest upbringing—or Blake's, from what she knew.

Michaela jerked from her thoughts when she caught sight of her lunch date rushing toward her.

"Sorry I'm late, Micky," Paige huffed as she leaned in for a quick hug, then squeezed herself into the seat on the other side of the booth. "I couldn't find parking anywhere. I swear, this city gets harder to maneuver."

"Especially when you're carrying two bowling balls in your tummy," Michaela quipped. "I wish you would have let me bring lunch to *you*."

Paige flapped a hand at her. "Very nice of you to offer, but I needed a change of scene. Having your office in your home has its upsides … and its downsides." She leaned toward Michaela conspiratorially and whisper-shouted, "And this way I can have something sweet without the dessert Nazi passing judgment." When Michaela's smile became a partial frown, Paige elaborated. "Beckett takes 'charge' of my diet every time I get pregnant, and while I love that he wants what's healthiest for the babies and me, the stubborn man always forgets what a bad idea it is to come between a pregnant woman and her ice cream." An evil gleam flashed in her eyes.

Michaela loosed a laugh. "I have a feeling you don't hold back when it's time to remind him."

"Not in the least," Paige agreed with a chuckle.

"What's that like?"

"What? Telling a hulking husband to shut it about my ice cream needs?"

"No," Michaela laughed. "Being married to a hockey player."

"It's ... different. Not for the faint of heart, especially if you're the non-trusting or clingy type. Honestly, I never pictured myself being married to a rock star—didn't think I could manage the never-ending hits to my confidence—but the right man came along, and the worry faded into the background like so much white noise."

*Huh.* "And you're happy."

Paige's eyes twinkled. "Deliriously."

"And you have a wonderful little family." Did Michaela detect a note of sadness in her own voice?

"Not so little," Paige chuckled.

They chitchatted until they'd placed their orders, then Paige folded her arms and leaned her elbows on the table. "So to what do I owe the pleasure of this lunch?"

Michaela clasped her hands in her lap, cleared her throat, and leveled her gaze at Paige's. *Here goes nothing.* "I wanted to let you know I'm on leave from Steadman, Fast & Hart until mid-December. I—" *Oh God, this is harder than I thought.* "I didn't want to tell you over the phone or in an email. You're my favorite client, and I felt I should let you know in person. Any work you need done in the next few weeks will be referred to a different attorney."

Paige's green eyes drilled into her, making her squirm. "Is everything all right?"

Michaela had practiced several partial truths and a few out-and-out lies, but they were tripping up her tongue. *Tell her the truth. Full disclosure.* Michaela looked down at her fingernails. They really needed a polish; pity she was cutting back on luxuries like manicures. She raised her eyes back to Paige's and launched herself into explaining about some of the peculiar happenings, without too much detail, leaving out the part about the billing irregularities. No need to raise the specter that billings might be off at her firm in any way, shape, or form to a paying client.

Paige took a sip of lemon water, keeping her eyes locked on Michaela. "So these ... glitches. Were you responsible?"

"God, no! I'm not sure I would know how to cause half of them, and I sure can't figure how I caused any of them accidentally. I'm still wrestling with that one." She released an extended exhale. What she had to say didn't get any easier. "I get that this doesn't put me in the best light, but I wanted you to know so you could make a change to a different attorney. There are several in the firm who—"

"Before you go there, let me tell you a story." Paige covered Michaela's hand with her own warm one, a concerned expression etched in her delicate features. "When I first started in real estate, I was with a big firm. I figured it was my best shot at learning and getting clients, and it was. When I'd been there a while and wanted to make a switch, I told myself I couldn't afford to. That my clients would stay with the brokerage, and I'd have to start over again. Imagine my surprise when my clients opted to stay with *me*, not the brokerage. They said they couldn't have cared less whose shingle I worked under." Paige squeezed her hand and released it. "I'm not telling you this to brag. I'm telling you because now that I've been running a business for a while, I understand you're only as good as the people on your team. And just like my clients that followed me that first time, I don't switch based on the company. It's based on the people I trust. I trusted you before, Micky, but by opening up and being honest with me, you've told me all I need to know. I'm Michaela Wagner's client, *not* Steadman, Fast & Hart's client. I go where you go."

Gratitude welled inside Michaela, stinging her eyes with tears. Their food arrived just then, giving her the moment she needed to recover herself. "Thank you," she finally said.

"No, thank *you*," Paige replied after the server left them. "Do you know how long I've been looking for a good attorney?"

Michaela shook her head.

"A loooong time, and I'm not giving her up." Paige winked at her.

They dug into their meals in comfortable silence. After a few beats, Paige asked, "What is it that drew you to real estate law, and is there one thing that really floats your boat? I'm guessing it's not filling your days with the sort of vanilla stuff you do for me."

Michaela swallowed a chunk of seared ahi. "Minerals."

An eyebrow dipped. "Like gems? Iron ore?"

Michaela chuckled. "More like oil and gas. I love unraveling mysteries from the past, like how a dusty document from a hundred years ago influences a property owner's rights today."

Paige seemed to assess her. "Do you get to practice much of that?"

"No. Right now we refer that type of work out." Michaela's attempts to get Steadman and company to keep the effort in-house had so far fallen on deaf ears. They were squandering an opportunity, though she'd had to tread carefully pointing out that fact to them. Colorado was ripe for more oil and gas attorneys. *We could even branch out into Wyoming. Talk about opportunity!* Michaela's excitement kindled, like it always did, when she pondered the possibilities.

A smile lifted the corners of Paige's mouth. "You should see your face right now. Have you considered going out on your own?"

"Someday maybe, but right now I'm still cutting my teeth."

Paige continued to watch her, calculations seeming to stream behind her eyes. "Oil and gas is a subject I know little to nothing about, but I *should* know. And other brokers are in the same boat. What would you think of me pulling together about ten of us, nothing formal, and you hitting the highlights for us? Help us learn the pitfalls and how to spot the red flags so we know when to call in an expert like you and keep our clients—and ourselves—out of trouble? While you're on leave would be a great time."

"You want me to teach a class?" Michaela spluttered.

"No, more like share your knowledge." Paige grinned. "I guess that's the same thing, huh?"

"Pretty much." An unexpected thrill coursed through Michaela. The opportunity to teach a subject she loved to geek out on? To a willing audience? Oh yeah!

Paige gave a little shoulder shrug. "Well, think about it. We would charge a fee to have them attend. It wouldn't net you much—maybe enough for a week's groceries—but you'd really be doing us a huge favor."

By the time they'd indulged in dessert and Michaela had paid the bill, she *had* thought about it. As she hugged Paige good-bye, she said, "I'd love to teach the class. You get the people, and I'm in."

Ten days later, Michaela sat on the edge of her rumpled bed and slid on her heels, her eyes glued to the tall, sexy man with his back to her as he buttoned his black shirt in front of the bathroom mirror. *Wow, he fills out that shirt nicely. The pants too.*

"Need help?" she called out.

"Not to get dressed." He caught her reflection in the mirror and waggled his eyebrows. "But later, when it's time to get undressed, absolutely."

She gave him a prim look. "And what makes you think I'll be around when it's time to get undressed?"

"Hope eternal? Unrelenting optimism that you'll want me to help mess up your bed again?"

Leaning back on one hand, she pulled in the scent of his cologne mixed with sex emanating from the sheets and switched from prim to seductive. They hadn't seen much of each other lately, so it was an easy transition. She was *so* not done with him today. "I have a feeling you'll get your wish."

He shot her a cocky grin. "I have a feeling I will too."

She gave him the requisite eye-roll.

He turned his attention back to his buttons. "Tell me about the class you taught. How did it go?"

The cloud of giddiness she'd been riding for the last few days slipped beneath her like Aladdin's magic carpet. "It was so much fun! They were a great audience, and we had a terrific discussion. I realized I enjoy passing on what I know."

"Sounds like you enjoy teaching."

"Yeah, I guess I do. And bonus, I've gotten calls from six of the agents wanting me to check into their clients' mineral rights and possibly represent them." He smiled at her in the mirror, and she drew in a breath and ran on. "*And* I had two other people call me wanting to know if I could help them with real estate issues separate from mineral rights. That's eight new people wanting to hire me in some capacity!"

"Wow! That's fantastic. Knew you could do it."

"Well, I don't have the clients *yet*, but..."

"I have no doubt you'll close the deals. Then you can tell Steadman to shove it and open your own practice."

Her mouth gaped. No way was she ready to go out on her own. "I was thinking more along the lines of bringing the clients to the firm and proving I'm a good asset."

He turned to face her fully. "M, you're such a good asset that you should work for yourself and yourself only."

"I'm a long way from that, Blake. I may never get there. I don't have the kind of resources—or the reputation—I need to open an office right now." *Or the confidence.*

"So don't open an office. Work from home. Meet them at their places or somewhere else, like how you met Paige over lunch. You don't need a lot of overhead to get a start. And I'll help."

She frowned. "I already told you, I don't want that kind of help."

He chewed up the space between them in two long strides, grasped her upper arms, and pulled her up from where she sat. "At least think about it, okay?" He laid a kiss on her that left her breathless and dazed. "I want to help."

"Why?"

Still gripping her arms, he let his eyes drift from her eyes to her mouth and back up again. Involuntarily, she licked her lips. "Because I ..." He swallowed hard, as if something was stuck in his throat. "I want the best for you, M, and I don't think it's Steadman's school of sharks." His eyes drilled into hers, as if he was trying to tell her something.

"What exactly does 'help' look like?"

"Like I said before, I help with your expenses. Hell, just move over to my place to make it easier."

"Easier for *whom*?"

"For the stubborn attorney who doesn't want to be a *kept* woman. If you're already living with me, you won't be *kept*. And full disclosure, it'd be easier for me too—I won't worry about you as much when I'm away." He grinned. "Seriously, my place is big enough for you, me, and your office."

"You worry about me when you're away?" she replied dumbly while she struggled to process what he'd just said.

He laid a soft kiss on her lips. "Always." He drew back, his green eyes piercing hers. "The way you're wrinkling your nose tells me you're not wild about the idea."

"It's just ... this is a big step. We've only known each other a short time."

"You keep saying you don't know what to get me for my birthday. I can't think of a better gift than you moving in." He winked.

"Wow. Pressure and guilt all rolled into one," she chuffed.

He grew serious again. "Look, M, this is new for me too. Maybe we take it for a test run for the next month. If it doesn't work, you still have this place." His hands fell from her arms.

"What about Owen?"

"Owen's a nonfactor. He's got his own place." His voice was completely flat, which only reflected the depth of his pain over whatever had happened between the two of them. Maybe she knew Blake better than she had realized.

"Are you two still friends?" she ventured. Blake hadn't mentioned Owen in so long Michaela had nearly forgotten about Flexing Ferguson.

"He's in Greeley and I'm here, so..."

*Not really an answer*. But something in Blake's expression told her to let it go.

He released a long exhale. "Let's just go to this thing and have some fun, okay? The discussion about you moving in will keep—if we even want to go there."

A stab of regret lanced her. She hadn't meant to shut him down; she'd simply been too startled to sort everything in her head before responding. Too late, he'd seen her raw reaction and had taken it for out-and-out rejection.

Her eyes followed him as he headed back into the bathroom to finish dressing. Did she want to move in with him? The idea had a certain appeal, but it also carried a heavy helping of uncertainty and fear, and she was already pretty dosed up with both. Making a monumental decision about her personal life right now—while the future of her career was damn sketchy—might not be the wisest choice.

Later, she told herself, when they'd finished making love and were snuggled in bed together, she'd let him know the subject wasn't closed. The brunch would last until late afternoon, giving them the whole evening alone together. Plenty of time for the kind of intimacy that would smooth his ruffled feathers, if any remained ruffled by then.

In the car a short while later, he picked up her hand and dropped it on his thigh, shooting her a quick grin when he turned his head her way for a beat. Had he already put the incident behind him? He was a flare-up, quick-to-cool kind of guy, she was learning, and it was one of the things she loved about him.

They pulled up to a valet at the arena, and Blake made quips about the guy's age. "He looks like the average thirty-nine-year-old. Think he's got a driver's license?"

She laughed—a little louder than necessary—relieved for a change of scene and a shift away from her rioting emotions.

When they walked into the staging area inside the venue—a sort of ballroom where other players and their significant others milled about—a blur of shapely redhead beelined for them from seemingly out of nowhere. She threw her arms around Blake's neck and dragged him in for a full kiss on the mouth. "You're finally here! I've been looking for you ever since I got here! God, I've missed you!" she breathed and ducked in for another kiss, which he barely avoided by pulling her arms off of him.

Slack-jawed, her stomach down around her knees, Michaela looked from Blake's flustered face to the redhead—*Sherry*—and back again. His angular cheekbones blazed crimson, the only bright spot in a scene that had Michaela's emotions twisting and tangling in a heap at her feet.

# Chapter 30

# Raising Funds and Frowns

How had Blake been transported into the fucking twilight zone? Sherry's perfume filled up his nostrils as he wrestled her octopus arms off him. Every time he pulled them away, she wrapped them back around his neck, her puckered lips coming in for another attack. Beside him, M looked as though someone had slapped her ... probably because someone had, figuratively speaking.

The tickle of Sherry's overpowering fragrance made him sneeze in her face. *Finally*, she pulled away. Astonishment flickered in her features. "I'll, um, catch up with you later." Without waiting for a response, she wheeled and headed toward an exit.

He exhaled in relief, only to look into fiery silver eyes beneath arched eyebrows. "M, I—"

"What *was* that?" The look of shock on her face mirrored the shock rippling through him.

He took her hand in his, intertwining their fingers in a solid grip. "I have no idea. I don't even know how she got—oh shit."

M's gaze followed his, landing on a grinning Ferguson heading toward them, his hand out for a shake, which Blake ignored. Sickly yellow-green stains still lingered along one side of his jaw. "Hey, ex-roomie. I see you already said hello to my date." Ferguson turned his attention to M, his eyes making a lusty sweep of her body that set Blake's blood ablaze. "Well, well, and if it isn't my beautiful neighbor." He leaned in for a kiss—the bastard!—and M turned her face in time, forcing his lips to meet her cheek.

"What the hell are you doing here, Ferguson?" Blake's jaw was ready to pop from clenching it so hard.

Ferguson's smirk widened. "Didn't you hear? I just got called back up for tomorrow night's game. Coach told me my presence was needed here." He looked around the room and shrugged. "Like old times."

"And what the hell is Sherry doing here?"

Ferguson gave M a fake look of apology before turning his dark gaze back on Blake. "Well, I didn't want to come alone, and she was available. Not all of us are lucky enough to score someone like M hanging on our arm." His gaze softened and swung back to her. "Very nice picture, by the way. Love the tat."

Blake flinched inside, all too aware of M's questioning eyes on him.

Ironically, Ferguson saved him by resuming his yammer, his gaze hardening once more as he leveled it on Blake. "Sherry's not a bad substitute ... which you already know *intimately*, bro." His eyebrows wiggled suggestively, and he made to tap Blake's bicep, but Blake blocked him. Ferguson held up his hands in mock surrender. "Whoops. That sort of slipped out. Yeah, guess I'd be a little touchy about my past hookups meeting my current, uh—"

A big hand clapped Blake's shoulder from behind at the same time a brunette wrapped her arm around M's shoulders. "Thought that was you." Mac laughed when Blake jumped. "Ready to serve up some chow for our guests?"

"Uh, yeah." Blake turned toward Ferguson, but he was gone.

Instead, he was greeted by the sight of Mia smiling beside M. "Hi, Blake." The four of them traded niceties Blake couldn't recall until Mia took M's arm in hers. "Why don't you boys go on ahead? We ladies will sit back and make sure the guests don't get too fresh." She winked at Mac.

Mac rotated his fist in a fake threat. "They *better* not get fresh with my girl, or—"

Mia scoffed. "I'm not talking about *me*. I'm talking about the women who are going to try grabbing your asses, *especially* when they see you strut your stuff down the runway for the fashion show."

"Yeah, guess we'll go," Mac sighed. "Ready, Bear?"

Blake leaned in and stole a kiss from M, whispering, "Are you okay?"

She gave him a brittle smile, noticeably struggling to get her imp on. "I'm fine. This'll be fun. Go knock 'em dead, *Blakey*."

He cringed at the nickname. The three little words he'd swallowed earlier at her place two-stepped on the tip of his tongue, but now was definitely not the time or the place to say them aloud—especially not for the first time. "I'll see you soon," he said instead.

"Yep."

As he turned, Mia's happy chatter sounded behind him, and he blew out a relieved breath. She'd take good care of M, not that M couldn't take care of herself, but this had to be all kinds of upsetting—not to mention downright awkward—for her. It sure as hell was for him. Now all he had to do was convince a very angry M he had nothing to do with Sherry being there—while dodging the redhead for the rest of the afternoon. *Yeah, piece of cake. Kill me now.*

Decked out in red aprons and chef's hats, Blake and his teammates served up the breakfast buffet and chatted with the long line of people who'd paid big bucks to attend today's event. His eyes continually prowled for M. She seemed at ease among the other SOs, spending most of her time with Mia, Sarah, and T.J. Shanstrom's wife, Natalie. The best-looking brunettes in the whole damn place. The whole damn city. He nearly laughed aloud when he realized one of those sassy brunettes belonged to him.

*Lucky me*. Wait. Did she belong to him? She sure as hell did, and he wanted the whole goddamn world to know it.

As much as his gaze sought M, Sherry's gaze continually tried to catch his. Ferguson, who stood about five guys away, seemed to hold little of her interest and vice versa. Had the two of them struck some sort of devil's bargain? Had Fergs brought her solely to make Blake squirm? To make M uncomfortable? *Asshole*. Blake planned to have a conversation with him about it later. Shit needed to be settled.

The serving of the meal over, he and the boys filed behind a stage and put on suits and ties to escort the real stars of the show, kids with varying disabilities for whom the fundraiser had been organized. Blake was assigned a shy little black-eyed cutie. To put her at ease, he went down on one knee and told her he was nervous and hoped she would escort him down the runway. She warmed to him, giggling and wiggling, charming the hell out of him. As he told her how pretty her dress was, his mind messed with him, imagining this was his little girl he spoke to. Something shifted deep inside him. Though she looked nothing like M, he imagined a miniature version with soft gray eyes throwing her skinny little arms around his neck and calling him *Daddy*.

*Whoa!*

Heart and hands trembling, he helped the little girl up on stage. She shed her shyness and strutted her stuff while he danced alongside her, and he was damn proud of her. Catcalls in the audience proved to be the sassy brunettes, Natalie's piercing wolf whistle the loudest of them all. He caught M clapping and beamed her a hopeful smile.

When they were backstage once more, he was back on one knee, thanking the black-eyed beauty for helping him out. Without warning, she threw herself into his arms, and he squeezed her back. "Something Just Like This" looped through his head. In that moment, he could admit he wanted this for himself.

Back in his black pants and black shirt, he was riding an emotional high on his way to M, a quick pit stop along the way. As he stepped out of the bathroom and into the dark hallway, perfume smacked him, and a pair of womanly arms snaked around him. "I've been waiting to get you alone all day." Sherry pulled his head down and locked her lips on his. She smelled of sour beer—lots of it.

With a gasp, he pulled away. "What the hell?"

Bewilderment and hurt flitted across her face, but she kept one hand on his chest. The other hand held a pint glass mostly full of beer. *That explains the smell.*

She thrust her bottom lip out in an exaggerated pout. "You said you'd call me. What's with playing hard to get?"

"What?" He shook his head as if it would shake out the confusing bits bombarding his brain. "I never said I'd call you," he blurted.

She tossed her red hair back, and his mind darted to the extensions fiasco. "No, because you didn't think I wanted to see you. But I do want to see you."

"Sherry, I'm here with someone else." He held his hands up so they couldn't accidentally come into contact with her—which unfortunately left him wide open, his back against a wall. Literally.

Her lips curved in a knowing smirk. "Owen said you'd say that." She stepped into him and took his bottom lip between her teeth. When he put his hands on her arms to pull her away, she bit down, and he let go reflexively. *Fuck!* She licked his lip and crowded him a little more, his shoulder blades in contact with the wall. "He also said you only brought your date to make him jealous," she whispered against his mouth, "and that you haven't stopped talking about me. I know what you want, Blakey. Now play nice."

Before he could protest, her hand cupped the back of his head in a viselike grip and her mouth was back on his, her big tongue probing, trying to work its way between his lips. He tried to turn his head from her grip, but she was fastened to him like a lifting suction cup. In a déjà-vu moment that might have been ironically funny if it weren't so damn disturbing, a throat cleared from several feet away. Sherry let up for an instant, and he tore his mouth from hers, wiping it with the back of his hand as he turned toward M.

"Practicing what you learned from your lessons?" M's voice was as glacial as her eyes, and his heart plummeted to his knees.

*Would saying "It's not what it looks like" be just too fucking cliché?* No doubt. Instead, he turned a glare on Sherry. "I don't know what bullshit Owen fed you, but what I'm telling you is the truth. I brought Michaela because I wanted to, not to make anyone jealous. I brought her because I'm *with* her." *I hope.* He was winding up, ready to launch another explanation or five, but before he could utter another word, cold liquid hit him in the face and ran in rivulets down his front.

"Damn it!" He shook his hands, flinging beer off of them.

Sherry stepped back, her narrowed eyes drilling holes into him. "Thanks for leading me on, asshole. If you want me, you need to apologize." She crossed her arms over her chest with a huff.

*I* don't *want you*, he wanted to yell. Right now, he was caught in a trap, and he didn't know what to do. Two impossible choices faced him: be a total douche to a woman he had no feeling for and have the woman he *loved* witness that douche-y behavior, or cave to the gentleman ingrained in him and risk having M believe he had some feeling for Sherry.

Rock, meet hard place.

Heart thumping wildly, he pushed a silent inhale through his lungs to get his breathing under control and darted his eyes toward M. Her arms were tightly folded over her chest, mirroring Sherry. He was bookended between two women, and not in a good way. He met Sherry's gaze, his mind running through ways to nicely say, "Get the fuck out of my life!"

But he never got the chance.

"You're either drunk or delusional. Or maybe you're deaf. Did you not hear what he just said?" M's voice was flinty, matching her eyes as she leveled them at Sherry.

Sherry's mouth hung open for several beats, but she seemed to snap out of it, turning her fury on him. "Are you going to let this little bitch do your talking for you, big man?"

Hearing Sherry call M a bitch set off a mini-explosion inside him. "There's only one bitch in this fucking hallway, and I'm looking at her. Michaela can do my talking for me all day long, *especially* if it makes you get it through your head that I didn't call you because I'm. Not. Interested. As for apologizing, you're the one who owes the apology—to *her*." He pointed at M.

Yeah, he was being an absolute dick. But Sherry had left him little choice when she attacked M. Without another word, Sherry shot him razor blades, then pivoted and stormed away. He dragged his hand across his jaw and slowly turned to face the fury of M ... only to see her back as she walked the other way.

"M, where are you going?"

She waved a dismissive hand over her head. "I'll just ..."

"Wait!" he shouted, the strength of his voice surprising even him. One quick stride and he'd caught her up. His hand wrapped around her upper arm, wheeling her to face him. "Where are you going?" he repeated.

She cast her eyes down and to the side, as if the pattern on the carpet had her hypnotized. "To find a ride home."

"You've *got* a ride home."

She blinked up at him. "You need to stay with your ... team. I can find my way back."

*What the hell is going through your mind right now, M?* He was flying blind here, and he blew out an exasperated breath. "Yeah, you're fully capable of finding your way back, but I brought you here, and I'm taking you home. Besides, I'm covered in beer, and I don't think it's a look the team would be too excited about in front of their big-time donors. Are you ready to go?"

He braced himself for pushback, but he got a short nod of agreement instead. So many words streaked through his mind at once, all of them some form of apology, promise, or explanation for something he hadn't done. But he had a fragile truce and decided not to blast it to shreds by opening his mouth. Shit, did they teach classes on this stuff? Maybe people came equipped to deal with it and that gene hadn't been included in his DNA chain.

Still grasping her arm, he walked her toward the doors. She looked up at him quickly. "Don't you need to check out or something?"

He shook his head.

"And what about Owen?"

"What *about* Owen?" he snapped, instantly regretting it. "I don't owe him a damn thing," he grumbled.

"Maybe a punch in the mouth," she said softly.

He came to an abrupt halt and looked down at her. The mischievous twinkle had returned to her eyes, and he forced out yet another lung-emptying exhale. "Been there, done that."

Her eyes widened. "You *hit* him? Recently?"

"When we were on the road, right before Thanksgiving."

"Oh! That explains a few things."

In the Range Rover, he started the ignition and backed out of the parking space. He stole glances at her rigid profile as she kept her eyes pointed straight ahead. "M," he finally sighed. "I'm sorry. I didn't mean to snap at you just now. I'm also sorry about what happened with Sherry. I didn't handle it well. It was just so ..." At a loss for words, he shook his head. How had he gone from being best friends with Ferguson to having the guy set him up like that? When had Ferguson developed such a vicious streak, and what had pushed him to unleash it on Blake?

"Why did you punch him?" M's soft voice pulled him from the questions churning in his mind.

"Why did I punch Ferguson?"

She turned her head to him. "Unless you're talking about someone else you punched recently?"

"No, he's the only one," he chuckled. "I, ah, punched him because he was being a jerk."

"A jerk about what?"

*Well, shit!* "About you."

She seemed to accept his vague response—for now—and turned her gaze to look out her window. They rode in charged silence, his mind ping-ponging between tearing Ferguson limb-from-limb to how he was going to keep M's picture secret from her. *You can't, dumbass. Ferguson will wind up telling her sooner or later, and you'll lose her for sure. Right now you stand a ten percent chance of keeping her if you're up front.* Suddenly, he was that kid caught on a stomach-heaving amusement ride, being spun and spun, with no control over the direction of the whirling machine. Did being in love with someone always twist your guts like this? And there it was: he was totally in love with the woman seated beside him.

When they reached their building twenty minutes later, his insides had settled down enough that he could filter his emotions one at a time—or at least focus on one while ignoring the others—and zero in on what was most important: finding his way back to solid ground with M.

Encased in the metal box moving up to their floor, time slipping away, he dared a look at her. Her arms were firmly fixed over her chest, her eyes trained on some spot on the wall farthest from him. "M, I'm really sorry. I never expected Sherry to be there. Even if I had, I still would have taken you. I just ... I could have been prepared. Prepared you." He tilted his head and peered at her.

"You only took me because Sarah twisted your arm."

"Sarah might have suggested it, but I *wanted* to take you. If I hadn't brought you, I wouldn't have brought anyone."

She flicked her eyes over him. "Smells like a brewery in here."

One side of his mouth hitched. "Because I'm *wearing* a brewery."

Her eyes lifted to his. "You need a shower."

He had his opening, and he snatched it, closing the distance between them. Leaning his forearms against the wall on either side of her head, he boxed her in. She blinked a few times but didn't break the gaze. He dropped his head so his mouth was only inches from hers and raised his brows in question. "What I *need* is you in the shower with me, scouring the stench off."

A spark lit her eyes, turning them quicksilver, and they dipped to his mouth, where they lingered a heated beat before rising to meet his gaze once more. "Do I get to use a coarse scrub brush?"

He ran the tip of his nose along hers, battling the urge to take her mouth with a crushing kiss. "Use whatever you want, gorgeous," he murmured. "Scrub me raw, if that's what you want." He kissed a trail across her forehead to her temple, burying his nose in her hair and drugging himself on her sweet, sweet fragrance.

The elevator door whooshed open, pulling him out of his trance. M slid out from under him, and he trailed after her like a puppy eager for its next treat, crowding her as she inserted her key in her door. She looked up at him and smirked. "I guess you're coming in?"

"I'm going wherever you go." Yeah, he was pathetic. So were most addicts.

She opened the door, and he closed it behind him. He was in! Fighting a smile, he basked in the victory. Scoring a hat trick wasn't nearly as gratifying as earning back M's smile.

She dropped her purse on a console table, looked at her phone, and frowned.

"What?" he asked.

She grimaced as she looked at him. "Do you mind doing that scrubbing alone? I have an opportunity with a new client, and I need to take care of it right away. It'll only take a half hour. You can shower here, or if you want to shower at your own place, I'll leave the door unlocked and you can let yourself in when you're beer-less."

He bit back his disappointment. "I'll shower at mine so you have some space. And don't worry. I'll rig your door so you don't have to interrupt what you're doing to let me back in." *And I don't have to worry that you* won't *let me back in. Yeah, I'm a sneaky bastard.*

She gave him the first genuinely warm smile he'd seen from her in hours. He shoved down the bristly question that kept coming back to him. When would be the right time to tell her about the picture?

# Chapter 31
# Commando

His shower finished, Blake yanked on a pair of sweats, and started pulling on a T-shirt before stopping himself. He slung the T-shirt over his shoulder, opting for shirtless. Hey, if it worked for Ferguson, he could make it work for him too. M never held back showing him how much she liked his chest, so why not flaunt it? Especially if the pecs tempted her to cut her client work short and start playtime with him. Play wasn't the only thing he wanted, though. He was desperate for the emotional connection, to get them back to where they had been before the catastrophic brunch, when it had been only her and him. A raw need to love her, to protect her, to fall at her feet and worship her surged inside of him.

His tipsy heart settled into his chest when he reached her door and realized she hadn't locked him out. Soon he was reclining on the couch, remote in hand, while M's eyes were glued to the laptop open on her dining room table. Outside, night encroached, though it wasn't yet five. Clicking through a cycle of channels, he stared at the TV without seeing what was playing. His thoughts were relentlessly drawn to her like a leaf skating on a river's surface that got pulled into an eddy, and he tried not to contemplate how his growing need for her left him wide open. She was as important to his survival as the air he breathed and the water he drank.

She'd swapped her dressier clothes for stretchy pants and a top that buttoned down the front. Stealing glances at her, his gaze lingered longer and longer on her small, unmoving, ramrod-straight form. A pencil rested between her teeth, and those fake black rims perched on the bridge of her nose. He laughed to himself. The first time he'd noticed her wearing them while she worked from home, he'd asked her why. She'd told him it kept her in the zone, kept her focused on what she needed to get done.

He understood keeping one's head in the zone, and honestly, though the glasses weren't real, they were hot as hell on her—maybe because of the memory they sparked of her in nothing but those and her heels. His mind, now under control of what lay below his waistband, meandered to an image of her work-rigid body softening, quivering under his touch.

He stood, rearranged himself, and ambled toward her, resting his hands on her shoulders. They could have been resting on planks. "Jesus," he exclaimed as his fingers moved automatically, digging into the knots. "You've got boulders in your shoulders. Maybe you should take a break."

Removing the pencil from between her teeth, she hummed and leaned into his touch, closing her eyes. "A girl could get used to this."

"Maybe she should," he murmured. *Come live with me.*

Spurred on by her soft moans, he worked his way around her neck, down her back, back up to her shoulders. He leaned down, his lips brushing her ear. "I can make you feel even better without these clothes in the way."

She cocked her head and looked up at him, her beautiful mouth curving in a smile. Facing forward again, she fluttered her eyes closed. "Do your worst."

He straightened, his fingertips working along the base of her neck, over her collarbones. "How about I do my best?"

"Mmm." She rolled her head to the side, giving him better access. He slid his hands to her top button and undid it, and she expelled a sighing moan that sent a jolt of electricity through him. He told himself to slow it down, not to rip her clothes off and give in to the beast inside. Not yet. For now, he would fend off the surging primal need to bury himself inside her. He craved that connection, but whether it was to love her or caveman-claim her, he had little clue. Maybe the two desires were inextricably woven together.

With almost painful deliberateness, he removed her glasses, returning to unfasten the second button, then the third, until he had them all undone. He leaned down and kissed her, upside down, slow and deep, his hands gliding down to cup her breasts. His thumbs brushed her nipples through silk, beading them into tight little pearls, and she gasped into his mouth. God, he loved how she reacted to him. He'd never been with anyone like her, and kissing her, touching her, making love to her made him come alive, as though liquid fire rushed through his veins.

Withdrawing his mouth from hers, he splayed her blouse wide, feasting on the view from above of her full, creamy breasts cresting the top of a pink bra that plunged low, exposing her mouthwatering swells.

"Pretty bra," he croaked. *But I want it off.*

Leaning away from him, she extended her arms so he could slide off her sleeves. *Fuck, she knows me too well.* Making short work of the shirt and bra, he tossed them somewhere over his shoulder as he took in her pale flesh and rosy-brown nipples calling him to touch, to suckle. He'd never get sick of this sight.

As he palmed her, filling his hands, she dropped her head back on a moan, and her body trembled, carpeting her silky skin in goose bumps. *He* was doing that to her, and it infused him with a sense of ... masculine rightness. Warmth joined the lust thrumming inside him.

He dipped his head, kissing the soft skin between her breasts, then latched on to one of her nipples. She arched into his mouth and pulled his head down, her fingers digging into his scalp and holding him tightly to her. Mewling sighs rose in her throat. He used his tongue and his fingers, all the while reminding himself to go slow, to show her he could be the man she deserved—skilled, patient, attentive to her needs and desires.

But she turned the tables on him when she twisted away, rose, and plopped her butt on the edge of the table. "Your turn," she declared.

Her hands skimmed his chest, feathering over his abs, and her eyes followed, hunger and appreciation in their depths. The way she looked at him made him feel like a fucking god, and his cock jumped. Hooking her fingers into his waistband, she tugged his pants down as far as she could reach, freeing his oh-so-ready dick. He shoved his pants off the rest of the way and kicked them aside.

Her lips tipped up in a sly grin. "You went commando?"

He gave her a casual shrug, belying the blaze building inside him.

She cocked a brow. "That's kinda hot." Before he could muster a witty comeback, she'd repositioned the chair and slid into it. One hand cupped his balls while the other one closed around his dick and began to stroke. He dropped his head back and shut his eyes, his limited brainpower entirely captured by her hand working his shaft and the other one squeezing his balls. Soon her swirling tongue joined in the fun. A groan he couldn't hold back rumbled in his chest. She closed her mouth on his crown and fucking *sucked*, sending ropes of heat lashing through him.

"Jesus fucking Christ, that feels incredible!" He opened his eyes, catching her silver ones peering up at him through long lashes. Hands still busily stroking and fondling, she used her hot mouth to suck and lick, driving him to the brink of insanity as she watched him watching her. Humming sounds from the back of her throat vibrated through his shaft, and he nearly lost it.

When he couldn't take anymore, he lifted her up, yanking her pants and underwear down to her ankles. She'd barely kicked them off when he grabbed her ass and hoisted her up, her slick warmth sliding against his lower abdomen as she locked her legs around his waist and looped her arms about his neck.

One goal driving him, he walked them to the red couch. "How do you want it?" he panted. "Hot and dirty, or slow and wet?"

Wriggling from his hold, she wordlessly clambered onto the cushions, placing her knees a foot apart with her hands braced on the back of the couch, presenting him her smooth, round, pale ass. She shot him a sultry glance over her shoulder.

"Hot and dirty it is," he growled. God, he loved this woman!

He fisted her hair in one hand as he tugged her head back so he could delve deep inside her mouth, tasting himself. While their tongues tangled, he dropped his hands between her legs and stroked her silky inner thigh before slipping two fingers inside her wet heat, making her moan and buck. Adding another finger, he worked in and out of her. Her nails dug into the leather as she writhed on her knees, her breaths hitching, coming faster, shallower, more ragged. She tried to break the kiss, but he wouldn't let her. Her whimpers became desperate groans. He loved possessing her this way, her body bending to his will. At times like this, she was completely his.

As she chased her pleasure, her thrashing grew more frenzied until she tore her mouth away and let out a cry. He withdrew his fingers and stared deep into her sex-dazed eyes.

"Was that good?"

"God, yes," she exhaled.

His ego swelled two extra sizes, but he didn't linger on it long. His shaft was heavy and thick, throbbing brutally, weeping for release, and filthy thoughts he normally bottled up tumbled out of him. "Get ready because I'm going to fuck you until you see stars."

He let her hair slide from his fingers and grabbed her hips, sliding his aching cock home in one savage thrust. Holding her hips in a bruising grip, he began pounding in and out, his speed and rhythm ramping up to a brutal pace. She wiggled and pushed back, her loudening moans adding fuel to his fire.

Conscious thought abandoned him. Primitive, guttural grunts—his—filled his ears. Fingers digging into her flesh as he gripped her hips, he slammed in and out, over and over and over until his balls pulled up and he emptied himself inside her, one pleasure-pounding pulse after another rocking him. Seconds later, she followed after him, her body convulsing, her muscles seizing, wringing him dry.

With what little strength he had, he slid out and pulled her down on top of him as he tumbled onto the couch, her back to his front. Wrapping his arms around her, nuzzling her neck, he caressed her belly and breasts, and she hummed her contentment.

When their breathing had slowed, she murmured, "Wow, you outdid yourself, big guy."

"I'm sorry I let go before you, M. I wanted you to come first." He nibbled her earlobe. "You have a way of making me lose what little control I have." He berated himself for not being able to hold off his orgasm while at the same time marveling at the effect she had on him. There was that next level with her he'd never known existed ... and he couldn't imagine living without.

"I like knowing I can drive you out of your mind." She flipped in his arms, her breasts pillowing against his chest. A sweet, satisfied smile tugged her kiss-puffed lips. "I'll let you in on a little secret," she purred.

He cocked an eyebrow.

Her long eyelashes fluttered. "*I* held off this time, but when you came? I lost it. Wasn't my plan." Her fingers twiddled with his hair, sending chills dancing along his spinal column, while her other hand scraped against his stubbled cheek.

He chuckled, easing inside. "You had a plan? That, I find fascinating." His index finger traced the vines along her upper arm, then drifted to her temple, over her cheekbone and jaw before coming to rest on her bottom lip. *Everything about you is fascinating*. She kissed his fingertip. His fingers tunneled into her curls, and he swept his eyes over her face. "God, you're beautiful," he sighed.

The corners of her mouth tipped up higher, and, holding his eyes, she whispered, "You make me feel beautiful."

*I love you, M.*

She nestled against his chest, and he wrestled back the words, holding them tucked in his heart. A different secret reared its ugly head instead. He quelled the urgency to tell her, reluctant to ruin their perfect dream state. He'd find another time—not during post-sex cuddling—when they were relaxed. The next road trip wasn't for a few more days, and he'd have plenty of opportunities to bare the ugly truth before he left.

*Yeah, that's how I'll handle it.*

He closed his eyes and drifted off on a cloud of sated slumber.

# Chapter 32
# Family Ties

Michaela sent Blake a sidelong glance as he guided his SUV through Denver's dark streets. They were heading home after his game—a losing game, though he'd played well—and she sat on eggshells. Not that he was about to flare, but he'd been acting funny the last few days, as if he was holding something back. Did it have to do with him leaving on an East Coast swing tomorrow? Or was it that Christmas was only eleven days away and he'd soon be dealing with his mom again?

Michaela had her own pressing issues: her looming meeting with Steadman and the end of her suspension. She still didn't know if it would result in her being asked to leave the firm or if they'd invite her back into their fold. Neither outcome appealed, which had her all kinds of twisted inside. Besides her conflicted emotions, she hadn't heard a word about the "investigation"—even April Super-Spy hadn't been able to uncover anything. Blake would be gone when she got whatever news was coming her way, and she realized how much that affected her. She'd come to lean on his strong shoulders, which also twisted her up. Having his support was ... wonderful. But was she turning into a starry-eyed mushball who relied on his presence in her life *too* much?

Ugh!

Then there was the man himself. What was she going to get him for his birthday and Christmas when he could buy whatever the hell he wanted? She'd picked up a book of silly trivia facts, but it seemed so … inadequate. And dumb. Maybe she could ask one of his teammates. Too bad he and Owen were on the outs. *Wonder what happened between those two?* A memory of something Blake had said, something she'd totally forgotten, winked on like a bright light.

So when he asked what had her thinking so hard, she replied, "You said something I've been wondering about."

Keeping a steady gaze on the road, he sprouted a wicked grin. "Was it about doing you in the elevator? Or when I told you how perfect your tits are and how much I love having my mouth on them?"

"What do you mean *when*?" she scoffed. "You say that like it was one time and not *every single time* you sneak your hand under my top, which, by my latest count, is north of fifty times a day."

The smile slid from his face. "And this is a problem?"

Damn, he was cute. She gave him the requisite eye-roll. "It could be if sex is all you think about whenever you look at me."

He pried her hand from her lap and kissed each knuckle before tucking it in his own hand against his thigh. "It's not, but I'd be lying if I said being naked with you doesn't occupy a huge chunk of my daily thoughts. Did you know men think about sex nineteen times a day on average compared to women at only ten?"

"Uh …" *Is he doing this on purpose? And I'm pretty sure I think about it way more than ten times a day, especially when he's around.*

"Then again," he rambled, "men think about food and sleep twice as much as women too. Which makes me wonder: What *do* women think about if they aren't thinking about sex, food, and sleep? Puppies? The mechanics of air-traffic control? Billboard's top forty hits?" He side-eyed her with an arched brow and a hint of mischief tugging at his lips.

"Something tells me you're avoiding my question."

"Uh, what was the question?"

"At the gala, you said something about why you hit Owen, that it had something to do with me. I never heard the rest of the story."

"Oh." He dragged his hand over his jaw, then pointed out the windshield. "We're almost home. Why don't we talk about it inside?"

An ominous silence settled over them. Michaela sank back in her seat on a sigh. She'd bide her time, but he *would* answer her, damn it, tonight, before he left on his road trip. *I'm probably going to need a few bracers of vodka—on top of the two glasses of wine at the arena—to hear whatever it is he has to say because this is* not *sounding good.* Slipping her hands under her thighs, she steadied herself.

His phone rang over the car's speakers, and Amanda's face lit up the dashboard screen. Blake hit the connect button with super-ninja speed. "Hey, little sis. What's shaking in Hawaii? Hopefully not a volcano."

"Blake, are you somewhere where you can talk?" Her voice sounded off, strained.

He hit a button, and the underground garage door lifted. "Just pulling into my parking spot after the game." He shot Michaela a quick glance. "M's with me."

"It's okay if she hears. In fact, I want her to. Tell me about your game while you guys go upstairs. I didn't catch any of the details."

His brows drew together in a frown. "Okaaaay." As he recited game stats and some of the plays, they parked and made their way up to Michaela's condo. Once inside, she kicked off her shoes and angled toward the kitchen, where she pulled out her bottle of Chopin and the largest shot glass she had icing in the freezer. Phone to his ear, Blake ambled in behind her and raised a questioning eyebrow as she poured herself a hefty helping. She threw it back in one go, letting the cool liquid slide down her throat. Blake's brows climbed higher on his forehead.

As she poured the second shot, he said, "We're in M's kitchen now, so I'm putting you on speaker."

Michaela was sipping her second pour when he laid the phone on the counter, hit an icon, and announced, "You're on speaker, sis."

"Hey, Amanda," Michaela called, forcing a smile into her voice.

"Hi, Micky. I hope you're keeping my big goon of a brother in line."

Michaela took another sip, catching Blake's gaze, and let out a humorless chuckle. "I'm trying my best."

Green eyes flashed, though she couldn't read what thoughts lurked there. The vodka sped into her bloodstream, its bite warm, and she felt her muscles ease a tic.

"So I've been wanting to discover who my birth father is," Amanda began, her voice shaky. "My adoptive parents used all kinds of arguments over the years to talk me out of it, which I never understood, so I-I finally bought a 23andMe test a few months ago without them knowing. I have the results."

Staring at the phone, Blake slid onto a barstool. "What did you find out?"

An extended exhale sounded on the speaker, and Michaela downed another quick gulp before Amanda spoke again. "I actually got the results weeks ago, but I had to dig to figure out the connections because it turns out my biological father isn't registered. But some of his relatives are, and I narrowed down his identity."

Blake's back went ramrod straight. "I'm listening."

"Blake, my dad is ... my dad."

"What does *that* mean?" Blake's voice held a sharp edge, and Michaela threw him a frown, but he ignored her.

"He's my adoptive dad. Our mom got pregnant by my adoptive dad. Now it makes sense why they didn't want me taking the test, but what do I do? I can't tell him."

"Have you spoken to DeeAnn about it?" Michaela asked softly. Blake's head snapped to her as if he'd just re-entered his body from some extended astral projection and wasn't happy to find her there.

"No, I haven't. I'm not sure how to approach it, and I don't need her going off on me right now."

"Why can't you talk to your biological father?"

"Are you serious?" Amanda croaked.

"Maybe not today, but now that the cat's out of the bag, don't you think he'd be relieved to know you found out?" Michaela posed.

"But what about his wife—my *other* mom?" Amanda near-wailed.

Michaela finished her drink with Blake's heavy gaze on her. He said nothing, looking between her and the phone, apparently waiting for her to continue skating with the puck. So she did. "Amanda, was your biological father married to your adoptive mother when they adopted you?"

"Yes," she sniffed. "But what if she doesn't know the truth? What if this breaks them up?"

"Chances are your adoptive mom knew about the affair when they adopted you. No one can be sure how people will react, but if *that* didn't break them up back then, how would having the truth out in the open break them up now?"

"I ... I hadn't thought of that." Amanda blew out another breath. "I don't want to do it alone, though. Blake, would you maybe come out here—"

"No!" His sharp reply made Michaela flinch. "Mom will find out, and it'll be one more reason for her to drink herself under the table." His eyes darted to Michaela's mostly empty glass, and she bristled inside at his silent meaning.

Instead of calling Blake out like Michaela wanted her to do, Amanda threw out another bombshell when she said, "I'll call Owen, then. I haven't talked to him since before your charity thing last week. Did you see him there, Blake? He said he was re-joining the team and I—"

For the second time in as many minutes, Blake chopped off her words with a growl. What the hell was wrong with him? "I saw him there—with his *date*—but I barely spoke to him. Why are *you* talking to him?"

A strangled noise came from the other end.

Michaela shot Blake a warning glare. “Amanda?” she soothed.

“Uh, I didn’t know he was seeing someone.” Echoes of pain threaded through Amanda’s small voice, and Michaela’s heart constricted.

“*Several* someones,” Blake snarled.

“Shut up!” Michaela mouthed at him, but he simply glared back at her. *You dense man!* She resisted the urge to throttle him.

Silence stretched so long Michaela asked Amanda if she was still there. The sob that came through the phone twisted Blake’s features with naked shock.

“He told me he didn’t have any girlfriends,” she cried. “Now I find out he has *several*?”

Blake swallowed, his Adam’s apple bobbing up and down. “’Manda, why does it matter to you who he’s seeing?”

She burst out in a tearful wail. “Because I-I hoped he was in love with me!”

Michaela covered her mouth to stifle a gasp.

Blake’s cheekbones flared crimson. “*What. The. Fuck?* Did he *tell* you he was in love with you?”

“Not in so many words, but it seemed obvious,” Amanda snapped back.

Michaela pressed her lips together as Blake dragged a hand over his face. “How, Amanda? How did it seem obvious? Fuck! Please tell me you didn’t sleep with him. *Please!*”

“I’m not telling you *any*thing.” Her voice was a series of tearful hiccups.

“Why did you do it?” He slammed the heel of his hand against the countertop. “Were you *deliberately* trying to hurt me?”

“Hurt *you*? This isn’t about *you*, Blake!” Amanda shrieked.

M’s hand shot out and rested on his forearm. He shook it off. “Not now,” he bit. She snatched her hand back and refilled her glass, biting back the urge to point out that Amanda hadn’t actually admitted to sleeping with Owen. Something clued her Blake didn’t want to hear it.

“Michaela?” came Amanda’s trembling voice.

"I'm here." She ignored the glare Blake swung on her.

"Can I call you tomorrow? I don't think I can talk anymore tonight."

Michaela's heart fractured for the foolish, heartbroken girl with the unreasonable, pissed-off brother. "Of course you can. I'll be around all day, so whenever you feel up to it, you give me a call, okay?"

Blake ended the call and tapped furious fingers on the countertop. Michaela held her breath, and when he leveled his gaze at her, his eyes were glacial green. "You knew, didn't you?"

"About Owen? I knew she'd seen him during Thanksgiving. She was about to bust with excitement, and Fiona and I were the only ones she trusted within hearing distance. She swore us to secrecy because she worried about how you'd react." *With good reason, apparently.* "I couldn't stop her before she blurted it out, or I would have asked her not to include me in her secrets. I didn't like keeping it from you, but she promised she'd tell you. Obviously, she hadn't gotten around to it."

"Obviously." His voice dripped with sarcasm. "So she trusted you, but not me?"

*Well, duh,* she refrained from saying. Instead, she gave him a blank look that appeared to poke the bear a little harder. "What is it with you and Owen anyway? Sisters fall for their brothers' best friends all the time."

He snorted, and his nostrils flared, but his voice was chillingly calm. "First of all, he's *not* my best friend. Not anymore. The guy's turned into an A-one douche. And you look like you're about to argue with me on that point too, so before you start talking about something you know nothing about, let me give you a little example. You keep nagging me about what happened at the charity event. Well, I'll tell you."

She didn't know what jolted her more. Being accused of arguing, nagging, or of talking about something she had no knowledge of. *Whose sister came to me because she couldn't talk to her brother? And now I see why!* Michaela folded her arms across her chest and held her temper in check.

"I have this picture," he said.

*Okay. Not what I expected.* She frowned in confusion. "Like him in some kind of compromising situation?"

Pain flickered in his eyes but was quickly doused with a shot of ice. "No. It's more like you ... in a compromising situation."

"Excuse me?"

"You heard me. I have a picture of you."

She eyed her shot glass. "I think I need another drink."

"You drink too much."

A mini-explosion detonated inside her, and she clamped down on the urge to throw him out—after throwing the shot glass at him. She needed to get to the bottom of what was going on, and *then* she'd throw him out. Meanwhile, thoughts bounced around in her head like superheated ping-pong balls because nothing made sense. "I'm going to be generous here and write off your snide remark to you being pissed at Owen or in a continual state of pissed-off-ness at your mother and taking it out on your sister and me, not that that gives you a pass to be callous." She gave herself an inner pat on the back for keeping her voice even. "So let's hear it. What kind of picture, Blake?"

His reply held a modicum of sheepishness. "I wanted a picture of you to ... to take with me on the road, and one morning while you were sleeping, I ..."

*Translation: I took a picture of you naked without your permission.* "You took a picture of me while I was *asleep*?" Owen's words swam back to her, suddenly making sense. *"Very nice picture, by the way. Love the tat."* She narrowed her eyes and pressed her fingertips hard to the underside of the counter to steady herself. Her breathing bottomed out, and her heart weighed heavy in her chest like a hunk of granite. "Oh. My. God! You took a picture of me naked without asking!—and you showed it to *Owen*? Who the hell does that?"

"I didn't *show* it to him," he thundered. "He saw it, and he's been giving me shit about it because he's jealous as hell."

"You still *have it*?" she yelped.

He had the decency to hang his head. “No one else has seen it, for what that’s worth.”

“It’s worth *shit*! Show me. Now.” She held out her hand. *No wonder I’m drinking!*

He picked up the phone, tapped and scrolled, and handed it to her. “I took it just for me, and I should have asked first, but—”

“Yeah, you should have, and you didn’t,” she finished for him. The picture on the screen wasn’t as bad as it could have been. An inch of her ass crack peeked above the sheet, and a slice of ass cheeks below. A sliver of side boob by her bent arm. And her tattoo in all its glory. But nothing revealing … in an X-rated kinda way. For a quick phone pic, it was actually kinda sexy and arty. But that did not make it okay!

“Did you take *other* pictures?”

He shook his head so hard he could have sprained a neck muscle.

“Is this part of your regular MO?”

“What do you mean?”

“Do you have pictures of other … conquests in your phone?”

His eyes widened with horror. “Fuck no! What do you take me for? Wait. Scratch that. Look, I’ll erase it right now.” Two taps and he handed her back the phone. “Go ahead. Scroll through my pictures. Yours is gone, and there aren’t any others like it.”

She scrolled quickly, vaguely registering pictures of teammates, hockey rinks, pucks in gloves, cityscapes, some cool cars, and a few of him and Amanda. Shoving the phone back at him, she said, “That was not cool. Or legal.”

“You sticking up for Owen and injecting yourself between me and Amanda isn’t cool either,” he fired back. “Just shows where your true loyalties lie, and they’re not with me.”

“*What?* Tell me you’re joking. How in the hell am I sticking up for Owen?” He shrugged, and she barreled ahead. “As for *loyalties*, Blake Barrett, take a look at yourself. I suppose you would have dragged Amanda to the town square by her hair and had her stoned?” He rolled his eyes dramatically and clicked his tongue, and she wanted to slap him. Instead, she gritted out,

"Yelling at her isn't cool either. No wonder she didn't come to you! Has that even gotten through that thick skull of yours? The poor girl can't go to her parents—*any* of them—and she can't go to her brother. Who's she supposed to talk to?"

He blew out a long, tortured breath. "Maybe I'll call you in a few days when you've calmed down."

It took a few moments of disbelief before his words registered and she detonated from the inside out. "Don't bother, you jerk! My calming down isn't going to do a thing to pretty up this shit-show, especially not now that we've exposed it for what it is." Brave words, and she carried them off with attitude, but the conviction was pure theatrics. Deep down, her foundation walls were crumbling.

"M, you're overreacting." He had the audacity to look icily calm, while inside she was a series of explosions.

Logic hopped a train out of town as her temper threatened to flare into an inferno.

"I mean it, Blake! We're done here. If I see your number on my caller ID, I'm not answering!" She paused to pull in a calming breath, willing her pounding heart to slow down. "I guess you were right about your juvenile vocabulary because the word 'apology' apparently isn't part of it."

He offered her another eye-roll. "Oh, come on. Cut the melodrama."

"You cocky son of a bitch! Are you serious right now? You don't get it. At. All." She pointed to the door. "Get out. Get the hell out."

He put up his hands in mock surrender. "Yeah, yeah. I'm going. And don't worry about my number popping up on your caller ID 'cause I ain't calling." As he let himself out, he turned to say something over his shoulder. She slammed the door shut just as his big frame cleared her doorway, cutting off whatever garbage he had been about to spew.

The adrenalin flooding her body had fueled her anger, and she twitched with energy that had no outlet. Cursing, she stomped around the living room, picked up a pillow and screamed into it, then hurled it across the room, sending candles flying from a table. The adrenalin finally ebbed after more pacing, cursing, and yelling, and she slumped into the red couch. Something inside her chest cracked, and like a failing dam, it gave way to a deluge of tears. They swept through her, and she curled up in a ball on the couch, pulling a pillow into her middle while she rode out the wave of pain.

He hadn't even tried. He'd just ... walked out without fighting back.

*Told you not to give up your heart*, Goody Two-Shoes whispered. The little devil fumed, spoiling for a pair of balls to kick with pointy-toed shoes. *At least you found out what a jerk he is* now. *Oh, and bonus, no need to fret over birthday or Christmas gifts.*

No amount of cleverisms from her shoulder advisers was going to heal the rip inside her. She'd only been with him a few months, yet she was torn in two as if it had been decades. Where did she go from here?

When she was sure she'd cried herself out, she marshaled herself into some kind of order and hit a familiar number.

Her voice wobbled. "Fi? I need you." A fresh round of tears she didn't know she had in her reserves welled up inside her again.

# Chapter 33
## Crickets

Blake prowled his condo, his head and heart reeling. A bonfire raged inside of him, blinding him to what lay around its edges. Yeah, M had thrown him out, but he'd been on his way out the door anyway. Eventually, they'd both cool down, apologize—she certainly owed *him* an apology—and they'd be back to where they had been before. *Right?*

Why did the little voice in his head feeding him this line of bullshit sound so reedy-thin? He tried to hide behind his bravado and convince himself these were truths revolving in his head, but the veneer was cracking faster than pond ice in the springtime. Deep down in his gut, a knot of dread was blooming.

And then there were the *other* warring emotions: One minute, he wanted to lash out at her for icing him; the next, he wanted to beg her to forgive him. Badly. *No, I get a pass. She loves me!* a voice loudly shouted down logic.

"She never told you she loves you, dumbass. *You're* the one who nearly let it slip. What if she was just using you for ... well, just using you?" he muttered aloud. This thought made his anger surge.

Herculean as it was, he pushed thoughts of M aside. He had other problems to solve, and they revolved around his sister. Amanda needed an apology from him, but he wasn't ready to do that until he'd confronted their mother and Ferguson. Too late for confrontation tonight, so he'd have to wait until morning. Which meant he got zero sleep, and though something tugged at him to go next door and make things right, every time he thought of Amanda running to *M* and not him, his wounded pride reared up and blocked him from following through. Never mind that Amanda *had* called him and he'd yelled at her. M had soothed her after he'd roughed her up more than she'd been at the start of the call.

But right now his head hurt too much to unravel it all.

The next morning, he locked his door on his way to practice and the flight to Nashville that would follow. He stole a few glances at M's still door and finally out-and-out stared at it as if her sunny smile would appear in the doorway. His phone buzzed with an angry text from Quinn, who was waiting for him downstairs. They were carpooling. *Hurry up, dumbass. Haven't got all day.*

"Right," he grumbled to himself and trudged with leaden feet away from M's door.

His mood didn't improve during practice or on the plane ride, and his teammates seemed to sense it, giving him a wide berth. Though he spent an impressive amount of time glaring at Ferguson, the guy never looked his way.

In the hotel lobby, Ferguson brushed past him, and Blake finally snapped. He yanked Ferguson's shoulder back, spinning him. Ferguson rolled his eyes as if he'd been expecting it.

"You and I need to talk," Blake said.

"About what?"

"My sister."

Ferguson's eyes went wide. "What about your sister?"

"You're *fucking* her," Blake accused through gritted teeth.

Ferguson sighed. "No, I'm not." He swiveled his head. "Maybe we should go someplace private and talk."

*What?*

"Look, Bear, there're some things I should have told you before, but we haven't exactly been getting along." One eyebrow dipped accusingly.

"Fine. Let's go."

They headed for the deserted mezzanine, and Fergs caught a waitress's eye. As they settled in at a small cocktail table, she followed and took their order, smiling broadly when Fergs slipped her a Benjamin and asked her to check in with them often. "We might be here a while." He grinned, and she amped up her smile to megawatt brightness before walking away with what seemed like an exaggerated sway.

Blake shook his head in disgust.

"What now?" Ferguson snapped. "You think every time I'm nice to a woman, I'm trying to get into her panties?"

"Because you are."

"No, I'm not."

"A little hard to tell with your track record lately," Blake said dryly.

To his surprise, Ferguson simply nodded. "Yeah. I can see that."

The waitress reappeared with Ferguson's beer and Blake's Coke and deposited a large bowl of bar nuts. Ferguson helped himself to a handful of nuts. Blake had no appetite, and once the waitress was out of sight, he leveled his gaze at Ferguson. "What's going on between you and my sister?"

Ferguson shook his head. "Nothing different than what's always gone on between me and your sister."

"She said you're in love with her."

Ferguson's eyes bugged out. "*What?* If she believes that, then it's in her own mind."

Blake straightened. "What the fuck is *that* supposed to mean?"

Ferguson blew out a breath. "I know she's your sister, so I never said anything before, but she's made it clear she has a thing for me. Probably only because she's known me for a while and looks up to her big brother's friend or some shit like that. Puppy love kinda stuff. As for being in love with her, no. I love her *like* a little sister, but I've never said that to her because I didn't want her taking it the wrong way." His voice dropped to a mumble. "Somehow she did that all by herself." He sipped his brew.

Blake's frown creased his forehead. "So you *didn't* sleep with her?"

"No. Doesn't mean I couldn't if I wanted to, though." He threw up his hands in defense as if warding off a blow Blake hadn't yet considered. "Just speaking the truth here."

Blake glowered at him in response.

"What I'm trying to say is," Ferguson continued, "while I knew I could take advantage, I didn't. It wouldn't have been right."

"Did you see her at Thanksgiving?"

He nodded. "I did. She said she needed to get away from your mom, and knowing what your mom can be like, I felt sorry for her. Once I realized it was more than just getting away from your mom, I cut it short."

"So where *was* she when she wasn't home?"

"I don't know. Once she figured out I wasn't interested, she ... she started crying and shit. I made sure she got home, then I gave her the brush-off. Felt like a giant fucking turd for doing it—she's your *sister*—but I figured it was better to let her think of me as a dick than to keep crushing on me."

"At least you *know* you're a dick. After watching you in that club with that girl, and after the stunt you pulled at the charity brunch, I didn't want you in the same *town* as me, let alone Amanda."

"Yeah, I know," Ferguson muttered.

"Why the fuck did you bring Sherry? Why did you tell her I was interested in her? That wasn't only a really fucked-up way to jack with me and M, but did you think about what you were doing to *Sherry*?"

Ferguson pushed out another puffed-cheek breath. "Yeah, I've had some time to think about that, and all I can say is I've been a little out of my mind lately. Between the demotion and watching your ass skyrocket ahead of me ... plus, you seemed to be finding something special with M while my thing with Tracy was going off the rails."

Blake gave an involuntarily headshake. "What thing with Tracy? I thought that was over."

One corner of Ferguson's mouth hitched with an ironic smile. "Yeah, well, that would have been the easy answer. The truth is *she* was done before I was."

"She dumped you?" Blake didn't bother hiding his disbelief.

Ferguson winced. "Why the fuck does it sound so much worse when *you* say it? Yeah, fucker, she dumped me. Said I was fun for a while but that she was looking for someone more *mature* for long-term." He let out a mirthless laugh. "And here I was, dumb fuck that I am, actually *thinking* long-term. Can you fucking believe that?"

"What? That you're not mature? Yeah, I totally believe that." *You and me both.*

Ferguson twirled his pint glass between his hands. "It's no excuse, but I think I sort of lost it there for a while, and you saw the worst of it. Sherry, the chick in the club, some other stuff I'm not proud of that only made me feel worse."

"Then why'd you do it?"

Ferguson shrugged, looking utterly miserable.

"And why were you acting like you wanted M when you wouldn't even ask her out?"

"I *did* want to go out with her at first, and I *was* intimidated. I don't have to tell you, but she's not like the girls we usually meet. I like a challenge, but she might've been more than I wanted to handle. I was working my way up to asking her out, and then I met Tracy, and we clicked. I just didn't want to admit how much I liked her. I kept thinking it was a fling, but I got in a little deeper every time I was with her. Then she broke it off and started seeing other guys. I've been trying to get her out of my system, but it's not working. Fuck, women can mess with your head!" He raised his glass. "But you wouldn't know about that. You and Michaela seem to be on solid ground." He winced again. "Sorry if I screwed anything up for you, man."

"No, you didn't," Blake sighed. *I did that all by myself.*

A few days later, after two games of piss-poor play, Blake decided M was messing with his head and he needed to put aside his pride and call her. The call went straight to voicemail. He texted instead, but hours went by without an answer.

*She said she wouldn't answer. Maybe she hasn't cooled down yet. Maybe she meant it. Maybe she doesn't want me back. Maybe she's just trying to prove a point.*

He called his sister instead. After the few requisite niceties were stiffly exchanged, he blurted, "I owe you an apology. I should have been willing to listen when you called with that explosive news."

"Yeah, you should have, you dick. But I forgive you."

He let out a relieved gust. "So have you talked to Mom about what you discovered? Or your parents?"

"No. I'm just not ready to go there yet."

"I'll help you with Mom at Christmas, Manda. And with your parents if you want, though that might be kinda weird since they don't know me."

"That's really sweet. Michaela said you'd probably come around and that I shouldn't stay mad."

*Huh.* "So, uh, have you talked to her lately?"

"Not since the day after you were such a jerk."

*Ouch.* But he deserved it. He'd been running the conversation through his head over and over, like a chicken rotating on a spit. He'd said some horrible things, but he'd assumed they could recover from their first real fight. Had he been so far off the mark when it came to knowing her, knowing the limits of their relationship? Because that's what they'd had: a relationship. Not some kind of fuck-buddies arrangement or a one- or two-night stand that ran its course in a week, much as he'd tried convincing himself of it in the beginning. Kinda like Fergs.

When Blake had first scrutinized his actions the night of his blowup with M, it hadn't struck him how badly he'd fucked up, how out of line he'd been, and he cringed every time he recalled telling her she drank too much ... among other things. He hadn't had a drop to drink, so he couldn't even blame his assholery on being intoxicated. No, that was *all* him being him.

Amanda pulled him back to the here and now. "She had some important meeting coming up at work, so I've left her alone. She doesn't need my problems too."

*Oh shit. The meeting with Steadman. I totally forgot.* His self-admonishment ramped up. How could he be such a selfish fuck? "Well," he said lamely, "if you talk to her, tell her ... uh, tell her good luck." After he hung up, for the first time since their fight, a hollowness grew inside of him.

For the rest of the road trip, he called and texted M every day, but he got nothing. Then he sent flowers. Still nothing. So he sent two more bouquets, but they got no response either. The silence thundered in his head, and the uneasy emptiness gaped inside of him. At times, he thought it might devour him from the inside out. He'd been so full of righteous indignation and wounded pride—and stupidity. Now that the toxic mix had drained out of him, he was left with ... less than nothing.

His birthday came and went without registering a blip on his radar. Life sucked.

And his play suffered for it because he couldn't fucking focus. Irony of ironies, Coach had toyed with the lines for today's matinee game—the last of the road trip—shifting Nelson back to center the first line, Ferguson on the second line, and Blake down at fourth-line center. If he was lucky, he'd see five minutes of ice time.

He resolved to pound on M's door when he got home tonight until she opened it.

Except when he strode down the hall from the elevator, his eye caught on three wilted bouquets outside her door. He turned and went straight downstairs to the security guard's desk.

"Have you seen Miss Wagner?"

"Not for at least a week. She said something about visiting family for the holidays, and that she'd be back after New Year's."

"There are three dead bouquets of flowers outside her door." *Sent by* me.

"I'm sorry, sir. We have a new kid that started, and he probably ran them up there without knowing she was gone for a stretch. I'll make sure the mess is picked up right away."

"No need. I'll handle it myself. Thanks for your help."

She was with her parents, he told himself, so at least she was okay. She was simply done with him.

# Chapter 34

# The Bleak Season

Blake stared out the window on Christmas Eve, taking in the bleak Oregon day shrouded in shades of gray. Raindrops peppered the window and slid down the glass, leaving a trail that obscured the yard beyond. A cup of steaming coffee appeared in front of him on the kitchen table, where he'd propped his elbows.

He glanced up and gave his sister a half-smile. "Thanks."

She slid into the seat perpendicular to his with a mug of her own. "No problem. You looked like you could use it."

"That bad, huh?" He blew on the dark brew.

"Let's put it this way: I've seen death warmed over that looks better than you do right now."

"Gee, thanks?"

She chuckled softly and sipped from her cup.

"I need to ask you something, and I don't want you to get upset."

She hitched an eyebrow. "Which means I probably *will* get upset."

"Well, try not to. Just remember I'm your big brother, and I may stick my nose in where it doesn't belong, but my heart's in the right place." He cleared his throat. "You said some things about you and Owen, and I jumped to certain conclusions." He turned up the softness in his voice. "Did you sleep with him, Manda?"

Casting her eyes down, she rubbed her fingertips across the table's ridged, distressed surface. "Did you talk to him?"

"Briefly. I want your side."

Still not looking at him, she shook her head. "Doesn't mean I didn't try, though." Her voice came out in a choke, and he covered her hand with his. She hid her face in her free hand, and her shoulders shook. "God, I feel so stupid."

"Hey, hey." He released her hand and pushed a hank of hair behind her shoulder. "Don't. He doesn't deserve you. Even *he* knows it."

Both hands covered her face now, and she leaned her elbows on the tabletop and sobbed.

At a loss for more words, Blake simply rubbed her back until her crying slowed.

"I've been in love with him for so long," she sniffled, "and I convinced myself he loved me back but that you stood in his way." She paused to hiccup. "God, I made a complete fool of myself." Her pitiful wail was muffled in her hands.

"I'm sure you didn't," he offered lamely.

She lifted her head, and her tear-filled eyes fixed on his. "Yeah, I did. Even if I hadn't, it wouldn't hurt any less."

"No, I guess not. Shit, this stuff is not for beginners like you and me."

"We didn't exactly have the best role models, did we?" she agreed.

"At least you grew up with a couple who cared about each other."

She shrugged. "Maybe. Honestly, I think they stayed together because they didn't know what else to do."

They sat in silence, sipping their coffees, listening to the rain patter against their mom's house.

"I'm sorry about Michaela," Amanda said softly.

He drew in a breath and blew it out. "I could've told you it wouldn't work. I just thought it'd take longer to fall apart."

"Cynical much? Your name should be Bleak, not Blake."

He shrugged. "It's realistic. I knew it was too good to be true. Why didn't I listen to myself?" *Guys like me don't get girls like her.*

"Because your *self* isn't always equipped to give the best advice."

"Wow," he snorted. "That sounds almost grown-up."

She shoved his shoulder good-naturedly, and they returned to a comfortable silence where his mind drifted where it always went: M. To the tiny pleats between her brows when she was mad or thinking really hard; to how she wore fake glasses because she thought she needed them to look smart; to how her eyes sparkled with mischief; to the adorable side of her she kept buttoned up behind her lawyerly façade, and how lucky he'd been to glimpse it. How being with her never felt like settling; it felt like being on top of the fucking world. How lucky some other guy would be when he captured her heart. How much he wanted to hear the smile in her voice right now.

*Yeah, maybe I'll change my name to Bleak.*

As if punctuating that thought, their mother drifted into the kitchen looking like death's death warmed over.

"Rough night, Mom?" He knew it had been. He'd been there. She hadn't screamed or thrown things, but she'd sat staring into nothingness, her elbow the only part of her body that was busy because it brought her drink to her mouth over and over and over.

"Don't be a smartass, Blake," she grumbled as she poured herself a coffee.

"Well, Merry Christmas to you too."

She shot him a bleary-eyed look over her shoulder. "Even I know it's Christmas Eve."

*Yeah, and only two days before I can politely escape and go home to my empty condo. Whoopee. That's what I get for letting myself believe in something as schmaltzy as love.*

As his mom approached the table, Blake pulled out a chair for her and she plopped down with a grunt. The silence that had filled the gaps in his and Amanda's conversation took on a turbulent quality. Was it his mom, or was it him? Was he just so damn apprehensive that he invited the uneasiness?

"Blake, while you're here, I'd like you to pull some boxes down from the attic for me."

"No problem. Just show me what and where you want them," he replied, relieved for something to *do* besides stare at his mother and sister. *Wonder if M's parents have invited over a ton of people for Christmas dinner? Bet their home is filled with fun and lively conversation. Of course it is, if M's there.* Warm fuzzies enveloped his chest as he recalled how nimbly and graciously she had done what neither Amanda nor he had been capable of even conjuring during their disastrous Thanksgiving dinner: she'd taken their mom under her wing, almost literally, and coaxed her with overwhelming kindness. She hadn't needed to, yet she had. That was M.

*Okay, idiot. Stop wallowing in M World.* "Did you know that most people only think they have one big attic when in fact there are—"

"Blake, stop!" his mother groaned.

He bit back his hurt. "Too early for trivia, huh?"

Amanda rolled her eyes. "It's *always* too early for trivia."

*M likes my trivia. If she were here ... She's not, dickhead. Get over it already.*

Amanda gave Blake a few head jerks like she was trying to tell him something, but he frowned back in confusion. She darted them to the ceiling as though looking for patience before training them on their mother. When Mom's mug was drained, Amanda quickly rose and held out her hand. "Ready for more, DeeAnn?" Since Amanda had someone she'd called "Mom" her entire life, she referred to their mother by her first name. Kinda weird, but then, what *wasn't* weird about their family?

Mom signaled she was ready for more coffee, and Amanda refilled her cup and placed it in front of her. Then she wrung her hands and sat down. "DeeAnn ... Mom ... I wanted to ask you something."

Their mom raised dull, watery eyes to her.

Amanda darted an uncertain gaze to Blake again and wrung her hands a little harder. “I found out something recently that I wanted to ask you about.”

*Oh shit*. He hadn’t cued in that they were having *this* conversation. How could he have forgotten so easily? His focus should have been on his sister, on this family melodrama, but it wasn’t—just like he struggled to focus on hockey. On anything but what he’d lost.

Their mother sipped at her coffee and waited.

“I took a DNA test,” Amanda said, her voice quavering.

The coffee cup slammed onto the tabletop and wobbled, and Blake reached out to steady it. Their mother’s wide eyes stared into Amanda’s. “And what did you find?”

“I’m ... My father is ...” Amanda burst into fresh tears.

Blake took one of his mother’s hands between his. Tears welled in her eyes too. “Mom, Amanda discovered that her adoptive dad is her biological dad, and she’s—we’re—wondering what happened.”

Their mother covered her mouth with her free hand and let out a gut-wrenching sob. Blake’s insides rolled, but he kept a stoic mask plastered on his face while she recovered. Amanda sniffled softly. “I wanted to tell you both for so long, but your father wouldn’t let me.”

“Dad wouldn’t let you tell us what?” Blake said softly.

For the next hour, Blake learned his father hadn’t been so selfless. After they married and she gave birth to Blake, his mother did settle down, but his father was away from home more and more, spending long hours with his buddies because “the kid cried too much.” Feeling neglected, she had an affair that resulted in Amanda. Blake’s father refused to let her bring the baby home, insisting it would be a daily reminder of his wife’s infidelity. He had even gone so far as to threaten to take his anger out on Amanda, so their mother did the only thing she could think of to protect her. She decided to put the baby up for adoption. When she told her married lover—Amanda’s biological father—he and his wife adopted and raised her as their own. They'd never been able to have children, and Amanda was a blessing they welcomed.

"Did Dad *know* her real dad adopted her?" Blake asked.

His mother shook her head. "I was afraid for him to find out, and frankly, he never asked." She looked from Blake to Amanda and wrapped her bony hands around Amanda's. "I didn't want to give you up, Amanda. It tore me apart."

Tears rimmed and spilled down Amanda's face. "Did you love my dad?"

Mom shook her head. "I thought I did, but looking back, no. I wanted to make Blake's father jealous. Stupid, silly, destructive games."

Blake's temper began rising. "But Dad said you didn't want to keep her."

She swung her gaze to him. "Yes, I know what your father said. That's what he wanted you to believe. I fought him on it, but I didn't win that argument. And you looked up to him so. I didn't want to destroy that."

"You made it worse!"

"I expect I did. For all of us. That's when I started drinking, and I never stopped. It's not an excuse. Just a reality."

"Dad wouldn't divorce you because he loved you too much," Blake accused. His agitated mind spun, trying to untangle the web of sticky lies. Amanda sat like a statue, her eyes riveted to their mother as if seeing her for the first time.

"Your father didn't love me. He loved a woman named Charlene, but Charlene married his best friend. Frankly, I think that's the real reason your father asked me to marry him. He was devastated, and he wanted to hurt her like she'd hurt him."

Blake shoved himself back from the table, the chair legs making an awful scraping sound. "You're lying!"

His mother looked at him blearily and shook her head. "Not about this. Those boxes I asked you to move? Your father kept journals, and it's all there in the attic. I wanted you to bring them down so I could throw them out, but maybe you should have them."

Blake sat back as though someone had shoved him. Someone had. His father, from the grave ... *if* his mother was telling the truth. “Is this the whole story you said I didn’t know?”

“Yes, the whole sordid mess.” She pierced him with a bloodshot gaze. “Your father and I were toxic together. I asked him for a divorce—many times—but he wouldn’t discuss it, even though he was in love with another woman. Maybe if she’d been free ... Well, it doesn’t really matter at this juncture. Too many lives were destroyed as a result, and I didn’t want to see that happen to you too. He forbade me ever telling you, Blake. He was so proud of you, and he wanted you to be proud of him. And I wanted that for both of you. Now I’ve destroyed that too.”

“Why did my father commit suicide?” Blake’s voice came out strangled.

Mom let out a slow, painful sigh. “Charlene died of cancer four years ago. Though their relationship ended when she married, your father still loved her, and I think he just couldn’t ... She was his ‘one,’ and I think he wanted to be with her, and he only knew one way to do that. You could say he died of a broken heart.”

Blake gaped. “So it wasn’t being married to you that destroyed him?”

“Being married to me didn’t help, but no, I didn’t drive him to it. I loved your father, but I couldn’t cope. My escape was in the bottle. I wasn’t much of a drinker when I met your dad, but I learned to become one. Not that it was his doing, because it wasn’t. I wanted to have babies and stay home, but your father liked watching games at the bars with his buddies. I tagged along at first because I thought that’s what a wife *should* do, and I liked being with him.” She smiled sadly. “And he was such a handsome devil; I didn’t trust the other women. Small consolation, but I needn’t have worried. He might have been in love with someone else, but he was loyal to me.”

The air seemed to have been sucked out of the room, and three people whose lives had been stitched together—not by choice, but by fate—sat in abject silence. Everything Blake had believed his entire life might have been a lie. He'd been the product of a bunch of fucked-up people who hadn't followed their hearts. Not knowing what to think, he let his mind go numb.

When his mother finally spoke again, he had no idea how much time had ticked by. "You know, I think I'd like to try rehab again. I'm getting too old to be this hungover all the time."

# *Chapter 35*
# SHENANIGANS EXPOSED

Michaela pulled in a breath and straightened her jacket in front of the imposing wooden door leading into the offices of Steadman, Fast & Hart. This was it. The moment of truth had arrived. Except she was armed with a few truths of her own that existed independently of whatever Steadman was about to tell her, and they were the reason she held her head high. Sure, her heart was hammering like a carpenter's nail gun, but *she* owned her future. No one else.

The receptionist gave her a curious look as she picked up the phone and announced Michaela's arrival to Mr. Steadman's assistant. Soon Michaela was ushered into a familiar conference room where she waited ... and waited. She'd been around the firm long enough to know this was a common tactic Steadman used. He enjoyed throwing his adversaries off balance. Did he see her as an adversary, though?

As the door swung open and Steadman's white head appeared, she inhaled a deep breath and crossed her hands in her lap. She was about to learn the answer to her silent question.

He gave her a cool glance as he took a seat, oddly, across the conference table from her and not at its head. "Ms. Wagner, it's a pleasure to see you again. How was your Thanksgiving?"

*Is he kidding?*

"As enjoyable as could be expected, under the circumstances." She offered him a guileless half-smile.

His expression unexpectedly softened. "Understandable ... and regrettable." He drew in a breath. "As you no doubt recall from our last meeting, I indicated our forensics team needed time to investigate the irregularities that had come to our attention. We have concluded that investigation and made some rather remarkable discoveries."

*Don't say too much. Don't give anything away.* She arched an expectant eyebrow. Just then, a knock sounded and the head of HR stuck her head in. "Ready for me, Mr. Steadman?"

He waved her in. "Yes, Judith. Please join us. You know Ms. Wagner, of course."

Judith offered a tentative nod and slid into the seat beside Mr. Steadman, placing a closed file on the table. Unsure what to make of the woman's presence, Michaela told herself having Judith here was preferrable to a cop with a pair of handcuffs ready to haul Michaela's butt off to jail.

Steadman cleared his throat. "As I was saying, we uncovered interesting facts, such as the extent of knowledge about the firm held by one of your colleagues."

Michaela's confusion must have shown all over her face because Steadman barreled ahead. "We had a saboteur in our midst, Ms. Wagner. A very clever one who—unbeknownst to us, naturally—schemed and gathered intelligence about our innermost workings, from client files to IT. He used this ill-gotten knowledge to cause trouble and, for reasons known only to him, aimed it at a bull's-eye he'd placed on your back."

"Who is it?" Michaela blurted.

"Mr. Hewitt."

Though Michaela had anticipated the answer, it still hit her square in the chest, and breath whooshed from her lungs.

Steadman's thick brows cinched together. "I assure you Mr. Hewitt will be dealt with appropriately. We have handed our evidence over to the DA's office. While I'm relieved we got to the bottom of the situation, I regret we had to put you on leave in order to do so, but we had little choice, you understand? To show our good faith, your pay has been reinstated retroactively, augmented by a holiday bonus, all seen to by Judith." Judith gave a solemn bob of her head. "Now about your future here at Steadman, Fast & Hart."

*Oh, this should be interesting.* Michaela had been up most of the night after receiving the "summons" to today's meeting, flipping through various scenarios in her head. She was about to discover how close to the mark her top guess about the firm's tack would strike.

"Ms. Wagner, we would like to offer you a swift path to partnership by awarding you the Fenton account." Steadman smiled, but it was calculated, without warmth. "I can think of no worthier candidate."

*Hmm. Not my first guess, but close.* The bigger surprise was how unmoved she was by the offer of the coveted account, especially after craving a bite at that dangling carrot for so long. The revelation bolstered the conclusion she had already come to.

Steadman's droning brought her back to the conference room. "If you agree to stay, and we hope you will, there will naturally be a substantial increase in your compensation to bring you in line with someone in such a lofty position." He sat back and steepled his hands.

*Naturally.* Michaela quickly sorted through the scattered debris from the bombshell Steadman had just dropped: First, Brad had been responsible for all the scheduling mishaps, the mysterious file movements, the billing questions, and all the other inexplicable crises that had plagued Michaela. Second, he had hoodwinked the entire firm for "reasons known only to him," which the firm no doubt knew but wouldn't divulge in order to limit their culpability. Third, while they'd "handled" Brad, they were paying her off to keep quiet and not file a lawsuit against them.

She darted a look to Judith and the nervous fingers the woman ran along the file. To Steadman, Michaela said, “And if I agree to accept this, ah, promotion, what are the next steps?”

He gave a noncommittal shrug that was more fake than her glasses. “Few, really. We will ask you to first sign an agreement to hold the firm harmless. After that, everything is back to normal, and you will be at your desk Monday morning.”

*Wrong. Nothing will ever be back to normal.* Since Thanksgiving, she’d had plenty of time to ponder the crossroads where she stood and which future she desired for herself. This, right here, left her with no doubt the path she was about to follow was the true one, the only one for her. And that future did not include slaving away in a pit of slithering snakes.

When Michaela didn’t immediately respond, Steadman slid a sidelong glance at Judith before his gaze landed back on her. “We appreciate that this has been a difficult time,” he said smoothly. “Therefore, if you would prefer to return after the start of the year, you have the firm’s blessing. Your pay raise will go into effect today, as soon as you sign off.”

Judith passed the file along the table’s smooth surface, and he corralled it with his fingertips. He plucked a document from the folder, scanned it, and placed it between himself and Michaela.

She didn’t look at it. She didn’t need to. “Thank you, Mr. Steadman,” she said with a graciousness she didn’t feel. “But I’ve made some discoveries of my own, and no matter how big the bribe, I will not be coming back.”

*God, that feels good to say!*

Steadman flinched, and Judith, whose guile wouldn’t fill a thimble, rocked back in her seat as though she’d been struck.

Steadman scrutinized Michaela. “May I ask your plans?”

Michaela pulled off her fake glasses, placed her clasped hands on the table’s surface, and leaned forward. “You may. I will be going out on my own. As to the rest, I’m not prepared to share those details until I’ve conferred with my attorney and we’ve worked out what’s in my best interest going forward.” The fact her attorney was herself was nothing he needed to know.

His eyes sharpened, and he regarded her for several beats, as if processing something that made no sense to him. "Might I suggest you will regret your decision, Ms. Wagner?"

"I don't think I will, Mr. Steadman."

For the first time since he'd entered the conference room, the old man's façade showed signs of cracking. "I don't understand. We made you a ridiculously generous offer."

She leaned back in her chair. "It's not always about money. Someone told me that individual effort is a solo journey. I may be part of a team—in this case, a legal team—but how hard I push myself, how high I climb, is purely up to me." *Thank you, Blake Barrett.* "Being away from this office made me realize the power in that statement, and I plan to take control of my destination and drive the bus there myself. Had you not suspended me, I'm not sure I would have recognized my own potential, so thank you for that."

Michaela cringed as she watched Blake turn over the puck for what must have been the fifth time in the game—and they were only halfway through the second period. Aiming the clicker at the TV, she muted the game and tried to look away, but it was like pulling her eyes from a car wreck. Some part of her just had to keep watching, had to assess the level of damage, no matter how horrible. The jumping muscles in his jaw told her he was trying to conjure confidence from thin air, and he wasn't succeeding. As he drifted in for the face-off, his usual tics and twitches were more pronounced than ever, and his eyes held a look that bordered on frantic. Where had his fierce determination gone?

Her heart sank like a stone. She'd watched every game, and a fresh crack had scored her heart whenever Blake's ice time had been shortened. Hockey was everything to him. The slide in his play and his role *had* to be killing the ferocious competitor inside him.

She had yearned to reach out and soothe him, but she had held herself back. Push, pull. During the past weeks, ever since she'd put Steadman, Hart & Fast in her rearview mirror, the familiar struggle had been going on inside her, and the only outcome had been paralysis. Was his poor play her doing? If she bothered to check in with him—hell, she hadn't even wished him a happy birthday—would his play improve?

"Oh, get over yourself!" she admonished aloud. "He's a pro who's going through a slump. You're not even a blip on his thought radar when he's on the ice."

Her phone vibrated, and she snatched it up, grateful for the distraction.

"Happy New Year's Eve, Micky-Dub!"

Michaela exhaled. "Same to you, Fi. Where are you guys now?"

"The Broadmoor in Colorado Springs. You should see this place! So luxurious and sooo romantic."

"Wish I was there too." The stab of envy in Michaela's heart physically hurt. An image of spending days lolling in a big fluffy bed with Blake popped into her head. They'd both be naked because why bother with clothes when—

*Stop it!*

"You could be. Just hop in your truck and—"

"You know the old saying. Two's company and all that."

"Well, maybe give that man a chance to grovel and we could be four. Then again, you'd have to talk to him first, wouldn't you?" Fiona said blandly.

Michaela sat at her parents' kitchen table, and she dropped her forehead in her hand, fighting back a sudden knot in her throat that made it hard to breathe.

"Shouldn't a best bud be on her bestie's side?" she choked.

"If the best bud thinks the bestie's right, then yes. But sometimes a best bud's job is to shake some sense into the bestie because her fake glasses are fogged up." Fiona sighed. "I want to see you happy, Mick, and you were happier with Blake than I've ever seen you. He was good to you. Yeah, you had a fight where some not-so-nice things were said, but that's heat-of-the-moment shit. He tried to apologize. Why not give him—give *yourself*—a chance?"

"I-I think it might be too late."

"How do you know if you don't try, Mick?"

"I'm just … I still have so much to sort out with the job change." And breaking up with Blake had dulled her ability to sort *anything* to do with her heart. She was a robot going through the motions programmed into her. Was she coming or was she going? This late in the game, was it even possible to backpedal and try to hit the reset button with him? The thought was daunting, like trying to undo the damage from a broken bone that hadn't been set properly right after the break.

The last few weeks had been upheaval on top of turmoil, and she'd shut down, made herself numb. But with time and her parents' doting care, the numbness was wearing off—which wasn't necessarily a good thing because she was emerging from her stasis with a great big hole where her heart was meant to be.

God, she missed Blake. Was there a way to let him know subtly so she didn't put him on the spot and could protect herself from the backlash if he was done with her? Trouble was, she wasn't sure she was sneaky enough to figure out how to orchestrate it.

She tuned back into the conversation in time to hear Fiona ask, "Have you heard any more from your former employer?"

"I just got a nice lump sum deposited into my account that I plan to use to get my new gig off the ground." Even that gave her heart a mere nudge instead of the big boost she should have relished, but the shift in subject managed to jump her to a different track where she could partially function.

"So you took the settlement they offered?"

Michaela scoffed. "No, I squeezed them a little harder and wrung a few more dollars from them. I also got a tidy sum for April, which will help when she comes to work for me after the New Year."

"Good for you! Those fuckers are lucky you're so nice and didn't slap them with a big fat lawsuit."

"If I'm being honest, Fi, they weren't the ones who did anything wrong. Well, except hire Brad in the first place. But he was a master conniver and manipulator. They had no idea that when he stayed late, he was letting himself into my office to mess with my stuff. They also had no idea how well he knew their IT systems and how capable he was of engineering trouble, that he was the one deploying their systems to invent catastrophes all along."

"You're giving him way too many props, Mick. He was a vengeful creep who wanted you and set you up because you didn't want him back."

"Whatever his motivation, he was masterfully deceptive, and they had no idea until it was too late. But I have a feeling he'll get his in the end." And *that* thought did give Michaela a lift.

"You mean beyond firing him?"

"Mm-hmm. The DA and Steadman are old chums from law school, and Steadman doesn't like egg on his face any more than he likes dishonest employees. There's a good chance Brad will end up somebody's bitch behind bars."

Fiona cackled. "I still say you should have accepted the big raise Steadman offered you just so you could torture the old geezer by reminding him, every day, how badly he screwed up where you're concerned."

"Honestly, as awful as it was, he did me a favor. The money won't be great to start, but I'm going to enjoy going to work so much more."

"Especially when work is in your lovely condo mansion."

Michaela blew out a breath. "About that. Looks like I'll be finding a new place to live."

"*What?* What happened to staying there through March?"

"The owner's project is wrapping up early, and he's returning in January. He wants his condo back."

"Where will you go?"

"Paige and Beckett have a carriage house above their garage, and they told me I could stay there as long as I wanted, so that could be a nice stopgap until I wrangle a permanent place."

"Hey, maybe you could give that Scott guy another chance!"

Michaela chuckled. "Don't think so. Apparently, he's got himself a girlfriend, which is great. He wasn't for me anyway." *I can only think of one guy who is.*

As if her bestie had read her mind, Fiona steered the conversation back to Blake. "Okay. So your professional life is back on track, which leaves your personal life. Obviously, Scott is out, but you still have option two: hot hockey player Blake."

"Gah! Stop, Fi. Let's admit I'm not good at picking men."

"I disagree, Micky-Dub. He's nothing like Anders, and he deserves a second chance. Anders had a stick up his butt and thought he never screwed up. Blake uses a stick for a living, and he screwed up but owns it."

"Is he paying you?" Michaela chuckled.

"He's the one for you, Mick. You just don't see it yet."

"I only knew him for two-plus months, and you knew him a few days. How can you possibly tell?"

"There's a lot you can intuit about a person," Fiona argued. "The way he looked at you at Thanksgiving told me volumes."

"Like he was hungry?" Michaela scoffed. "It was sex, Fi." Even Michaela didn't believe the words she spewed because there had been an undeniable deeper connection she couldn't explain.

Honestly, Fiona wasn't telling her anything that she hadn't recently admitted to herself, and while the memory of what Blake had said to her during that fight still stung, the sting didn't hurt nearly as much as missing him did.

"No, not like a guy who's hungry. Like a guy whose heart was quicksand—shifting and gooey and sucking things in. Okay, so not the best analogy. But I watched him watching you, and he was so focused on you that he was blind to everything and everyone else—well, except his mother when she spiraled out of control, but kinda hard to be blind to that spectacle. Then he looked like he was in hell, but again, it seemed centered on how it affected *you*, not himself or anyone else. And just look at how shitty he's been playing since you two broke up. I'm telling you, Mick, that man would give up his world for you."

Too dumbfounded to respond, Michaela let the comment slide for a beat. He *had* been playing shitty. "I hate it when you're stubborn. You're like a dog with a bone."

"You hate it when I'm *logical*, which is the opposite of what you are right now," Fiona countered. "Tell me what made you fall for him the first place. Other than how he looks, that is, because we both know there's more to him than that."

Michaela let out a resigned sigh. "He makes—made—me laugh. He's smart, thoughtful, protective. He has a really good heart. He genuinely cared about what affected me, and he tried to fix things, whether I wanted him to or not." She let out a soft chuckle. "I like that sexy brooding thing he's got going on."

*He put me first, spent time trying to figure out what he could do to make me happy, and I've never felt like that with anyone but my parents.* Hadn't that kind of caring deserved the second chance she hadn't given him?

Her breath stuttered in her chest as an image of his eyes drilling into hers popped into her head. They'd haunted her dreams, night *and* day.

"His eyes," she blurted. "He had a way of looking at me ... maybe it's what you were describing from Thanksgiving." *He made me feel beautiful and adored and like I was the most important part of his world.*

She caught herself and snapped out of her Blake trance. "Two months isn't enough time to know someone well enough to commit to more." *Is it?*

"Yeah, well, five years didn't tell you everything you needed to know about Anders either."

"Brutal, Fi."

"The truth often is, Mick, but it doesn't have to be."

# *Chapter 36*

# MILA KUNIS CURE-ALLS

***MID-JANUARY***

Blake parked his Range Rover and strode to the Cooper Lounge, where he was about to meet his date.

*My date.*

He was flying blind here, as in he was on the first blind date he'd been on in over a year. First *date* he'd been on in months. But was it really a *date* when he was merely helping Ferguson out? The guy had just gotten back together with Tracy, and her best friend was in town for the holidays. Ferguson had begged Blake to join them for dinner so she wasn't the proverbial odd-man out.

"Believe me, Bear, you'll be glad you came out of your hole for a few hours," Ferguson had enthused. "Tracy's girlfriend is hot, hot, hot, and unless you really screw things up, sex is on the menu tonight—which is something you need, dude. Badly."

No, he didn't need sex on the menu. Well, he *did,* but only with one woman. *Horny-specific.* Wasn't that the term he'd used with Michaela when he'd been hammered a lifetime ago? God, no wonder she was done with him! Not only had he been stupid drunk, he'd been just plain stupid.

Now he was firmly mired in his Michaela misery, along with being mired on the team's fourth line, battling in vain to get himself back to the second line. Hell, even the third line seemed like a long shot. He needed to break out of this funk because he was hurting his team. None of them were playing well, and he couldn't help but feel it was his fault. The slide had started with him, and it hadn't stopped. Their shot at a playoff spot was sliding right along with their record.

Everything had gone south after he and M broke up—the breakup he hadn't even realized *was* a breakup until its obviousness clobbered him over the head. By then, it had been far too late to put it back together again.

After trolling relationship websites for advice, he'd suffered through a self-imposed "no-contact" period. Had it been long enough? Was it time to try again? Her answering silence from before had been painfully deafening—was *still* painfully silent. Its sting poked at his frustration, and anger flared along with the same inner debate: he'd fallen over his skates trying to apologize. Didn't she owe him *at least* the courtesy of a response, even if it was a "Go fuck yourself"? That sudden flash dissolved into a fresh stab of disappointment and hurt. Maybe it *was* good he was getting out tonight.

As he entered the restaurant, Ferguson stood and flagged him over to a table where Tracy sat beside Fergs and a Mila Kunis lookalike sat next to an empty spot in a booth. She was ... Fergs hadn't exaggerated. The girl was stunning. When she gave him a dazzling smile, his battered ego bumped upward an inch or two.

"Lisa, this is Blake Barrett," Ferguson said before retaking his seat.

She tucked a piece of her long brown hair behind her ear. "I've really been looking forward to meeting you. I'm a huge fan."

Blake gave her a polite half-smile as he slid into the seat beside her. "Nice to meet you too." A flowery sort of fragrance assaulted him. Sweet, but not too overpowering.

"I've heard this place is really, really good." She flashed big hazel eyes at him and made a moaning sound that would have been sexy ... if it came from M.

*Stop thinking about M.* He gave himself an inner head slap. "Yeah, it is." He tried to work himself into the small talk without his awkwardness blazing like a beacon, mostly listening in while the three chatted.

Lisa was fairly easy on the eyes and ears. Pretty. Enthusiastic. Maybe *too* enthusiastic. Her hair was the same shade as M's—maybe not quite as rich or shiny—but she had soft waves instead of corkscrew curls like the ones he'd wrapped around his fingers for months. The thought it might not all be hers jolted him in his seat.

Dinner was decent, though he couldn't remember what he'd had hours later as they sat at a reserved table in Vinyl's upper mezzanine, not too far from the table he'd shared with M, Quinn, and Sarah Halloween night. Head on a swivel, he found himself looking for M everywhere, torn between wanting to see her and hoping like hell she wasn't there with some other guy.

Lisa tapped his forearm and pointed at his club soda. "You don't drink?"

"No."

She frowned, the vertical lines between her brows deeply creased, like frowning was a normal expression on her ... which brought to mind M's soft dimple and the tiny creases bracketing her mouth whenever she smiled.

*Focus, dumbass.*

"My mother's an alcoholic," he explained. An alcoholic who'd just entered rehab. Blake had talked to her several times before she started on the program, and she sounded determined. Hopefully, it would stick and she wouldn't fall off her wobbly wagon. The fact she'd enrolled herself was a victory, one M would've celebrated with him.

"That's too bad," Lisa said. "So you protest her drinking by *not* drinking?"

*"You drink too much."* He cringed inwardly as he recalled his words during his fight with M. God, what an ass he'd been. And yet he couldn't tell her that, could he, because she hadn't fucking called him back! How hard would it have been to send a text saying she was doing great? Not that he wanted to hear she was doing great—he wanted her to be as miserable as he was.

Lisa's brows furrowed with concern, and her hand squeezed his arm. "Are you okay?"

"Uh, yeah. Having a great time." He flashed her a fake smile.

She fluttered her eyelashes at him. "Want to dance?"

Ferguson and Tracy had left to dance some time ago. Dancing wasn't Blake's favorite pastime in the best of times, but he definitely wasn't feeling it tonight. Still, he needed to break out of this bleak mood he was in. "Yeah, let's do it."

The dance floor was packed, forcing him and Lisa close together. She gave him a sultry smile and started doing this undulating thing with her hips. She was good at it, and it should have been a turn-on, but he found himself shrinking away from her.

*Fuck me! Is it time to go yet?*

Someone poked his shoulder, and he whirled, surprised to see Fiona behind him. He bent down and squeezed her so hard she squeaked. "Where's James?" he yelled above the music.

"I left him with our friends." She waved to a table, and James waved back. Blake gave him a nod as his eyes strafed the other people at the table. *No M.* "I saw you dancing out here and thought I'd say hi," Fiona added.

*"Where's M?"* he wanted to blurt but held back. "Thought you guys were headed to Maldives or someplace like that?"

"We leave in a few days. We diverted to the Springs because James wanted to check out a business opportunity that came up." Blake's eyes roamed the dance floor. "She's not here," Fiona added.

"Who?" His innocent tone rang hollow in his own ears.

"Weren't you looking for Micky?"

*I totally was.* "Uh, no. Have you seen her lately?" The casual note he was going for didn't fly when he was shouting.

"Just saw her for lunch, as a matter of fact."

His heart pounded, competing with the music in his ears, making it hard to hear. "How is she?"

"She's doing about as well as you seem to be doing, which is somewhere between okay and not-so-great."

Now his pounding heart fell. "Can we go someplace and talk?"

Fiona pointed behind him. "I think your date wants your attention."

*Oh shit.* He whirled back around, meeting Lisa's frustrated glare. "Sorry. An old friend. Let me introduce you." He did, and it was awkward as hell. No judgment on Fiona's part, but plenty on Lisa's. Fiona seemed to sense his discomfort, and she pushed up to her toes and lined her mouth up beside his ear. "I don't think your date appreciates me taking you away from her. Text me tomorrow and we'll find some time, yeah?" She slipped a card into his hand. Lisa probably saw and misinterpreted the gesture, but he didn't give a fuck because finally, *finally*, he would get some answers.

He nodded vigorously and mouthed "Thank you" as Fiona danced back to her table. He would have a hard time sleeping tonight, and it had nothing to do with the fact that he'd be sleeping alone.

"How did the rest of your date with Lisa go last night?" Fiona shot Blake a coy look over her latte. He had texted her at 6:00 a.m. the morning after seeing her, unable to contain himself any longer.

"It wasn't so much a date as it was me helping my buddy Ferguson out. I went home alone, in case you're wondering."

Fiona gave him a noncommittal nod.

"Why won't Michaela call or text me, Fiona?" he blurted. No reason to beat around the bush, was there? "I just ... I want to apologize for being such a dick." He sat across from her and James at a local coffee shop before practice. And now not only was he a dick, but he was a whiny, *pathetic* dick. Hearing himself made him sick.

Fiona's eyes softened with sympathy, but her voice was full of skepticism. "Really? That's *all* you want?"

"No," he admitted.

"Good. Then she needs to understand that."

He groaned. "That's what I'm *trying* to do, but she won't let me. I don't know what to do. I'm not good at this stuff."

She lowered her brows at him. "None of us is, Blake, but somehow we bumble along until we get it right. Tell me something. Did you know how to play hockey the first time you strapped on skates?"

"No, of course not."

"But you learned, didn't you? Because you loved the sport. You pushed yourself, got better and better. You fought to get where you are. I expect you're still fighting."

He stared for a beat, two, three. "What you're saying is I should treat Michaela like hockey?"

"Give the man a ribbon! In your case, the Cup. Yes. Exactly."

"Okay. Got it. Now how do I get her to listen to me?"

Fiona pursed her lips. "Well, between you and me, that part's a little trickier. I've known Micky my whole life, and she's fiercely independent and doggedly determined, which I admire about her. However, there's a flip side that also makes her blindly stubborn. You have to understand, she never expected to be bowled over by you, but I'm trying to get her to come around and see reason."

He blinked a few times. "Are you saying I bowled her over?" Fiona nodded. "And that she's being blindly stubborn by not communicating with me?"

She nodded again. "I understand why, but I don't necessarily agree with her. Nor do I believe her stonewalling is in her best interest."

A breath of relief squeezed from his lungs. There was hope! Did he have an ally? "Since you understand why, would you please explain it to me?"

"She stormed into a corner, and she's not quite sure how to back herself out without appearing wrong. And her appearing wrong is, in her mind, a big chink in her armor, if that makes sense. Her confidence is a little shaky after what she's been through at work." Fiona filled him in on the developments at Steadman, Fast & Hart, and he sat back in stunned silence as she went on. "More than anything, Micky doesn't want to appear weak or stupid."

"But she's not! She's the strongest, smartest woman I know. Who else could come through what she just came through in her professional life and land on their feet? Jesus! She's my freaking hero." *I'm in awe of her.*

"You and I see that, but she doesn't. And this rule of hers doesn't apply to other people in her life. No, she reserves that collar for herself alone. She sets herself a high bar. This is what I mean by 'tricky.'"

"So by giving me a chance, she's what? Admitting to herself she was wrong and therefore weak?"

"Something like that. Because she shouldn't have shut you out in the first place, and deep down she knows that, but it's like she's stuck on this train track and doesn't know how to get off."

He sat back, feeling more defeated than when he began. "I'm not sure I know how to solve that."

"Maybe she just needs a little more time to wriggle out of the situation she's put herself in. Can you be patient with her?"

"If you think I have a chance, then fuck yeah! I can be as patient as she needs."

Fiona grinned. "See? Patience and persistence. Just like your approach to hockey."

"I love her *more* than hockey." *Whoa.* He'd said it out loud, and it felt ... right.

Fiona smacked her palms on the table. "Good! I knew you were the best one for her."

"I'm not so sure I am—"

"You gonna let that stop you?"

"Fuck no."

She held up both hands for high fives. "Yes! You've got this, Blake."

Blake wasn't sure he had a firm grip on exactly what the plan was here—or if there even was a plan—but he was buoyed by having Fiona on his side.

James, who had been quietly listening to their back-and-forth, sat forward. "What you need is a grand gesture."

"What? What the hell is that?"

He shrugged. "It's something women really like us men to do to show them they're important to us." He dropped his voice and mumbled, "As if all the other shit we do doesn't prove it." Then he flashed a smile. "Pretty sure it involves prostrating yourself, though."

Fiona scoffed. "The grand gesture can come from either party, and in this case I'm thinking some mutual grand-gesturing is in order to get you both to the finish line. Er, goal line. I need to brush up on my hockey-isms. Anyway, as long as you do your part, Blake—and I have no doubt you will—I'll see if I can move Micky's end along a bit." She winked at Blake, and his spirits lifted a little higher.

Several days later, in the locker room after practice, Blake asked Ferguson what the "grand gesture" was—assuming Fergs would be familiar with the term since he'd recently patched things up with Tracy. Big mistake.

"Oh shit, bro, I think it's basically where you lie prone in front of your woman and beg for forgiveness. Invite her to stomp all over you in front of your closest friends." He grinned. "If I were you, I'd lie on my stomach and let her walk all over my back with spiky heels. Hopefully, she'd be willing to do it naked."

Blake threw a roll of tape at him. "Stop picturing my girlfriend naked."

"Oh, interesting. So she's your girlfriend again. I guess you haven't given up entirely yet, huh? Which means you're not as big a loser as I pegged you for. Then again, even a blind squirrel finds a nut once in a while."

"Are you calling Michaela a nut?"

Ferguson laughed as he snatched the tape out of the air. "If she wants to be with you, she might be certifiable."

Blake fired a second roll of tape at him.

"You know he's needling you so he can get your tape, right?" Cam Blue grunted from where he sat on the bench, pulling off his skates. Blake blinked at him—it was the longest series of words he'd heard the guy string together in a while. "And you're playing into his hands like the dumb fuck you are," Cam added helpfully.

"All right, asshole," Blake growled. "What grand hand gesture have you used?"

Ferguson hung his tongue out and mimicked jacking off. "What, you looking for a *grander* way to do it? Try using your left hand."

Now Cam chucked a roll of tape at Ferguson. "*Grand gesture*, dickhead. There's no 'hand' in there."

Quinn piped up from his stall. "You want to win her over with a *grand gesture* so you don't *have* to use either of your hands."

Ignoring Quinn and Fergs, Blake arched an eyebrow at Cam. "You were saying about your experience with grand gestures?" He figured Cam's spare use of words made him some kind of sage.

"Don't ask me," the sage responded. "I've never grand-gestured in my life."

"You mean you never pissed a woman off so badly you needed to resort to it?" Blake asked. "The grand gesture, I mean, not your hand."

With a chuckle, Cam went to work loosening the tape around his socks. "Didn't say that. I've pissed off plenty of women. Just haven't been interested in reversing their opinions of me."

Blake might have growled in frustration at being more confused than ever, but his lips quirked with a grin as he busied himself with the rest of his gear. Despite his race to the bottom of the stats sheet—or maybe because of it—his footing with the boys seemed more solid than it had ever been. Was it because he and Fergs had patched things up? Did the struggles in his non-love life make him more sympathetic? Who knew? There hadn't been many bright lights these last weeks, and this was one that outshone any other. So there was that.

"Hey, dumbass," Fergs hollered at him.

Blake narrowed his eyes.

"You're heading home, yeah?"

"Yeah, why?"

"I still have some stuff I left behind at your place I want to swing by and get." He looked at his phone. "Oh shit. I better hurry. I have a stop to make first."

"Yeah, whatever." Blake arranged and rearranged his bag a few more times while he listened to the boys swap stories. By the time he left the locker room, Ferguson was nowhere in sight. Not that he was looking for him. No, his head was occupied with ways to find his way back into M's life.

He was still pondering and discarding alternatives as he stepped off the elevator. A grunt came from down the hall, and he paused, taking in a sight he wasn't quite sure his eyes were reporting correctly to his brain.

M's red couch was wedged in her doorway, and a body was draped over its arm. The ass belonging to that body stuck up in the air, all round and perfect and having an effect on things south of his waistband. No one else caused those kinds of stirrings. It could only belong to one person.

Right now that one person huffed in a muffled voice at whoever was on the other end where Blake couldn't see. "Seriously? This is the best you've got? I thought you knew what the hell you were doing?"

A male voice clucked somewhere inside her condo. "God, you're sassy!"

"Well, you're slowing me down! When do you think Blake will be home?"

"Blake's right here," Blake announced, feeling all kinds of stupid for talking about himself in the third person, but his brain wasn't firing on all circuits at the moment.

M swung up from the waist, pivoted, and fell on her ass on the couch, her legs splayed over the arm. "Oh, hi. What are *you* doing here?" Her bright gray eyes went wide and round, matching the shape of her open mouth. Her cheeks flushed pink.

"Uh, I *live* here? Need some help?"

She shook her head, and her curls bobbed. "No, I got this. I've got a helper." She jerked her thumb over her shoulder.

Ferguson stuck his head out of M's door, a shit-eating grin all over his face. "Hey, Bear. Didn't know you'd be here."

Blake parked his fists on his hips. "Yes, you did, jackass. I just saw you at—"

Ferguson smacked the side of his head. "Oh, would you look at that!" Except he wasn't looking anywhere but at the back of M's head. "I totally forgot what time it is, and I need to be somewhere else." He raced over the top of the couch, sidestepping M. Patting Blake's chest, he jerked a nod. "I'm out. You can handle it from here, right?"

Blake gaped at him.

"Just say yes, bro." Ferguson speed-walked to the elevator, where he spun and winked. "Consider this payback for my douchebaggery."

"Fergs, wait. I thought you had stuff you needed—"

"No, I'm good." He pointed at Blake as he waited for the elevator doors to open. "Watch out. She's got mace."

"Pepper spray," M hollered at him, though she seemed to be fighting a laugh.

"But you love me. You know you do." With that, he hopped on the elevator and was gone.

Heart trying to bolt from his chest, Blake swung his gaze to M. "What was that all about?"

Hoisting herself up, she sat on the arm of the couch and cinched her arms over her chest, blew a curl off her forehead, and shrugged. "I needed help with my couch, and he offered to help."

His eyebrows hitched. "So you just *happened* to be here, and Ferguson just *happened* to be helping you?" he replied dryly, corralling the effervescence in his veins. She was dressed in jeans, a soft gray sweater that matched her eyes, and hiking boots. Her cheeks were rosy, her full lips a deeper shade that invited kissing, and her dimple peeked out. She was fucking gorgeous, and his knees dipped a bit.

"I'm sorry I, er, um... The guy who owns this place is on his way back, and I need to be out. The couch is the last piece I had to move, and um, Ferguson offered to help. Ah ..."

He gaped at her. "You mean, you've been in and out of here, and I didn't know it?"

"Um, yeah?"

"Why didn't you knock?"

She flinched. "I-I'm not sure. Nervous, I suppose. I was afraid you'd slam the door in my face as soon as you saw it was me."

*Oh wow!* He scratched the back of his neck. "Is this a grand gesture?"

She looked up at him through thick, sooty lashes. "A what?"

"I have no fucking clue, except if this is something you set up, then it feels like it might be."

She blinked at him a few times. God, she was adorable. It struck him like a slapshot to the chest how much he'd missed her.

His lips twitched as he battled the smile that wanted to split his face. "M, you don't have a sneaky bone in your body, yet somehow you're up to something."

She blew out another breath. "I was watching you on TV the other night, and you didn't have the best game"—she winced—"and I thought, I don't know, maybe I could help somehow, and ... God, that sounds lame. The truth is I wanted to see you and I thought it would be easier on both of us if it was an accidental kind of meeting."

"Except this isn't accidental, is it?"

She shot him a sheepish smile. "Nothing about this is accidental. Fiona and I cooked it up, and Ferguson helped."

The breath fled from his lungs, and he swallowed to pull in more air. "So you went to all this trouble just to see me? Why didn't you just pick up the phone?"

She rolled her eyes. "I don't know. I didn't want to appear so deliberate, I guess. That way, if you wanted nothing to do with me, it would be less humiliating." She shook her head, muttering, "As if this ridiculous setup would be *less* embarrassing. God, what was I thinking? I'm so bad at the conniving thing." She dropped her head against the couch and peeked at him, one corner of her mouth curving upward, mischief sparkling in her pretty eyes. "Well, the guy *is* coming home, and I *did* need my couch out, so it's not totally fake."

Blake ran his hand over his jaw. "Where are you moving it?"

"To a storage unit."

"Huh. You know, I'm kinda partial to this couch." He pictured some of the things they'd done on that couch, and his fondness for the thing grew. "Bet we could find room for it at my place, if you're okay with storing it there."

Her expression suddenly turned shy. "Yeah, I guess that would be okay. Think you can unwedge it from the door? Owen got it stuck pretty good."

"It's what Owen does best. But between the two of us, we'll figure it out." He slid his bag off his shoulder. "Is this the part where I pull off my shirt?"

# Chapter 37

# Kissing Lessons on a Red Couch

If Blake kept wiggling his stupid eyebrows and kept that cocky grin plastered on his chiseled, unshaven face, Michaela wouldn't be able to stand up. Her knees were the consistency of aspic as it was, not helped by her rapid-firing heart and her somersaulting stomach. Damn near an entire cheer squad had apparently taken up residence in her belly.

"No, please keep the shirt on. One Owen is enough." *Him, I can resist. You, not so much.*

Blake's smile slid from his face. "Don't tell me he pulled that stunt again just now."

"Okay. I won't." *Because he didn't.* She pushed up to her feet and steadied herself, resting her hand on the couch. "Did you know that Hugh Jackman wouldn't consume any liquids for thirty-six hours before filming his shirtless scenes in *Logan*?"

Blake's gaze flickered as though he was processing this bit of trivia. "So you've been studying up on trivia?"

"Well, it's Hugh Jackman, so ..."

"Huh. Why did he do that?"

She shrugged, feigning a nonchalance completely opposite to her jangling nerves. Picturing him—Blake, not Hugh Jackman—in person these last few weeks was one thing. The real deal took her breath away, and no amount of ogling him on TV could have prepared her for six-two, blond, green-eyed perfection. She'd given devil girl the heave-ho in favor of her more responsible, boring side, but somehow the girl was back, whispering all kinds of inappropriate suggestions in her ear that made her blood come alive for the first time since she and Blake had split up.

Her mind was made up of cottonwood fuzz, causing her to question why she'd stayed away for so long. Pride. Confusion. Fury and hurt had driven her decision-making at first, and by the time the anger had fizzled, she'd been neck-deep in survivor mode, shut down to the point where she could barely tie her shoelaces. What mental capacity she'd possessed had all been thrown at navigating the debris that had been her career, leaving the other big stuff—like how to handle Blake reaching out to her—beyond her scope. It had been easier to tell herself she'd confront her feelings and unravel her tangled emotions the next day and the next and the next. By the time *that* altered reality had worn off, she'd been at a loss.

And now here she stood, staring at the man who owned her heart. Emotions were still a jumble, but her excuses for avoiding him had slipped through her fingers like fine grains of sand, and she was primed to take her life—and him—back.

He tilted his head, reminding her he'd hung a question out there. She curled her fist and dug her nails into her palm to keep from getting swept up in his gaze before she could say what she wanted to say to him. God, he had beautiful eyes!

"It had to do with wanting to look really ripped for the scenes," she croaked, "so he used some bodybuilder dehydration diet." *Which you definitely do not need.*

"Huh. Thought he was some big-time dancer?"

"Wolverine?"

Blake let out the warm, lusty laugh she craved hearing, and it uncoiled an overly tight spring inside her. "No, I was talking about Hugh Jackman," he said casually. "Got his start in song and dance. Did you know he graduated with a BA in Communications? He needed more credits, so he took a drama course in his last year of college. The class put on a production, and he was the lead. And did you know he was a last-minute addition to the cast of *X-Men*?"

His rambling gave her courage. She wasn't the only one whose nerves were fraying in this hallway. "I did not know that."

"Here's something else you might not know. It takes between ninety seconds and four minutes for someone to make up their mind whether they're attracted to someone else. And men typically fall in love faster than women. They're usually the ones who say 'I love you' first."

Hope popped and fizzed in her bloodstream. She let go of the sofa and took a step toward him, swallowing around the lump in her throat. "And have you found somebody lately that you were attracted to in less than four minutes?" *Please say no.*

He shook his head vigorously. "I did go on a date last week, though."

*Oh.* There was a jab to the solar plexus, and she couldn't breathe. She took the same step back.

"In case you're wondering," he ran on, "I spent nearly three hours *trying* to make myself attracted to her, but I failed. Miserably."

A silent breath left her body, but jealousy collected in her gut like bubbling green acid. The thought of another woman spending time with *her* man ...

"No? Wasn't she pretty?" She forced the words from her mouth.

"She was *really* pretty."

*Oh God, not helping, big guy!* The jealousy inside her heated and fanned out, pricking every nerve in her body like a bad rash. Michaela frowned at him, though deep down she admitted she *might* deserve the medicine he was spooning out.

Before she registered what was happening, he closed the distance between them and leaned down, his face mere inches from hers. Pulling in citrus and spice and him, she resisted the urge to stick her nose in the crook of his neck and inhale his skin. A corner of his mouth hitched, and he murmured, "She wasn't as pretty as you—no one is—but what she really had going against her was she *wasn't* you." He straightened, widening the space between them.

"Oh. So why did you go out with her?"

"Because the woman I *wanted* to go out with hasn't called or texted me back in weeks, and Ferguson was being a pain in my ass about taking out his girlfriend's BFF, so I thought I'd kill two birds with one stone: shut him up and try to forget you. I shut him up all right, but the other part? Didn't work. How about you? Done any speed dating lately?" His fern-green eyes gave absolutely nothing away.

The quick shift threw her off guard, but relief flowed through her body nonetheless, and she released a shaky breath. "I don't have time for dating, even the speedy kind, because I'm building a new practice of my own." *Although I had plenty of time to mope.* "Besides, I'm not so sure I buy that whole 'the one' business anymore. I'm beginning to believe it's all fairy-tale tripe."

He swiped his thumb across his lip and gave her a thoughtful look. "Really? That's just downright sad because I've come around to the opposite way of thinking. Unfortunately, though, it's really fucking up my game."

Confusion shrouded her partially functioning brain once more. "Are you talking about hockey?"

"Hockey, my personal life. Everything," he chuffed. "They're tied together. Have you watched any of our games lately?"

"All of them."

Surprise flitted across his features. "*All* of them? Then you know how much my game sucks. I need to get it back on track, but I can't do that if I'm distracted."

"Distracted?"

He answered her by way of a pointed look.

*Make your mouth move, Michaela.* "So this woman who wouldn't call you back ... you said you *wanted* to go out with her, past tense?"

"Did I? Huh. Didn't even realize I'd done that. Must be a Freudian thing." His eyes bored into hers with heat and intensity, making her squirm as though a swarm of eels had been let loose inside her. Not a good kind of squirm.

When it became obvious he wasn't going to rush in to placate the raging doubts she'd just stupidly stirred inside herself, her heart sank. Until that moment, she hadn't even realized how badly she'd been *hoping* he'd say a present and a future were still possible. The precarious house of cards she'd built for herself was upended, and merely looking at him made her unable to distinguish top from bottom, wreaking havoc inside her.

"Here's the thing, M. This one's on you," he murmured, "because I let myself get out of control."

"I-I'm not sure I understand." She wasn't doing a good job reading between his cryptic lines because emotion continued gunking up her synapses.

He puffed out a breath and darted his eyes to the ceiling before leveling them back at her. Hope for a happy outcome was fading faster than a plucked wildflower as more realization dawned and her eyes opened wider. What they now clearly saw was pain and frustration in her future, and her heart verged on splintering.

"You're dancing around this thing, and you're killing me here. Just come out and tell me what a bastard I am and get it over with. I know I was out of line. *So* out of line. I've been trying to apologize for weeks, but you've avoided me at every turn, and that's not fair to either of us. If you're asking if I still want to be with you, the answer is God, yes. But am I going to keep chasing you when you don't want to be caught? Or twist your arm into saying you want to be with me too? My life's fucked up enough as it is, and I can't keep beating my head against a wall if I want to hang on to a shred of sanity." He let out a mirthless laugh. "Then again, I can't focus on anything but you, so I may not have a choice." He paused, shaking his head. "I know I'm supposed to come up with some grand gesture, but I'm not sure what I can do to prove to you that you're more important to me than anything. How do I convince you to give me another chance? I love you, M, with my heart and soul. You're holding them both captive in the palm of your hand, and I'm kinda stuck until you let them—and me—go."

His unexpected speech nearly knocked her ass back on the couch again. "Do you *want* me to let them, um, you go?"

"No. I want you to hold them forever." A bright sheen coated his eyes, and he looked at her with such sadness that tears welled up and jammed her throat. At the same time, her heart grew wings, ready to soar out of her chest. Jumbled emotions be damned! What mattered most crystallized.

Swiping at her wet cheeks, she whispered, "As grand gestures go, that ranked right up there."

His eyebrows crept up his forehead. "*What* grand gesture?"

"Everything you just said. You bared your soul—*that* was a grand gesture."

"It was? Here in the hallway? I had a little different setting in mind." He looked utterly dumbfounded, which only made her want to hug him more.

She nodded, and her tears fell freely down her cheeks. "It came from your heart, so yeah, it's an epically grand gesture. Especially for a skeptic leery of having his heart broken like his father's." She covered her heart with her hand.

"Yeah, well, being with you these last few months has helped me learn a few things."

"Like?"

"Like, where did your glasses go?"

The surprising question didn't slow her stride. "Don't need them anymore. My new boss thinks I rock without them."

He nodded. "That's a smart new boss you've got. Want to know what else I have on my mind?"

She nodded a little too eagerly and held her breath.

Reaching out, he toyed with her hair. "Your curls. They're pure satin. I think about wrapping them around my fingers." Running a finger along the side of her face, he paused by her eye. "And your eyes are ... they're ... Every time I look at them, I think of a moonlit lake. People with gray eyes are supposed to be strong, creative, and flexible. Just like you. Did you know that gray eyes are most common in Northern, Western, and Central Europe?" he rambled. "And they're similar to blue eyes, only there's something in them that reflects the light differently.

"And God, your skin. It's so fucking soft. I can't get enough of it." He cleared his throat. "Well, that's some of what's on my mind."

*Wow. Okay. Just wow.* She gaped at him for an instant, fresh tears rimming her lower lashes and threatening to spill over before she gave herself an inner slap to rattle loose the speech she'd been turning over and polishing in her head. The speech was lost, but words began filtering through.

"Killing me here," he prodded.

"I've had a lot of time to think—too much time. I've missed you so much," she burst, not censoring what she said before it tumbled from her mouth. "I love being with you. I love talking to you. I love your trivia, and I love how you make me laugh and how you make me feel. I love watching you play hockey. I'm so sorry I missed your birthday and Christmas and New Year's. I was mad, but then I wasn't, and I didn't know what to do or if you'd still want to be with me. None of this is a good reason to have shut you out the way I did, and I'm so sorry. I hope I'm not too late and that you can forgive me for the stupid—"

He pulled her against him, and she tightened her arms around his waist resting her cheek against his chest. For a frozen moment, neither of them uttered a word, and she soaked in his familiar scent and the wonderful feel of his hard planes. *Home. Safe. Warm.*

"Shh," he murmured against her hair, "there's nothing to forgive. You had every right to be mad about the things I said to you. I was wrong. You scared the shit out of me for weeks when I thought I'd lost you. I don't ever want to go through that again."

She cried into his T-shirt, hiccupping, "You never lost me. I thought I'd lost *you*. I love you, Blake."

He kissed her head, her temple, and banded his arms around her. "God, M, I love you so much. Never knew I could love anyone like this."

She'd never felt safer. *This is where I belong.*

He lifted her chin with his knuckle and cradled her face, scanning it, as though he wanted to reassure himself she was real. His mouth hitched in a half-smile. "Michaela Wagner, I am ... dazzled. I am a believer of 'the one' because against all odds, I found my one. And I am not letting you go, so you'd better get used to having me around."

Now she was a blubbering, running faucet of happy tears. She buried her head against his chest once more. "I don't want to be a distraction. I want to make your life better, add to it. Not take away anything."

"Just being around you adds to it, more than I could have ever expected. And I want that for you too." He grasped her shoulders and set her apart, drilling into her eyes. "I want to make your goals easier to reach, take away whatever stands in your way. Will you let me do that?"

"I'm open to negotiation."

"Speaking of negotiation ..."

She giggled through her tears. "We're negotiating now?"

"I know. Never negotiate with an attorney. But I'm kinda rusty on the kissing thing. I think I need lessons." He wrinkled his nose, and she melted a little more.

Still giggling—she was having trouble stopping now—she dried her eyes on her sleeve and crooked her finger at him. "I'd be happy to help. Maybe you should show me what you got first, sailor."

A laugh rumbled through his chest, brightening his entire face, stoking a riot of joy inside her.

"Don't laugh," she fake-scolded while she struggled to corral her laughter. "This isn't middle school. It's a clinical lesson, not a make-out session."

"Well, that's all kinds of disappointing." Grinning, he narrowed his eyes. "Are you gonna pull your pepper spray on me too?"

"I don't know. Are you going to misbehave?"

"Probably."

"Good. In that case, I will *not* pull pepper spray on you." Surging up on her toes, she cupped the back of his head and pulled his mouth to hers, leading him in a tender, languid kiss he took without hesitation. He quickly seized control and deepened the kiss, turning it into something filled with need and want and love so exquisite it scorched her from her scalp to her toes. Before she knew what had happened, he'd maneuvered them to the couch and had her flat on her back, the comforting weight and warmth of his big body settled on top of hers. She hitched a leg over his hip and kissed him back with everything she'd held back these excruciatingly long weeks.

Breathing nearly as heavily as she was, Blake broke the kiss and looked down at her with a tenderness that made her heart open like a blossom in the spring sun. He wrapped a curl around his index finger. "What do you say, Curly? Ready to move this into my place and continue our, ah, lessons before we embarrass ourselves out here in the hallway?"

"Ready. But I want to make one thing clear."

He cocked an eyebrow at her.

"You absolutely do *not* need kissing lessons or any other kind of lessons." She pulled him back down, nipped his earlobe, and whispered, "I have heard, however, that practice makes perfect."

"Then we'd better start practicing. Now."

Hours later, Blake lay in bed, on his back, drifting blissfully with his arms encircling M as she snuggled against him. She drew lazy circles on his skin, her curls tickling his jaw. His world was right-side up again. The couch sat at a cockeyed angle in the entryway, where they'd scooted it in just far enough to close the front door.

A laugh rolled through him, and M kissed his neck. "What are you chuckling about?"

He craned his head and peered at her. “You went to a lot of trouble setting up this couch-moving scenario. I had no idea you could pull off something so sneaky.”

She grinned wide. “I guess when it truly matters, I’m capable of getting my sneaky on. And it worked.”

“True, but now you have me worried what else you’re capable of.” His eyebrows arched.

“Don’t worry. It was more Fiona than me, and besides, the sneak factor only came into play because I was desperate.”

He hugged her to him. “I guess I’m glad you have a latent sneaky streak, then.” His shoulders shook with laughter.

“And this is funny why?”

“That’s not what I’m laughing about. I can’t believe you actually *like* my stupid-ass trivia.”

She shifted, throwing a leg over his knees. “I believe I said ‘love.’ Speaking of love, Ferguson explained he wasn’t firing on all cylinders because he was loopy for Tracy, which made me wonder how Amanda’s handling her crush falling for someone else.”

“Not sure. I think she still blames me, which might be easier for her than believing he wasn’t into her. And thank God he wasn’t.” Blake blew out a relieved breath. He and Ferguson might have patched up the majority of the damage between them, but that didn’t mean he wanted the guy touching his sister.

“I have a feeling Amanda won’t hold you responsible forever. In the meantime, maybe she’ll meet some nice surfer boy in Hawaii to take her mind off Owen.”

Blake snorted. “Are you *trying* to upset me?”

“No,” she giggled.

“Then stop it.” He settled back with a sigh and tightened his hold on her. “Fergs was insane long before he met Tracy, but I can see where she might have pushed him over the edge. Especially since he wouldn’t admit how much he cared about her. Reminds me of someone I know.”

M parked her chin on his chest. “Who?”

“Me.” He twined a few more curls around his fingers.

“Are you saying you’re insane?”

"For you, yeah. I'm fucking nuts."

"Aw, you say the nicest things." She kissed his nose. "I love you too."

He chuckled. "Speaking of nuts, my mom entered a rehab program. On her own." He filled M in on the story his mother had shared at Christmas. "I'm not holding my breath—we've been down Rehab Road before—but this time feels different, like maybe she's turned a corner after getting some heavy shit off her chest."

"Do you believe her?"

He nodded. "I read my dad's journals. It's all there."

Concern etched her features. "How was that?"

"Not easy. I had to deconstruct a lot of what I'd believed about him all these years, which sent me into a bit of an emotional tailspin."

"I'm so sorry I wasn't there while you were dealing with it."

*Me too.* The ache from what he'd learned about his dad lingered, though it was more blunted. "Ironically, I feel closer to him now than I ever did—like I know him better. It's a new reality that Mom, Amanda, and I are adjusting to, and it's still confusing. As hard as it was to learn all that shit about my dad, knowing my mom isn't pure evil somehow balances it out. And maybe because she's the surviving parent, it's actually a little easier to deal with. I don't know. Like I said, it's still confusing." He shrugged. "We're pulling together, though, and we'll help each other through."

M's thoughtful quicksilver eyes studied him. "What will you say if your mom wants to come live with you when she's through rehab?"

"No," he said unequivocally. "That wouldn't benefit either of us; in fact, it would drive us *both* to drink. There's only one woman I'm inviting to live with me."

Her breath stuttered so loudly that he heard it.

"A discussion for later," he added, totally unrattled. Yeah, he was determined. M was his, same as he owned that twisted wrister title he was about to reclaim. "Speaking of drinking, I owe you a colossal apology for what I said. For the record, I don't think you drink too much. I was being a prick and vomiting crap out for the sake of vomiting."

She offered him a soft, warm smile. "I don't know that I'd describe it in such colorful terms."

His heart sat heavily in his chest. "I'm sorry I hurt you, M. It's nothing I ever want to do again." He kissed her gently, relishing the feel and taste of her lips. "You're sorry you weren't there when I found out the truth about my dad, and I'm even sorrier I wasn't there for you when you went through the Steadman crap. Fiona told me what you did, and I am so damn proud of you. I can't believe how that asshole Hewitt set you up." Jesus, just thinking about the lengths Brad Hewitt had gone to in order to hurt her made his blood boil over. "I knew I didn't like the guy, but if I'd known what he was capable of the night I met him, I would have done more than threaten him. And if I ever see him again, I'm following through."

"If *I'd* known what he was up to, you would've had to get behind me while I unloaded the contents of my pepper-spray canister in his face." With a small laugh, she laid her head back down, and her index finger returned to tracing loops on his chest. "After I had a chance to process what you said about my drinking, I realized maybe you struck a nerve and that I was getting into some bad habits and blaming them on stress. I've cut back, and I feel better, physically *and* mentally."

The subject made him cringe inside, but her words eased his guilt a fraction. "Does this mean life is less stressful?"

"I wish," she laughed. "In some ways, it's *more* stressful, but it's more freeing at the same time. I'm looking forward to establishing my own practice. I know it'll be crazy, but it'll get better."

He traced her tattoo from her shoulder to her elbow while he pondered how he could help her. "Where did you move to? How safe is it?"

"Well, it's a little carriage house above Beckett Miller's garage. Not only does a hockey player live close by, but construction guys go in and out all the time. It feels pretty safe."

*Not as safe as a secure building ... with a different hockey player close by.* "Shit! You're living above all those classic cars? Does Miller keep you up all hours revving engines?"

"Hardly," she laughed. "He's up all hours with Paige, taking care of their twins."

"Oh yeah. I heard about that. Two more girls. Ha!"

"What's wrong with girls?"

"Absolutely nothing. I *love* girls. Especially the one whose curls are tickling my chest. Must get pretty noisy around there, though, huh?"

She sighed. "At times. Now that the weather's warming up, I keep the windows open more. They have a big house, but sound carries."

He adjusted their bodies so he could look into her eyes. "Like I've said before, I know a quiet place close to downtown where you can live and have plenty of space for an office too. The guy who lives there is gone half the time, but when he *is* home, he'll try his damnedest to give you your space. Well, during work hours anyway."

"Doesn't it worry you that we've only known each other—"

"Four months. Lots of people are already engaged at this point in their relationship."

Her eyes startled wide.

"Yeah, that's right. I said the *M* word."

"I think that's the *E* word," she stammered.

"Technicalities. *E* leads to *M*. You're cute when you're nervous, by the way."

"You're *not* nervous talking about this stuff?"

"Nope. When it's right, it's right." Nothing had ever been more real or more crystal clear. Being with this woman pulled the whole man at his very core from his deepest depths to the surface where he could breathe. She completed him. He would never let that feeling stop.

He would never let her get away again.

# Chapter 38

# Doesn't Take an Einstein

Blake pulled Michaela against him, her back to his front, as he tried to get the bartender's attention. The bar they stood in was raucous, crammed with Blizzard players, the coaching staff, and their SOs celebrating tonight's victory. Elation thrummed in Michaela's veins, spilling over from Blake and the rest of his teammates. The team had closed out round two of the playoffs in six games, and now they awaited the as-yet-undetermined winner of the other Western Conference series. While those two teams duked it out, though, Blake and the boys would get a few extra days to rest up and heal as best they could before the start of the brutal third round less than a week away. Which was a good thing, considering how many bumps and bruises and pulls and sprains her man had.

Yep, *her* man.

Her man, who had centered the second line through the first two rounds. Who'd ticked and twitched for every face-off and was tied with Gage Nelson for best face-off percentage in the playoffs. Who had scored seven goals and four assists. Who had gotten his mojo back, and then some, and was a force the other teams weren't sure how to contain.

She leaned back against him, soaking up his heat and his hard angles, pride surging inside of her that he was all hers.

Arms banded around her, he leaned down and pulled the shell of her ear between his teeth. “Hang on. I’m trying to get us some drinks.”

She tucked her arms on top of his and craned her neck to look up at him. “I’ve got all I need right here.”

“Here!” Two drinks were thrust at them, and she looked up into Ferguson’s grinning face. “Chopin for you, right?”

She nodded and accepted both drinks, nudging Blake with her elbow to hand off a bourbon on the rocks.

“Hey, thanks!” He raised his glass to Ferguson.

Ferguson matched the motion. “To a hard-fought series and the Blizzard’s goal-scoring machine.” Ferguson took a sip of a pale gold liquid in a shot glass. “So which goalie would you rather meet in the Finals?” he asked Blake.

“Does it matter?” Michaela posed. “Bear can beat any goalie. Nobody stops the Twisted Wrister.” Both men stared at her a beat, then broke into laughter.

“Well, hot damn, buddy!” Ferguson said. “I guess you’ve got yourself an honest-to-goodness mama bear.”

Blake kissed the top of her head. “And I am one lucky son of a bitch.”

She lifted her chin an inch or two, tilting it toward Ferguson. “And you’d best remember it next time you try any shenanigans.”

“You still haven’t forgiven me, have you?”

She shook her head and smirked. “Not yet, but keep trying. You might get there. The fact that Tracy likes you is a point in your favor.”

“I can’t disagree,” he chuckled. “Speaking of Trace, I need to go find her before one of my asshole teammates tries to steal her away.” He winked at Blake. “Drink up, Bear. Time to cut loose. You’ve earned it.”

“Oh, I’m cutting loose all right.”

Ferguson moved off, and Blake hauled Michaela into a less-rowdy part of the bar, where he pinned her against a wall. One hand braced by her head, the other held his cocktail as he leaned down to her. “About cutting loose. You know what an easy drunk

I am, and I haven't had a drop in months. I'm expecting to have my bones jumped as soon as I get you home." He paused to rotate his shoulder and grimaced with the motion. "Maybe we should leave jumping off the menu, and you're probably going to have to do most of the work."

She grinned. "I'll be gentle, I promise. Then again, with your mom and sister staying with us, it's probably best to put the frisky stuff on hold altogether." He'd flown them in for the game, and Amanda had ferried his mom back to the condo. Still on shaky recovery ground, DeeAnn didn't need to be around an inebriated bunch of guys celebrating themselves silly. Besides, DeeAnn had developed a new addiction: astrology. Michaela giggled inside every time she thought of Blake's mom poring over charts, telling Michaela about her houses and moons and planets ... and a future that looked quite rosy.

"They'll be asleep when we get home, and their rooms are at the other end of the condo anyway, so they can't hear you scream," Blake countered. "But if you're worried, you could take advantage of me *before* we get home."

She shot him a questioning look, and he wrapped a curl around his finger. "I'm told they have big bathrooms here." He waggled his eyebrows. "A few more bourbons and I'm all yours."

"Are you saying you have to be drunk to have sex with me?" she chided.

He pulled back, dismay in his eyes. "Fuck no! Just saying I'll be putty in your hands. You can have your way with me."

She quirked a grin. "I usually do."

He wagged his head back and forth. "True. Did you know oxytocin is released during sex, and it boosts feelings of love? All that oxytocin must be why I love you so much. And did you also know that sex is about connection more than it is about lust?" He poked her collarbone with his index finger, nearly tipping his drink on her.

"Really? So lust is out? Damn."

He sipped his bourbon. "That's not what I said." Now he nudged her elbow to encourage her to drink her vodka.

She sipped, letting the icy liquid burn a cold path to her stomach, warming it when it landed. “I haven’t been drinking either. So are you trying to take advantage of *me*?”

“Always. A smart attorney like you should know this by now.” His expression suddenly shifted, and his green eyes filled with tenderness. “I can’t tell you how damn glad I am that you’re here to celebrate this with me. I’ve won other stuff, but it’s never felt like this before, and that’s because of you, M. I can’t wait until we win the Cup and you’re with me at the parade.”

His misty eyes had her choking up, and she blinked rapidly and downed another sip. “I love you, big guy.”

He rubbed her nose with his and plastered his wide grin back in place. “If I’m going to win the Cup, there’s something I need from you first.”

She tilted her head. “What’s that?”

“I need a new picture for luck. *With* your consent this time.”

Her eyes widened. “Are we talking naked pictures here?”

“Oh, I get more than one? Sweet! And we’ll probably need to take a bunch to get just the right pose.”

She spluttered, then eyed him skeptically. “I don’t know if you can be trusted with a picture. Who’s going to see—”

“Just me, I promise.”

“Hmm. A picture or two might be good for your twisted wrister mojo, since you’re chasing the Cup and all. But instead of being naked, I have a better idea.”

“What could possibly be better than naked?”

She batted her eyelashes at him. “Whipped cream.”

His mouth dropped open. “We’re stopping at Costco on the way home,” he croaked.

“It’s closed.”

“Don’t care. I’m breaking in.”

“Michaela?”

She and Blake turned their heads at the same time, and she froze in place.

“It *is* you! I don’t believe it! How long has it been since I’ve seen you, and you’re here, of all places, with—” Anders’s eyes swept Blake from head to toe. He stuck his hand out. “Hi. I’m Anders Einstein.”

Blake’s eyebrows hitched up above his round eyes. He seemed to shake Anders’s hand out of reflex.

At first, Michaela wished the wall would swallow her up. But she reminded herself that was a leftover feeling from a long time ago, and her voice grew strident. “Anders, hi. It *has* been a while. This is my ... this is Blake Barrett, my fiancé.”

Blake and Anders were mid-shake when Blake swiveled his head to her, his eyebrows climbing a few inches higher. Anders’s eyes were nearly as wide, but they were assessing Blake, which made the whole thing cosmically comic. She was a terrible liar, though, and she reeled a bit from her blatant deception, but Blake gave her a cockeyed smile that made her heart stutter in her chest. Apparently, he *liked* her lie.

He released Anders’s hand.

“Nice to meet you. Blake Barrett, is it?”

“Yes, Michaela’s fiancé.” Blake’s grin widened as he threw an arm around her shoulder and hauled her against him in a staking-his-claim, caveman-like move. She loved it.

“That’s ... what wonderful news. I’m really happy for you, Michaela.” As Anders reached out a hand to her, she looked from him to Blake and back again. *Past, meet Future.* She’d traded up—*way* up.

As she grasped Anders’s hand, the vestiges of hurt and anger he’d left her with dissolved away. How she had ever been in love with this man was a mystery to her, just as it must have been a mystery to him when he found his “one.” And she couldn’t be happier for him—and herself. If he’d never found his one, they might have settled for one another. Instead, she’d won the ultimate prize—the man beside her—whose fern green eyes looked at her with love so deep and so profound he breathed life into every part of her being while wrapping her up in his warmth and safety. Whose raw power caged in a beautifully sculpted frame made her heart gallop and her knees turn gelatinous. Every. Single. Day.

God, she'd barely had one sip of vodka, and she was waxing mega-mushball poetic. Blake had that effect on her, and she was okay with that. Deliriously okay.

"Well," Anders said awkwardly, "Pamela's waiting outside for me. She forgot her coat in our rush to escape when the ... group arrived. A little more excitement than we were up for." He patted a coat draped over his arm and gave Blake a man-nod. "Congratulations on the win. Your team has brought a lot of excitement to the city."

A few quick good-byes and good lucks, and he was gone.

Blake turned to her, his eyebrows practically glued to his hairline. "Einstein?"

She wrinkled her nose. "I know. Can you imagine me having *that* for a last name?"

"No, but I *can* imagine you having 'Barrett' for a last name." Eyes holding hers, he pointed in the direction Anders had gone. "You called me your fiancé. Was there a proposal in there somewhere?"

"I, um ..."

"Because if there was, I accept. Although I wish you'd stop stealing my grand gestures."

A laugh escaped her chest. "Were you planning to ... to propose?"

"It had crossed my mind ... about a hundred times. Or more. I was thinking maybe on top of that bus during the Stanley Cup parade in downtown Denver a few months from now."

"And on the off chance your team doesn't win?"

"Doesn't matter." He rested his forehead against hers and dropped his voice. "Michaela Wagner, having you in my future, forever, is more win than I need or deserve." His index finger traced a vine of her tattoo. "I might get one of these. A twisted vine with your name inked in it. Are you in my future? Forever?"

"Just try and get rid of me." Butterflies danced in her stomach, and she wasn't sure she would ever be able to eat again. She looped an arm around his shoulders, steadying herself against his strong frame, something she planned to do the rest of her life.

"Never gonna happen." He took her drink from her and placed it with his on a nearby shelf. "Who needs alcohol? I'm intoxicated just looking at you, and that's a better high than I can get anywhere. Let's go someplace quiet and compare notes about this future. And take pictures."

"Anything to help my man win."

"M, just knowing I'm 'your man' is all the winning I'll ever need."

**THE END**

## Want more of Blake and Michaela?

Go to my website at www.gkbrady.com and download your free copy of two (yes, two) bonus Epilogues! (Here's the direct link: https://gkbrady.com/bonus-content/tw/)

HE'S BEEN BURNED by commitment. She can't seem to find the one. Here's an excerpt from *Besting the Blueliner*, Book 8:

It was no small surprise when an unfamiliar white pickup towing an empty trailer pulled up in front of Cam's house.

The second surprise came when the driver bounded from the vehicle carrying a load of something cloaked under a red-and-white-checkered cloth. It looked like a tablecloth his mother might spread over a picnic table. The stun factor had him rooted in place until a loud knock came at the front door, pulling him from his fog. Grace, who was far sharper than he this morning, already stood at the front door, inhaling the air in the crack between the door and frame.

Terra beamed from under a nylon hood when he opened the door. "Hi!" She pushed her way inside.

"Hi?" He suppressed the urge to ask what the hell she wanted, watching her back as she took a few more steps inside his house, her coat shedding raindrops all over his floor. Only Grace's greeting stopped Terra's advance, like an invisible force field. His dog wiggled from head to rear, her tail doing a fine imitation of a helicopter rotor. This was how she usually greeted *him*, not a sworn enemy. He needed to have a talk with his girl as soon as he could shoo the drippy one back out from where she had come from. "Can I help you?"

Terra pivoted and held out the checkered tablecloth to him. "I brought you something."

He arched a skeptical eyebrow. "Will it explode? Does it bite?"

Her face fell, and he instantly regretted his snark. She recovered quickly, flashing a smile as she whipped the tablecloth off of the bundle it cloaked. A tray of colorful cupcakes sat under a thin layer of clear plastic, perfectly swirled thick blue icing as high as the cake part with a perfect chocolate bean adorning it. They looked like the kind of treats that tempted him from his favorite bakery's case, and he realized too late he'd licked his bottom lip, giving himself away. If he stared much longer, he'd drool worse than Grace when bacon was on the menu.

Terra gave him a triumphant grin. "I took a chance you liked cupcakes, so I made these for you. They're chocolate with cherry filling."

*Chocolate? With cherry filling?* Well, shit! How had she zeroed in on his Achilles' Heel? His internal alarms sounded—she had to want something from him, like everyone else who ever offered him gifts, food or otherwise. "I thought you were afraid of Grace ... and maybe even me?" He cocked a questioning eyebrow at her.

"Having the great equalizer helps."

"The great what?"

She jerked her head to one side, and his gaze dropped to the sidearm barely concealed by her raincoat; he hadn't noticed it before.

*Huh.* "Yet you had the 'great equalizer' last time you were here, and you were still intimidated," he pointed out.

"I wasn't intimidated. I was simply ... frazzled." She patted the pistol. "I do know how to use it." Her sunny smile was completely at odds with her mildly veiled threat.

"As you should," he replied dryly. He pointed at the cupcakes. "What are they for?"

"For helping me yesterday." Her voice dropped. "And today." She thrust the tray at him, revealing his neatly folded flannel shirt beneath. "And I washed your shirt. Thanks for the loan."

He resisted the urge to shake his head and got to the important bit hiding in the unsolicited fanfare. "Today?"

"Um, yeah. I was hoping you could help me get the side-by-side on my trailer? Seeing as how you have those big muscles and all." Her eyes did some weird blinky thing he could only interpret as an attempt at Olympic eyelash-batting or clearing out a gnat that had splatted against one of her irises.

Relieving her of his shirt, he shoved the tray of cupcakes back at her. "I'm busy."

Those big blues of hers took a tour around the room before sweeping him from his bed head to his bare toes. "You don't *look* busy. What are you busy doing?"

His hackles, tempered by amusement at her boldness, rose. "Not sure that's any of your business." He took an extra loud slurp of his coffee. "Are you always this nosy?"

Grace, who had been sitting patiently beside him, cleaning the floor with her tail, lunged toward Terra—to get better acquainted, no doubt. Terra's eyes bugged, and she jumped backward with a squeak, smashing the back of her head into a hall tree too rickety to hold anything beyond a ball cap. She sent it and the tray crashing to the floor.

He wasn't sure where to turn his attention first: Terra's head, the toppled hall tree, or the cupcakes smearing his floor.

Get *Besting the Blueliner* at Amazon and find out what surprises are in store for Cam and Terra when they're thrown together in the isolated mountains of Colorado.

SEVEN PLAYMAKERS COUPLES unite for a winter wedding getaway, but there's trouble in Paradise. Claim your free copy of *Puck the Halls* at www.gkbrady.com and see if they can find the spirit of Christmas—and each other—before it's too late.

# A Note from the Author

Thank you so much for reading *Twisted Wrister*! I loved the idea of a superstar without the swagger, and so Blake was born. The trivia nerd side of him bloomed as I wrote, and I found myself looking up all kinds of fun facts. I loved pairing him with sassy attorney Michaela. I'll let you in on a little secret: I didn't consider how long her name would be to type over and over, but by the time I realized it, she was Michaela and no other name would do ... hence, the nickname "M" that Blake gave her.

If you enjoyed Blake and Michaela's story, I would love it if you would leave a review on Amazon, BookBub, or Goodreads to help readers like you find the story. And if you do leave a review, I would love to read it! Email me the link at gkbrady@griffin-brady.com.

Be the first to know about upcoming releases, bonus content, giveaways, and discount deals by joining my newsletter. Simply go to: www.gkbrady.com/contact/.

**Trouble is brewing. Disaster strikes. Can they conjure a mistletoe miracle?** Claim your free copy of *Puck the Halls* (Book 7.5), a Playmakers novella, when you join. Download it at www.gkbrady.com/bonus-content/pth/ or scan this code:

Listen while you read! The playlist for *Twisted Wrister* can be found on Spotify.

# *Acknowledgments*

My readers, you are the reason I write. Thank you from the bottom of my heart for reading my stories. And thank you for helping me pick Blake's cover!

My ARC readers, for your enthusiasm and for your steadfast support. I am a fortunate author indeed and so honored to have you on the team.

Jenny Q., for yanking me back on the right path every time I stray too far. Your insights are pure gold. And of course, the gorgeous cover! I love collaborating with you.

Jodi B., for boldly going where no one has gone before. Namely, for wading through that rough, rough first draft and helping me smooth it out. And thank you for believing in Blake!

Word Servings, for keeping me on the straight and narrow so the prose makes sense and so I don't unintentionally invent new slang terms. I'm so glad you're willing to wade through my words.

Stephanie H., for spending your nights and weekends creating gorgeous graphics and for taking care of details I can't even begin to list. I've said it before, but it bears repeating: not only do you make everything work, but you make it beautiful and polished without seeming to break a sweat.

My husband, Tim, for still making me laugh after all these years and for cheering me on without ever seeming to tire of that constant arm-waving. Good thing you've been building up those guns. ;-)

# *Also by this Author*

## The Playmakers Series®

## The Fall River Series

## The Love in Destiny Series

# *About the author*

Since childhood, all sorts of stories and characters have lived in G.K. Brady's imagination, elbowing one another for attention, so she's thrilled (as are they) to be giving them their voice on the written page.

An award-winning writer of contemporary romance, she loves telling tales of the less-than-perfect hero or heroine who transforms with each turn of a page.

G.K. is a wife and the proud mom of three grown sons. She also writes historical fiction under the pen name Griffin Brady. She currently resides in Colorado with her very patient husband.

Connect with her on these platforms:

www.amazon.com/author/gkbrady

www.twitter.com/GKBrady_Writes

www.facebook.com/AuthorG.K.Brady/

www.bookbub.com/authors/g-k-brady

www.goodreads.com/author/show/19488321.G_K_Brady

www.instagram.com/authorg.k.brady

www.pinterest.com/gkbrady0993/

www.ingramcontent.com/pod-product-compliance
Lightning Source LLC
LaVergne TN
LVHW010556100826
845148LV00014B/2734

* 9 7 8 1 7 3 6 3 6 0 6 6 8 *